UNSPOKEN
Temptation
TREY'S STORY

Book Four of the Unspoken Series

Gabbie S. Duran

Unspoken Temptation
Book Four of the Unspoken Series
Copyright © 2015 by Gabbie S. Duran

Cover art by Rebecca Marie of The Final Wrap
Photographer: Mandy Hollis of MHPhotography
Cover models: Julio Elving and Ashley Edmund
Editing done by Edee M. Fallon, Mad Sparks Editing
Proofreading done by Sarah West of Three Owls Editing
and Missy Stegman
Formatting by Stacey Blake of Champagne Formats

Champagne
Formats

Printed in the United States of America First Edition: May 2015 Library of Congress Cataloging-in-Publication Data # 1–2270761961

ISBN-13: 978–0692421208
ISBN-10: 0692421203

Other Books by the author

Unspoken Series

Unspoken Memories
Unspoken Promises
Unspoken Endings

Clarity

With Me

Dedication

To my daughter, Stephanie, my inspiration behind Trey.

Chapter One

Walk of shame

Nearly three years earlier...

Trey

I WATCH ABIGAIL walk away, irritated with myself for agreeing to come to this stupid event. I only did it because Matt made me feel guilty about Abigail coming alone. Now I'm regretting letting myself be convinced, but no more. From now on, when it comes to Abigail, I will not cave. She obviously belongs to Matt, so her shit is his to deal with. Turning my head, my eyes lock onto the rigid princess they left behind.

From the moment I walked up to them, I knew she was part of this crowd. If her pinched up nose wasn't sign enough she came from money, then her designer clothes and jewelry were a dead giveaway.

"What?" she snaps out as I stare at her. Her attitude

doesn't faze me. I'm used to stuck up bitches like her turning their noses up at me. This one isn't any different.

"Nothing," I clip out, trying to find the nearest exit to make my escape. When my eyes find her again, she's already turning to leave when she runs into an older gentleman. Her body bounces back and she loses her balance, causing me to catch her out of pure instinct. She lets out a giggle that is clearly a result of her drunken stupor.

"I'm sorry, sir. She clearly didn't see you there," I apologize for her, earning me a curt nod before he irritably walks off.

With my help, she steadies herself. "Thank you," she says, looking embarrassed.

"No problem," I reply, taking the empty glass in her hand and placing it on a passing waiter's tray. She's about to reach for another drink when I stop her. "I think you've had enough," I tell her.

"What, now you're my babysitter?" she asks with a scowl on her face.

"No, the last thing I want is to be is your damn babysitter, but you've obviously had enough for the night," I state.

She sways in my arms and it's clear my words are true.

"How about we get you some fresh air," I suggest, already tugging her towards the nearest exit. Thankfully, it's the same one I entered when I arrived with Abigail, which tells me I can easily bail when I'm done with this chick.

"I'm fine," she states as we walk, but somehow I don't fully believe her. I stay silent as I lead her from the room.

"You have a room here?" I ask, hoping she does, so I

can happily dump her ass in it and leave.

I'm left disappointed when she shakes her head at me. "I have an apartment, but I can't seem to remember where it's at right now," she blurts out, tilting her head to the side as she lets out a sigh.

"How can you not remember where you live?"

"Because I just moved there. I know it's on the Upper East Side," she says.

Great. It's further proof that she's made of money.

"How about I take you back to my place and let you sleep it off?" I ask her, knowing full well I'm probably out of my mind.

"Oh, I bet you use that line on all the girls."

"No, it's not the one I usually use because they're not usually sleeping," I say, unable to resist throwing it back at her.

"It's obvious you're wasted and since you know Julio, he'd probably kick my ass if I left you here in your condition," I admit. "Julio is staying with us, anyway. I'll take you back to our place and let him deal with you," I tell her.

She gives me a drunken nod, making her sway again. Leading her outside, I flag down a taxi. Once inside, I give him the address to our hotel.

When we arrive, I reach for my credit card to pay for the taxi, not expecting the outrageous fare. The girl reaches into her small, dangly purse and yanks out a hundred before shoving it through the plastic divider.

"Keep the change," she orders.

I feel a pang of aggravation from knowing she's just paid for the taxicab without hesitating over the price. I tell myself that she's made of money and that a hundred is probably petty cash to her.

Pulling her out of the car and guiding her to the elevator, she's already clinging to my arm. In the elevator she starts to doze off against it, causing her to keep losing her balance. Giving up the notion that she'll actually be able to walk, I scoop her up into my arms and wait for the elevator doors to open. She wraps her arms around my neck as her face relaxes into the crook of my shoulder. Her nose nudges against my skin and I hear a contented moan. The sound alone is enough for me to get ideas in my head that don't need to be there.

Thankfully, I'm saved when I hear the familiar ping of the elevator. Briskly walking out, I rush over to our door and upon reaching it, I realize the key card is still in my pocket.

I shake the girl to get her attention, earning me a grumble. "I need you to reach into my coat and grab the key card," I tell her.

Without hesitating, she does as I request. When her hand slowly glides against my chest, I start to grow hard. How the fuck is one simple touch making me react this way? Pushing the thought aside, I start to think of ugly old ladies as she continues to search, trying to force my dick to go limp again.

Eventually, she digs the key out and swipes it. When the green light appears, she pushes the handle down and I shove the door open and enter. Kicking it shut behind us, I carry her straight to Julio's room.

On the way, she starts nuzzling her nose into my neck

again, this time letting out a moan as she licks it. I nearly fucking trip on my own feet when she does it. I quicken my steps towards the bedroom and place her on the bed. I reach for her arms to unwrap them from my neck, but she tightens her grip and tries to pull me down. I have to force myself to breathe as I brace my arms on the bed to keep from collapsing on top of her.

"I don't think this is a good idea," I groan out, knowing damn well that it isn't. She ignores my words and starts kissing and sucking on my neck, still trying to pull me down on top of her. I try to gently shove her away so I can make my escape, but I lose the battle when her lips find mine.

She opens her mouth to allow me inside, our tongues slowly glide against each other's and I can taste the alcohol she was drinking. She moans into my mouth as my tongue continues to explore hers, the breaking point of my struggle to keep away from her.

I don't know how long I hover above her as I kiss her, but when we eventually pull apart, we're both breathlessly panting as I stare down at her.

"Please," she begs for God only knows what, but I know what I want.

"I'll be right back," I tell her, giving her one quick kiss on the mouth before rushing out of the room to my bag that's sitting in the living room. Scrambling through the side pockets where I put the condoms I brought, I grab the entire box, hopeful I'll put them all to use.

Entering the room again, I lock the door behind me. With the glow of the city lights entering through the windows, I take in the view in front of me. She's completely naked as she lies back on the bed. How the fuck did she manage to get her clothes off that fast? At this point, I tell myself to be grateful she's ready and willing. Within a minute, I have every piece of clothing removed from my body and I'm back on top of her, this time snugly between her thighs.

Slamming my lips back down onto hers, I deeply kiss her, already needing to have my tongue in her mouth again. Ending the kiss, I start trailing my tongue down her body to taste the rest of her. Her skin is soft against my lips. I don't know whether to take my time and savor each inch of it or get straight to the point. Since I'm an impatient man, I choose the latter and make my way down.

When my mouth finds the heat of her, she's already wet. Lapping my tongue against her lips, the sound she delivers drives me wild. I continue tasting every inch between her thighs, her nails digging into my scalp as she tries grabbing onto my head, but unable to because of the lack of hair on my head. Instead, her hands find their way onto my shoulders and she lifts her hips to further grind against my mouth. Within minutes, she's screaming at the top of her lungs as my mouth keeps sucking at her clit. Her juices explode into my mouth and the taste of them is practically making me come as I lap up every ounce she released.

When I lift my head, she's staring down at me with a satisfied smile on her lips. Slowly, I start to kiss my way up her body and make my way back up to her.

"Do you want me to keep going?" I cautiously ask,

not wanting to force her, knowing damn well she's drunk. This isn't the first time I've fucked someone while they were drunk, but somehow this time it doesn't feel right. I feel like I'll be taking advantage of her.

She answers me with a nod, and it's the only sign I need to pull away to grab a condom. She watches me as I roll it on, the entire time her eyes never leaving my dick as she hungrily stares at it. Normally, with a look like that, I'd make the girl service me back, but I can't wait to be inside her.

I grab her leg to hook it around my waist and she automatically pulls me towards her with it. Her arms move to my shoulders as her eyes lock onto mine as I gradually enter her. Inch by tantalizing inch, I push myself inside her. She's so fucking tight and the thought of her being a virgin occurs to me, but I'm proven wrong when I don't meet any resistance as I thrust the last couple of inches inside her. She does let out a gasp when I'm all the way in to the hilt.

I stay still above her, knowing from the clutching of her eyes and the digging of her nails into my shoulders that she must be in pain. Already regretting seeing her like this, I start pulling out. When the tip of my dick is at her entrance, her other leg wraps around my waist. She lifts her hips and begins urging me forward. Giving in to her request, I thrust back into her, earning me a pleasured whimper.

At first my thrusts are slow and cautious, not wanting to hurt her any further. Her screams demand more, causing me to completely lose it. In the midst of thrusting in and out of her, Julio starts banging on the door. His angered request to open the door should be enough to make me stop, or go completely limp. The encouraging words being screamed from below me are enough to shut Julio's words out.

I know I'm going to get my ass kicked by him when he finds out who I'm fucking, but at this very moment as my dick glides in and out of her tight walls, I know it's worth taking the beating for.

It isn't long before I feel her walls clamping down around my dick and she explodes, screaming at the top of her lungs. It's all I need to quickly follow her over the edge as I internally shatter right after her. When I'm done, I stay hovering over her, keeping my weight on my extended arms at her sides as I look down at her. She looks just as breathless as I feel as I finally collapse at her side. My heart is racing and my body is drenched in sweat as I stare up at the ceiling. She rolls over to drape her body over mine and I can't resist wrapping her tight to my side. I've never once allowed a girl to cling to me after sex. Normally, I'd be pushing her off the bed or jumping off it to get dressed. This time I do neither as I tilt my head to the side to take in the scent of her hair. She smells of something fruity and I leave my nose buried in her hair, enjoying her scent.

I start drifting off to sleep when I feel her leg rubbing back and forth over my groin. I'm about to warn her not to tease me when she climbs up to straddle my hips. She places her lips onto mine as her pussy grinds against my dick. Within second, it's hard again and my last thought before I grab for another condom is: Fuck sleep. It's overrated when you have a girl as horny as the one on top of me.

Victoria

I roll over, refusing to wake just yet. Clutching the pillow, I take in its scent, realizing it's unfamiliar. My eyes snap open, alarmed by my surroundings. This is not my room. In the distance, I can hear a shower running. Panicking, I try to figure out where I'm at as my eyes search the room.

Frantically sitting up, I realize I'm naked. My heart is racing as I try to remember why I'm here. The act of sitting up makes my head hurt, as if I have hammers pounding in my head. Groaning, I'm still trying to take in my surroundings. By the looks of it, I'm in a hotel room. Closing my eyes, the last thing I remember is being at the charity event. Searching my mind, I further remember speaking to a redneck guy.

Oh, God. Did I really go home with him? Let alone have sex with him? The panic inside me is increasing with every second. Doing the only thing I can do, I climb off the bed and search for my clothes. I *have* to leave before God knows who gets out of the shower. I can't even remember his name.

Although I can't remember most of the night, now that I think about it . . . Just thinking about it makes my cheeks blush as I recall the things we did and the way he made me feel. Pushing the thought aside, I have to focus on getting dressed.

In record time, I'm dressed and rushing to the door, relieved to be leaving the evening behind me. Opening the door, a smile lifts my lips as I make my escape without him knowing. My face falls as I unexpectedly walk into a room full of people—recognizing two of them.

"Victoria?" I hear the familiar voice ask.

Shamefully, I hang my head as I focus on the front door, quickening my steps. My cheeks that were blushing from the thoughts of last night are now red in shame. My legs can't move fast enough as I yank open the door and pray nobody will follow me. The last thing I need is to have to explain why I woke up in a stranger's room.

Now in the hallway, I take in my surroundings. Finding the elevator, I push the button to demand its presence on my floor. Within seconds, the elevator doors open in front of me and I let out the breath I was holding since I stepped out of the room.

I watch the doors close and tell myself I should be grateful this part of my life is behind me.

Trey

As I step out of the shower, I grab the towel off the rack and dry myself. Once done, I wrap it around my waist and head into the room. My need to wake Victoria with sex is overtaking me. The only reason why I'd taken a shower is because I woke up smelling of sweat and I didn't want her smelling me that way.

As I open the door to the bathroom, I find the bed empty.

"What the fuck?"

Perplexed, I search the room for any sign of her, but

there isn't any besides the rumpled bed I'd awakened from. I'm pretty sure I wasn't dreaming about last night. When I woke up, she was still in bed. I know because I was staring down at her angelic face.

Turning to the door, I see it cracked. Rushing over to it, I open it to find Julio and Abigail in the living room wearing confused expressions as they look at me.

"Where is she?" I ask.

Abigail's jaw looks like it might fall off her face as it continues to hang open. Her speechless expression tells me she knows exactly who I'm talking about as she points to the door with her finger. I don't hesitate to run out the door in hopes I can still catch her.

Rushing down the hallway still in my towel, I head straight towards the elevator, but I'm too late. When I reach it, it's already closing. Pushing at the button in hopes it will re-open, I'm disappointed when it doesn't. Banging at the metal door staring back at me in anger, I contemplate whether or not it would be worth taking the stairs.

Laying my head against the door, I bang at it, feeling a sense of heartache and loss. I knew last night she was out of my league, but that doesn't mean I would ever forget her. No, her smile will be forever engraved in my memories.

Voices

Present day

Victoria

THAT VOICE. I recognize it. It haunts my deepest memories, captivating my thoughts when the chance occurs. Awake or in my dreams, it doesn't matter which state I'm in; it's the only memory I hold of him. My body comes to a halt and my legs grow weak, unable to keep moving. Cowering in the safety of the hallway leading me to the waiting room, the wall keeps me vertical as I close my eyes and surrender to the agony of my mind playing tricks on me. Just this morning, I had awoken from another heartbreaking dream, torturing me by keeping him on my mind the entire morning. This is what must be happening, my mind playing another trick on me.

The booming of his laughter snaps my eyes open.

There is no possible way I've imagined the sound. It echoes clear as the night I heard it the first time. Trembling, I gradually find the courage to take a glimpse to ease my wayward mind. My breath hitches while my heart momentarily stops beating. It's him. The one I walked away from. The one and only regret from a night in which I constantly wish I could turn back time and return to. It was the *only* night I've ever felt free.

Why is he here in Seattle? The last time I'd seen him it was in New York, so I had assumed that was where he resided, leaving me to also ask why he would be seeking out a lawyer. He is sitting in the waiting room of the law firm I currently work at.

A wailing distracts me from his form and has me looking to his side. Sitting next to him is the same girl who attended the charity event with him. Another cry vibrates in the room and she tries her best to calm the baby, but it's effortless.

"Is she hungry?" he worriedly asks.

Rocking the baby back and forth in her arms, she looks just as concerned.

"She can't be. I just fed her." She seems to consider his theory while looking down to the baby.

"Feed her again," he commands.

"She isn't hungry," she snaps. "Anyway, I'm trying to wean her, remember?"

He bleakly looks down to the baby as if contemplating other options. "Maybe she needs to be changed."

"I already changed her," the woman replies with a fierce look aimed at him. "You really need to stop lecturing me. I know how to take care of my own baby," she bites back. "She's probably just gassy." Patting the baby's back, she attempts to soothe her.

"She's probably just pissed because you won't give her the tit. I would be," he grimly replies. Looking down at his watch, he appears frustrated. "How much fucking longer are they going to take to call us back?"

"Trey! Language."

"I'll stop lecturing you about the baby when you stop lecturing me about my language," he throws at her.

Who is she to him?

His girlfriend?

The thought has an unwelcome feeling traveling through my veins. If she is, how come she never came searching for him when she returned from the event? Knowing she was his date that night still signifies they are close. From the way he looks down at the baby with tenderness, she must be an important part of his life. By the age of the baby, something more may have developed between the two and she is the result. It *has* been a few years since I'd last seen him and it was clear he was a typical man whore willing to screw anything that came his way. The bitterness of my thoughts has me seething as I continue to spy on them both.

The baby's cries have calmed to whimpers. Completely ignoring the reprimand from the girl next to him, he focuses solely on the child she's holding. His eyes turn affectionate as he smiles down to her and pinches her cheeks. "I'm sorry, baby girl, but these assholes are testing my patience, too," he says, making me chuckle at his complete disregard of obeying her request.

"Trey!"

Oh, yes, now I recall his name.

The baby's whimpers have returned to cries. He's lost his patience and grabs the baby from her arms. Bringing her up close to his chest, he immediately begins rocking her. All cries and whimpers vanish and she is silent in his arms.

"See. I know how to make her happy."

The girl looks defeated. "I don't know how you do it," she grimaces. "But I'm serious, Trey, you really do need to watch what you say around her. I don't want her first word to be a curse word."

He rolls his eyes and continues to rock the baby.

The girl is looking around in search of something. "Have you seen my phone?"

"Did you take it off the charger in the car?"

Her eyes go up as if thinking. "Crap. I think I left it in the car."

"And you're lecturing me about my language?"

Her lips go flat, as if at a loss.

"Victoria!"

My name is shouted from behind me, startling me at the precise moment I catch him whipping his head in my direction. The blood drains from my body in reaction as I cower behind the safety of the wall, my heart erratically racing at this point.

"Victoria?"

"Shhh!" I lecture to Melissa, another junior associate, who is now standing in front of me with a perplexed face.

"Is there something wrong?" she asks me.

"No." My body trembles as I answer. Her doubtfully arched brow tells me she knows I'm not being truthful.

"Jones is still waiting for the file he requested."

"Shit!" I whisper harshly. It's the reason why I was on my way to the front desk. Hearing his voice distracted me from my task.

"Would you do me the biggest favor and grab it for me?"

Her brow rises higher. "And why can't you do it?" she draws out.

"It's complicated."

She's skeptically waiting for further details, but now is not the time, nor the place.

"Please," I plead. Before she can answer, I see Trey and the girl walking in our direction. My eyes go wide in fear before I yank Melissa by the arm and pull her through the open door at our side. Just as quickly, I shut the door behind us.

Melissa takes in our surroundings. "Why are we hiding in the file room?"

His booming voice can be heard outside the door. Both my heart and breath come to a standstill as I stare wide-eyed at the door, as if it would spontaneously open by him. The sound of retreating footsteps has me releasing my breath.

"Victoria?" Melissa asks.

"Like I said, it's complicated," I breathlessly answer.

Her lips go flat and her earlier expression returns. Melissa knows I won't be disclosing any information, which is why she's irritably staring back at me.

"Complicated or not, you have a file to retrieve," she orders, yanking open the door.

No longer having the fear of coming face to face with him, I step into the hallway to complete my earlier task. Requesting the file for the new client whose appointment is now running late because of my distraction, I rush it back to Jones, one of the partners from the firm.

"What the hell took you so long?" His impatient reaction to my delay is no surprise.

"Sorry," I utter, the only answer I can give him.

He takes the file, dismissing me just as fast. Returning to the small office I share with Melissa and two other junior associates, my mind cannot stop wondering why Trey would be in our office. Is it because of the baby?

Unable to resist, I use Google to research the night of the charity event. Within minutes, I'm reminded of the name of the guest speaker, Abigail Adams, the legendary former model turned runner.

Of course I wouldn't have known the full details of her personal life, regardless of how popular she is. Gossip is the reason why I don't read the tabloids. Lord knows I would run the risk of reading about my father at some point. I already live with enough disappointment from his actions. Thankfully, my mother spares me the details during our conversations when I am mandated to call her. With as little details as there are, there is no mention of him at all.

My research is interrupted when a message from Benjamin, another partner in the firm, requesting me to his office pops up on my laptop. Disappointed I've hit a dead end, I leave my *research* behind. Entering Benjamin's office minutes later, my heart stops as I stare at the back of the same person I was cowering from not so long ago.

"There she is," Benjamin announces, extending his arm in my direction when he sees me walk in. "Victoria will take it from here. You have no worries at all."

Trey turns to take me in and the blood drains from my body when our eyes meet. For a moment, there is no sign he recognizes me until his lips curve up into a smile and his eyes light up.

"You." He grins.

"Victoria!" Abigail excitedly let's out as she recognizes me.

"You know each other?" Benjamin asks as he looks between us with confusion.

Answering with a forced smile, I say, "We have a mutual friend," reminding me Julio isn't with her as he had been the last time we met.

"Where *is* Julio?" I brave to ask, knowing if she answers he is no longer in her service I will somehow grow disappointed.

"He has the day off." Abigail looks to Trey. "This is perfect! Don't you think?" she enthusiastically asks him.

He doesn't share the same reaction as her. Instead, he's scornfully looking at me, as one would eye their long time enemy, before he answers.

"Yes, I would say it's perfect," he says, full of sarcasm.

A frown mars Abigail's face before Benjamin cheerfully replies, "Well, then. Everything is set. Victoria will keep in touch, but please don't hesitate to contact her with any concerns."

His statement returns my attention back to him. "What is it exactly that I am taking over?"

Benjamin waves my question off. "Ms. Adams has requested we review her most recent contract. Simple stuff." He extends her file out to me, then dismisses me soon after.

It's his normal behavior, which is why I'm allowed to leave, and gives me the chance to escape. I leave Benjamin's office as quickly as my legs can take me, needing to escape Trey's much too gleeful cast.

In the confines of my office my ecstatic mind is finding trouble coming back under control. I feel as if I've returned to the morning of waking up in his hotel room, lost and confused over how to react. A silhouette standing at my door draws my attention, my eyes crashing into *him* when I look up. His head is cocked to the side, arms crossed over his chest, eyes narrowed down into slits.

His athletic build was obvious compared to most men in the room, but it was his striking blue eyes that drew my attention to him the very first night we met. I'd seen him from across the room and was instantly mesmerized. Never would I have thought I'd be leaving with him that night. The clearing of his throat draws me back to the present.

"Is there anything I can help you with, sir?" I ask, masking the trepidation coursing through my veins.

"Actually, there is," he says with the same mischievous grin from earlier.

The simple answer has my breath hitching and my

heart just as rapidly coming to a halt. Swallowing, I wait for him to continue.

"Why did you walk out that morning?" he curiously asks with raised brows.

I was dreading that question, hoping he wouldn't ask.

"I'm sorry, sir, but I don't know what you're speaking of."

His jaw tightens, his expression turning annoyed, the complete opposite of the tender kisses I once received from the same mouth.

"Is that so?" he draws out.

I may have been intoxicated the previous evening, but it didn't take long for me to remember what had occurred after shamefully walking away.

His frown is expected, only it doesn't remain because his lips curl up again to one side. "Would you care for me to remind you? I'm pretty sure I can think of several ways to boost your memory," he says, wagging his brow while asking.

I'm left muddled over how to correctly respond.

"Trey?"

He doesn't turn when his name is called, instead keeping his focus entirely on me when he answers.

"Yes, Supermodel?"

An odd name to call her since she is no longer a model. His broad frame takes up most of the entrance, but from her response, I can tell she's standing directly behind him.

"Umm," she tries to answer, sounding apologetic. "We need to leave if we're going to make it back in time for Matt's game."

He's expressionless for a moment before resuming his conversation with me.

"I guess I'll be seeing you around. Maybe then I can restore that memory of me," he delivers with a wink before turning, leaving me to watch him walk away without a backwards glance. Abigail is oddly gazing at his retreating form then turns to me with an apologetic smile.

"It was nice seeing you again," she says before waving goodbye.

I take in my first breath, thankful he had no longer pursued our conversation, but still dismayed he hadn't. It leaves me with an endless amount of reasons why he's done so.

Rejection

Victoria

MY DAY IS uneventful. The reviewing and preparing of our clients' files done, my usual phone calls complete. Five more minutes and my day will be over, my week for that matter.

"Victoria, you have a client on line two." The sound of the click immediately follows before I have a chance to inquire who is calling. Sighing, my gut tells me this phone call will be keeping me busy for a while. Picking up the receiver to answer the call, I say, "Victoria Montgomery speaking."

With a deep baritone voice, I hear from the other end, "Montgomery. It has a ring to it." The sound has my breath catching.

"May I ask whom I'm speaking with?" I ask, already

knowing who it is, but continuing my façade from yesterday.

"Let me see. You never did refer to me with a specific name, but "harder," "more," and "oh, God," were repeatedly screamed from your lips. Very sexy lips, if I recall. But, please, remind me of what my name is. Or were you too uncaring to want to find out?"

"Mr. Johnson, if this phone call has nothing to do with your client, Ms. Adams, then I apologize, but I will have to end the phone call."

"So you do know my name?"

"Yes, in fact, I do. It's my job to know very important details about our clients to better provide them with the best service possible. I did some research after you left to be better prepared for our next meeting."

"In other words, you were stalking me? That's good to know."

I blush, because I did in fact do more research than needed past Abigail Adams herself.

"Research, Mr. Johnson," I answer, hearing a groan from the other end upon saying it. "Solely for research purposes only, as I said," I continue, but knowing it's still a lie. I refuse to willingly admit the fact, though.

"You know, I really do look forward to hearing you moan Mr. Johnson from those same lips."

I'm appalled he would say such a thing, especially since he's called our office.

"You are aware this phone call is costing your client three hundred dollars an hour?" I remind him.

"Chump change for Supermodel."

"How considerate of you to waste her money," I dryly let out.

"Whatever it takes to get your attention, Ms. Montgomery. Or is it Mrs. whatever that cheating asshole's last name is, now?"

Rubbing my temples, I sigh. "No, it's still Montgomery," I reply. Then it occurs to me, I know I would have never disclosed details of my relationship to him. "May I ask who it is you're referring to?" I bravely ask.

"Julio mentioned you were dating some guy when we slept together."

His comment has me closing my eyes and silently groaning as he reminds me of the mistake I had made.

"So did you dump the asshole?" he inquires.

"You keep referring to him as an asshole as if you know the man personally," I say fearfully. I hope it isn't true, although from the years we've put between us, he never once did reappear in my social circle.

"You don't need to know a man to consider him an asshole."

I find myself asking, "Are you speaking from experience?"

"Maybe," he replies with a half-hearted laugh. "But it's probably best you discover for yourself. The first time we didn't have adequate time because you seemed to be in a hurry to get somewhere."

"It won't be necessary," I snap back, still in dismay over what occurred the first time we met.

"You sound sure of yourself on that one," he mocks.

"*I am.*"

"Whatever, princess," he growls before becoming silent, as if he's ended the call.

"Mr. Johnson?" I risk asking to inquire if he's still on the line, but the echo of my voice confirms he's hung up.

Hastily searching my desk for Abigail Adams's file, I find it still sitting in the center of my desk. Opening it up, I know I've come across a contact number for him at some point in time. Dialing it, I impatiently wait as it rings, but get his voicemail.

"Sorry I missed your call. You know what to do," his recording says, making me slam the receiver down onto its cradle without leaving a message. Sitting and continuing to grow frustrated over the phone call will get me nowhere.

Silence surrounds me, as I'm the only one left in the office. Late nights are normal for me. Dedication over personal life has been my family motto since childhood. My own career hasn't been any different.

Abigail Adams's file stares back at me. I know it from beginning to end. There isn't any more than his name and phone number in her file. The two addresses noted for Abigail are in Portland, Oregon, and the other in Riverside, California. Odd, but not unusual for her type of clientele. Most celebrities usually have more than one home.

Closing the file as if it would shut out his memory, I return my attention to the case I had been working on before taking his call. Two hours later, my mind is still in turmoil over the phone call. Surrendering, I pack up my laptop and close up my files, neatly organizing them in a pile.

It's Friday. I'm going home, drinking a glass of wine,

and putting the day behind me.

Trey

Cute little debutant seemed so sure of herself. Not much of her demeanor has changed from the first night I met her. I guess I shouldn't expect it to have by her actions the following morning. I knew from the night I fucked her I wasn't in her league. I should have listened to my conscience to leave her be, but my stubbornness wouldn't let me forget her. All I've been able to accomplish in the last three years is to dull my memory of her, nothing more.

She may have walked away the first time, but she isn't going to get the chance to do it again. I already have my plan in place. It's initiating said plan where I may have a problem. If she doesn't break down the walls of her pretentious ego, it will never happen. My dick doesn't seem to understand he's going to have to be patient until I can. Until then, I just need a distraction. Someone new. A fresh piece of ass, it's exactly what I plan on finding tonight.

My eyes are closed and I'm desperately trying to let my mind savor the sensation of the girl's warm mouth wrapped around my shaft, but I fail. Her little moans cause me to snap them back open, it sounds too similar to the memory of the girl I am trying to push from my head. Looking down at the girl vicariously sucking away, I'm left disappointed when it's confirmed it's indeed not the girl of my imagination.

My dick automatically goes limp in disappointment and the girl between my thighs is looking at it in confusion. Her drunken expression doesn't help how I feel.

"What the hell?"

Ignoring her slurred comment, I force my eyes shut and dig my fingers through the girl's hair, imagining it's someone else between my legs. It works, helping my once limp dick rise to the occasion and get what it was waiting for: completion.

My drunken guest is already rising to take her clothes off, but fails miserably as she loses her balance and stumbles to the floor. Sighing at the pathetic sight, I stand to help her up.

"How about we get you home?"

"But, I thought we were going to fuck?"

Fuck . . . Exactly what I *would* have done, but I'm no longer in the mood.

"Sorry, babe. You're too far gone for me to enjoy it," I tell her, using the only excuse I know will work.

"What does me being drunk have to do with it?" she purrs, already reaching for my dick. Pushing her hand away, she scowls back at me.

"I don't do drunk girls. It's not my thing."

The words are bitterly eating away at my conscience as I remember the last time I thought those words. Only then I had intended to keep them, but failed miserably.

"Fuck you!" she shouts, trying to step back, but stumbles again. I catch her, thinking to myself: *drunken girls*.

They can never last long before they pass out.

Not true.

The last drunk girl surprised the shit out of me.

"You know, you're a real asshole."

"So I've been told," I remark. "Is this your place?"

The girl turns, her drunken smile returning. "Yeah, you want to come in?"

Shaking my head at her, I would have thought her throwing up in the parking lot earlier would have cleared her mind a little.

"No. I'm good."

"You're just ditching me?" she whines.

"You're lucky I was a gentleman enough to get you home," I bite back.

Another girl opens the door. She surprisingly looks at me for a moment before she turns to the girl in front of me. "You her roommate?" I ask, hitching my thumb at the drunken mess at my side.

She crosses her arms over her chest as she delivers a glare. "Yes," she growls at me. Taking a better look at her, I notice she looks familiar. Surveying the building better, I realize it also looks familiar.

"Did you screw her, too?" the girl at the door asks.

"No," I quickly reply. "I don't screw drunk girls."

Anymore, I should say, but I'm not going to. "Do I

know you?" I brave to ask.

"You should since you screwed *me*."

Oh. That's why she's glaring at me. My bad. How am I supposed to remember every girl I fucked?

"Here, get her ass to bed," I demand, shoving her roommate into the apartment and turning to walk away. My ass needs to get away from here and the roommate as fast as possible.

I'm already at my car driving back to my place when my phone starts ringing. Looking down at it, I'm perplexed. I don't recognize the number and it's almost one in the morning. Matt better not be in jail, or Abigail, for that matter.

"Hello?" I answer with the car's Bluetooth.

"Are all men assholes?" The question comes out in a slur through the speakers of the car; it almost makes me laugh when I recognize who is speaking.

"Do you always drunk dial men?"

"I'm not drunk!" she screeches. With the volume in the car set loud, it makes me wince. "Tipsy?" I correct.

"You haven't answered my question."

I sigh. "Not always."

"Good, because I really don't want you to be an asshole. I have enough of those in my life." Her remark has me smiling again.

Somehow the way she's responded leaves me hopeful. I still don't know why, but I'm hopeful, nevertheless.

"Princess, why are you calling me?"

"Why are you calling me that? I'm not a princess."

"You haven't answered my question," I mock.

"I tried calling another asshole and he lectured me for being drunk. I hate when he lectures me," she replies. "It's all they do," she finishes with a sigh.

"Who would this asshole be?"

"Not you."

Somehow, she's managed to make me forget why I'm asking her. She remains silent for a couple of seconds. I know she hasn't ended the call because it's still connected on the Bluetooth.

"Princess?"

"Huh?" She sounds startled.

"Did you pass out on me?" I can't help but laugh at imagining her doing so.

"No, I was just laying here thinking of you."

My brows rise. Curious, I have to ask, "You're in bed?"

"Yes," she answers in a husky tone.

Fuck, now she has me asking, "You naked?" I joke.

With the same husky voice, she says, "Yes."

My car jerks and the car next to me honks. I was *not* expecting her to answer with a "yes."

"You okay?" she asks, sounding concerned. "What are you doing?"

"Trying to not kill myself," I mumble under my breath.

Another "Huh?" comes from her.

"Never mind. Why are you naked?" I risk returning to the conversation.

"I took a bath," she replies. "And I like to sleep naked," she casually adds.

Groaning, I briefly close my eyes and remember how

delectable her naked body looked below me. When my eyes open my dick is as hard as a rock. Pulling up to a red light, I look down at my groin and complain, "Now you decide to be hard?"

"Who are you talking to?"

"My friend Hector."

Another honk, this time behind me, has me breaking my thoughts.

"Why do I hear so much honking?"

"Because I'm driving."

"What?" Another screech. "You're in your car with someone named Hector?"

Throwing my head back, a bellow of a laugh comes out.

"Don't worry. I'm alone."

"Then why did you say you were speaking with your friend Hector?" she asks, sounding completely confused.

"Hector is my dick."

"Why in the world would you name your dick Hector?"

"It's better than calling it a pecker."

The truth behind the story is when I was a child and my father would refer to it as "my pecker," I would respond with "*Hector.*" Regardless of all the times he would try to get me to correct it, I couldn't. The name just stuck.

She sighs on the other end. "Hector did do a good job that night."

My eyes go wide and my hands grip tightly on my steering wheel to keep from swerving again.

"Princess, you're not helping with my hard-on." I'm

already pulling into my driveway when I say it. Thank God. I don't know how I would react if she were to speak anymore dirty thoughts while I was on the road. Killing the engine, the phone call still continues.

I can hear her heavy breathing as she asks, "Were you serious about reminding me about that night?"

Now I'm the one practically panting.

"Yes."

"Then remind me."

Swallowing deep, I contemplate whether to take her offer or not.

"I can't truly do it with the distance we have between us," I say as I remember she's in Seattle and I'm now back in Portland. Hector is telling me to start the engine and speed over to her, but my mind is the only coherent one at the moment, informing me it would be a waste of time. I have to take advantage of what I have: her voice.

I can hear her disappointed sigh.

Closing my eyes, I remember every detail of the night.

"Every inch of your body felt like silk," I huskily tell her. "I couldn't get enough of touching you. I still dream about it to this day." She rewards me with a moan that echoes throughout the car.

"Your kisses tasted of the champagne you drank that night. I've never liked the taste of champagne until I kissed you. You make me crave it."

Hector is straining to be let out at this point. Reaching down, I try to shift him in my pants, but it makes it worse as my hand makes contact and she lets out another moan.

"Why did I leave?" she complains.

It's the bucket of cold water I needed to remind me of how she marched out of my life the next morning.

"Why *did* you leave?" I ask, wanting clarification myself.

"Because it shouldn't have happened." Another cold bucket of water returning me to reality.

"I think I better let you go," I regretfully inform her.

"What if I don't want to let you go?"

The admission has me stiffening in my seat.

"Let me ask you something, *Victoria.*"

"What happened to *princess?*"

Ignoring her question, I get to the point. "Why did you *really* call me tonight?"

I receive silence for a couple of seconds.

"I don't know," she admits.

"Then I think it's best I let you go. Goodnight, Victoria." Pushing the button on the screen, I end the phone call.

The satellite radio returns to playing music, and ironically it's playing "*Am I Wrong.*"

I don't receive another phone call immediately after hanging up on her as I did earlier, which is for the best. I already know I shouldn't be playing with fire, and she is the flame of desire. But I've learned from my first mistake with her: Never mess with an intoxicated girl; it will lead to regret.

Maybe she's right. There shouldn't be anything occurring between us. I've always told myself I wouldn't be pathetic enough to fall prey to being trapped and her actions in the past are a clear reminder of why I kept telling myself I wouldn't. She isn't the first girl who has given me a reason to harden my heart, nor will she be the last, because there is no fucking way I will ever let a girl tie me down.

Or have I already done so?

Because since the day I met her, she's all I can ever think of.

Closing my eyes and throwing my head on the head-rest, I let out a heavy sigh, thinking of her as I've done for hours. I don't know what the hell I got myself into, but there is no one who will ever compare to her. I was stupid enough to think they could. She's champagne when all I ever drink is beer, far beyond what I'm allowed to have.

Defeat

Victoria

WITH A SMILE, I stare down at the document in my hands, satisfied with my work. Weeks' worth of back and forth negotiations to give Abigail the best possible deal has been my primary focus. She had left me with enough details of exactly what she required and from the tone in her voice during our only conversation, she wasn't taking no for an answer. I admired her for it.

I had made the dreaded call to her manager, bracing myself for his expected rejection, but he didn't answer. Being *this* phone call was for professional purposes, I was forced to leave a message this time. Thankfully, it was she who had returned my phone call, and not her manager.

Ready to return the contract to Benjamin to have Abigail sign, I enter his office minutes later.

"I'm done with Abigail Adams's contract. It just needs her signature and we can return it to their lawyers," I say, referring to the sports magazine, which she plans to do a photo shoot and interview for.

I had never heard of contracts needing to be involved when it came to interviews or photo shoots, but Abigail and her manager were adamant there be a contract in place prior to the date it was to take place. Since my sole intention was to stay clear of the media, who am I to know what was involved with these things? My specialty will be family law, which is what our office focuses on. How we obtained Abigail Adams as a client and are representing her for the type of industry she's in is still a mystery to me, but Benjamin speaks highly of her and claims he has been with her for years and wouldn't turn her away when she is in need of a lawyer.

Negotiations are negotiations, regardless whether they are made in court, our office, or on paper. I thrive on the thrill of attaining the win in the end. It's why I gave no argument when ordered to draw up her contract.

He holds out his hand for the document, and I pass it to him, waiting while he reviews it. I've left tabs on the side pointing out the areas in which I made changes. It takes him quite some time to review each change, the entire time I stand and wait for his approval. Reaching the last page, he looks up at me with a satisfied smile.

"Looks good," he says, holding the contract out to return it to me. "Have her sign it."

Taking it from him, I say, "Of course. I'll call her

now."

Leaving his office, I exit with pride. For something I was never expecting to ever have to handle in my life, I am proud of myself for accomplishing it.

This time I call the number Abigail had informed me to call when done. She answers after a few rings, but I was not expecting for her to say, "I need you to come to me. I can't go to you."

"I'm sorry, but I don't believe that will be possible," I politely inform her.

The wail of her baby shrieks through the phone.

"There isn't any other option. I need that contract returned by tomorrow morning so I can do the shoot on Sunday. I'm caught up in training all day today so I can't leave the city. You *have* to come to me." The baby lets out another cry, keeping me from denying her once again. "I've got to go. You have my Portland address. I'll meet you later today." She hangs up on me as soon as she's done.

She hung up on me!

Do they both have the habit of hanging up on people as if it is normal? Slamming the receiver down as I let out a frustrated huff, I'm now discovering this is becoming one of *my* bad habits.

Sending Benjamin a message to inform him of my conversation with Abigail, I'm confident he will side with me and agree that she has no choice but to come in and sign the contract or lose the deal.

What I don't expect is his response.

Victoria: I've spoken with Abigail Adams via phone and she insists we take the contract to her to have it signed.

I informed her it would not be possible. She is aware the contract needs to be returned by tomorrow morning, but still insists she cannot come to us.

Benjamin: Why can't you take her the contract to have it signed? You have the address in her file.

Victoria: She lives in Portland.

Benjamin: You have a car. Take it to her.

Victoria: When did we begin to provide out of town courier service?

Benjamin: TAKE IT TO HER.

He used shouty caps on me!

At this point, I'm ready to throw my laptop across the room. I want to type out "Are you serious?" but that would be pushing it too far. He does have the ability to fire me. I'd already pushed the limits with my first response.

I'm left with no choice but to call defeat.

Knowing it would take three or so more hours to drive to her, a look at the time tells me it will be around 7 P.M. on a Friday by the time I reach her, meaning I am going to get stuck in traffic there if I don't leave soon.

Fine.

I'll just drive there, stand at the door while she signs the document, then leave. She states it's *her* address. He's her manager. I know for a fact he can't be at her side every minute of the day, so I won't be running into him.

Yes. That is the plan and I have nothing to worry about.

Checking the address on the gate and comparing it to what

I had written down, I confirm it's the correct house. The navigation on my car did not steer me wrong. My only roadblock is a giant security gate keeping me from entering the premises. It's strange. I'm in a modest residential area. All the houses are simple and far from extravagant. The gate has it standing out compared to all the others, but I do remember she was a celebrity of some sort at one point. It must be for privacy reasons.

Rolling down my window and pressing the button on the security box, I wait for admittance.

"May I help you?" An older female voice replies from the box.

"I have an appointment with Ms. Adams."

"Please hold."

I'm expecting the gate to immediately open, but instead I'm left waiting for a few more minutes. I'm about to press the call button again when the gate finally begins to creak open. Driving my car forward, I'm not surprised to find a modest looking house similar to the others in the neighborhood. Parking my car in the only space available, next to a shiny black Escalade, I turn the car off.

Grabbing the document from my briefcase, I exit the car and walk towards the front door. As I'm raising my hand to knock, it opens before I can make contact. My jaw drops and my eyes are the size of saucers when I take in who opened the door.

Him!

"Can I help you?" he slowly draws out, glaring at me.

Checking the numbers indicating the address, I find I'm at the location listed. "What are you doing here?" I choke out.

"I live here."

Just as rapidly, I throw back, "I thought Abigail lived here."

"She does."

Now I'm shocked speechless. It also confirms all my speculations whether he has a relationship with Abigail or not. It's obvious he must if he lives with her.

Finding the breath to speak again, I say, "Abigail sent for me."

"She's not here. Come back later," he says then slams the door in my face.

My jaw drops to the floor. The audacity of this man! I pound on the door, demanding he open it. It opens, but it's an older lady apologetically staring back at me.

"I'm sorry, ma'am. Mr. Trey wasn't expecting you. Please, come in," she insists, widely opening the door to grant me entrance.

I'm trembling from anger as I step across the threshold. I immediately see him on the phone, bellowing out, "You knew she was coming?" A second passes before he adds, "I told you I never wanted to fucking see her again!" Spinning in my direction, his mouth falls open when he eyes me.

I turn to leave, refusing to be in the same room as him for his comment. I'm barely taking the first step when he's shouting. "Where are you going?" I ignore him, already reaching the front door. "I'll call you back."

A large hand slams down against the door, keeping me from opening it. Freezing, I debate whether to turn.

My heated blood still has me trembling in my spot. I can feel him standing directly behind me, the warmth of his presence radiating directly at me, making my heart pound against my chest. Bravely, I turn to face him, my heart now lodged in my throat when I face him, mere inches from me.

"She said she would be here."

Removing his arm from my side, he folds both over his chest. "She's in L.A. She arrives in the morning," he discloses. "You weren't supposed to hear what I told her," he delivers, expressionless.

Whether I was intended to hear it or not, I did. What I'm more concerned about is why Abigail would order I drive up here when she never intended to meet me. "She told me she was here, in Portland, training."

"She lied," he grits out.

My head jerks back in surprise.

"The contract has to be signed by tomorrow. She knows that."

"Exactly. She had me schedule a courier a couple of hours ago to pick it up at noon. Now I know why."

Feeling the disapproval of me being here, I thrust the contract at his chest. He confusedly looks down at it as he takes it.

"Abigail's contract for her to sign. Normally we wouldn't leave unsigned contracts with our clients, but under the circumstances, I have no other choice. I've labeled exactly where she needs to sign," I say, pointing at the tabs sticking out on the edge of the pages. "Make sure it gets to them on time or else the agreement is void," I command.

He frowns. "Isn't it your job to make sure it gets there

on time?"

"How am I supposed to do that if she's not here to sign it?"

"Like I said, she'll be here tomorrow. You can return then."

Now I'm irritated. It would mean I'd have to return to Seattle and drive back early in the morning.

"Fine," I clip out. "I'll be back tomorrow." I try to take the contract back, but he firmly holds on to it.

"You can't take it yet. I have to review it."

"I heeded every order she requested. There is nothing but perfection in this contract." Once again, I try to yank it back. He pulls it from my grasp, holding it up in the air at his side where I can't reach it.

"You hungry?" he asks. "I'm hungry," he says. He's completely lost me.

"What does you being hungry have to do with the contract?"

"We can go over the terms and conditions of the contract over dinner." He opens the front door urging me outside. "I told you. The contract is perfect," I argue. "Besides, any changes made would require me to formally draw up a new contract. I can't do that here in Portland." By this time, he's steered me to the passenger side of the car. Opening the door and urging me into the seat, he shuts the door quickly after I climb in.

I'm furious at him for not listening to me. Seconds later, he's climbing into the driver's side.

"Where are we going?"

Without looking at me, he answers, "I told you. Dinner."

"Weren't you just complaining you didn't want to *ever* see me again?"

He flinches. "I already told you, you weren't supposed to hear that."

"Well, I did." Asshole is what I want to finish the sentence with. "Thank you for the offer, but I will have to decline. I'm here on business."

As soon as I answer, he jerks the car into motion, preventing me from exiting the car. "Trey!" Mischievously, he smiles. "Stop this car and let me out!" I protest, but it does nothing as he keeps driving away from the house.

Crossing my arms over my chest, I pout in frustration. Coming to my senses, I ask, "What about Abigail?"

"I already told you. She'll be back tomorrow morning."

He doesn't comprehend my question. "Won't she be upset you're taking me out to dinner?"

His eyebrows draw down in confusion. "Why would she care?"

I'm appalled at how he treats his relationship with her.

"You really are an asshole," I throw at him.

"What the hell is your problem?"

"You!"

"Is this about earlier?"

Throwing my hands up in exasperation, I say, "This is about *you.* I can't believe you would cheat on Abigail. I don't know her on a personal level, but I know from personal *experience* she doesn't deserve it."

His laughter renders me speechless.

"You think I'm dating Abigail?" My mouth opens to speak, but nothing comes out, allowing him to continue laughing.

"Aren't you?"

"You have a lot to learn," he comments with a shake of his head.

Needing to distract myself, I ask, "This is your car?" I imagined he would have something different.

A sports car, maybe.

"I needed something safe to drive Emily in."

"Who's Emily?"

Still looking straight ahead, he answers, "My baby girl."

Knowing he's willingly giving up information, I continue to probe. "So she's yours?" I ask, bracing myself for his admission.

He briefly glances at me with a smirk. "You're all about asking questions tonight, aren't you?"

"I'm always asking questions. I prefer facts instead of rumors—a lesson learned from personal experience."

His smirk widens. "Good," he says, turning to focus on the road ahead of us.

He still hasn't answered my question, nor confirmed or denied my earlier speculation. But my mind is too distracted on his physique to insist he answer. The couple of times I've seen him, I've not been allowed the luxury of fully taking him in. The first night we met, I had no intention of engaging in any type of personal connection with him upon our meeting. He'd instantly repulsed me with his attitude. But actions speak louder than words and by the end of the night, I was putty in his hands, both physically and mentally.

Our last encounter was similar to the first. He immediately reminded me of why I had been repulsed by him in the beginning. His condescending demeanor had kept me from wanting to rekindle any exchange we had in the past.

It was for the best. I shouldn't be allowing myself to stray from my initial reaction and form any type of friendship with him that would cause me reason to call myself a hypocrite, leaving me to wonder why I'm accepting his offer of dinner.

Feeling the vehicle come to a slow stop in a parking lot, my thoughts break. Taking in our surroundings, I'm confused. "Where are we?"

"The Brewhouse." He turns off the engine and exits his side. Deliberately taking my time to exit my side, I'm still trying to decipher exactly where we can possibly be.

With me at his side, we walk to the entrance. Entering, he bypasses the hostess with a nod of greeting and heads straight through the restaurant. We pass several empty tables, but he doesn't stop until we've reached the far back of the building to a specific table he seats himself at.

To say it's a table is quite an overstatement. It's more of a wooden picnic bench sitting near a wall full of flat screen televisions. He takes a seat directly facing them, his focus already on a specific one. Looking over his shoulder where I'm standing and staring at him with perplexity, he asks, "Aren't you going to sit?" He nods to his side.

Hesitantly heeding what I believe is his request, I struggle to take my seat with what I'm wearing. The tight pencil skirt I most favor as my work attire leaves me with a difficulty to casually seat myself. The entire time I attempt to gracefully take my seat, Trey is humorously watching me.

My skirted suit is a far cry from the casual attire everyone else is wearing, making me stand out. I'm not dressed for this kind of environment.

"I thought you said we were going out to dinner?" I ask at the precise moment a waitress hands Trey a tall glass of beer.

"Another one?" she remarks, staring right at me. I scrunch my nose at the reasons why she must be making the comment. "Where in the world do you boys find these girls?"

"Shut it, Carol," he snaps at her.

Her eyes pierce me with a glare. "Is she as brave as the last one to drink a beer?"

Before I can answer I would *never* drink beer, Trey is ordering, "Bring her some water."

"With lemon, please," I add. She snickers while turning away to grant my request. "Was it necessary to bring me to a facility where your past liaisons would want to gouge my eyes out?"

This makes him chuckle. "If you think Carol and I have a past, then you're wrong. That was Matt's department. I have a very specific rule to not mess with any girls my friends have fucked."

"How mindful of you," I mutter. "Is her attitude part of the service provided?" I ask as I fully take in the interior of the restaurant.

"Are you always this stuck up?"

This has me snapping my head in his direction. I'm gawking at him for his question. The waitress has conveniently returned with my water, keeping me from answering.

"You ready to order?" she asks from the end of the table. I'm staring in front of me, baffled as to how I am to order food if I was never given a menu.

As if reading my mind, Trey replies, "We're going to need a minute." He grabs a menu sitting near the napkin holder then hands it to me.

The waitress leaves and I look at him to answer. "No, I'm not always this *stuck up,* as you've so kindly put it."

"Then what's up with the snotty comments about the place? Not even Abigail acted this way the first time we brought her here, and she *has* money."

I've brought his reprimand upon myself. "I've never been in a place like this," I admit, knowing it's still no excuse for my poor behavior.

"To a brewery?"

"If it's what this is called, then yes." Considering all the places I've eaten, I add, "Or anywhere similar to this establishment."

"You've never been to a bar?"

"I've been to a bar," I defend, but it's he who finishes my argument. "Just not *this* kind of bar," he says, his head curiously cocked, waiting for me to deny his assertion.

Shaking my head to answer, I feel somewhat ashamed for it.

His brow rises high. "You really are from the other

side of town, aren't you?"

"What side would that be?" I ask, testing his opinion of me.

He's silent for a moment. "The rich side," he mumbles before pulling the contract from his back pocket.

Knowing it will now have a crease down the center, I cringe. Perfection is my downfall. Without accomplishing it, I feel like a failure. Opening it up and flattening it with his hand, he begins to peruse it, slightly turning his body to better face me.

"Looks good," he comments.

"You haven't even read it," I say, still upset over the scene he made back at the house over needing to review it.

"I trust you."

Now I'm agitated that he has wasted my time. "That's it? You're putting the security of your client in my trust?" I ask, pointing down at the contract. "What kind of manager are you?"

His chest puffs out and he's clearly upset. "The kind that isn't going to let her get screwed over," he grits out. "I've gotten Abigail out of the most difficult situations time and time again. It isn't my job on the line if she gets fucked over. It's yours."

He's correct. Benjamin knew what Abigail's needs were from this contract. If it were to show any inconsistencies out of her original request, it *would* cost me my job. Not him, or Trey.

"You're right." This is the one argument where I have clearly been defeated. "But you have nothing to fear. It's as you've both requested and more."

This catches his attention. "Really?"

Pointing out where I made my changes and had negotiated on Abigail and Trey's behalf impresses him.

"See, my trust in you was merited."

The waitress has returned to take our orders and when she leaves he returns his attention to the screens in front of us, completely ignoring me.

The building is surrounded by noise of every kind, however the silence between us is heavier than the decibels vibrating off the walls. His earlier comment pointing out our differences is still lingering in my mind. We may have started off despising each other because of a poor first impression, but I can't deny he fascinates me. It's rare for it to occur with someone I've just met. He's like no person I've ever met, and for that reason I'm unable to keep from wanting to be on the same side as him.

Chapter Five

Infatuation

Trey

VICTORIA MONTGOMERY.

Had you told me nearly three years ago I'd be having dinner with her, I would have snorted at you. Then I would have mentally pictured the scenario with a yearning for it to become true. She's been a constant memory I return to every so often, one I refused to permanently forget, nor allow myself to recall on a regular basis. Nevertheless, after discovering she may have been in a relationship when I slept with her, I figured it was most likely the reason why she bolted the next morning, I swore to never touch her again.

She never admitted to still being with the asshole when I asked her the other day and there is no ring on her finger, so in my eyes she's a free agent.

My eyes keep traveling down to her skirt, imagining what it'd be like to lift it completely up and around her waist. My dick has been semi-hard from the moment she tried seating herself. Shit, to be honest, it's been hard from the moment I answered the door and fully took her in. The professional demeanor is a turn on.

Her chocolate colored hair cascading down her shoulders is longer than the last time we were together. Then, it had reached just below her shoulders. Now it flows down to the center of her spine. The color is a perfect combination with her honey colored eyes. Both have been engraved in my mind from the very first night I met her.

Her figure is much slimmer from then, but not thin enough for concern. Perfectly matched for her form. At first, I would have believed it was due to the pressure of watching her figure, but to my surprise, she had casually ordered a burger and was now blissfully eating it.

The sound of a satisfied moan breaks my current thought and sends me returning to one of our past.

"Good?" I cannot help but ask as she wipes her mouth with her napkin. Her stiff posture and the dainty dabs she makes at the corners of her lips signify the blue blood she comes from.

"Very," she happily answers.

"Have you even had a burger before?"

With sneering eyes, she replies, "Of course I have. I'm beginning to believe every assumption you make of me is going to be compared to royalty." I'm ready to remark how it's her actions giving me a reason to think so, but I think better of it. "As a matter of fact, our cook used to make me burgers all the time as a child. Her burgers were the best. The entire staff said so," she continues.

"Cook. Staff. Next you'll be mentioning your nanny."

Her expression is relaying just how offended she is by my comment, but I continue. "With words like those, you're baiting me to call you royalty." She remains silent, but I know she cannot deny my presumption.

"I'm sorry if my upbringing offends you, but it wasn't my choice," she retaliates, unable to keep the resentment from her tone in her answer.

She pushes her plate forward, not completely done with her burger, but from the gratified expression and holding of her stomach, I know she's full. I've been finished for some minutes, allowing myself to lose my thoughts to her.

"Is it true what they say? You don't really have a life?"

From what little information Julio has given me of how he knew her, she has lived a secluded life. Julio still worries because she doesn't currently have her own bodyguard. What kind of life does she lead to make him worry?

"It's the only life I've ever known, but no, I didn't have a normal life." She sighs at the end of her answer. "You're right. We are royalty. Just without the crowns and titles. My family has always played a very important political role of some kind for centuries." Perking up with a smile. "My ancestor was one of the founding forefathers of the Declaration of Independence," she proudly conveys.

This has my eyes bulging out.

"But it also has its disadvantages. We are bred to uphold our reputation to continue the family legacy, to gain power and ensure it progresses into the next generation.

There is pressure from the moment you take your first breath up until the last. With power comes money, and with money comes threats. I may have never had need of anything growing up, but I also didn't live a normal childhood. I *was* surrounded by staff of every kind you can think of. I *did* have a nanny, but I also had a family bodyguard always watching from the shadows."

She mockingly looks at me. "I bet you had free range to do whatever you wanted."

"Most times, but I was also raised to work hard. All hands on deck was our family motto. Not money or power." I hadn't meant for the last to come out so defensive, but it did. "We have a big family, so it was just normal for us," I voice with a shrug of my shoulder.

This makes her smile. "How big?" she asks, sounding interested to know more.

"Too big."

"Oh, come on," she begs.

Dammit. The begging. Another memory making my dick twitch.

"I have one brother and two sisters. They're a pain in my ass, by the way. Four uncles, all married. My mom was the only girl. Twenty-six cousins, including myself. We all live in the same small town within a ten mile radius."

Her eyes bulge and her mouth parts slightly.

"Like I said, too big."

"It's perfect." This has me snorting. "Think about it. You were probably never lonely because you always had someone to play with, and I'm pretty sure every day you had some sort of excitement that didn't have you fearing it would end up in the tabloids or involve your life being in danger," she protests.

"Oh, my life was in danger a couple of times, but it was because I found it."

"Exactly," she says dryly. "Not the kind you were forced into."

Now I'm intrigued for more information. Urging her to speak, she takes a deep breath before she begins.

"When I was four, I was kidnapped. I don't remember much, a result of wanting to repress a traumatic event according to my childhood therapist. But according to details I've been drilled to remember, someone managed to come onto the grounds of our Hampton home during one of our holiday parties and they took me. They didn't make it very far because of the excellent security detail my family had, but it happened."

"It's why Julio has been insisting you have your own bodyguard?"

She nods. "He wasn't necessarily *my* bodyguard, but my father's. We always had several on hand, so I never actually had my own. I preferred it that way. Most can be emotionless, like robots. They're trained to stay in the background and never be seen unless necessary. Julio was different, though. He always sneaked me chocolate when he could and smiled at me when no one was looking. He showed me more emotion than my own father in the six years he was with us. I was really sad when he left."

"If I didn't know any better, I'd think you had a crush on him," I tease.

"I did at one point," she responds with a blush.

"The man is old enough to *be* your father!" I exclaim while my blood slowly rises in envy.

"I know, which is why it was only infatuation," she laughs out. "I was a minor then. It would have never happened, anyway."

She may claim it was only infatuation, but I'm sure as hell not going to leave them alone in the same room from now on. She's an adult now.

Completely taking her in, she's a fucking smoking hot adult. I'm not taking any chances.

"So how did you do it during college? I remember Abigail and Julio talking one day and he mentioned you refused a bodyguard while you were away."

"Was this before or after we met?"

"Before," I'm quick to answer. But I remember the day of the conversation, and although I may have been playing video games that day, the conversation of an unknown girl was intriguing. I'd held onto every single word discussed between them. Who would have known it'd be the same girl sitting at my side? Or the same girl I would have had mind-blowing sex with?

"I used my mother's maiden name in college. It was easy to do, as it's my middle name. They altered my first, so it helped hide me." Her hand extends forward for me to shake. "Hello, my name is Stephanie Mason," she relays with a smile. Shaking her hand with amusement, she returns my smile. "I was only allowed to attend with the promise to never have a social life that would put me in danger. I kept to myself. I had my own apartment, alleviating the need to have roommates. My sole purpose was to attend school and graduate. I lived a pretty boring life during college." She shrugs off the last sentence, but I can see the sorrow in her eyes.

As Julio has explained to Abigail, this girl has lived a secluded life and is happy with it.

"So you weren't the crazy college girl?" I joke.

"No," she casually answers.

"Not one party," I push.

She chuckles. "I went to parties, but they were social events involving my family in some way. They normally have detailed security involved so it eliminated the chance of any danger."

"So family shit?"

"Normally. Yes."

Her somber expression returns and I remember back to the night we met and she was alone. It wasn't a family event. No wonder why she was drunk off her ass. She didn't have anyone around to judge her for her behavior. She was free of her normal lifestyle.

"How did you meet Abigail Adams?" she asks, as if needing to change the subject.

"She showed up at our door one day looking for someone," I inform her. It is partially the truth, but I am not going to reveal the true reason why Abigail came knocking on our door that day. I may have slept with this girl, but I don't trust her enough to disclose Abigail's secret.

"You?" she questions.

It's almost as if I've picked up on an ounce of jealousy in her tone.

"I *was* the one who answered the door," I relay. "And

she kept coming back. As a matter of fact, she moved in not too long after."

"So you *are* a couple?" she rasps out, tormented eyes match her reply.

I've come to the conclusion she's speculating I have a relationship with Abigail. I had wanted to correct her the very first time, but taunting her is amusing.

"It's getting late," I say, reaching into my pocket to pull out some cash to pay for our dinner then throw it down onto the table, ready to leave. Grabbing the contract and stuffing it into my back pocket, I walk us back to the car, wanting to get her back to my place.

Most of the car ride back to the house is made in silence, until we are mere blocks from my driveway.

"Why did you take me out to dinner?" she demands to know. I can't help but smile at the sauciness she's put behind the words.

"It was dinner time. I was hungry," I nonchalantly answer.

From the corner of my eye I see her lips go flat in disapproval of my response. Seeing her pissed is a turn on. I just want to fuck the shit out of her to make her smile again. The thought makes my dick hard.

We reach my driveway and I'm expecting her to keep bantering me about the subject, but the moment I put the SUV into park, she climbs out of the vehicle, the door slamming behind her. I immediately rush after her, refusing to let her escape. Stopping her before she can open her door, I turn her and trap her against her car. She attempts to shove me away but fails as my lips slam down onto hers. Her body stiffens for a moment before I feel it surrender in my arms. Her nails dig into my skin as they grip my forearms to pull me closer. An image of those same nails digging into my back while I fuck her hard has my dick straining in my pants. Pushing my hips into her body, she whimpers from the contact. Her actions will have me exploding in my pants within seconds if she doesn't stop.

Ending the kiss, we're both panting, her mouth slightly gapes open as my chest rapidly rises and falls. My entire body is humming with the need to take her. Right here. Right now. Against her car if I have to.

"There isn't anything between me and Abigail," I breathlessly let out.

"Oh—" she confusedly replies. "But, you were with her the night of the charity event. Before we left to . . ." she stops speaking, biting her lip as she shyly looks down at the ground.

"Before I took you back to the hotel?"

Her head snaps up, looking relieved I didn't point out what we did. "In the office. You were both comforting the baby. You keep referring to her as yours." This has my lips going up to one side. "The baby is yours, isn't she?"

"I wish." She looks completely perplexed. "She's Matt and Abigail's baby."

"Who's Matt?"

"Abigail's husband."

Her jaw drops open. "She's married? But it doesn't say that in her file," she quickly recovers.

"I'll explain everything inside." Grabbing for her hand, I pull her towards the entrance of the house. Once inside, I lead her to the couch so she can take a seat.

I'm already walking into the kitchen when I ask, "Want a beer?" Quickly glancing over my shoulder, I catch her scrunching her nose.

"I'll take a water instead."

"If you're going to be hanging around with us, you better learn to like it," I convey, already grabbing both.

I don't want to look at her expression from my comment. I know she most likely still has her nose up high in the air, but it's the truth. I plan on breaking this girl of her snobbish customs so she can ultimately start having some fun. Better late than never. On the way back I spot the bottle that will help her do so.

Returning a couple of seconds later, I'm now juggling my beer, a bottle of water, a shot glass and bottle of Patron. Placing all items on the side table next to her, I begin filling the shot glass. Grabbing my beer, I stand directly in front of her. She strains her neck to look up at me as she waits for my next move.

"Which one will it be?" I ask, lifting both in the air.

Looking appalled, her eyes dart back and forth between the two before stating, "I'm not drinking with you."

Great. Exactly what I should have been expecting.

"Too good to drink with a *commoner?*"

"That has nothing to do with why I won't drink with you," she defends, looking back at both as if they're foreign objects. "I didn't come here to drink. I came here to have Abigail sign her contract."

"I'm not a dumbass. I know what you came here for, but there isn't anything you can do about it tonight. So why not relax a little?" I encourage her to take the glass.

At first I think she'll refuse it, but she takes the shot glass from my hand. "I've never taken a shot before," she admits. Her comment has me practically choking on the beer I'm drinking.

Swallowing what's in my mouth, I ask, "Have you ever seen anyone take a shot before?"

"I've seen it done in movies." Rolling my eyes at her, I think, of course. I'm pretty sure rich people aren't throwing back shots at their parties.

Kneeling in front of her, I say, "Here, I'll show you," as I take the shot glass from her fingers.

Her eyes are entirely focused on the shot glass I'm holding. My own stay focused on hers as I lift the glass up and toss the liquid into my mouth. The tequila gives a slight burn as it travels down my throat, but nothing compared to the fascination radiating off her eyes.

Refilling the glass, I return it to her. "Your turn." She shakes her head in refusal. "Or are you too scared to do it?" I tease.

She purses her lips and lifts her chin. "I can do it," she clips out. "But I won't because I need to drive home tonight." She shoves the glass back at me. "And back tomorrow morning, for that matter."

She's already standing and I follow her lead. "Whatever, princess," I mock while she keeps her eyes locked onto mine.

"Why do you keep calling me that?"

"What?"

"Princess," she seethes out.

"Would you prefer Tory?" I ask with a tilt of my head, waiting for her answer. The look of disgust on her face proves she doesn't.

"Victoria will do just fine, thank you," she proclaims.

"Okay, *Victoria*," I drag out. "How brave are you?" I taunt, still holding the shot glass for her to take.

She yanks it from my hand and lifts it up, the glass hovering inches from her lips. My brow arches high, challenging her. Parting them, she lifts the glass up and tosses the liquid into her mouth. The back of her hand comes up to cover her coughs.

Taking the shot glass from her to refill it, I'm just as quickly putting it back in her hands. "Here, the rest of them should be a breeze from now on."

"I'm not taking anymore," she complains between coughs.

In the brief moment before she took the shot, I discovered just how competitive she is. "I should have known you'd chicken out."

Once more she yanks the glass from my hands and throws the liquid into her mouth. As before, it's followed with a bout of coughs. I smile, realizing just how fun this night will be.

"That a girl," I praise with a wink. She doesn't look satisfied, but since she's a newbie, it won't be long before she knows just how much trouble she's gotten into.

Urging her to sit back down, I take the seat at her side. Tilting her head, she looks to be considering something.

"If Abigail is married, then why hasn't she changed her last name?"

I feel reluctant to answer, more for the reasons Abigail has chosen to remain *Abigail Adams.* "She has. Legally. But to the public she's still Abigail Adams. We trademarked her name for business purposes. It's the name that made her who she is, so she's decided to keep it for promotional reasons," I answer, hoping it will satisfy her curiosity.

"Why are you living with them? Can't you afford your own place?"

"Yes, I can, but why should I when I'm happy where I'm at?" I defensibly throw back at her.

It isn't the first time someone has mentioned my living arrangements. Yes, I *can* afford to purchase my own home. At one point I'd offered to buy this one from Matt, but Abigail refused to relinquish it. It holds memories for us all. It was they who had insisted I continue living in the house. They didn't like the idea of it being vacant while they were in California. Who was I to argue? Besides the house I grew up in, this was my home in my heart as well, and it's the home we *continue* making memories in.

Her eyes roam the interior of the house, still perplexed.

"Why does she live here when she can easily afford something more lavish?"

"What's wrong with this house? Not flashy enough for you?" I probe in return, gruelingly containing my arising temper.

She's picked up the offense in my tone. "No. It's just . . . It's simple," she gently conveys. "It's perfect."

I give no further details as to why she's living here, or the fact that she owns something just as *simple* near Los

Angeles.

Her eyes grow weary and I know the alcohol is kicking in. It won't be long before she's passing out and morning will quickly come. I watch her eyes grow heavy and her breathing begin to slow. Suddenly, she's alarmingly popping them open.

"Was there anything ever between you and Abigail?" she asks, seeming urgent to know.

"Why are you digging for information on her?" I grow defensive. "The tabloids pay you for it?"

"No! I hate the media."

"Then what's with all the questions?"

"What are you hiding that you won't answer them?" she throws back at me. It makes me smile. Her angry eyes have returned, which also has me shifting in my seat. She's made the problem between my legs return.

"We're all just really protective over her, that's all."

She opens her mouth as if to ask another question, but quickly shuts it. She's pouting like a child now.

"When we met her she had a cheating fiancé who was embezzling her money. She confronted him and it didn't end well. That's when she came to us for help and has been living with us ever since."

"But it still doesn't answer the question of how you met her."

"She knew Matt through his sister," I answer, taking a swig of my beer as an excuse to not explain anymore.

She takes in my response with a pondering silence. Her eyes begin to slowly wander around the room. My defenses go on high alert, until she rasp out, "She's lucky to have found you guys," is all she says.

Victoria

My head has slowly grown hazy during the last couple of minutes. Shrugging my shoulders causes me to lose my balance, even while sitting. My body sways to his side and he wraps his arm around my shoulder to catch me. My conscience is screaming for me to pull myself from his embrace and walk away, but my heart has been demanding to stay. I feel comforted in his arms, a feeling I crave on a daily basis.

Silence overtakes the room as I inhale his scent. His smell is captivating. It's not cologne or aftershave, but it's the same smell as the first night we met. Nudging my nose closer to his skin, he stiffens in my arms.

"Princess, you need to stop." His voice is husky and deep, my mouth catching the feel of his deep swallow when he delivers his request.

"Why?" I hear myself whine, my words vibrating against his skin. The arm embracing me tightens its hold. "You smell good," I confess, inhaling once more.

He groans, and it vibrates against my lips.

"Do you taste just as good?" I ask, letting my tongue graze against his neck.

I feel myself being shoved away, causing me to disappointingly look at him. Before I can voice my dissatisfaction, he kisses me. The feel of his tongue exploring my mouth has my hands gripping his shoulders to steady my-self. Internally, I'm igniting as sparks travel up and down my skin.

Pulling away, he asks into my mouth, "Do I?"

"Perfect," I breathlessly answer.

His mouth returns to kissing me, slowly they begin trailing down the side of my cheek. Closing my eyes, I let the darkness increase my senses as his mouth travels down the side my neck, leaving behind a tingle with every inch they travel until he severs contact.

"I wonder how good *you* taste, princess?" I hear him ask.

My incoherent mind does not realize his intentions when he slowly moves down my body until he's kneeling directly in front of me, his body in between my thighs. My hands hold him by his shoulders, fearful he will try to stand and walk away. The feel of his warm hands gliding down my legs sends a tremor through my blood before the tips of his fingers glide back up into my skirt, taking it with them. The brisk cool air can be felt as the skirt rises, caus-ing my sensitized skin to intensify the quiver in my blood. Biting my lip to keep from vocally whimpering, my thong can be felt being pulled down my thighs and voluntarily my hips rise to allow him to pull it off. Pushing my thighs wide open before he lowers his head, my eyes go wide.

"What are you doing?" My hands struggle to shove him away.

His head snaps up, bewildered over my question. "You really need to stop asking questions, princess," he voices before returning to his previous position and the warmth of his tongue meets my center. Letting out a gasp, my fingers have returned to digging into his shoulders, needing something to hold.

My breath becomes heavy and my head is thrown back as my body begins to stiffen.

Every glide of his tongue from his wicked mouth torturously works its magic on me, making my whimpers grow into intensified moans with every minute that passes. Minute by minute, he sends me higher to the pinnacle I'm rarely ever sent to.

My conscience is advising me to force him to stop, but the struggle to withhold my desire is defeated. My eyes close and I let out a moan of satisfaction as he shatters my body into a thousand pieces.

"Damn, princess, I don't think I've ever made any girl come that fast," I hear him boast.

My mind is screaming in warning it isn't something I should be hearing, but my baffled mind is equal to that of my trembling body still in aftershock. I'm still attempting to calm my erratic heart as his mouth returns to the center of my heat, grazing his tongue up and down the folds once more.

Seconds later, the loss of his head in between my thighs has my eyes slowly coming open to gaze down at him. His tongue is licking at his lips while his hooded eyes gaze back at me. The sight has my breath increasing with knowing exactly what he's licking from his lips.

"You taste delicious, princess," he says, rendering me speechless.

I am unable to distinguish whether it's the alcohol disorienting my mind or the mind-blowing orgasm he's just given me. Regardless of the cause, I have no complaints. I'm exactly where I wish to be. A satisfied smile arises upon his lips, having me return one to him. Remembering just how wonderful he makes my body feel has me pulling him towards me to kiss him.

"I want more," I say against his lips.

I feel his smile. "It will be my pleasure," he says as he picks me up, walking us out of the living room.

Holding on tight, I'm already eager to find out how much pleasure he will bring me with the promise.

Chapter Six

Imbecilic

Trey

A TORTUROUS GROAN vibrates into my neck. The sound frightens my eyes open. Who the hell is in my bed? Inhaling a breath, her scent hits my nostrils, reminding me of who I fell asleep with.

Fuck . . .

Another night I broke my own rule. I had sex with Victoria. I told myself it wouldn't happen again, that I wouldn't take advantage of her while she was drinking like the first night. Unfortunately, my carnal needs kept me from keeping my word, or remembering the vow. I had her in the bedroom as fast as my legs could take us both and within minutes I was making her moan my name.

I got my wish. Several times I had her screaming "*Mr. Johnson.*"

I blame the lecherous notions that were constantly on my mind. They were the driving force that made me whisk her off to my room and have my way with her the entire night.

Hearing voices coming from the living room advises me that Matt and Abigail have arrived. Searching for my phone, it shows it's close to noon. It won't be long until they are looking for me if I don't emerge from my room. Especially since I *know* Victoria's car is parked outside.

Carefully, I try dislodging her wrapped limbs so I can climb out of bed, but I fail to be discreet. The moment I move she awakens and slowly sits up to stretch. Her arms are high in the air and the perfect silk skin of her back faces me. Her body is bare of any clothing, giving me the perfect view of her ass sitting at my side.

"Good morning, princess."

Realization hits her, causing her body to go rigid. Slowly, she turns to face me with a dazed expression on her face when she takes me in. Her disheveled hair and doe eyes have me feeling pleased with myself. I've gotten this look many mornings, but never leaving me to feel content with the result.

"Oh, no. Not again," she rasps out, her hand covering her mouth as she shakes her head in denial. It pushes all sense of satisfaction from me.

I'm ready to rebuke her reaction, but I'm stopped when there is knocking at my door.

"Trey? Whose car is outside?" Julio asks from the other side as I suspected he would do. He's asking for security reasons. When Emily was born, we all made a rule that no unknown visitors were allowed in the house, another infraction to add to my list this morning. However, in my defense, this one was not of my doing, but of his boss's.

Anxiety overtakes her. "Oh, my God. Is that Julio?" she asks in a whispered panic.

"Yup. You better get dressed, princess, because if I don't answer the door in the next minute he's going to bust it open." She turns ashen from my response.

Victoria begins scrambling off the bed in search of her clothes.

"Shit!" she whispers when she can't find her shirt. The sight of her frantic movements has me chuckling. Picking up my shirt from last night off the ground, I hand it to her. She looks ready to refuse it, but Julio's pounding on the door has her yanking it from my hand and hastily putting it on.

"Give me a minute," I shout at the door as I stand to put my jeans on. Making sure Victoria is decent enough, I finally open the door.

Julio is sternly staring back at me, unhappy with the delay.

"Good morning," I smirk. He ignores me, looking past my shoulder, his jaw slightly dropping open. "Where's Abigail?" I ask, attempting to distract him.

Bringing his attention back to me, he says, "She's in the living room." He looks back to Victoria. "What is she doing here?" he demands.

"She's here to have Supermodel sign her contract," I inform him.

"What is she doing in *your* room?" he clarifies.

I can feel her standing directly behind me. "I'm not doing this again. She's a big girl and she makes her own decisions," I say, remembering back to the first morning Julio had given me a lecture for sleeping with her.

The door is opened and slammed behind me. The force used tells me it's Julio. I was expecting him to come barging in here, I'm just not in the mood to deal with him at the moment.

"What was she doing here?"

Turning to directly face him, it's I who is pissed at him.

"I only brought her back here because of you," I inform him.

He looks taken aback. "How is that so?"

"She tried leaving last night, but was drunk off her ass, so I brought her here so you could babysit her."

"You took advantage of her!"

"Look, man, I never planned on sleeping with her," I defend. "My plan was to bring her here so you could deal with her when you got back. She came onto me," I say with my finger pointed at my chest.

In his thick accent he declares, "Liar. She isn't like that," he growls. "I know you. You have no shame who you sleep with." Now he's testing my patience.

"That may be true, but I never *intended to bring her back here for that reason. I only did it because you're my friend. From what you've said about her, the last thing she needed was to end up in the tabloids with a picture of her looking the way she did."*

"Her walking out of this room with you following her in nothing but a towel isn't any better." He may be big,

but I'm not scared of his ass. If he continues with his comments, I may just beat the shit out of him.

"She was the one who walked out on me. You remember that."

"Do you have the paperwork I need to sign?" Abigail's voice brings me back to the present.

She's currently wearing a guilty expression on her face. She should. This is all her doing and she knows it.

"I put it on the counter," I inform her, walking past Julio and into the living room. I can hear Abigail's footsteps following closely behind. Glancing over my shoulder to make sure Victoria is not within hearing distance, I demand to Abigail, "Why did you have her come here last night?"

She doesn't stop until she's reached the island near the kitchen, then grabs the contract.

"I knew you'd want to see her again," she voices, staring down at the document in her hands.

"What made you think that?"

Looking at me, her teasing eyes are sparkling with delight. "From the way you've been moping around since we saw her in Seattle."

"Trey, moping?" Matt laughs out. He's standing at Abigail's side with Emily in his arms.

"I was not moping," I declare. "You need to control what your woman does," I demand, pointing at him. This makes him laugh harder.

"Why should I when it's entertaining to see you this way? It's your turn now, buddy," he says, patting me on the shoulder.

Before I can protest his statement, Victoria joins us. Taking in the oversized t-shirt she's wearing, it looks ridiculous paired with the pencil skirt she has on. "Now that you've arrived you can sign the contract and I'll be on my way as soon as the courier gets here," she informs Abigail.

"Why do you need to leave so soon? Wouldn't you like to catch up with Julio?"

"That would be pleasant, but unfortunately I didn't plan to stay the weekend. I have no change of clothes. Thank you for the offer, though," she politely responds, but from the strain in her jaw, I know she's lying off her ass. She's looking to run out of here the first moment she can.

Abigail dismisses her reply with a wave of her hand. "I've got plenty of clothes here for you to wear. I'm pretty sure we can find something you'd like."

Leave it up to the supermodel to come up with a solution to her clothing dilemma. She isn't lying with the offer of clothing. Abigail occasionally receives clothes from designers hoping she will be photographed wearing them. Most she donates to her favorite charity for abused women, but what little she chooses to keep she rarely has time to wear. Most of her days are spent in training, and when she isn't she prefers to be casual if she isn't out in public. It's what she's most comfortable in.

Looking between the both of them, they are similar in height and size. There is definitely no excuse for her to not take her offer if she chooses to stay.

"Again, I appreciate the offer, but I really can't stay," she repeats.

Abigail looks ready to protest, but I cut her off. "Let her go. She probably wants to get back to her royal life." Victoria pierces me with a glare. "Don't worry. We won't be offended if you see us as beneath you," I add, walking away from them.

"Trey Johnson!" Abigail bellows at my back as I leave them to return to my room.

Reaching my room, I hear the door slam behind me. Turning, I'm ready to face Abigail and her reprimand, but instead it's Victoria and her words attacking me.

"What is your problem?"

"It's you. From the day I met you all you do is act like I'm unworthy to be in the same room as you unless I'm fucking you!"

"That was never supposed to happen. Either time," she argues.

"Why not, princess, because I'm not from your side of town?"

Her chin rises from my speech. "That has nothing to do with it."

"Then why are you always in a hurry to leave?"

Her mouth opens to answer, but quickly shuts. I impatiently wait before she replies, "I have my reasons."

"Please, enlighten me."

She sighs this time. "It's not what you think. Us sleeping together was an imbecilic decision on both our parts. It should have never happened." Her refusal to answer my question has me growing angrier.

"I like you, Trey. I really do, but I have my reasons why there can never be anything between us," she continues to explain.

Her declaration is a dagger to my heart.

"Just leave," I order, giving her my back, refusing to look at her any longer.

Seconds later, the opening and closing of my door is heard. I continue to stare off into the distance, stunned over what has occurred. How is it I can't force myself to discard this girl from my mind like any other?

Regardless of the reasons, this time I have to face the reality. She isn't the one worth bestowing my heart upon.

Victoria

My heart is heavy as I leave Trey in his room. I never intended for this to happen, but it's a decision I have to make. Walking back over to Abigail, I face her wavering smile.

"I'm sorry, but I think it's best I leave now. I heeded your requirements for the contract so there shouldn't be any discrepancies." Pulling out a business card from my purse, I hand it to her. "But if there is, please don't hesitate to call me."

She takes the card from me. "If you would just give him a chance, you'd learn he's a really great guy."

"I know he is, which is why you're all lucky to have him in your life."

Those are my last words before I leave the house and climb into my car. Today has proven something valuable.

Now I truly know what it is to be wanted. It was clear

in Trey's anguished eyes. It wasn't love staring back at me, but an emotion just as strong.

Need.

Want.

Desire.

All of which I've never known before, even while in a relationship. My body knew what it craved; it was the man I walked away from minutes ago. Nevertheless, it wasn't meant to be. It would be unfair to give him false hope.

My cellphone rings. When I look down at it, I see it's Abigail calling. I'd programmed her number in my phone to distinguish her and Trey's numbers. Of course, it meant also programming his into my phone.

"Hello," I answer into the phone, already bringing up her file on my laptop, preparing for any request she may make as a client.

"Hello, Victoria," she cheerfully greets. "I hope I'm not bothering you at the moment."

"I am at your disposal whenever you need me, Mrs.—" I cut myself off, still unable to figure out how to address her.

"Abigail, please. Actually, this isn't a business call," she tells me. The alarm bells in my head are ringing as I wonder if she is about to discuss Trey. "I'm calling about Julio's birthday this weekend."

I've never known this piece of information, and I feel guilty for my lack of knowledge.

"I have a meeting with the designer for my running company in Seattle this week, so I'll be in town and I wanted to celebrate while we were there. Since you already live in Seattle, I thought it would be nice if you'd join us."

I'm about to decline her offer when she adds, "I don't know any of his family or friends, besides his mom, but I thought it would be nice if you'd be there. For him."

When she puts it that way, how can I refuse? My only concern is I'll have to endure being in the same room as Trey. After the way our last encounter ended, I know it will be an awkward situation.

"It would be an honor to be there. Thank you for the invitation," I say, knowing that I *will* like being there for Julio.

"Great!"

The next minute is spent with me taking down the information to the restaurant, with the promise to be there. I know I will have to endure being in the same room with Trey and his antagonizing glares, but they are well deserved on my part and it's best I face them now rather than later.

"You did what?" I exclaim.

"Shh!" Matt angrily demands so I don't wake Emily.

Abigail defiantly lifts her chin up to me as she lightly rocks the baby's car seat after she whimpers. "I don't care what you think of her, Trey. She's coming for Julio, so I don't want you doing anything to upset her and cause her to leave."

I let out a frustrated growl. It's like she's refusing to let me breathe during dinner. "You really need to stop this shit, Supermodel. I put up with it the last time because I had no choice, but not this time."

She sighs this time. "I know how you feel, but I understand now," she says, eliciting a snort from me.

"Sure you do."

"Trey, you really need to stop berating yourself." If we weren't in a moving vehicle, I would be walking away. I hate her pity. She looks over to Matt with a smile. "Sometimes love is worth fighting for."

"How many times do I have to tell you, Supermodel? I'm not in love."

She rolls her eyes at my comment. "It may not be love, but I know you. You're mad because you can't have her."

Silence overtakes the car. I want to protest, but it would do no good. She's right. I'm furious over how Victoria reacted during our last encounter.

"Whatever," I mumble under my breath.

"It's Julio's birthday. He's part of this family as much as me and you," she announces. "So you *are* putting up with *her.*"

"It's only for the night," Matt apologetically conveys, understanding my dilemma.

"Fine," I clip out.

Abigail's referral to us being a family has me defeated. I may not share the same blood as them, but they *are* my family. On days like today, I wish I could disown them.

Matt and I have had the discussion about Victoria. He'd awoken late in the night with Emily and I was in the living room drinking my sorrows away. I'd admitted my side of the story to him, from the very beginning of the very first night I'd slept with her. He hadn't judged me for my actions, but he was able to sympathize. He was at one point in my shoes with Abigail—wanting to be with someone knowing you couldn't be with her because of your past. Only difference was he had pushed Abigail away in fear of hurting her. I was on the opposite end of the spectrum. For once in my life, I was willing to give up my playboy lifestyle for Victoria, but she was the one pushing me away because of my assumed upbringing. She never hesitated to slap me in the face with how different we are.

The SUV I rented slowly pulls up to the venue, bringing my thoughts to a halt. Abigail is right. This night is for Julio. He's done so much for us and *he is* a part of our small dysfunctional family, so he deserves nothing less than for me to be cordial tonight. We enter minutes later and my body is already humming in anticipation of seeing her.

The restaurant Abigail had me book for the celebration has a private room in the back where we will be eating. When we enter, it's empty. As if reading my mind, Abigail says, "Maybe she's running late."

"Or maybe she changed her mind." My words are full of the pent up resentment Victoria had left me with.

Abigail doesn't hide her disappointment, either towards my reaction or the realization my comment may be true. It wouldn't surprise me if she doesn't show up.

Unfortunately, Victoria proves me wrong. Abigail's elated smile has me turning to see her walking into our private section.

As always, she looks stunning. Her black lace, fitted dress looks practically molded to her sleek figure that I'm very familiar with. It's as if it was specifically made for her. Her normally long hair is pulled up in a loose bun, showcasing her slender neck; a neck my tongue is longing to run across. The hem of her skirt stops halfway down her thigh, between her ass and knees, the perfect length to emphasize her slender legs. Legs I know wrap perfectly around my waist.

Dammit! What am I doing to myself?

As I watch her she walks directly in Julio's direction, embracing him when she reaches him. The sight has me vibrating with jealousy. I didn't expect for it to happen, but knowing how good she feels in my arms has me craving the affection she's giving him.

Pulling away from his arms, she looks over to Abigail with the same smile, but when her eyes meet mine she instantly frowns, recuperating with a forced one in an instant. Stopping the waiter as he enters to order my beer allows me to break eye contact with her while Abigail walks over to greet her. To sanely make it through tonight, I'm going to need a drink.

Minutes later, Abigail is requesting everyone take their seat so we can order dinner. My intention is to sit as far away from her as I can. However, since Julio is the guest of honor, Abigail seats him at the head of the table, leaving Victoria and me to sit side-by-side across from her and Matt.

Thanks to my mother's insistence to behave like a gentleman while growing up, I carry out her most cardinal rule: help a lady seat herself at the dinner table. Who would have known I'd be carrying out my father's nightly habit towards my mother? It's when I take a seat and my leg brushes up against her thigh that my body ignites; it's the simplest of touches, but it travels all the way up my body. My eyes catch her sheepishly glancing at me, as if she felt it as well. The thought has me remembering how good her bare legs felt gliding up and down my skin. Thankfully, I have the table to hide the hard-on growing between my legs.

"So, Victoria, how have you been liking Seattle?"

"It's beautiful. It's different from New York. Much more laid back, but I like it."

"Were you raised in New York?" Matt asks her.

"Yes and no," she replies. "I spent most of my time in New York, however my family owns a house in both the Hamptons and Washington, D.C., so we alternated between the three." Abigail's brows raise, along with Matt's. Her response doesn't surprise me though, having heard of her background from our last dinner conversation.

"Which was your favorite of them all?" Abigail curiously asks.

"The Hamptons."

"Typical," I mutter under my breath. "She enjoys living the life of the rich and famous."

This has her coldly peering at me. "It was my favorite because it's where I felt less trapped," she defends.

"I don't think I've ever been to the Hamptons," Abigail comments. Victoria whips her head back in her direction, looking baffled. As if knowing it's the perfect time to wake, Emily lets out a wail. "She must be hungry," Abigail says, smiling while she reaches down into the car seat to retrieve her.

Out of her car seat and in Abigail's arms, Emily quickly starts to quiet her cries down to a whimper. "Sorry, it's her bedtime," Abigail states, as if needing to explain.

Matt is already helping place a blanket over Abigail's shoulder to cover the baby to prepare to feed her. Realizing we have a newcomer who isn't accustomed to her breast-feeding Emily in front of us, Abigail apologetically looks over to Victoria. "I hope you don't mind me feeding her at the table. If I feed her she'll fall right back to sleep."

"By all means, go ahead. I don't mind at all," Victoria quickly responds. "How old is she?"

"She'll be a year next month."

With a smile, Abigail returns to her task and from the absent cries, I can tell Emily is already drinking away. I catch Victoria compassionately staring at Abigail as she feeds the baby. As much as I try to avoid looking at her, my eyes are automatically drawn to her. The insensitive characterization I've associated on account of our previous encounters is faintly pushed aside. Victoria shyly turns away and our eyes meet, betraying I was watching her.

The waiter takes this moment to ask for everyone's drink order. To my surprise, Victoria orders an entire bottle of wine, which he returns with minutes later. Going through his routine of opening the bottle at the table and handing a sample to her to approve, which she does with a happy nod. He fills her glass and turns to the remainder of the table to offer to pour for anyone else. As I'd expected, everyone else kindly declines.

"Are you sure? It's a wonderful vintage," Victoria encourages.

Abigail speaks first. "I can't drink," she says, pointing down to the baby still in her arms.

"I'm a beer kind of guy," Matt remarks.

Julio, on the other hand, never drinks and she must know, as she doesn't look to him for an answer. She politely dismisses the waiter, and when he leaves she gives me a stern look. "Don't let me drink more than two glasses. I'm a lightweight."

This makes me chuckle. "Don't I know that?"

As if needing to further defend herself, she says, "I also need to drive home."

Should I offer to drive her home? My mind is chivalrously already offering, but my thoughts have been far from honorable since the moment we sat down and I risk reverting to what is perpetual between us: one night stands.

At least it's what would most likely occur with the track record Victoria and I have. The conversation returns, this time with reminiscences between her and Julio from when he was employed by her father.

Her beaming eyes and laughter keep me focused entirely on her. My hand has been idly spinning my bottle of beer, unable to finish it. My wary mind has been warning me to leave it be, as if predicting I may need a clear mind for later. My watchful eyes have been keeping track of Victoria during dinner since the bottle arrived, and she's close to finishing her first glass. At the pace she's drinking, I'm predicting she won't be driving herself home.

"How is it Trey came to be your manager?" she inquires, immediately bringing my attention to their discussion.

"He has a big mouth," Matt teases, looking to me to rebut his declaration. "But I'm pretty sure Abigail and I wouldn't have the deals we do without him."

"I doubt you would," I banter.

This seems to surprise Victoria. "He manages you, too?" she asks, as if eager for Matt to confirm.

"Again. He has a big mouth." He smirks before taking a drink of his beer.

"It still doesn't answer how he came to become *both* your managers."

"What's with the interrogation, *Victoria?*"

"Trey!" Abigail's reprimand slides completely past me as I look directly at Victoria. "I'm just curious to know. She seems to be full of questions when it comes to you."

The sound of Julio clearing his throat overtakes the bitter silence filling the room.

"Victoria has always had an endless supply of questions on hand for anyone she meets. It's nothing to concern yourself with, Trey."

Victoria and I are still intensely gazing at one another. My eyes are still full of displeasure for her meddling questions, while hers are irritably looking back at me.

"Forgive me for wanting to know you better. Clearly it was a mistake," she says with a fictitious smile before turning to face Julio. "Please forgive me, but I think it's best I leave." She reaches down for her napkin and boldly throws it onto her plate as she stands. "I hope you all enjoy the remainder of your evening," she says before turning to leave immediately after delivering her words.

Keeping my back to her as she walks away allows me to catch Abigail viciously glaring at me. Exhaling in defeat, I soon follow Victoria's footsteps.

"Victoria." The quickening of her steps informs me she's heard me calling her name but is refusing to stop. Exiting and stopping at the valet, she searches her clutch for what must be her ticket, giving me the perfect opportunity to catch up to her and pull her aside a few steps.

"Let go of me, Trey," she snarls, trying her best to free herself from my grip. There are several couples staring at us while entering the restaurant. I, of all people, know we do not need an audience.

Releasing my hold of her arm, I wrap my own around her waist. "Come on," I urge, leading us farther away from the entrance.

She doesn't falter in her steps, however her sharp tongue can't seem to resist. "Whatever it is you wish to say, I don't want to hear it."

Her words do not surprise me. Regardless of what she says, I'm not letting her leave until she listens.

Chapter Seven

Comprehension

Victoria

"YOU DON'T HAVE a choice."

I hate those words. They've been delivered all my life. It's as if I was born to be repeatedly told them.

"Fuck you!"

This stuns him, and he brings us to a halt, giving me the opportunity to free myself from his hold. I don't make it more than a couple of steps before he wraps his arm completely around my waist and jerks me to a stop.

"Whoa there, princess."

Spinning around, I'm mere inches from him as I say, "I refuse to be ordered about," hoping the remark will rid me of him. From the crooked lift of his lips, I know I have failed. "What's got your panties in a wad?"

"You!" I angrily throw back before spinning back around to continue on to my destination.

He's persistent. This time when he detains me, my back is flush up against the hard frame of his chest. The sensation of our bodies molded so closely together has me frozen to the spot, and I can't resist wanting to stay in the safety of his arms.

The warmth of his breath near my ear sends a shiver down the column of my neck. "I'm sorry," he says, remorse laced in the whisper of his words.

"Apologies are nothing but words," I tell him.

He stiffens behind me, the intent of my statement understood.

"My friends are my family, and I'll protect them anyway I can. You were asking too many questions and it made me nervous."

"They were only questions," I defend.

It takes him a moment to respond. "I know, but there are things you aren't ready to know just yet."

Secrets.

They have their own bond of trust that keeps the outside world from coming in. This is what has him on guard. I assume it's the reason for his declaration of protecting them.

I am not one to argue with the importance of keeping secrets. I have many of my own in which I am not ready to disclose. I would be a hypocrite if I insist he reveal his.

Both arms have wrapped around my waist, securing me tightly within his embrace. I surrender to his hold, a pleasure that is still a rarity.

"I want to trust you, Victoria, but you should understand why it's hard for me."

"Please, remind me why it is so?" I test, full of sarcasm. Turning me so I'm facing him, his dark eyes peer back at me. They're nearly expressionless.

"Because all you've ever done is walk away." His reminder is a dagger delivered straight to my heart.

There is no denying his proclamation. My chest tightens as guilt overcomes me. The feel of his lips beginning to graze across my skin sends a shiver to replace it.

"Don't leave." The plea vibrates against my skin.

"You have to stop ordering me around," I deliver in a demand instead of a request.

His hand comes up to grasp the side my face, the base of his thumb gently gliding across my chin. "That's all they've ever done with you, isn't it?" he asks. My silence is his confirmation.

A part of me despises he's discovered a part of the puzzle that is my life; one of many I'm still trying to unpiece.

Tears begin to build, but I refuse to allow them to emerge. I am stronger than the weakness threatening to show. I have always been.

He lowers his head, our mouths connecting to fuse as one. With weakness, I willingly surrender to the kiss without protest. My heart pounds against my chest with excitement, my legs slowly becoming unsteady. Thankfully, it is impossible since he has tightened his hold. My feet are still firmly on the ground, but my entire body feels as if it's floating in midair when he deepens our kiss.

"You really have to stop doing that," I breathlessly deliver when the kiss ends.

Our foreheads are touching, his nose nudging against my own. "What is it that I have to stop doing, princess?"

"Kissing me," I voice. I'm beginning to like it too much, I think to myself.

"What if I were to tell you I like kissing you? Among *other things*." I don't need to view the smile I know he's wearing.

"Why are you so hard to resist?"

Pulling apart to allow me to watch his lips curve, his current smirk widens into a satisfied smile. I hadn't meant to relay my question out loud, again another statement, which was to be conveyed in my thoughts only, but silence was not on my side.

"Because you like the way I make you scream," he breathes into my ear.

This has me gasping in a combination of both shock and humiliation. Blushing, my eyes cast down to the floor.

"Don't be ashamed. It means I'm doing something right with you." Only he would see the positive in the situation.

His pocket lets out a ping. He pulls out his cell phone to check who is calling. His brows draw down and his smirk vanishes, turning into a frown. "It's Julio. He's texting to check up on you." From his uneasy expression, it's obvious the question offended him in some way.

"I should let you go," I assert, feeling a sudden urge to leave.

Deeply gazing into my eyes, he pleads, "Don't. Why

don't we just go back inside so he can see for himself?" he suggests.

Without allowing me time to make a decision, Trey leads me back inside. How easily I'm returning is a mystery to me; his suggestion could be held against him as another one of his commands, however I hold regret for leaving the way I did.

When we return, I'm greeted with hesitant smiles. No surprise, as it was expected.

"Everything okay?" Abigail asks eagerly.

"Of course," Trey quickly answers with a coy smile. Abigail's wary eyes can see completely through him. The waiter returns to take our orders, giving us the perfect distraction from the subject. He's also quick to refill my glass of wine. With the tension still simmering inside of me, I'm quick to empty half the glass just as fast. The waiter hastily refills it, allowing me to take another sip.

Trey leans in next to me, his mouth mere inches from my earlobe. "Is this when I need to remind you to slow down?" The way he's addressed the question sounds far from an inquiry, but his way of mocking my earlier request.

Placing the glass on the table as if it's stinging my hands, he lets out a chuckle.

"Did Emily fall back to sleep?" Trey asks from my side. From the tone he used, it's as if he's trying to distract every one from the situation I left them with. Abigail answers with a happy nod. Until our meals arrive, their conversation consists of small talk amongst the four of them: schedules, trainings, or designating baby duties.

"We all know when it's your turn to watch Emily you'll most likely be stinging her ears with curse words," Abigail snickers.

Failing to appear offended, Trey responds, "Shit, as long as the girl talks, you shouldn't be too concerned." Matt laughs, Julio as well, but is quick to clear his throat when Abigail looks to him for support. "Sorry," he apologizes.

"Pushover," Trey coughs out. This time Matt lets out a bellow of laughter, and not even Abigail's chastising glare can stop him. He simply kisses it away when his mouth meets her lips.

I'm both envious and feeling out of place in the presence of these four carefree personalities. By the way they comfortably banter with each other, it is clear they spend a great amount of time together. It leaves me feeling as if I'm in a room full of strangers where I don't belong. My only distraction is my wine since I can't contribute much to the conversation.

Thankfully, the food soon arrives and dinner is quickly ending with Abigail pointing out how late it's gotten and would prefer to get Emily to a proper bed.

We all say goodbye and before long I'm off in the direction of the exit, thankful I made it through the night without embarrassing myself for a second time.

Trey

It's clear Victoria will not be driving herself home. Internally, my emotions are vibrating as I try to come up with a solution as to how to end the evening, but I'm quickly shot down with three simple words.

"No sex tonight," she orders. "Whenever I drink you take advantage of me."

I laugh. "If I recall, you are the cause of us sleeping together when you're in this state."

"I'm not drunk," she defends.

"Whatever, princess." Pulling her tighter to my side, she surrenders to my hold, resting her head on my shoulder. I can't resist placing a kiss on her temple, her response a contented sigh.

Minutes later, her car arrives and I lead her to the passenger side door. "You're driving me home?"

"You didn't think you were driving yourself, did you?" Without answering, yet holding a wide grin, she climbs into the car. Once inside, she states, "I would have thought you'd call a taxi to take me home."

"Not on my watch, princess," I say, already driving away from the restaurant.

"Why do you keep calling me that?"

Confused, I ask, "What?"

"Princess," she declares.

"I like it."

"Because it's your way of mocking me?"

"No. I just like it," I repeat.

What more can I say? Openly admitting it was my first thought from the moment I set eyes on her is asking for another argument. Her pompous behavior from the moment she took me in was the reason for her current title. At the time, it *was* meant to mock her, but it is no longer the reason. It's come to be the only endearment I can give her without coming across as a pansy.

I've always sweet-talked girls to get them into bed, but never meant the words I delivered. With Victoria, I've never needed words. Sex was unforeseen by the end of each night we spent together, however it inevitably happened, except for tonight. According to her "*no sex*" command, we won't be having any.

We'll see.

"Where do you live?"

Leaning forward, she begins entering the address in her navigation system. Soon a male voice is delivering commands.

"There. Bill will lead the way."

"Bill? You named your car Bill?" The name leaves a bitterness on my tongue.

"What's wrong with Bill?"

"Nothing. It's your car. Call it whatever you want," I sneer.

"Why do you do that?" she barks back. Before giving me a chance to respond, she continues. "You make me feel valued one minute, then you turn back into an asshole the next." This has me taken aback. "It's starting to get old. Pick one. Are you a guy worth risking everything for, or one who I *know* I shouldn't have left with?"

I'm speechless.

Thankfully, I have instructions to follow and a road to focus on, or else I would be standing in front of her, gawking like a fish out of water, unable to defend myself.

What in the hell does she mean by her speech?

Glancing to the side, she's sitting stiffly in her seat, arms crossed over her chest as she pouts.

The bright city lights on the exterior of the car are welcomed. They're a distraction, along with the instructions coming from *Bill* to ease my mind. Soon, we are pulling onto her street. My eyes are quick to take in her building. Of all the residences, why am I not surprised she resides in the Newmark Tower? I only know of it because of Abigail's running route along The Pike. The building is tall and visible on the route. There have been several times I've had to run with Abigail in Julio's place. Something I *do not* enjoy, but know it must be done for her protection. I may not reside in Seattle, but I know it's one of the most sought out locations with those who have money.

Shit, I'd considered it at one point, so I know how much one of these condos cost.

Driving in to her parking garage, she leads me to her spot with the point of her finger. Parking the car, we sit in silence for a couple of seconds. I'm debating what my next step will be.

It's I who breaks the silence. "I'll walk you up," I say, already opening my door to rush to her side and help her out. The alcohol is still affecting her, as her first step is a small stumble.

Securing her close to my side, I lead her to the ele-

vator. With a press of the button, the doors open and welcome us in. She encloses us when she presses the button
for the eleventh floor.

"No penthouse?" I taunt.

"I prefer the eleventh floor. It's my favorite number."

It isn't the response I was expecting, but it's another
piece of information I've learned about her. The ding of
the elevator comes too soon and she leads me out into the
hallway. To the right and a couple of doors down, she stops
at what must be her condo.

She's anxiously staring at me. "Would you like to
come in?"

"Yes," I'm quick to answer . . . too quick. I sound like
a desperate, teenage boy eager to get laid.

I've had the worst case of blue balls since the last time
I've seen her and tonight with the dress she's wearing, it's
only getting worse.

She opens the door and steps through, allowing me to
follow her. We're both greeted with the screech of a drawn
out crackled cry.

Looking down at my feet, I notice there is something
standing at Victoria's feet. It's still dark in her apartment,
but from the shadow alone I can tell this thing is huge.
Victoria turns on the light in the foyer and scoops down to
pick up the object.

"What is that thing?"

Without looking at me and instead rubbing her chin
across its cheek, she answers, "My cat. Mr. Whiskers."

"That's a cat?" It looks more like an over-sized raccoon. It's so big that it takes up her entire chest as she

holds it. The cat glares back at me before he hisses.

"Mr. Whiskers! Be nice," she reprimands. "I'm sorry. He's not used to strangers," she apologizes. I swear the cat is mocking me with his mischievous eyes as he contently purrs in her arms.

Bending down, she gently releases him onto the floor. He scurries off down a long hallway to what must lead to her bedroom.

"Would you like something to drink?"

"You wouldn't happen to have some beer, would you?"

She tilts her head down into frown. "Sorry, I don't."

"Water is fine," I say, more for her benefit than mine.

She walks over to her kitchen area and as expected, she returns with two bottles of water, handing me one. With a tilt of her chin, she directs me to the living room.

Her décor is exactly how I pictured: fresh, light, yet simple with a modern feel. The dark gray is a contrast to the whites, light grays and blues she's chosen.

Victoria removes her shoes, neatly placing them on the floor. Odd, most women would have let them drop where they landed. Lifting my eyes to look back up to hers, she's already eyeing me with a deadpan expression.

"What's with the seriousness, princess?" I laugh out, hoping to break the tension.

"I'm still trying to figure you out." This has me on high alert. She's still trying to dig for information. "You fascinate me," she admits.

She's amused me. "How is that so?"

"You're nothing like the men I'm used to being

around."

"Because I'm not arrogant?"

She smirks. "Oh, you're arrogant alright, but not like them."

Right now I wish I had a beer. At least the alcohol would help me relax. Her responses have my heart slowly increasing with each beat.

"I like you. More than I know I should."

"We've returned to pointing out the differences between us."

"You're no different than I am, Trey Johnson," she replies. "I know for a fact you make just as much as Abigail does yearly. You have several athletes you are currently representing, including Abigail's husband, who I know is a well-known athlete. You make a *very* decent salary." Her brows are arched, daring me to deny her claims. "So you see, money is not a factor you can use to distinguish our differences."

"Money doesn't affirm who a person is," I point out.

"Exactly, which is why I like you so much. You are not one to flaunt what you have. You continue being true to yourself regardless of the wealth you have."

Her declaration has me looking around the room. "As you do?"

Dismissing my reply with a wave of her hand, she says, "My mother insisted on decorating the place. The only opinion I was allowed was to choose the colors."

"Doesn't look like she did a bad job. It fits you." I meant it as a compliment, ironically it came out sarcastically.

"You should see the bedroom." This makes me groan, while it makes her laugh.

"You're a tease."

Standing, she looks directly into my eyes as she huskily whispers to me, "Teasing is leaving you here on this couch to wonder what I'll be doing in that bedroom." She points behind her.

This intrigues me. A sheepish grin spreads across her face before she spins and saunters away. She tosses a smile over her shoulder as she steps into what I assume is her bedroom. My pulse increases as my eyes follow her every step. The sway of her hips has left me in a trance before she disappears down the hallway.

Thickly swallowing what nerves I have left, I wait a minute before I quickly follow behind her. My feet lead me to the end of the hall to a bedroom matching the same color tones as the living room, the same sleek, elegant décor I had left behind. Entering, I find myself alone with Victoria nowhere to be found.

The same drawn out cry from earlier captures my attention, averting my eyes to the bed. Her raccoon of a cat is curled up on her bed, glaring at me.

"What are you looking at?" I hiss back to it.

As if he couldn't care, he rolls over and closes his eyes.

The sound of a toilet flushing tells me the closed door to my right is her bathroom. Seconds later, running water is heard, indicating she must be washing her hands. I remain rooted where I'm standing as I wait for her.

The door opens and she exits, her hand landing on her

chest with a gasp when she eyes me. "What are you doing in here?" She's removed her dress and is standing in front of me in nothing but her strapless bra, thong, and a garter belt holding up her stockings.

I may have been rendered speechless from her words earlier in the night, but I'm completely at a loss of what to say at the sight of her.

Fuck pledges I've made to myself.

Fuck her order of no sex.

There is no way I'm obeying her request because I'm going to fuck *her.*

Chapter Eight

Vulnerability

Victoria

H E STALKS FORWARD, like a predator hunting his prey. The sight sends an anxious shiver down my spine, a distinct reaction I've come to expect when peering into those eyes, even when he isn't touching me. He halts his steps inches in front of me, close enough for me to watch the pupils of his eyes dilate in hunger.

"What happened to your dress, princess?" His husky voice drops low as he speaks.

His finger grazes across my bare shoulder. The touch robs me of coherent thoughts as sparks glide across my bare skin. His lips find the hollow of my neck, the exact spot of my beating pulse.

"Trey," I say after swallowing, unable to manage anything more before he cuts me off with a smoldering kiss.

Holding onto his shoulders to keep from collapsing, his hands grasp me from behind and urge me forward to meet the straining erection in his pants.

Closing my eyes, I allow myself to enjoy the sensation, moaning into his mouth as he dominates me with his kiss. With clumsy footsteps, he leads us over to the bed, my body descending onto it as his body descends over mine. My hands tug at his shirt, demanding he remove it. In one swift motion it comes off, allowing me the pleasure of grazing my palms against the hard muscles of his chest.

Warmth from his hand traces every inch leading down to my thighs. "Fuck. I don't know whether I want to fuck you with these on or off," he says, referring to my stockings. To tease him, I glide my leg up against his side, earning me a strangled groan.

"I've decided. They stay on," he says, making me chuckle.

There is no question as to whether my bra will stay in place. His mouth is already tugging the cup to close his mouth over a nipple. Firmly suckling on the peak, I release a whimpered moan. His mouth moves to the other, elongating the pleasure he's delivering. How much longer will he make me wait?

"Please," I beg, struggling to pull him lower to meet me. The desperation in my plea has him moving.

A mischievous smile spreads across his face. "I hope these aren't your favorite," he claims, before ripping my thong with a force straining across my skin. The sound of it shredding intensifies my erratic pulse, and desire.

Opening my legs to allow him access, he stares down

at me with the same hunger in his eyes.

"Beautiful."

My hands reach out to the button of his jeans, but he gently shoves my hands away, unfastening them himself. Without hesitation, he pushes them down his thighs and my eyes don't stray from the erection standing proud in front to me. Lowering himself back down to meet the center of my heat, I feel him at my entrance and the anticipation to have him inside of me increases.

"Shit," he lets out in a frustrated growl. "I forgot to put another condom in my wallet."

"I have some in my side drawer," I inform him.

Without hesitation, he reaches for the drawer and removes the brand new box of condoms I had placed there. I hadn't bought them until recently. An impulse had me buying them, as if knowing this night would come.

With expertise, he rolls the condom over his shaft, his eyes never wandering from mine. Seconds later, he returns between my legs, grabbing my thighs to tug me to the edge of the bed. The animalistic action sends a shudder up my spine.

"You ready?" he asks before guiding his shaft to my center and entering me in one full thrust. The force of him stretching me has me gasping out loud. Regardless of the many times we've had sex, I have yet to adjust to how he fully fills me. As usual, he pauses, giving me the opportunity to adjust. He's hesitant for a moment, until I wrap my legs around his waist to lift my hips, inviting him to move. It's all the encouragement he needs to begin pumping his hips.

Trey has never failed at making sure to please me. There is no doubt he's skillful with his lovemaking. Each thrust against my core leads me closer to the pinnacle. I feel his lips kissing their way across my neck, the touch of his hands roaming up and down my body when they are not fiercely grasping at my ass as his hips pump in and out of me. I have never felt this way with anyone. I don't think I ever will.

His mouth meeting my own to capture the screams of my completion as my body erupts into an explosion of ecstasy has me smiling moments later. Our labored breaths and aftershocks are, as always, a result of what can only be described as mind-blowing sex.

He gazes down at me with a satisfied beam. "That was crazy."

Nodding my head, I try to catch my breath.

Leaning down, our lips gently touch. Once. Twice. The third time he passionately kisses me. "I don't know what you're doing to me, princess," he huskily relays against my lips when done. "But I can't get enough of you."

Contentment spreads through me.

Lifting his weight off me, he drops to my side, pulling me to drape across his chest. The beat of his heart eases my worried mind and silence overtakes the room while his hand strokes up and down my back.

My mind has completely forgotten the reservations I've held against him. My conscience is screaming with the repercussions to come, but my heart is demanding just one more night.

I suppress a yawn behind my palm, another that has escaped. Now naked with nothing but our bare skin touching as we lay side by side, he comments with a smirk, "I did my job well."

Smacking him on his chest, he catches my hand to bring it up to his mouth, placing a tender kiss on my palm. The endearment makes me sigh. I've always wished for it to happen to me, but until this day, I never thought it was possible. I'd come to believe it was a fictional act, meant only for fairytales or movies.

"I'm just sleepy," I mock, but he's correct. It is his fault that I'm exhausted. Turning onto my side, I rest my head on my hand to look down at him and ask, "Are you always this sweet with women after sex?"

He grows uneasy. "Do you want the truth or for me to sugarcoat it?" His response sends a quiver to the center of my stomach. The fact he is willing to be honest with his answer expands my heart, yet, there is no doubt in my mind he isn't celibate. Without waiting for my response, he says, "I'm not one to hang around."

Does this mean he will be leaving soon? My panic arises. I don't want him to leave. The emotion must be clear on my face because he adds, "I'm not going anywhere."

Mr. Whiskers must have sensed it was safe to return, since he jumps onto the bed, startling Trey with his meow. "How in the fuck does he not scare the shit out of you?"

"I've had him for so long," I laugh out, already petting Mr. Whiskers behind his ear.

Trey eyes him as if he holds the plague. If it weren't for half my body draped across his chest, he would most likely be off the bed by now.

He begins to relax, then asks, "How old is he?"

I consider the question before answering. "He'll be sixteen this year."

This has his eyes bulging wide. "How in the hell is he still alive?" he asks as he eyes the cat in amazement.

"I've taken very good care of him," I say. The response has my thoughts returning to the day I received him. "I had begged and begged my parents for a pet. I wanted a puppy, but my dad is allergic to most breeds. Occasionally a stray cat would wander on to the property. One of them must have had kittens because out of nowhere this little ball of fluff came out of the bushes," I say, continuing to pet Mr. Whiskers. "I snuck him into the house and fed him some milk. I intended to release him when he was done drinking, but my father came home early. I feared punishment for bringing him inside and knew I couldn't go outside without being caught, so I took him upstairs to my room. He never left after that day."

Trey skeptically looks at me. "You kept him without anyone ever finding out he was in the house?"

"For the first week, yes, but he eventually attacked one of the maids while I was at school," I shamefully admit. "They tried their best to catch him, but couldn't. He was fast. When I got home, he jumped into my arms. I cried my eyes out until they allowed me to keep him."

"Were you one of those spoiled little girls who got whatever they wanted?"

The amusement in his voice keeps me from taking offense. "Yes," I answer, earning me a snicker. "My parents were always busy with one thing or another between work and their social life. It was easier to replace their love with materialistic items than to pay attention to me," I say, simmering with dejection.

"Mr. Whiskers was the only companion I had growing up. It's why I love him so much."

His expression turns quizzical. "You weren't one for a unique name were you?"

"Hah, hah," I muse. "At least he's never judged me."

"That bad, huh?" he somberly asks.

Resenting his comment, I say, "It could have been worse."

"I would always bitch because I had some family member up in my face every day, while you had this raccoon for company," Trey says, pointing his index finger at Mr. Whiskers who has made himself comfortable at the edge of the bed. He's crawled into a ball and is sound asleep.

Shrugging it off, I say, "You get used to it."

This doesn't amuse him. "Was it like this during college, too?"

"How come you get to ask all these questions and I can't?"

By the look on his face, he's realized his error. "I'll tell you what. For every question I ask, I'll answer one of yours."

I agree, since I know this might be my only chance to discover more about him.

"Okay. I would love to know how you met Matt and Abigail. It's clear there is more than just a manager client relationship. Were you friends when you decided to become a sports manager?"

"I went to college with Matt. I played center on the football team and he was the quarterback. It was my job to never let anyone get near him. It's sort of like what I do now when Julio isn't around." He chuckles. "I never intended to become their manager. It sort of happened on accident." The sincerity in his eyes is accompanied by his reply. "Abigail needed saving one day and I was there to rescue her."

My heart swells. "That's my goal in life. To be someone's heroine." His brows arch. "It's why I chose to be a lawyer. My parents think it's because I wanted to follow my father's footsteps, but in reality I want to help people."

"Did you always want to be a lawyer?"

Blushing, I answer, "No. I wanted to be a teacher. My family's library was the one place you could always find me. I loved learning. So I wanted to give back what I learned."

"Why didn't you?"

My shoulders drop in defeat. "It would have never been an option with my family. The only options are those which can benefit the family reputation."

"I was supposed to return to my family's farm and help expand the business," he sorrowfully admits.

"Did you go to college on the west coast?"

He nods. "Yeah, in Portland."

"That's how you ended up over here," I say, pointing out the obvious. "Are they disappointed you didn't return?"

It takes him a moment to reply. "They say they're proud of what I'm doing. All I can do is believe them." A sense of envy overcomes me from his response.

"Do you miss your family?"

"Do you miss yours?" he's just as quick to ask.

Shaking my head, I answer, "No. When they're not around, I feel as if I can breathe." He frowns. "You didn't answer my question," I remind him.

"Yes and no in regards to my family. I haven't seen them since I graduated college and went home for a couple of months. Matt and Abigail's careers have kept me busy and I haven't been able to go home since. If it wasn't for technology, I wouldn't get to see them." His statement has my heart aching. "But I have my own dysfunctional family on this side of the country to keep me company."

Comprehension spreads across his face. "How did *you* end up on this side?" he asks.

"I wanted to acquire a position on my own, not through my father's connections. I can't complain. It gives me the sense of freedom I was searching for."

"You have a lot in common with Abigail. She's determined and independent," he compliments. It should leave me gratified, but my mind returns to the reason why I've had to work so hard.

"Try telling my father that," I bitterly say. "He keeps insisting I come work for his law firm. It'd be boarding school all over again where he makes all the decisions."

"Please tell me it was a Catholic one. Or better yet, an all girls boarding school." I roll my eyes at his suggestion.

"Let me guess. So you can show me what I've been missing?" I relay.

Looking smug, he says, "Exactly."

I laugh. "You don't need to pretend. You already are," I confess, trying to lift myself from the bed. He catches my body and rolls it underneath him so he's looking directly into my eyes. He looks pleased from my confession.

"All the other guys couldn't compare to what I give you?" he says, thrusting his hips between my thighs when he utters the words, igniting my desire for him once again.

"I'm pretty sure you weren't a virgin the first night we had sex, but from the shy little smiles you give, I know I've shocked you a few times."

This has me slightly blushing. "True," I rasp out.

"Then let the lessons commence," his deep voice says against the crook of my neck. Before I can stop him, he's already hard and grabbing for another condom. This man is insatiable, but I can't deny him, nor do I have any complaints.

I'll have to remember to refrain from surrendering to my weakness the next time I find the opportunity to confess why I'm so inexperienced. Until then, I'm going to enjoy how Trey makes me feel at this very moment.

Trey

The ringing of my phone awakens me from my slumber. Most people would ignore it, but I can't. My life revolves around this device. It can pertain to any one of my clients. It's the life I live.

Victoria's annoyed groan is heard from my side, advising me to make the sound stop, quickly.

"Hello," I half whisper into the phone.

"Where are you?" a concerned Matt asks. Pulling myself out of bed, I walk down the hall to Victoria's living room.

"Since when do I have to report to you?"

"Are you still with her?" The unpleasant tone he is using makes me livid.

"What is it to you?" I throw back at him.

Matt's heavy sigh has me picturing him raking his hand down his face. "I'm just calling you to warn you about the tabloids today."

"What the fuck did you do? Or is it about Abigail?" I ask, already irritated I'm going to have to clean up someone's mess.

"It's not us they're talking about. It's you this time." Now I'm confused. "Someone managed to get a picture of you two outside the restaurant last night. It's in every tabloid you can think of."

Doubtful he's referring to Victoria and me, I have to ask, "Are you sure it's us?"

"Yes, I'm sure," he states.

"What the hell do they want with us?"

Instead of answering my question, he drops another bomb on me. "It's not you they're after. It's her." This pisses me off even more.

"It still doesn't explain why they would want to target her."

Silence overcomes him for a moment. "It's because she's engaged," he faintly says.

My mind is telling me I've misheard him. "Engaged? Are you sure?" I'm still in denial. "Maybe they're mixing her up with someone else."

"They pointed her out. *By name,*" he admits.

At his point, I look towards the bedroom, only to clash eyes with Victoria standing in the hallway. Her curious expression advises me she has no clue as to what I'm speaking of.

"I've gotta go," I tell Matt, hanging up the phone without waiting for a reply.

Quickly searching the Internet myself, I find the article within seconds. As Matt had stated, there, staring back at me is our picture with the headline to prove her infidelity.

Glaring back at Victoria, I force myself to ask, "You're engaged?" I didn't want to believe Matt, but there is no refuting it now.

She shakes her head in denial.

"Don't fucking lie to me!" She flinches. "It's all over the papers, Victoria," I say, holding my phone out towards her, as if she's able to view the screen from where she's standing.

She's still shaking her head in dismay. "It's not what

you think."

At this point, I'm seething as bitterness courses through my veins. "You were with him the first time I *fucked* you, weren't you?"

She pales. There is no denying the truth. I knew days after she walked out on me, so she doesn't need to answer for me to know the truth.

"When the fuck were you expecting me to find out? When you sent me the wedding invitation, or when you were walking down the aisle?" I snarl as I walk past her and back into her bedroom to dress.

"You have to listen to me. I'm not engaged to him anymore," she cries to my back.

Without turning to look at her, I shove my legs into my jeans. "Quit fucking lying to me, Victoria. That's all you've ever done."

"I thought I'd be able to resist you when I saw you again, but I couldn't," she protests. "It's why I told you there couldn't be anything between us when we met again, but it's not like that anymore."

I spin around to finally face her. "I don't want your pitiful excuse as to why you slept with me. You should have just stayed the fuck away!" I declare, marching my way towards the door.

"Trey, wait. Please. You have to let me explain." She grabs ahold of my arm to stop me. Yanking my arm from her grasp, she stumbles back, giving me the perfect opportunity to resume my exit.

"Trey, stop!" she calls.

I stop a few feet from her doorway and spin to face

her. She has tears streaking down her cheeks. "What is there to explain, Victoria? Was this your plan the entire time? You'd come crawling to me so I could fuck you because he can't keep you satisfied?"

"I told you I'm not engaged to him anymore!" she argues.

"Were you engaged to him the night I fucked you back in Portland?" She remains silent, a single tear trickling down her cheek. There is no denying her guilt. "That's what I thought. You're no different than the cheating father you were bred from."

Those are my last words before I leave her apartment.

I may not know much of her family's personal life, minus the few clues Julio had disclosed long ago, but what little I did learn of her from my own prodding, I know her father is known for his affairs.

This entire time I believed she was different, nothing like the family she speaks of, but it's evident the apple doesn't fall far from the tree.

Chapter Nine

Rescued

Victoria

MY DRIVE TO work was eventful, to say the least.

The day before, most of the paparazzi had left when they discovered I wouldn't be leaving my building. Mariam, my father's publicist, had done a wonderful job of deferring the tabloids onto another story, but there were some that were persistent; those lingered and followed. They hadn't gotten more than a couple of pictures of me on the drive to work, but it was dangerous enough. Several times, they nearly caused an accident trying to get their much-needed photo.

Believing I would be safe inside my work building was a mistake. They found a way to breech security then tried to lie their way through the receptionist by claiming to have an appointment with me. It hadn't convinced her, of course. Security was called and they were escorted off the premises. However, they weren't giving up.

Late into the night when my day is complete and I am leaving my office to head home, the first flash of the camera throws me off guard upon stepping off the elevator. The shouting of my name adds to my fright.

"Victoria! Do you still plan on marrying?"

"How does it feel to follow in your father's footsteps?"

"How long has the affair been going on?"

Question after question. Flash after flash. I have only taken several steps from the elevator and I can't manage any more with my disoriented mind. The bright flashes have my head spinning and all the shouting has my heart erratically beating out of control. Panic kicks in. No matter where I turn, I face a camera flashing in my face. The tears have built, but I refrain from crying, as it would do no use to save me.

"Get the fuck away from her!" a voice booms through it all.

A body slams up against me at the same time a strong arm wraps around my waist. I frantically attempt to push at the chest of the man who has me wrapped in his arms, but he firmly holds on.

"Trey!" I hear another man shout, notifying me who has me safely embraced in his arms. He's here . . . with me . . . He's rescuing me.

"Trey! Are you taking her off for another rendezvous before the wedding?" My eyes are still full of tears, but my ears catch the sound of someone grunting.

"I'm going to sue you for that!"

"Whatever!" he shouts back.

Burying my face in the crook of his neck, I take in his familiar scent, which instantly helps to calm my internal storm.

"What are you doing here?" I incoherently ask. He remains silent, quickening his steps, ushering me away.

The sound of an alarm disengaging has me slightly lifting my head to see we've reached his SUV.

"Keep your head covered," he orders before pushing me into the seat and slamming the door shut.

I do as told and bury my face in my jacket, leaving just enough of a gap to watch his actions. The roar of the engine is heard as he pushes his way through the crowd to the driver's side. Once he's inside, he engages the locks before slowly beginning to drive us through the hoard of paparazzi still flashing away with their cameras.

It isn't until minutes later when I know we're far enough away from the building that I emerge from my coat. "Where are we going?"

"I don't know!" he angrily shouts.

"You don't have to yell!"

"I'm sorry. I wasn't expecting it to be that bad."

"How did you know they would be there?"

"I didn't." I'm confused. "I showed up a couple of minutes before you came out," he explains.

"You still haven't answered why you were there." And he still doesn't. Instead, he uses the distraction of driving to avoid answering me. I'm still trying to comprehend what has happened myself.

"Where are we going?" I demand to know.

"Back to your apartment. I need time to think."

"What if they're there? Won't it make it worse?"

He pierces me with his glare. "Look around you! Regardless of where we go, they're going to follow. If you have a better idea, then speak up," he furiously states. Silence is the only answer I can give because I don't have a better idea. "That's what I thought."

My eyes continue to watch his jaw tighten and his nostrils flare when he returns his focus on the road. Fear continues to bubble in my chest knowing our situation will only grow worse. The paparazzi have gotten what they've been patiently waiting for: Trey and I together once more. It wasn't planned, but the media won't care about the truth.

As I assumed, they are waiting for us as we near my condo. The flashes resume when we pull up to the building. Once in the confines of the parking garage, Trey parks his vehicle.

"Get inside," he orders. The slamming of the door startles me back to reality.

The headstrong part of me wants to resist his commands to prove a point, but the rational part of me is yelling at me to listen. Knowing it's always best to heed to the rational part of myself, I do as he says. With him once more at my side, he leads me inside the building, and as a couple of nights ago, we ride the elevator up to my apartment.

Through the chaos of it all, my body still reacts to having him so closely at my side. Butterflies are fluttering in my stomach. My heart rate increases with every breath.

A simple touch of his hand on my back to lead my way sends sparks traveling up my spine. It's a reaction he's always brought out of me, which no one else has ever accomplished.

Especially not Andrew.

The ping of the elevator is a welcome distraction. Just as quickly, I am reminded of the situation we're in when Trey pulls me to stand behind him, checking first left, and then right before turning to grab for my hand.

"You didn't think they would be able to get into the building, did you?" Without hesitation, he says, "You'd have to be stupid to believe they couldn't."

One moment this man has me feeling emotions I'm still trying to decipher, the next he has me wanting to strangle him. Obviously, it's my rational side keeping me from following through with the latter.

"Are you always this arrogant, or am I just privileged enough to have to endure it?"

We are standing at my door when I make the comment. His arm flanks out the moment I open the door, blocking me from entering.

Rage is in his eyes when he asks, "Why do I have a feeling you always have to have the last word?"

Refusing to allow him to frighten me, I say, "I look forward to the day when you may shock me into silence."

He narrows his eyes before his face becomes expressionless when he removes his arm and steps aside to grant me access. Our eyes stay locked for a second before his chin is thrusting forward, gesturing for me to move.

He shuts the door behind us, safely securing the lock

then walks over to the doors leading out onto the balcony. He checks them, reassuring they, too, are locked.

"What now?" I ask, needing to know.

"I don't know. It's not like I planned on having to rescue you." The animosity is evident in his tone.

"Nobody said you had to."

He stalks over, stopping inches in front of me. "What would you have preferred I do, leave you there to fend off the wolves all by yourself?"

Lifting my chin, I refuse to show him weakness. "I would have been perfectly fine. I'm sure security was probably on their way down."

He snorts. "Whatever," he retorts before he turns to pace away.

"You still haven't answered why you were there." I demand to know why, and I won't stop until he tells me. He remains silent, pulling out his phone and punching at the screen. "Why do you keep doing that?"

He continues to ignore me, now speaking into the phone. "I need you to fly back. Seattle this time." He listens to the caller on the other end, his brows furiously narrowing down. "Yes, tonight," he insists. He's silent for a moment. "I don't give a shit what you're doing right now. You better remember who issues your paychecks," he barks into the phone. "Good. I'll see you then."

He ends the call then looks at me.

"Who was that?" I ask.

Without replying to my question, he orders, "Go pack."

I stand, grounded to my spot, defying his request.

"Why?"

"Because we're leaving. The pilot will be here in a little over two hours." He called a pilot. Why? Where does he plan on taking me, and how in the hell does he have a pilot on standby?

Nevertheless, I can't go.

"I'm not packing."

"I didn't ask you."

"Stop doing that! I refuse to let you bark orders at me like I'm some kind of dog whose obedience you demand." Stepping forward, I close the distance between us to snarl at him. "You never ask, you demand, just like them."

"Who's they?" he challenges.

Raging, I answer, "My father and all his minions. You are no different than everyone I left behind, and because of that I refuse to heed to your commands." Crossing my arms over my chest, I continue to stand my ground.

His eyes grow darker before his shoulders drop down. "Unlike them, Victoria, I'm willing to protect you. It's all I'm trying to do," he says then exhales deeply. My heart melts from his admission.

"You better remember it's because of you we're in this situation," he adds. And just as rapidly he shatters my emotions to pieces.

"Thank you. I appreciate it," I sarcastically relay through clenched teeth. "But I still can't leave."

He steps back, his arms spreading wide. "What is it now?"

"My job." Is he really that ignorant? "I have responsibilities. I can't just leave without notice. I can be fired. I worked too damn hard to lose what I earned on my own."

A hint of comprehension spreads through his eyes. Turning, he gives me his back. Although I'm curious to know his next decision, I remain rooted to my spot, mute, refusing to say anymore. When he brings his phone up to his ear, a sense of satisfaction spreads through me, thinking he's calling off the pilot.

"Benjamin. It's Trey." My heart stops for a beat. "I'm with her," he relays. With his back still facing me, I'm unable to read his facial expressions. "Yeah, I agree, which is why I need you to give her a couple of weeks off." I watch his head snap back as he snickers. My heart has resumed beating, only this time erratically out of control. "Alright, I'll keep you updated."

Pulling the phone from his ear and spinning to face me, he says, "It's done. You're off until the end of the month. Now go pack."

My mouth gapes open. "You can't just call Benjamin and order him to give me time off," I claim, as if it hasn't already been done.

"It wasn't so hard since your *daddy* already called him ordering he do it. He's expecting you to go running home."

Fury spreads inside of me. "Even more reason to stay and continue doing my job."

Trey frowns. "Benjamin didn't sound so sure your dad was going to let you," he claims. "It's your choice, Victoria. Run home to daddy or I take you with me. What will it be?"

Hating my options, I still ask, "Where exactly do you plan on taking me?"

"Home."

Chapter Ten

Homecoming

Trey

PROTECT HER.

Those two words fuel the adrenaline still coursing through my veins.

I had no intention of returning to Seattle after dropping Matt and Abigail off at the airport earlier in the day. Instead, my mind was on autopilot, already heading north on the freeway returning to Seattle, driving to her place of employment. It was there I'd seen her being invaded by the paparazzi.

Instinct kicked in. There was no way I would allow them to hurt her. All animosity dissipated within a split second and my drive to protect her had replaced it.

I'm still trying to wrap my mind around how I allowed it to happen. It's been years since I've made an irrational decision of this sort. I have become a man of well thought out plans. The days of ludicrous decisions are behind me. They were left behind the day I took on being Abigail's manager, the same day responsibility for others became of the utmost importance. Maybe it's the same reason why she's sitting to my side while I drive us to the airport.

The drawn out cry from Victoria's cat has my thoughts breaking. She refused to leave without him. We'd argued back and forth for almost an hour, but in the end, she won. She stuck to her insistence of bringing the damned thing.

"Is he going to cry the entire trip?"

She looks down to her lap where the Louis Vuitton carrier sits. "He'll be fine," she states, immediately adding with a hint of doubt, "I think."

Great. I'm going to have a psychotic cat to deal with as well.

My phone rings, saving me from having to comment further. "Hello," I answer, already knowing who it is.

"Everything is ready. Security knows your license plate number, along with the make and model of your car. They are expecting you to drive through the gates."

"Julio?" Victoria confusedly asks as she listens to the phone call airing through the speakers thanks to the Bluetooth.

"Good. We'll be there in another couple of minutes. See you then," I tell him, immediately ending the call after my last word. It cuts off the chance for either of them to communicate.

Within minutes, true to my word, we're driving up to the airport. "You have a private jet?" she asks, sounding astonished at the possibility.

"This little trip will go smoothly if you stop asking so many questions," I inform her.

She mumbles a snarky response low enough under her breath preventing me from making out the words. Instead of retaliating, my eyes stay focused on the purpose ahead, getting us safely to the plane. My eyes have been closely watching the paparazzi in my rearview mirror. They've been following us since the moment we left her building. I was expecting it, which is why I called Julio before leaving to make precautionary plans.

Driving through the gates and leaving them behind, I bring my SUV to park as closely to the jet as possible. Julio is already at Victoria's door attending to her, leaving me to play bellboy to her luggage. Nearing them, I see Julio's extended hand.

"Victoria, may I have your phone, please?"

Giving him a baffled look, she asks, "Why do you need my phone?"

"Your father most likely already has his security team tracking you. It'll be safer for both of you if the trail ends here." Concern is in his eyes when he looks over to me while he explains.

Comprehension hits her. She cautiously looks down to it before surrendering it to him. They're fucking acting like her father is part of the mafia.

"Thank you," Julio grants, tucking the item into the pocket of his blazer. "Be safe," he encourages, urging her towards the steps of the aircraft.

"You're not coming?" She frantically looks to him

when she asks.

Julio glances to me for a brief moment. "No. I'm driving the vehicle back to Portland," he says, signaling me to hand him my keys. She hesitates for a short moment before stepping up into the plane.

Julio waits until she is no longer in sight when he orders, "I need your phone as well." He holds out a replica of the one I own.

Staring down at it, I ask, "You sure I need to?"

He gives me a curt nod. "I wouldn't be surprised if he's already tracking it." I hand my phone over to him as if it will catch on fire any second, exchanging it for the one he's offered. "I've already entered your most important contacts, including your family."

"Tell me again why the fuck I'm doing this. I've got too much shit to do for me to be babysitting a debutant."

"I've already informed your assistant you have a family emergency overseas. That way, if she slips, they think you've left the country," he explains, as if understanding my frustration.

Georgia may have signed a non-disclosure agreement when I hired her two years ago, but I wouldn't put it past her to crack under the pressure.

"You're doing the right thing, Trey," he reassures me, but I'm still skeptical. "You'll make sure to call me if anything changes?"

"Of course."

"You ready?" The pilot questions, bringing our conversation to an end. Giving Julio one last nod, I, too, make my way up the steps. When I'm inside the plane, the pilot pulls me into the cockpit. "Is this really the destination you want me to fly to?" He looks doubtful while staring down at a manual map.

"Yes."

He's still uncertain of my request. "I don't know if this is an actual airport."

"It's not. It's a landing strip for crop dusters," I disclose.

His eyes bulge out of his sockets. "Are you crazy? I can't land a plane this size on a crop dusting runway."

I roll my eyes at him. "I've seen the runway myself." It was part of my life growing up. "It's wide and long enough for you to land."

"I still have to get clearance to land there before we take off."

"No you don't. It belongs to my family so you don't need it." His lips irritably go flat. "I have every bit of confidence in you," I encourage with a grin.

"Fine, but if you kill us, I'll make sure to drag you to hell with me."

"Got it." Slapping him on the shoulder, I leave him to return to the seating area.

I find Victoria already sitting in one of the ten seats in the interior. "Is the plane yours?" she asks again.

Taking my seat at the other end of the aisle from her, I explain, "It primarily belongs to Matt and Abigail, but I'm free to use it when they don't have a need for it."

"So they travel a lot?"

My eyes narrow down, considering just how much information she's probing for, but she most likely already knows most of what I'm going to tell her. "You already know they have two houses." She nods. "They spend an equal amount of time between California and Oregon because of their schedules. Plus they insist on being at each other's events as much as possible."

"That would require a lot of flying," she points out.

"Which is why it was beneficial to buy a plane. It cost just the same after all the traveling they do. Plus, this way we don't put the baby at risk with the public."

Her eyes turn sympathetic. "She's important to you," she comments.

"I would kill for her."

Victoria remains silent from my declaration. The sound of the pilot shutting the door overtakes the tension in the room. He requests for us to buckle up for takeoff, and after doing as instructed, she continues her questioning.

"Is Julio's plan to distract them back to Portland?"

"Yes."

"Wouldn't it have been safer for him to just come with us? Who's going to protect us when we get there?"

"Are you doubting my ability to do a good enough job?"

She doesn't respond, but instead gives me a glare before she turns to look out the window. The roar of the engines notifies us we are ready to taxi for takeoff. Within minutes, the aircraft is speeding down the runway and elevating into the air to soar into the sky. Using the controls near my armrest, I dim the lights to help relax both our anxious minds. It isn't long before her eyes begin to grow weary and she's fighting to keep them open. Soon she loses the battle and her head is leaning against the panel of the wall. Unbuckling my seat belt, I move over to her side and engage the control to flatten her seat so she can better rest. She must be completely exhausted, since she doesn't stir at all.

Staring down at her, I have to keep asking myself what the hell it is I'm doing. Whatever it is, it must be because I've completely lost my mind.

Hours later, she stirs awake. Her arms reach up first to stretch, seconds later her entire body stiffens when I say to her, "Good morning, princess."

Frantic eyes are staring at me before she lets out a relieved breath.

She shyly smiles. "Good morning." As if comprehending our greetings, she snaps her head to look out the window. The soft glow of the sun preparing to rise is reflecting back at her.

"What time is it?"

Looking down at the phone Julio gave me, I notice it's already on local time. "Nearly 6 A.M." Her wide eyes turn to me.

"That's impossible. Portland isn't that far away from Seattle by plane."

"No shit, Sherlock."

"You said you were taking me home," she reprimands.

"I am," I verify. "To Tennessee."

Her face turns ashen, her mouth gaping open. I've accomplished what I believed to be the impossible: I've rendered her speechless. She looks to be searching her mind, but is kept from speaking when her cat lets out his usual cry. Strange how I've become accustomed to the sound in a matter of days. He was curled up in the seat next to her, but is now arching his back and stretching out his front legs.

"You let him out?"

"He kept crying. It was driving me nuts," I lie to her. It was only once he complained, but I'm not going to admit how I felt sorry for the animal. "He looked cramped up in that thing." Which is the real reason why I took him out.

There's a hint of a smile at the corner of her mouth. "Thank you. He does hate being in it."

"No problem." Her eyes soften with a glow, causing my chest to tighten up. "Put your seat up, we're about to land in a little bit," I instruct, breaking the mood before she gets any ideas.

I can't allow her to affect me any longer. It's what got me in this situation in the first place. Victoria gathers up her cat and against all protest, she returns him to his carrier. Within seconds, he's crying to be let out, making me chuckle.

"Did you sleep?" she asks.

With a light shrug, I try to disguise the weariness I still hold. "A couple of hours."

The pilot announces we are about to land and my eyes find the window to look out onto the miles of land, which is my past. I've never regretted growing up here, however it isn't who I am any longer.

It's been years from the last day I stepped on the soil I was raised on. I've always meant to return, but thankfully for technology, I've been able to keep in touch. Nevertheless, no video chat will compare to seeing my family in the flesh.

We feel the light bounce of the aircraft wheels landing and the engines coming to a roaring halt as we slowly taxi to a stop, my heart erratically beating in anticipation of seeing everyone. Knowing I'm on home ground has an excitement I hadn't expected kindling inside of me.

We come to a complete stop and Victoria is skeptically looking out the window.

"Is this even an airport?"

"Something like that." She's confused by my reply as the pilot exits the cockpit, looking pleased with himself.

"Whew. Didn't know if it'd be possible."

"I never doubted you, Russell," I laugh out.

Grimly looking at me, he doesn't seem to agree.

"Let's go," I tell Victoria, unbuckling my seatbelt to stand. She does the same and the sound of the hatch opening has me taking a deep breath. The beam of the morning sunrise radiates inside the aircraft seconds before the humidity of the southern air hits me in the face with force. Descending the steps, my ears hear, "Well, look at what the tumble weeds blew in."

The familiar, thick accent of my childhood greets me as I step off the plane. Embracing my cousin, Jimmy, in a half hug when I reach him, I say, "It's good to see you, too, Jimmy."

Pulling away, I see his eyes looking past me and spying Victoria.

"Finally brought someone home to meet your momma, huh?" he hoots out, referring back to all the times I refused to bring *any* girl home.

"Not exactly."

He arches his brow in question.

I declared long ago I wasn't bringing just any girl home. It was going to be the girl I was marrying, and only when I already had a ring on her finger. I couldn't chance her being scared off by my crazy family.

Glancing over my shoulder, I now have to bite back my own words.

"She's *just* a friend."

Jimmy's amused eyes laugh back at me. "In that case, it means she's available." Taking Victoria's hand, he brings it up for a kiss.

"What would your name be, pretty lady?"

"Victoria," she says, now blushing.

"It's a pleasure to meet your acquaintance, Ms. Victoria."

Johnson men are notorious for their flirtatious ways. It's what gets us laid. Nonetheless, there is no fucking way I was letting Victoria become his latest victim.

"Back the fuck off her, Jimmy. She isn't here to get mauled by the likes of you."

Victoria's cat lets out a frustrated cry from his carrier, making Jimmy look down with a suspicious glare.

His lips lift up into a smirk. "I see she has a pussy, too."

She isn't used to our filthy mouths, and her eyes go wide as saucers, increasing the blush on her cheeks.

"Watch your fucking mouth unless you're looking to

have a swollen lip," I snap at him.

My threat does nothing. "Not if you want me to knock you into next week." Our threats are just banter, nothing has ever really come of them. However, he has me at the line of following through this time.

Before I get a chance to retaliate, the pilot is stepping up next to us. "I've done my job here. If you don't need anything else, I'll be heading back now."

"You sure you're good to fly?"

"I'm going to take a nap before heading out to the nearest airport to fuel up."

"Sounds good, Russell. I really appreciate it," I say while shaking his hand to thank him.

Giving me a curt nod, he heads back to the aircraft and closes the hatch. Facing my cousin once more, I ask, "You think you can give us a ride home?"

He snorts. "Of course. You think I'm going to miss seeing your momma's expression when she sees the both of you?" he says, wagging his brows.

"We're just friends," I repeat.

He's glancing at Victoria when his lips curve up to one side. "It's not me you have to convince," he mocks over his shoulder after spinning on the heels of his boots, now heading towards his truck.

Country music, cowboys, and thick southern accents are

just a few of the things I expected to see when we arrived in Tennessee. I had also imagined the cowboys driving old, muddy pick-up trucks. The kind where city girls like myself would fear getting into. It's what I envisioned in my imagination.

I was correct about most of my assumptions.

Jimmy is a cowboy from head to toe, his accent giving me shivers as it rolls off his tongue. And under the layers of caked on mud, I'm pretty sure is a brand new truck, four doors and most likely to the year. Oh, it screamed country from front to end. At least, I wouldn't have to fear it breaking down. The faint lyrics of a guy singing about a girl declaring how this was her favorite song keeps me distracted from the two men sitting in the front seat.

Jimmy keeps stealing glances from the driver's seat, giving me a flirtatious smile each time. All I can do is keep biting my lip to keep from smiling in return. I'm sure with the bright sunlight peeking through the tinted windows he is catching the hint of a blush I've been holding from the moment he kissed the back of my hand.

Looking between the two men sitting ahead of me, they may seem like two different characters by the way they are dressed, but the similarities in their features are completely alike. It's obvious they are related. They both have bright blue eyes, a light complexion, and hold the same body frame. Even their hair color is similar. They can easily pull off being brothers instead of cousins.

Jimmy glances over his shoulder to ask, "I take it you're from Junior's side of town?"

"Junior?" I ask, confused as to whom he's speaking

of.

"It's what my family calls me," Trey explains from the front seat.

Hitching his thumb to his right at Trey, Jimmy says, "He was named after our granddaddy."

With an ecstatic smile, I say, "Really? I was named after my grandmother."

"Explains the old lady name," he laughs out.

I'm far from amused. "At least it's a respectable name. How far back does Trey go in the historical archives?"

Challenging me, he turns so he's looking directly in my eyes. "Oh, so just because your name comes from royalty, it's more important than mine, princess?"

The truck slightly swerves, startling me.

"You're a princess?" Jimmy asks.

Shoving his shoulder, Trey demands, "Keep your eyes on the damn road, Jimmy!"

Jimmy's eyes are still bulging when I reply, "No, I'm not a princess. Trey just has a way of making me feel as if I'm part of some aristocratic world."

"You act like it," Trey says, facing forward. I can't fully see his entire face, but from the side mirror, I catch him staring outside, looking edgy.

"I do not!" I defend.

He snickers, but it's Jimmy's disoriented voice catching my attention. "So you're not royalty?" he asks, sounding baffled.

"No," both Trey and I bite out at the same time.

My arms bitterly cross over my chest and I, too, am now staring out of my window.

"Y'all are a strange couple."

"We're not a couple," Trey declares.

The declaration has my chest tightening as my heart shrinks. It's evident in his tone that he sees me as nothing more than an inconvenience he's unfortunately stuck with. I have to force myself to bite my tongue instead of demanding clarification as to what the hell I am and why he has me here. Thoughts of regret begin to fill my mind, as anguish wraps around my heart. It's the rope of sorrow keeping the remaining pieces of my shattered heart together.

With my eyes focused to my right, I can't help but notice the miles of land we are traveling through. Trey has never specified what it is his family does, nor did he ever mention specifically where it was he was from.

Unable to resist, I ask, "How long has it been since you came home?"

My question is directed to Trey, but it's his cousin that answers for him. "Almost three years. We were beginning to think he'd never come back."

"I've been busy," he defends.

Trey's eyes never waver from his focus of looking out of the window. I do catch the deep breath he exhales, a sure sign of the anxiety he must be sheltering within himself. The sight has my heart aching a little. I may not be on good terms with my family, but the mandatory family events I'm obligated to attend allow me to see them every so often. I've never spent more than a couple of months apart from them, so I can't imagine not seeing them for years.

"Well, nobody is going to be happier to see you than

your momma," Jimmy indicates.

The moment he declares it, an iron arch with the stating of *"Johnson Ranch"* comes into view. Minutes later, a house comes up ahead. It's a modern looking, one-story home with a porch wrapping around the entire house. From the view of the exterior, it's obvious it's full of love.

Jimmy pulls up near the back of the house, putting the truck into park and turning off the engine.

"Welcome home."

Two words I've never heard in my entire life whenever I returned to my own home, yet they have more meaning than any flat smiled greeting when you walk through the door of my own residence.

Trey looks over his shoulder to me, a hint of anxiety in his eyes. "You ready?" It isn't me who should be nervous about being here, yet he still looks to me to ensure I'm with him one hundred percent of the way.

I'm already replying when he exits and opens my door. "As ready as I'll ever be." The humid, southern air hits me, as it had done earlier when departing the plane.

"Is it always this humid?" I ask, pulling at my shirt already sticking to my chest.

Stepping from the truck, he gives me a bemused smile. "It's springtime, so the humidity is going to start rising, but for now it's nothing compared to how it gets."

My breath catches as I step out, placing the shoulder strap of Mr. Whiskers' carrier over my shoulder. "Please tell me we won't be here long enough to experience it," I complain.

Turning so he's mere inches from my face, I notice the

sneer before he says, "Trust me, princess, if I could return you now, I would."

Without a backwards glance, he turns to walk up the front steps of his home. Swallowing the blow he's delivered, I watch him disappear through a backdoor.

"Does he always act like he's got a thorn up his ass?"

"For as long as I've known him, yes."

I walk around the truck to retrieve my luggage from the back, but I'm beat to the task. "Allow me," Jimmy offers, already grabbing it for me. "My cousin seems to have forgotten his manners in the big city."

"Did he ever have manners?" He tilts his head as if considering my question.

"As far as I know, we were all raised with them." Snickering, I try to imagine Trey with manners. "Give the boy two nickels for a dime and he thinks he's rich and doesn't need them anymore, I guess."

Confused, I ask, "Am I going to need a dictionary to decipher what you just said?"

This amuses Jimmy. "Not if you stick with me, pretty lady." Looping his arm into mine, he leads me up the same steps Trey just traveled.

Entering the house with Jimmy, I find Trey tightly embraced in the arms of an older lady. Pulling away, she keeps his face in her palms. "I can't believe the luck the good Lord has blessed me with today." She sniffles. "My boy is home," she adds, before pulling him back into her arms.

My heart begins to mend at the sight I'm beholding. He keeps her wrapped in his arms as if he's the one frightful of her disappearing. My chest tightens as tears build and my throat constricts. My vision becomes glassy from the love radiating from this one embrace, and a longing to for once have the same. A welcome embrace is something I have never experienced

Jimmy wraps his arm around my shoulder, pulling me tight to his side. I'm so lost in the display in front of me that I forget whose arms I'm in and lean into the chest comforting me. Trey pulls away to look over to us. The once affectionate expression he held disappears when he takes me in. It's one of a monstrous scorn.

His mother's eyes beam when she spots me. "Oh, who do we have here?"

Giving me a light shake, Jimmy says, "This here is Trey's *friend,* Ms. Victoria."

Trey groans from the elated expression his mother now holds. I couldn't have imagined her eyes shining any brighter.

"She's just a friend, Momma, nothing more," Trey sternly clarifies. "It would do you some good to take your arm off her, Jimmy," Trey threatens the man holding me. I could have sworn a hint of the same accent Jimmy speaks with accompanied the command.

"You just said yourself she isn't anything to you, so why you getting all pissy?"

Trey steps forward, the look of a bull ready to rage. It's Trey's mother who stops the feud. Clapping her hands, she catches their attention. "Both of you stop with this pissing contest," she huffs out. "I won't be having this nonsense in my house. Y'all are some grown men now, not the boys you once were." She scowls at both of them.

Moving away from Jimmy's grasp to keep a war from developing, I'm thankful when Mr. Whiskers distracts us all when he lets out his usual cry.

"What is that?" Mrs. Johnson asks, pointing at the bag at my hip.

Holding up the carrier to look into it, I see Mr. Whiskers completely annoyed that he's still trapped.

"It's her cat, Momma," Trey informs her.

She gasps. "There is no way that creature is staying in my house. Put it out back," she declares.

"Please, Mrs. Johnson. He can't. He's declawed so there is no way for him to defend himself," I explain, pleading with her.

She narrows her eyes at the bag while I nervously clutch it to my chest. "There is no way he'll be scratching at my furniture?" she questions. Shaking my head, I say, "No, and he's neutered so he won't spray either." I'm ready to drop to my knees and beg if I have to.

Her lips go flat as she contemplates her answer. My heart begins to race in fear she'll deny my request.

"Fine. But he's your responsibility. Don't be expecting me to clean out his box." Nodding my head in agreement, I finally let out the breath I was holding.

"Thank you, Momma," Trey tells her, placing a kiss on her temple.

His mother takes a deep breath. "Now, why don't y'all go and wash up. I'll start making breakfast," she orders with a dismissal. "You can put her in Chrissie's room and you will stay in your old room." She narrows her eyes at

Trey. "Alone. They'll be no funny business under my roof if y'all aren't married yet."

Shocked from the assumption she's made, my mouth gapes open. "I already told you, Momma, she's just a friend," Trey repeats, sounding more like a whine towards the end.

"Whatever she is, she deserves to be respected like a lady. That goes for the both of you." She turns to glare at Jimmy as she states the last part.

"Of course, Aunt Viv."

"Thank you, Mrs. Johnson."

She looks to me with her smile now returned. "You can call me, Viv, dear." Her palm comes up to touch my cheek before stepping around me and into the kitchen. It was nothing more than a touch, but it was a mother's touch. The affection makes my heart expand ten times larger than when I walked in the door. Looking towards Trey, who is looking back with a blank expression, leaves me feeling envious. He has no clue as to what treasure he holds. Or maybe he does, which is why we are now here.

With a tilt of his head, I follow him past the living room. Pointing to a door on the way, he says, "We'll have to share this bathroom, so if you are OCD about cleanliness, now is the time to get over it." I shoot him an indignant look when he delivers that comment. Pointing to a room next to it, he stops and stands next to the doorframe, but doesn't enter. "This is my sister Chrissie's room. You'll be staying in here." He steps back, allowing me to enter it. Turning full circle, I take in the white and lavender tones overflowing throughout the room, a perfect combination of colors to represent a young lady. Posters of young teen boys hang from the walls, with fashion magazines lying around the room.

"How old is your sister?"

"She'll be seventeen this year."

When my eyes find him, he's staring at the surroundings in the room. "This room used to be filled with nothing but dolls and stuffed animals."

"Is she at school?"

He nods his head. "Yeah, they have to catch the bus really early here." Still looking around the room, I remain silent, waiting for him to speak again. "You can have the shower in the hall now, I'll take the one in my parents' room. If you need anything, give me a holler," he says before turning to leave me standing alone in the room.

A sense of heartache remains with me as I watch him walk away. Mr. Whiskers demands to be let out by jolting around in his carrier bag.

Kneeling down onto the floor, I put him down and begin to unzip the bag. "All right. You win, but you are to stay in this room," I clarify when I pull him out. He looks agitated, most likely from the time he's had to spend in the carrier. "Don't give me that look," I tell him. "You would have been in there longer if Trey wouldn't have let you out during the flight." In answer, he gives me the stink eye.

Sitting back on my haunches, I watch him hesitantly look around the room before he jumps up onto the bed. He makes two full circles before lowering himself down into a ball. Laying his head down, he closes his eyes and falls asleep. How he can become so comfortable with his surroundings so quickly is a mystery. The first two members of Trey's family may have already welcomed me with smiles and warm greetings, but it still leaves me feeling out of place in a world I am unaccustomed to. Had they greeted me with dreary smiles and directions on what was to come in the day so I could be prepared what to expect, I would have felt right at home.

Sighing to myself, I know I should be grateful for where I am, considering where I could have been: my own family's residence.

Knowing it's pointless to wallow in my misery, I grab a fresh pair of clothes from my suitcase and head to the shower. An hour later, I'm refreshed and comfortably dressed in skinny jeans, a casual blouse, and a pair of flats. Upon exiting the bedroom, the sound of many voices, along with the clanking of dishware, escalates the closer I walk towards the dining area.

Entering, a jubilant young lady around my age with a round belly spies me and waddles her way over. "You must be her." She opens up her arms, engulfing me within them. Her protruding belly sits between us, yet it doesn't stop her from squeezing the air out of me. "It's so nice to meet you," she squeals into my ear.

Awkwardly patting her back, I say, "It's nice to meet you, too," even though I have no clue as to who she is.

She pulls back, a wide smile still on her face. Her eyes roam my body, and I can't help but feel as if I'm being politely scrutinized. "Oh, you're a pretty one."

"Leave her be, Becca," Trey's booming voice says from behind me before we both turn to face him. The sight of him has my mouth gaping open.

Walking towards us is a Trey I would have never imagined. He's wearing a light blue flannel shirt with the sleeves folded to his elbows, but it's clear it's small in size, tightly showcasing the muscles my palms love grazing across when we're alone. The jeans are not the usual well taken care of designer pair I'm used to seeing him in. These are well worn and snug perfectly around his thighs, sending my thoughts back to the memory of what my legs felt like wrapped around them. My eyes keep traveling lower to where he's replaced his designer shoes with a pair of cowboy boots. The entire ensemble is far from the casual businessman I've come to see him as the few days we've been together. Now standing before me is the southern boy I had envisioned in my mind when he mentioned growing up in the south.

"I had to see you with my own eyes to believe it," the girl standing next to me laughs out. Trey reaches out and engulfs her in his arms. The delighted expression on his face sends a pang of jealously coursing through me. All of Trey's reactions upon seeing me have been far from ecstatic. Most of the time they begin with him glowering at me.

"I've missed you so much," she tells him.

Pulling away to place both his hands on her stomach, he says, "Damn, Becca, you're one horny girl."

Becca smacks him on the chest. "It takes two to make a baby." She points down at her stomach. "You can blame your brother for my condition."

They both chuckle right before Trey says, "Hopefully

this time it's your girl."

"It better be or I may just castrate your brother."

"Scary part is you know how to do it," Trey comments, flinching at the same time. They both laugh together while I'm left standing awkwardly, looking around the room, feeling out of place. A hand on my arm catches my attention.

"Are you hungry, dear?" Trey's mom kindly asks.

"I'll have coffee if you have some."

Viv nods with a smile. "Come," she says, leading me over to the table in the kitchen. "You sit here while I get you a cup." She urges me to take a seat, and I find myself glancing back in the direction I was pulled from to find Trey still conversing with Becca, both of them quietly speaking with their heads forward in concentration. It's obvious from their body language and curious glances they are speaking of me.

"Here you go, dear," Mrs. Johnson cheerfully says above me.

The aroma of freshly brewed coffee wafts up to break my attention, and I avert my eyes then search for my phone, realizing I don't have it. Normally, it's the one distraction I seek to shut myself out from the world, yet it's in the world I escaped from.

Staring down into the mug of black brew, I contemplate how it currently matches the color of my emotions. My throat tightens and tears well in my eyes. Reality has finally sunk in. I've fallen down a rabbit hole, and there is no one to blame but myself. I'm in a strange, unfamiliar world and the only person I know in it is the same person who seems to despise me. I *have* made a mistake, and I am not ashamed to admit it's entirely my fault.

Inquisition

Trey

"**S**HE DOESN'T LOOK too happy." Becca gestures towards Victoria.

Glancing to see what she's referring to, I say, "She isn't here for happiness."

Seemingly addled by my statement, Becca asks, "Why is she here, then?"

Regardless of the countless times I've tried to avoid the question, I know my entire family will keep asking until they learn the truth. Best to start with Becca, who will understand. "She's in a bit of trouble," I admit.

Looking worried, she asks, "Are you in the same trouble?"

"It's not as bad as you think." Knowing it's best not to stress her with details because of her condition.

Still pushing, she says, "Is she one of your clients?"

"No. She's *actually* Abigail's lawyer."

"How is it a lawyer gets herself in trouble? Aren't they usually the ones pulling people out of it?"

Staring at Victoria, I feel lost as to how to answer. "It's complicated," I respond, remembering specifically what got us into this situation. Maybe I *am* in trouble as well.

"Complicated or not, the poor girl is miserable and from the way you're looking at her it doesn't take a fool to see you're taking it out on her." Leave it to my sister-in-law to get snappy with me on the first day of my arrival. The moment I'm about to defend myself, she's lifting her hand to silence me. "You may have forgotten where I came from, Trey. I wasn't always the country girl I am now. I keep up with tabloids and gossip, so your *"just friends"* excuse isn't going to work on me," she announces with a wicked smile.

She turns to leave me gaping at her, unable to deny her allegation. Comprehension hits me that she may just announce it to the whole family. "Becca," I half shout to her back before she can enter the kitchen.

She stops, spinning to face me with a teasing smile. Lowering my head so only she can hear, I ask, "You're not going to go blabbing to everyone are you?"

Tilting her head to the side to consider my request, I realize she's baiting me. "I should, but this isn't my tale to tell," she proclaims, allowing me to breathe. "But you better tell them the truth soon before they find out for themselves, or you'll be finding yourself in a heap of trouble for keeping it from them."

I silently groan inside. She's right. There is no denying the truth in her words. My family would have a field day with their tongue-lashings if they were to read the tabloids instead of me telling them the truth. Becca resumes her steps, entering the kitchen area and walks straight to my mother. Considering Victoria, she's as my sister-in-law indicated, appearing miserable at the kitchen table, staring down into her cup of coffee.

The thought that I may have made a mistake passes through my mind.

"You hungry, Junior?" Hearing my mother ask me automatically pushes the thought aside. The scent of my mother's homemade biscuits and fried eggs has my stomach grumbling in answer.

Rubbing at my stomach, I say, "I'm so hungry I could eat a whole cow," making her chuckle.

Taking the seat across from Victoria, I wait for her to lift her head. When she does, she has the hint of unshed tears in her eyes. Rapidly blinking them away, she instantly produces a forced smile.

"Are you really that miserable here?" I'm unable to keep myself from asking.

Shaking her head, she wipes her nose with the back of her hand, stifling a sniffle. Shit.

"I'm fine."

I know she's lying. Before I get the chance to call her out on it, the smell of bacon burning and the smoke alarm going off draws my attention over to the stove. I find Becca swatting away a ton of smoke while my mother opens the back door to air out the smoke.

"You trying to burn the house down?" I tease, getting up from my chair to head over to the stove where Becca is pulling burnt strips of bacon from a cast iron pan.

"Shit!" she complains, disappointed with the outcome of her cooking. "Your momma needed help, but you know I can't cook to save my life." Obviously.

My mother frowns at the result of Becca's cooking.

"Damn, girl. We want cooked bacon not charbroiled to death. The pig's already dead."

Becca scowls at me. "Do you think you can do any better?"

I snort. "Probably."

Shoving the fork at my chest with a huff, she says, "Then you do it," before stomping off to take a seat next to Victoria, leaving me with the burden of cooking.

"Leave it be, Junior. I'll cook it after I'm done with the gravy."

Seeing my mother overwhelmed with all of her tasks has me feeling uneasy. "I've got it, Momma," I tell her, wondering if I remember how to do this. She hesitantly eyes me for a moment, but I ignore her. "Matt may know how to cook pancakes, but he's got nothing on my bacon," I mention over my shoulder.

Both girls queerly look at me, as if I've lost my mind. It's the challenge of the task at hand I'm focused on. Twenty minutes later, I'm pulling the last bacon strip out of the pan and placing it on a paper towel to dry with a sense of satisfaction. My mother places the last of the biscuits on the table when I take my own offering towards this morning's breakfast. Placing the plate on the table, I'm about to take my seat when the back door opens and in walks my dad with Jimmy, who was sent to retrieve him. He eyes me with a delighted smile on his face.

"I thought your momma was pulling my leg when she called me," he says, right before holding out his arms for a hug. Embracing him, I take in the smell of cow manure, most likely from being out and doing his morning duties. Sweat and animal is a scent I will always associate with my father. He would tell me it was the smell of a hard-working man. I never doubted him.

"Dear Lord, Everett, did you bring the entire farm back with you?" My dad and I both laugh at my mother's question.

Shooing him away, she orders, "Go wash up. We've got a guest and I don't want her thinking you lot are a bunch of savages who stink." My father looks confused until he takes in Victoria sitting at the table curiously looking up to him. A smile spreads across his face, just like my mother's when she spotted her earlier.

"Who do we have here?" he asks in his polite manner.

"According to Junior," Jimmy draws out, but before he can say anymore, I finish up for him, "Her name is Victoria and she's a really good friend of mine, Dad."

Jimmy's mouth is still opened, as if he's about to continue. "She's just my friend," I add, as usual.

Frowning in disappoint, Jimmy says, "I was about to tell him that, you fool, but you beat me to it," then pouts, as if disappointed he didn't deliver the news.

My dad looks to me for any doubt and I give him a quick shake of my head. "I'll explain later," I inform him.

With a curt nod of understanding, he casts his eyes back to Victoria with a smile. "Nice to meet you, young lady."

She stands from her seat to properly greet him, but he stops her with a command of his hand to stay as she is. "It's a pleasure to meet you as well, Mr. Johnson," she says before taking her seat once more.

With the same smile still on his lips, he slaps me on the shoulder. "In that case, I'd best be doing as your momma ordered and go wash up." He steps around me and heads in the direction of my parents' bedroom.

I stay focused on the hallway he's disappeared down, wondering how it is I'm going to explain this entire situation. I could never lie to my parents; however, they won't be too happy with how it all began. Adultery is frowned upon in this family. If they were to get wind of the story the tabloids are portraying, they may no longer treat Victoria so kindly. My reaction will be minor compared to theirs, which is the warning Becca was trying to mention. One thing is for sure, I'm going to have to make sure my father is the first person I speak to. I've always been able to converse with him knowing he would understand, which is why I know he'll help me figure this whole mess out before it can get any worse.

Victoria

The sight of a man standing behind a stove in hip hugging jeans cooking bacon is mouthwatering. Every cord of muscle is emphasized with the tight fitting shirt he has on. Never would I have thought the sight of a man cooking would drive me insane . . . in a good way. I've sparsely listened to Trey's sister-in-law speaking at my side. My entire focus has been on stealing glances of Trey in the kitchen at the stove. It isn't just the aromas wafting through the air giving me an appetite. I hadn't had an appetite this morning due to my nerves, but now I do. Only, it isn't for food.

"So how long do you both plan on staying?"

The question catches my attention, as I am curious to know as well. "To be honest with you, I don't know," I convey.

Waving her fingers in the air, Becca says, "I take it this wasn't entirely planned, then?"

Somberly looking down into the empty cup in my hands, I try to figure out the best way to reply. I wasn't prepared last night to be whisked away to the country, yet there is no logical way of explaining it, either. I'm not prepared to explain why we are here, and I also don't know what Trey plans on telling his family. I would hate to go against what he has planned.

I'm completely lost in my thoughts when Becca speaks. "I know who you are, Victoria," she declares in a whisper for only me to hear. My head snaps up to face her.

"How?"

I'm expecting to find distaste staring back at me, instead I see sincerity in her eyes. "I'm from Philadelphia. We know all about the famous Montgomerys." It truly is sympathy staring back at me.

Dread fills my stomach. "What exactly do you know

about me?" I apprehensively ask.

"Enough to know why you're here. I keep up with the gossip," she relays, taking a sip of her orange juice. My heart is erratically starting to speed up, while my chest feels as if it's tightening.

I bravely ask, "You're not going to talk to the tabloids, are you?"

"Don't worry. I already promised Trey I wouldn't say anything."

She may have given *him* her word, however it doesn't mean she will keep it. Panic must still be evident as she places her hand on top of mine, giving it a gentle clutch. Slowly my heart begins to calm. Taking my first breath to fill my empty lungs, I swallow around the lump sitting in my throat.

"Thank you."

Peering over to Trey, Becca asks, "Just how serious are things between you and Trey?"

I don't know whether she's asking out of curiosity or to gain more information. "We're just friends," I tell her, using the same justification Trey has been using.

Arching her brow, she states, "That's not what it looks like."

"Those articles were taken out of context. You know how the media will use any lie they can to earn money," I defend.

She grins. "It's not the tabloids I'm referring to." I'm trying to decipher what it is she's trying to say. "He's protecting you." Her suggestion has me lighting up inside. I knew he was, but to have someone else point it out eliminates the small doubt that I could have been wrong. "Why would he bring you home of all places? To his family?" she inquires.

The tone used indicates growing protectiveness herself. "I didn't know, I swear. Had I known, I never would have allowed him to. The last thing I want is to put your family in jeopardy."

She waves off my concern. "Trust me, honey. We have enough guns to protect ourselves," she jokes. "The fact is he brought you *home*."

"I don't understand. I'm sure I'm not the first girl Trey has brought to meet his family."

She looks at me as she considers my comment. "Actually, you are," she reports with a mischievous smile spread across her face. "Which is why you're going to need to protect *yourself*," she smugly replies.

"Why?" What the hell does she mean?

My expression must be conveying my thoughts, as she's now laughing. "Johnson men don't just bring any girl home. They bring *the one* home," she explains.

Now I comprehend all the looks I've been receiving. "You mean to tell me they think there's something serious between Trey and me?" I choke out. "Trey already told them we're just friends."

She chuckles, then crosses her arms over her chest. "That excuse of *'just friends'* isn't going to fly with this family." A wide grin is now plastered on her face. "Luke brought me to visit and I never left," she adds with a wink, making my mouth slightly gape open.

Frantically, I look over to Trey who is sauntering his

way over to the table with a plate stacked high full of bacon. He's curiously eyeing both Becca and me until he's distracted by the back door opening.

The man walking through the door is without a doubt Trey's father. He's an exact replica of Trey with years of hard work and wisdom carved into his features. The heartfelt embrace shared between the two men have me once more full of envy. In spite of how I feel, I'm still delighted to be a part of this, regardless of the circumstances that sent us here. It leaves me to wonder how much longer would Trey have gone without coming home had it not been for me.

Mr. Johnson eyes me with the same gleeful smile I've been greeted with from everyone who has welcomed me.

Minutes later, after a very brief conversation, he excuses himself then disappears into another part of the house. Jimmy is already making himself comfortable in the seat next to me at the table, his usual flirtatious grin greeting me. It makes me seek out Trey to see where exactly he'll be seating himself, since Becca is sitting on my other side. It's the same seat he'd taken earlier, directly across from me, only there is no hint of a smile looking back at me this time. Instead, he's completely lost in filling his plate full of food to distract himself, from me I presume. My eyes roam the entire table, overwhelmed by the sight in front of me. The table can easily seat twelve, and food is covering most of the table in an abundance of different varieties of breakfast dishes. It looks like enough to feed an army when there are only five of us—six when Trey's father returns. Who in the world will be eating all this food? Before

I can finish the thought, the back door opens and in walks three more visitors.

All cheerfully greet Trey with their usual hugs and round of teasing. Becca stands, making her way around the table to greet one of the visitors with a kiss on the lips. This, I'm assuming, must be her husband. The other two consist of another older gentleman and older lady. When everyone is done greeting Trey, they all look to me with curious faces.

Holding out her hand, Becca introduces me. "This is Victoria," she informs them. "She came along to visit with him."

The older lady is quick to smile. "Is that so?" she asks, giving Trey a playful smile. I'm beginning to understand Becca's earlier warning.

Holding my hand out to shake theirs, I explain, "We're simply friends." I seem to find myself telling them this time, saving Trey from the ordeal of having to repeat himself. She seems to grow a little disappointed when she shakes my hand. "I'm Trey's aunt, Mary Anne. This is my husband, Trey's uncle, Finn," she says, gesturing to specify the man to her left. He, too, gently takes my hand to shake it. "You're a pretty one, aren't you?" he comments. Both his casual southern accent and comment have me blushing.

"Yes, she is," Becca's husband jokes. "What penance are you paying to get stuck with my brother?"

Becca swats him on the chest. "Stop, now," she teases, but just as quickly quirks her head. "Well, depends on how you see it. Trey isn't that bad of a punishment," she says, making us all chuckle. "This is my husband, Trey's brother, Luke," Becca introduces.

"How do y'all not know I didn't get stuck with her instead?" Trey counters, a hint of a southern accent rolling off his tongue.

I know he truthfully relayed the remark to defend himself, but in reality, he *is* stuck with me at the moment. But everyone else sees it as a joke.

Jimmy's arm loops around my waist, tugging me to his side. Our bodies slam together and I flinch from the contact. "Just let me know what it is I have to do to get stuck with her," he teases, squeezing my waist with his hand.

Everyone in the room laughs, while I, on the other hand, am staring into Trey's narrowed eyes aimed straight at my waist. His jaw is tight and the fury is evident in his eyes—a side of Trey I'm becoming accustomed to experiencing.

"Now, leave the poor girl alone. She just got here and y'all are going to scare her off," Mr. Johnson scolds with a wink of his eye directed at me when he returns to the room.

Dislodging myself as politely as I can from Jimmy's embrace, I can faintly see Trey's scornful gaze watching me as I seat myself. It has me squirming in my seat and the feeling doesn't dissipate until he returns to his earlier task of filling his plate. Minutes pass before everyone is seated and casually conversing.

"You aren't going to eat, dear?" Mrs. Johnson aims the question at me. Giving her a polite smile, I say, "I'm fine, thank you. I don't normally eat breakfast."

Everyone pauses, a complete silence overtaking the

room.

"You're not one of those girls who starves themselves, are you?" Mary Anne asks with an appalled tone.

"No, Ma'am. I'm usually in a rush in the morning. A cup of coffee is enough." The explanation is still not sufficient. "No wonder you don't have any meat on your bones," Trey's Uncle Finn criticizes. "Don't you feed this poor girl?" He directs the question towards Trey.

Trey stops his chewing and swallows what's in his mouth before replying, "It's not my job to feed her."

His reply is the truth, yet the manner in which he answered leaves me feeling dejected. A bowl is shoved in front of me, the contents a white looking substance. "Here, have some grits," Mary Anne instructs.

I'm staring down at the bowl in front of me wondering what in the world it consists of. I've heard of them, but never once would have imagined eating them.

"How is it you both know each other, again?" Luke asks, distracting me as I lift my head to look at him.

"She's Abigail's lawyer. Y'all remember Abigail, right?" Becca relays, as if trying to defuse the subject. Smiles spread across everyone's faces. "Such a sweet girl." Mrs. Johnson sighs.

Waving his fork between the two of us, Luke says, "So you met through Abigail?"

"Yes, the law firm I currently work for represents her," I proudly express.

"So how is it you ended up here with Trey?" Luke questions, still pressing for answers.

Dread courses through me, unknowing of how to respond. Admitting we met at a charity event because he had to escort my drunken body away before I embarrassed myself is not a logical answer. Let alone the fact that we ended up sleeping together isn't smart, either.

The loud clank of Trey dropping his fork draws everyone's attention over to him. "I'm only going to say this once, so y'all better listen," he declares. A lump forms in my throat. I was already full of dread, however with Trey's declaration, I'm burning with fear as to how everyone will handle the truth. "I didn't bring Victoria here for y'all to be grilling her with a thousand questions, nor did I bring her here as my girl. So get that idea out of your heads." He points to everyone when he declares this. His aunt makes a sound as if she is about to say something, but Trey silences her by lifting his hand in the air. "I'm not going to go into full details over why we're here, but you do have *her* to thank. Otherwise, I wouldn't be here visiting with y'all at all." A heavy silence overtakes the room from his speech, but no one argues or continues to question him.

Grabbing for his fork, he scoops up a large amount of food and stuffs it into his mouth to resume eating. A couple of seconds later, everyone else proceeds to do the same.

My eyes cast down to the bowl in front of me, using the excuse of trying to decipher exactly what to do with the contents as a distraction. The bowl suddenly disappears from my view. When I snap my head up, I find Trey replacing it with a plate full of bacon taking up more than half of the plate, a scarce amount of scrambled eggs, and potatoes on the side.

"I won't be able to eat all this," I say with astonished

eyes. Lightly shrugging his shoulder, he says, "Eat what you can, but I know you won't like the grits."

"How would you know?"

"Because I've seen you eat. You prefer meat," he states. His statement sends me back to the night we had dinner.

"Thank you," I shyly reply, grabbing for a strip of bacon and taking a bite.

The crunch of my first bite of bacon echoes in my ears. Mouth-watering flavors burst throughout my mouth, and a small whimper escapes as I chew.

"Good?" Trey questions with a hint of a smile.

With butterflies floating in my stomach, I reply, "Perfect," unable to contain the smile I give with it.

Satisfied, he returns to eating while everyone is already lost in their own conversations. I tune everyone out except for Trey as I return to stealing glances at him while I eat. As predicted, I don't eat all the contents on my plate. Actually, the bacon was what I mostly ate. With each bite I took, I had to keep myself from blushing while I remembered exactly who cooked it, and the sight of him while doing so. Bacon will never be the same again in my mind, nor will it ever be forgotten.

Enticement

Trey

VICTORIA TAKES THE last plate from my mom, insisting she take a seat and finish conversing with my family at the table. It gives me the chance to follow. She's placing the dish in the sink when I come up behind her to place my own. She stiffens at the feel of my chest up against her back. Slowly she turns, my arms reaching down to each side of her, locking her into place when she faces me. We're standing so closely together I can feel her breath sliding across my chin. She swallows, as her brown eyes stay locked directly with mine. It's a sure sign of her nervousness of our close proximity. It's oddly gratifying to know I have this effect on her. The feeling is quite mutual when she's near.

Taking in how I have her trapped, her eyes wander

over to the table and mine do the same, finding my family lost in conversation. My eyes find hers again and narrow down into slits.

"What are you doing?" she chokes out.

I'm asking myself the same question. The answer could be I'm still stirring with animosity over the events of breakfast. Or it could be from seeing Jimmy's hands on her earlier. Could it be how tempting she seems while she trembles right in front of me? Despite the many reasons, having her so close at the moment has my blood turning to fire, my fingers begging to touch her.

"I don't know," I shamefully admit, glancing again towards the table to ensure no one is paying attention.

"Breakfast was delicious," she says, drawing my attention back to her. "Thank you."

I'm fighting the smile wanting to match hers. "I only cooked the bacon."

"It was the best I've had," she stammers out.

My restraint to hold in my smirk is slowly dissipating while I find myself still leaning onto the counter. I can't find the strength to move. More like I'm unwilling to move. The scent of her floral shampoo is still fresh in her hair from this morning's shower. I'd come to associate that particular smell with her as we lay next to each other and I inhaled the scent while sleeping. The exact memory has me recalling what it was that led us to sleep.

"Really? Would you say the same about my sausage?"

Her brows draw down in confusion. "You didn't cook sausage," she says, completely overlooking the innuendo.

"I wasn't referring to the kind you eat," I state, watching her slowly comprehend my meaning. She sucks in a breath, her eyes turning wide. Her cheeks flush pink as she blushes.

Knowing I'm the cause of her reaction has me beaming with satisfaction. It's selfish, but I haven't been blind to her heated glances all morning. It's been driving me completely insane. Against all will, she has opened emotions inside of me I had vowed to block away from her.

Lust.

Desire.

Yearning.

All without having to try.

She deeply swallows before asking, "What do we do now?"

I'm completely at a loss as to what she's referring to. "About what?"

"Do we just stay trapped inside all day, or are we allowed to leave to go do something?"

"Bored already, princess?"

Yanking her head back, she answers, "No, I just would love to explore a little. I've never been to a ranch before."

Considering all the things we can do, my eyes begin to rake over her body as I ask, "Do you know how to ride?" My thoughts are still lost to my earlier memory.

"A horse?"

Her two-word answer has me returning to my deepest of carnal thoughts. Lowering my mouth near her ear so only she can hear, I whisper, "I already know you can ride me, princess. Pretty well, in fact." A strangled sound resembling a mixture of a groan and whimper vibrates from her throat, causing me to grow hard.

The sound of a throat clearing to our sides has me retreating from her to cross my arms over my chest. Victoria has retained her crimson blush as both our eyes peer toward my brother curiously eyeing both of us. Becca steps up behind him.

"What do you want, Luke?" I ask, releasing my frustration in the inquiry for disrupting us.

From the curiously arched brows Becca gives us, she may know exactly why I'm irritated. "We were wondering what Victoria was planning on doing today. I have to run some errands, but I'm willing to take her along so she doesn't get bored," Becca offers.

Victoria's eyes light up at the suggestion, but I already have other plans for us.

"I was actually going to show Victoria the lands," I inform them, remembering she still hasn't answered my earlier question, a fault of my own since I intentionally distracted her.

"Do you know how to ride a horse?" I ask her, making sure to clarify this time what I meant by my question.

"Oh, a horse. Yes," she answers far too quickly, making me chuckle from knowing why. My brother, on the other hand, looks confused by her reaction.

"Well then, I guess we'll see you both later tonight," Luke informs us both.

"Tonight?" I find myself asking, wondering what they're up to.

"Yeah, momma is planning to cook dinner for all of us, so you better bring an appetite to that meal, Victoria,"

Luke indicates with a wink.

"She's not planning on inviting the entire family, is she?" I have to ask. Because if she is, I better have that conversation with my parents soon.

"No. The big one is tomorrow night," Becca laughs out.

Her answer still isn't reassuring and has me inwardly groaning.

"I guess I'll see you tonight. Have fun today," Becca expresses, reaching out to give Victoria a hug. It catches her by surprise as she awkwardly pats her back. I've come to discover Victoria isn't used to being friendly with people. She's in for a surprise with my family and their gestures.

"You better treat her nice or I'll be castrating you instead," Becca firmly states, directing the threat at me with a pointed finger.

"I'll make sure you don't find out," I tease as I hug her, receiving a roll of her eyes when I let go. She steals one more glance towards Victoria then walks away.

"I'm going to go put on some better shoes," Victoria conveys, excusing herself from me and my brother, who is still lingering.

"Friends, huh?" he smugly asks when she's no longer in hearing distance. "Because from what Becca has told me, she seems to be in a heap of trouble. I can't see you bringing *a friend* just to keep her out of trouble."

"It's complicated," I tell him with a defeated sigh.

"It always is in the beginning," he laughs out.

"Glad I can be of some amusement."

"You're the one who started it when I brought Becca home," he reminds me, taking me back to the day he showed up with her. Only he never denied how he felt about Becca then. It was her that was in denial.

"I don't know what the hell is going on," I admit. "But this girl always finds a way to get herself in trouble and I find myself stuck saving her," I say with a grimace.

"She must mean enough for you to keep saving her, then."

I can't help but snort at how foolish it sounds.

"They always start out as friends, though," Luke comments, referring to Becca.

"That's the problem. This one was never supposed to be a *friend*. I wanted nothing to do with her." He looks confused by my comment. "It's a long story," I relay, feeling defeated.

"Friend or not, she's growing on everyone. So you may be the one in trouble now."

He could not throw any truer words at me. I've seen the way everyone has responded to Victoria. Our families may be complete opposites, but she treats everyone with politeness. It's a value my family respects.

"I've never seen you react this way with a girl before. It's sort of . . ." he pauses, tilting his head to look me over. " . . . fascinating. You're growing up, little bro," he finishes, patting me on the shoulder and following his wife out the back door.

Confused and wondering what the fuck just happened, I find myself at a total loss for words. I went from fawning all over Victoria like a teenage schoolboy, to my brother complimenting me over it. Not what I was expecting, but it shouldn't surprise me. My brother always did taunt me that my day would come, only I had denied it would ever happen. I kept telling myself I wouldn't be as foolish as them to bring a girl home.

Victoria appears at my side again, pulling me from my thoughts. "Ready?" she asks, curiously peering at me. Before I am able to answer, my mom shows up at our side with eager eyes when she hears Victoria's question.

"Where y'all going?"

"I plan on taking Victoria out riding," I explain.

My mother's eyes light up. "Oh, let me pack you some lunch to take."

"That's not necessary, Mrs. Johnson. We had a really big breakfast," Victoria tries telling my mother.

Clucking her tongue, she says, "Nonsense. You need to eat," she protest. Exactly what I knew she would do.

Victoria looks to me for help as my mother walks over to the pantry. I shake my head to advise her not to argue, already knowing the outcome of this little discussion. We're not walking out of here without the food.

"Just take the food or else you're going to piss my momma off," I inform her. She opens her mouth to argue, but I'm quickly cutting her off with a whisper. "If you think I get mad, it's nothing compared to her." I glance over my shoulder as I point my thumb in my mother's direction.

Victoria's mouth snaps shut for a moment before it opens again with a smile. "Thank you, Mrs. Johnson," she says to my mother, making me laugh. Victoria pinches her lips at my reaction, upset she can't argue.

We both watch as my mother happily continues her task, and minutes later hands me a shoulder bag full of food. Giving her a kiss on the cheek, I promise to be home to help her with dinner, although I already know it isn't me who will be helping.

"Let's go." I gesture toward the door, leading the way for Victoria to follow.

"Where exactly is it we're going?"

"Somewhere," I say, the only response I'm going to give her for now.

"Is this somewhere the start of our tour?" Her curiosity makes me chuckle.

"Have you always been this way?"

"How?"

"Always wanting to know every detail," I say, making sure I watch for her reaction. As expected, she isn't too happy with my comment as her lips go flat. "It's almost like you *have* to know," I tell her. "I take it you're not like typical girls who like to be surprised?"

"I'm rarely surprised. This trip is the biggest surprise I've ever had."

My steps falter from her response. "That's impossible. You're rich, so didn't you always get spoiled with surprises?"

"Money has nothing to do with surprises," she states. "Yes, I was spoiled, but it was usually something I *asked* for, never anything out of the blue."

This has me stopping in my tracks to take in her words. She stops with me as I say, "I don't believe you."

She sighs. "This isn't something I would lie about."

"That sucks." It's all I can say.

Locking her arms behind her back, she steps closer so she's only inches from me. Standing up on her tippy toes, the warmth of her breath whispers into my ear. "Not as good as you." Spinning on her heel, she resumes walking. "Is that a stable?" she asks, full of curiosity.

I can't answer as my breath is caught in my throat from reluctantly forcing the images her statement conjured from my mind. Quickening my steps to catch up to her, I'm at her side when I say, "I can't wait for the day when you show me how well you can suck."

This has her stopping again. Her arms are still locked behind her back as her brow arches in curiosity. "What makes you think there will be a chance?" she coyly asks. "According to you, there isn't anything going on between us. I sort of like the terms you've laid out for the both of us. *Just friends,*" she points out.

"Friends have sex all the time."

"Do they?" she asks, sounding disappointed. Her eyes narrow into slits while she remains silent for a moment. I can practically see the wheels turning in her mind. "Because I was beginning to wonder what I was to you," she expresses with saddened eyes.

"I'd like to consider you my friend," I admit, watching her eyes light up at my admission.

Her eyes cast downward before coming back up to meet mine. "I'd like that, too," she replies with a bashful smile.

The sound of a horse whinnying breaks our gazes. Victoria peers behind her shoulder. "You actually have horses on the property?" she excitedly asks, practically skipping when she resumes walking.

"What the hell do you think I meant when I asked if you knew how to ride?"

She shrugs her shoulders. "I don't know. I thought you were just asking." Her eyes light up. "I can't believe we're actually going to ride a horse today," she practically exclaims with excitement as we make our way towards the stables.

"You seem a little too eager."

"It feels like forever since I've ridden a horse. I miss it."

This has me puzzled. "Don't you have stables on your ritzy properties?" It's what I envisioned when she explained her residences growing up.

"No. I would have to go to an equine club for my lessons, and those were only when I was a child," she replies, not hiding the disappointment in her reply. Normally, I would push for more information, but I refrain this time. From the expression in her eyes, I know I was hitting a sore spot.

Walking into the stables minutes later, Victoria's eyes grow wide with amazement. From the outside it may look modern sized, however it isn't until you walk in that you're able to take in its size. The stomping of the many horses still in their stalls and the constant snorts and whinnies they make fill the air.

"How many horses does your family have?" she asks in amazement, still trying to fully take it all in.

"Over a dozen last time I was here."

Victoria is wide-eyed when she turns to me. "Really?" she asks, full of exhilaration. "What is it your family does?" she suspiciously asks. I remain silent, contemplating how to respond.

"Are you going to start with your, *'No, I'm not going to tell you'* crap?" she asks, using her fingers to quote the line. "You probably wouldn't have ever told me had I not asked, would you?" she bites out.

Halting directly in front of her, she's forced to a stop. "I never told you what they did because I didn't think I would ever have to," I reply.

"Why not?"

I can't seem to answer.

Placing her hands sternly on her hips, she says, "You let me spill my entire family history to you, yet you still keep yourself locked up."

She's right. I purposely do it with everyone.

"Never mind. It's probably safe I don't know," she angrily lets out.

Addled by her declaration, I ask, "Why not?"

"Yeah, why not?" A voice from my past asks from behind me.

Victoria glances past me, seeming to be taken aback, before her perfectly shaped brow arches high. "Another family member?" she asks.

Crap, I would have preferred to never have to be in this situation. "No, this is Callie," I tell Victoria, turning to face the other female in the room. "Callie, this is Victoria. A friend."

It's Callie who is curiously looking at Victoria now.

"A city girl, I take it?" Callie inquires, still eyeing Victoria from head to toe.

"Don't worry about it," I reply.

Callie snickers, and from the irritable grimace Victoria delivers in return, she isn't happy with the response.

Knowing I need to diffuse the situation before they have time to speak to each other, I say, "I'm going to need two horses. Who needs their exercise today?" I direct the question to Callie.

"It's nice to see you again, too," she sarcastically replies. "How have you been? Me, I don't know, still here where you left me," she adds through clenched teeth.

Grabbing the bridge of my nose, I know I'm playing with fire. "Now's not the time, Callie."

"When is the time?" she throws back at me.

"Not now," I growl.

Her pinched lips tell me she's received the message. Glancing at Victoria, she asks, "Does she even know how to ride a horse?"

"Yes," Victoria and I answer at the same time.

She doesn't seem all too convinced, but she finally answers, "Thunder and Betsy haven't been run in a couple of days, but I have a feeling it'd be safer to put her on Jasper. He's still worn down from yesterday, so he'll be easy on her."

"Saddle up the first two. She can handle Betsy." Callie looks doubtfully at Victoria, who still is not moving. "Just do it, Callie," I order this time.

Glaring straight at me, she steps toward me, inches from my face. "Your days of giving me orders are over,

Trey Johnson. You had your chance to keep doing that and gave it up," she delivers before stepping back. Letting out a frustrated breath, I catch Victoria with her arms crossed over the chest.

She's the one skeptically looking at Callie, who still hasn't moved. "Callie's an old friend," I explain, watching her eyes narrow.

"Just like the kind of friend I am?" she asks.

Shit, I know this is a trap. Taking in the two women standing side by side, there is no easy way to answer, and the lapse of silence while considering how to reply to Victoria has allowed her time to come to a conclusion of her own.

Rolling her eyes, she says, "Just what I thought," as she marches towards the exit.

Catching up to her, I bring her to a stop. "What's wrong?"

"Nothing," she hisses, trying to dislodge herself from my hold.

Wrapping my arm completely around her waist, I make sure this time to keep her from escaping. "No. I want to know."

She is still trying to get away, but I hold on tight. "Go catch up with your *friend*. Maybe she holds the secret to becoming more," she spits out.

What fire got up her ass, and what the fuck did she mean by her comment?

"I don't understand why you're pissed."

"Then you're an idiot."

Before I can continue pushing the subject, Callie is

butting her nose back in.

"He was always an idiot," she snickers behind us.

"Since when is she allowed an opinion?" Victoria throws at me while I exclaim, "Butt out Callie!"

"Are you really going to ride? Because I've got better things to do than stand around and wait for your lovers' spat to end."

"We're not lovers!" I yell, but Victoria looks heart-stricken from the declaration before her eyes fill with anger.

"Why do you have to always be an asshole?" she snarls, while Callie answers, "He's always been an asshole."

Victoria looks ready to tear Callie's eyes out, and strangely it's turning me on.

Pointing at Callie, I say, "You go do your damn job before I fire you!" I don't bother waiting to see if she heeds my command as I'm already tugging Victoria into an empty stall, kicking and screaming with every step.

"Let me go, Trey!"

"No," I say, locking her up against the closed door I've just shut. "I wouldn't be an asshole if you wouldn't make me one."

"I changed my mind. I don't want to go anywhere with you."

Keeping her from escaping, I lock my arms on each side of her head. "Too bad. You're stuck with me now, just like I'm stuck with you." The sound of the horses stomping with their whinnying adds to our high-pitched replies.

"This wasn't my choice!"

"It wasn't mine either, princess, but it's because of you we're here!" I yell, earning us another loud whinny from the stall next to us.

Edging her face forward so it's a mere inch from mine, she says, "Is that going to be your only excuse? Because of me? No one made you choose to come home, that was all you, buddy." Shoving her finger into my chest, I feel her breath glide against my chin. "The way I see it, you should be thankful we're here. At least your family is. So stop trying to make it seem like this is all my fault."

Yanking my head back, I ask, "How the hell did this end up about me?"

Victoria throws her hands up in exasperation. "I don't know!" she frustratingly yells. "This is all your fault!"

"How the hell is it my fault?"

"Y'all need to quiet down. You're pissing the horses off!" Callie shouts at us both.

Victoria couldn't care less. "Because . . . Because . . ." Her eyes take in our surroundings. "You brought me here," she says, waving her hands around the stable. The stomping gets louder. Raking my hand through my hair, I realize I'm so fucking confused. From the corner of my eye, I see Callie trying to soothe Jasper, trying to calm him down.

It suddenly hits me why she's pissed and I can't help but grin. "You're jealous?"

"You wish," she snorts.

"You are. Or else you wouldn't have cared who she is," I say, referring to Callie.

Victoria's mouth opens and closes, as if speechless. Holy fuck. I never thought I'd be so ecstatic in my life knowing I've done this to her.

"Stop gloating!" she snaps over the whinnies of the horses.

"Stop yelling!" Callie exclaims right after Victoria.

Her eyes come to an angered slit. "I don't want to be here." I can feel the hostility seething from her pores. It's why the horses are agitated.

Inching my face forward, I say, "What if I want you here?"

She goes rigid, her breathing quickening. "Don't lie to me. I know you don't," she chokes out. The tip of her tongue comes out to lick her top lip and I lose all self-control and kiss her.

I hadn't meant to do it, but remembering how sweet her mouth tastes and feels makes me lose all self-control. Being distracted by her sweet taste causes me to lose my balance when her hands grip the center of my shirt and she tugs me forward to close the gap between us. My hands find her waist, pulling her hard against my hips, allowing her to feel the proof of just how much I want her. A soft whimper vibrates in my mouth, sending a jolt straight down to my dick, hardening it completely.

"I see you found a way to shut her up." Callie startles us both from outside our stall, causing us to jump apart.

"Shut up, Callie!" Victoria shouts to her, making me laugh.

If I weren't already hard, seeing her furiously ready to tear Callie's eyes out would have done it. She's pretty damn hot when she's pissed, and I know exactly how pleasurable her fire can be.

Victoria

"I don't know why I couldn't ride the pretty white horse," I whine once more, as I've done from the moment Trey told me he was riding the white stallion and I was to take old Betsy.

"First off, Thunder is taking offense to you calling him a pretty boy," Trey jokes, patting the side of his horse. "Second, Betsy is going to buck you off for rejecting her. So I'd be nice if I were you," he says, gesturing toward the dark brown mare I'm riding as the giant beast between my thighs sways me back and forth.

My eyes cast downwards while I tighten my knees, just in case she does attempt to throw me hearing his suggestion. "She'd really buck me off?" I frightfully ask, trying to calm my worried mind so the horse doesn't react to my emotions.

Trey's booming laughter isn't too convincing. With his humor, there is no telling if he's serious or not. Taking in the animal between my thighs, I can't complain. Betsy is just as beautiful in her own ways as Thunder. I just hadn't expected Thunder to be so enticing.

Referring back to his comment, I mumble, "You're cruel, *Trey Johnson,*" as I adjust my position on Betsy. "Then again, you already knew that," I add.

"Are we back to this again?" he comments from my side. "Do I need to remind you why it is we're both in country town, *Victoria Montgomery?*"

"No," I clip out, choosing to drop the subject while taking in more of our surroundings. I can't help but sigh happily.

For miles around us, there is nothing but magnificent land to look out onto. We've been riding for close to an hour and it feels as if it will never end. Trey hasn't yet mentioned we are coming upon the borderlines where we need to turn back, which leaves me to wonder how much land we plan to ride through.

"How much of this land belongs to your family?" I bravely ask, risking the chance he'll refuse to answer as he's so commonly done in the past.

"Roughly over a hundred and twenty thousand acres."

I practically choke on my breath when I realize what he's said. "A hundred and twenty thousand?" I exclaim back to him for clarification.

He nonchalantly shrugs his shoulder, as if the amount is no big deal.

"How in the world can your family own that much land when you've more than once pointed out our differences in lifestyles?" Trey remains silent, allowing me to continue berating him. "I'm beginning to believe all the guilt you made me feel about my family money was for nothing."

The wolfish grin confirms my prediction.

"My family primarily raises beef cattle." I'm dumbfounded as he continues. "But we do more than just raise and sell cattle. My Uncle Finn also grows and sells alfalfa. The fields are spread out throughout the land and are the primary source for over a hundred miles. He's the reason why there's an airport for the crop dusters," he explains. "The cattle business goes back as far as my great-grandfather, who started it. But it was my grandfather who found ways to expand the business so we wouldn't have to out-source anything."

"When you say outsource, you mean you don't have to buy from anyone else, therefore profiting more?" I ask, risking pushing too much.

Giving me a nod to imply I'm correct. "Besides alfalfa we grow our own vegetables and other produce. Whatever is needed to keep our animals and family fed. What we don't utilize we sell."

"Your family is just as rich as mine, aren't they?"

It takes him a moment to answer. "Probably, if not more," he says, leaving me speechless.

"You hypocrite!" I throw at him. "You kept using my family's wealth against me when you're just as rich."

"The money isn't all mine, Victoria. It never will be. You have to earn your wages here. Money isn't easily giv-en to me like it is with you. The difference between you and me is every day I was on this land was spent working my ass off for my family. Can you say the same for your-self?"

Now he's just being bitter and attacking me. I know I *don't* do anything to contribute to my family's wealth; I've never had to.

"Exactly," he bickers, using my silence to drive the nail further into my wounds. There is no denying he's cor-rect.

"Whatever," I comment. "But the next time you call me royalty, I'm going to call you a prince," I ridicule. His snort suggests I've won this part of the argument.

"What exactly is it you had to do growing up?" I'm curious to know. His only response is a raised brow, which elicits an eye roll from me.

"It's either that or I keep pushing for you to tell me exactly how much of a friend Callie was," I mock, hoping he won't really choose to discuss the latter.

I know I've won when he begins to enlighten me with his story. "I did a little of everything. Johnson men are trained from the moment they can walk to learn the ropes of the business."

"Is that what you meant by coming back home and continuing the family business?" I ask, remembering him mention it the other night.

He thinks hard for a moment. "Something like that," he voices. "I majored in business management in college, hoping to come back and do more than shovel manure or round up cattle. I wanted to run the financial part of the business."

It also reminds me of how it is he came to do what he does. "It's what you meant by becoming Abigail's manager? It kept you from returning?" The disappointed expression he holds suggests he isn't happy for not following through and returning as planned. "Do you regret it?" I have to ask.

"There are times I ask myself if I should have ignored what I *wanted* to do and returned, knowing my family would have benefited from my degree," he notes, instead of truly replying to what I've asked.

"Wasn't it you who told me your family is proud of what you do?" I say, reminding *him* of his own words. He delivers a curt nod. "Then stop blaming yourself for your decisions."

"Is that what you tell yourself every day, princess?"

"Yes," I declare without any further reasons, knowing I should change the subject before we begin arguing again. "A hundred thousand acres, huh? So does that mean I won't be trespassing into any forbidden land anytime soon?"

"No. Why?" Trey inquires, seemingly lost as to why I would ask.

"Because I'm about to show you exactly how well I can ride a horse and have you eating my dust," I tease, leaning forward and digging my heels into the sides of the mare to send her into a gallop.

The beast increases her speed and a sense of power travels through my veins. Every ounce of anguish from our discussion begins to evaporate as she takes me flying through the land. Peering over my shoulder, I see Trey closing the distance between us, making me dig my heels harder into the side of the horse. This may be the only time I have him chasing after me. Better make it worth remembering.

Juice leaks down the side of my mouth from the piece of fruit I just bit into. My hand is about to come up to catch it when Trey's thumb wipes it away. Retracting his thumb, his mouth closes over it, sucking the drop off it. "Hmm, sweet," he says around his thumb, sending a jolt to travel straight down between my thighs.

The sight of him lying propped up on one elbow as we both relax, along with pleasurable sound he makes has me clenching my sore thighs, making me wince.

"What's with the face?" he asks.

"I seem to be a bit sore," I confess, trying to adjust my sitting position to get more comfortable, which makes me wince once more. "It's been years since I've been riding," I remind him.

He finishes the bite of sandwich in his mouth, then says, "Didn't seem like it with the way you were pushing the poor girl."

Old or not, I recall how well of a pace she kept on her own. "She did a great job putting you and the unicorn to shame," I jest, using the nickname I began teasing his stallion with the moment we called a truce and brought them back down to a trot.

"You're really trying to piss my horse off, aren't you?" He frowns, glancing to where they're both tethered to a tree.

"I'm not the one who has to ride back in shame," I retort with a smirk before trying to eat the last piece of fruit. Trey yanks it from my grasp and pops it into his.

"Hey!" I scowl at him as he chews it.

"I got tired of you teasing me with it."

Glowering at him, I ask, "How was I teasing you?"

"You were making me want to kiss you with every bite you took." Whoa, not what I was expecting to hear. Blinking to bring myself back to reality, I find him coyly staring at me. "And you call me a tease," I defend, earning me a full grin to match my own.

Closing my eyes to absorb the sounds of my surroundings, I take a deep breath from the fullness of the meal. I hadn't thought I would be able to eat another bite after the large breakfast this morning, but the ride had given me a small appetite. It wasn't long after we brought our horses back to a trot that Trey declared we should give them a break.

He'd chosen a small patch of trees next to a lake with a house nearby. It wasn't until we began to eat that I started a small conversation and got up the courage to ask who the house belonged to. Apparently, this is where Luke and Becca reside.

Opening my eyes, I find Trey staring off into the distance, completely lost to his thoughts. I'm about to ask what it is he's so deeply thinking of when a ringing disrupts him. Reaching into his back pocket, he retrieves a phone and I'm quick to complain, "Hey, how come you got to keep yours?" I know I sound like a whining child, bitter over not being able to keep my own.

"This isn't mine. Julio gave me an extra we keep on hand for emergencies," he explains before answering the phone.

"Hello." Trey's eyes lock with mine when he comments a minute later. "Yeah, she's with me and still alive."

"Who is that?" I ask in a whisper. He silently mouths out, "Julio."

"How's everyone doing?" he asks, returning to his conversation with Julio. The next five minutes are spent with me listening to a one sided conversation before he eventually ends the call. His pained expression when he's done has me asking, "Everything okay?"

"Yeah, just fine," he curtly murmurs under his breath. His reaction and how he's chosen to stare off into the distance puts me on edge.

"We should head back," he comments and retrieves the bag we brought the food in. He begins packing the remains of our picnic we'd brought along in silence. During the small amount of time I've known Trey, I've come to discover how easily he can close up his emotions. It can be quite disturbing at times.

Without a word, he begins walking back to the horses, leaving me no choice but to follow. My inner-conscience is screaming to point out how rude he is acting, however I refuse to add to his fury by provoking him. I'm climbing back onto Betsy when I'm reminded of the ache I'd come to have.

"Are you going to be fine for the ride back?" Trey chuckles as if he noticed my discomfort climbing onto the mare.

"As long as you don't demand a rematch, I think I'll be fine."

The mischievous grin he grants me with has me thinking otherwise. "I think the horses can handle it," he indicates, proving me right. "Last one back has to help my momma cook dinner," he says before racing off.

Digging my heels into Betsy's side, I silently plead to the horse she doesn't disappoint me this time, because I don't want to embarrass myself when I'm burning the food. Becca isn't the only one who doesn't know how to cook, and I'd hate for Trey's family to want to disown me for burning down the house.

Empathy

Trey

MY MIND CAN'T help but wonder how Victoria is doing. I've been tempted to call the house to check up on her for the past hour to make sure she's doing fine, but the antagonizing glare she gave me when I left has kept me from doing so. I already know I'm going to receive her wrath the moment she can throw it at me; I'd rather wait until we're alone so she can deliver her anger in private. At least then I will be able to do something about calming her down.

"That's the last one," my father says as he points to the bale of hay I'm grabbing off the back of the truck. Carrying it into the stable, I let it fall to the ground when I reach where it needs to go. It lands with a hard thump, trickles of hay falling from its sides. I'm wiping away the sweat on my brow when Callie walks in. "Didn't think you still knew how to do manual labor by the way your hands look all pretty now," she ridicules.

Removing my gloves, I place them in my back pocket. "Just because they're not calloused anymore doesn't mean I don't use them," I grunt.

"Yeah, I remember how well you used to use them," she chides. Her eyes rake up and down my bare chest. "At least you haven't lost your figure." For some odd reason, the kindling in her blue eyes has an uneasy shiver running down my spine.

"Don't even think about it, Callie. Our episode is over," I warn, already knowing why she's looking at me that way.

Overlooking my warning, she asks, "Did you tell her about us on your little ride?"

"No."

"Why not? You afraid your little city girl can't handle the truth?" she asks with a teasing smile. "The Trey Johnson I remember wouldn't give two shits about what a girl thought. At least, that's how you made me feel," she says with a frown.

Before I get a chance to clarify there was nothing ever between us, my father clasps my shoulder. "If you're ready to go, we better get back to the house to wash up before your momma comes looking for us," my dad proclaims, reminding me of who I have waiting for me at home with my mother. "We're cooking out tomorrow night in honor of Junior coming home. We look forward to seeing you and your family there," he says, extending an invitation to

Callie.

I know he's only inviting her out of respect for her family.

A boasting smile spreads across her face when she replies, "Wouldn't miss it for the world, Everett."

"Great." My father may be satisfied from her accepting his invitation, but the unsettled feeling I'm developing is far from his reaction. Giving her a tip of his hat, he turns to return to the truck while I remain behind for the sole purpose of warning Callie.

"I don't need you going and stirring a pot full of shit while I'm here, so stay away from Victoria," I say, knowing what she's capable of.

"I feel sorry for the poor girl. She has no clue how deceiving you can be."

"She doesn't need to know, either."

She shakes her head with a disappointed look upon her face. "You're never going to change, are you, Trey? You'll always be the heartless bastard I grew up with," she delivers, then spins on her boot heels, leaving me to watch her walk away. The action reminds me of the last time I'd seen her, a reminder that my career wasn't the only circumstances that kept me away.

Making my way back to the truck, I climb in a minute later to find my dad curiously taking me in. "Everything okay with you and Callie?"

My father isn't oblivious to my situation with her. I'd warned him of what had happened in case she came protesting to my parents.

"Yeah." He doesn't seem convinced, but doesn't pry,

and thankfully changes the subject as we drive away. "So is there something I need to know about this new girl?"

My father isn't one to jump to conclusions, but from the way he's asking, I'm beginning to believe he's siding with everyone and hoping Victoria is my girl. "It's not what you think. We seem to have gotten ourselves in a bit of trouble," I find myself declaring on behalf of *both* of us. It's the first time I've not entirely blamed Victoria for everything.

"How bad is it?"

Overcome with how to correctly answer, I take a moment before I answer, "Not as bad as the gossip pages are making it out to be."

"You're the one always telling us they're all lies," he's quick to remind me.

"She was engaged to be married when they caught us kissing and decided to . . . let the entire world know about it," I say. "Or at least, they are claiming she was. She denies she was still engaged when the photo was taken, but she *was* still engaged when we started hooking up a couple of weeks ago."

"Is it because of who you are they're targeting her?"

"No. It's because of who she is they're targeting *me,*" I allege. The poor man looks lost at my reply, obviously needing further explanation. "Her father is in the running to be the next president this year. Her fucking family goes all the way back to hanging out with George Washington for Christ's sake," I bellow, still unbelieving myself.

I receive a slow drawn out whistle from my father.

"Help me understand why she's here again?" he wonders.

Maybe if I clarify it to my father, I can better understand it myself. "She was being attacked by the paparazzi and it pissed me off. I knew no matter where I took her in *our* world they would find her. So I brought her here." This earns me a chuckle.

"Running home isn't always the answer, boy," he tells me. "But I'm not complaining you're here and I'm pretty sure your momma isn't, either," he conveys. "I think it's best you keep this from your momma. You know how she'll react to all this."

Scrubbing my face with my dirty hand, I'm back to admitting he's right. "I know."

"There's one thing I need you to be honest about," he demands. "Just how serious is it between you and her?" He holds up his hand to keep me from replying just yet. "Don't be giving me that bullshit that you're just friends. I see the way you look at her." Fuck, does everyone watch my every move with her?

Shamefully, I admit, "I don't know what to tell you, Dad."

"Because you can't figure it out for yourself," he finishes for me. It's not the exact wording I would have chosen, but it keeps me from having to clarify why I don't know. "All I can suggest is you take the time you're here to figure it out. Y'all are going to have to return to reality at some point and your problems are still going to be there. It's up to you whether you're going to stand by her side as her man, or let her be and deal with it on your own. Either way, it isn't right for you to be messing with her mind like you did with Callie because you weren't honest with her."

Throwing my head back on the headrest, I let out a groan while I take in his words, thinking to myself: *How the fuck did I let my dick get me in trouble again when I vowed to never let it happen?*

Victoria

I'm staring down at the ingredients Mrs. Johnson placed in front of me minutes ago, completely lost as to how I will be able to accomplish the task. I am not one to turn down a challenge, but neither am I going to risk the lives of an entire family because of my cooking.

"The sooner you start mixing it, dear, the sooner I can get those biscuits in the oven," she says, seeing how confused I am.

Crap. I'm under pressure now. I'm still contemplating ways to make Trey pay for making me do this. The moment we walked into the kitchen upon returning from our adventure, he informed his mother that I would be helping her with dinner. The way she lit up from his offer left me with no choice but to follow through and help her so I wouldn't appear rude. He left with a mischievous grin on his face. He's the one who lost the race for the second time; it should be him making these darn biscuits for dinner.

The gloating smirk after kissing his smiling mother goodbye is still fresh in my mind. Had it not been for the fear of his mother defending him, I would have strangled him right then and there. I would have done it. I'm sure I can wrap my hands completely around his thick neck to accomplish the task.

"The biscuits are not going to make themselves, honey," Mrs. Johnson asserts from across the room.

Snapping back to reality, I begin reading over the recipe once more. It makes constitutional law seem like a casual read at the very moment. I have to keep repeating: *I can do this. How hard can it be to mix a total of seven ingredients?*

Trey's time with his father better be as strenuous as this recipe. Grabbing for the bag of flour first, I pour it into the bowl. My watchful eyes are near the bowl when it lands, and I receive a giant, white puff cloud to my face. Using the dishrag she included for wiping my hands, I wipe away the evidence of my first step from my face.

First step done.

Grabbing for a can labeled baking powder, I pour it in the bowl next. All other ingredients follow soon after, and when there is nothing left, I contently mix them all up.

Walking over from the kitchen counter, Mrs. Johnson holds out her hand and says, "May I have that can of baking soda, please?"

Grabbing for the empty can, I hand it to her, receiving a baffled expression in return. "You used all of it?" She peers down into the bowl in front of me.

"The recipe said to use it," I say, pointing to the paper on the counter next to the mixing bowl.

Mrs. Johnson's eyes widen as she stares down at my bowl full of ingredients. My once joyful emotion has completely perished to non-existent.

"Oh, dear," I hear in a hushed tone from her.

Frightfully, I ask, "Did I do it wrong?"

"You were supposed to use measuring cups," she says, pointing to a set of utensils still sitting on the table. "That's why there are numbers before the ingredients.

"I thought you were just supposed to mix everything together." Picking up the paper, I point directly to the instruction stating, "See? Right there. It says to mix all dry ingredients together."

She gives me a skeptical look. "Have you ever cooked before, dear?"

"No," I shamefully confess.

I can feel the tears building, knowing I've failed Trey's mother and myself in the biggest way possible. My lips begin to tremble while I fight to hold back tears.

Rushing around the table to my side, she wraps her arms around my shoulders, nudging my face into her chest to comfort me. "I'm sorry," I choke out, still trying to fight back the tears. How is it one simple task can make me feel like a complete failure?

Patting my head, she says, "There, there, dear. We can always try again."

"Do I have to?" I plead, not wanting to fail a second time.

Her laughter vibrates through her chest and into my ear. "Your biscuits will be the talk of dinner tonight. You just wait and see," she confidently boosts, while I sit in her arms thinking to myself: *They won't be able to talk about my biscuits, because everyone will be choking on them.*

I'm ready to throw in the towel sitting on my lap when Trey walks in the door. The sight of him and knowing my current failure is still sitting directly in front of me has me letting out the whimpered cry I was containing. I told myself I wouldn't cry. I have no reason to cry, but seeing him broke the dam inside of me.

"Why you making her cry, Momma?"

"It's my fault, not hers," I bawl, digging my face into my white powdery hands. "I messed up the biscuits," I cry into them.

"It will all be fine, dear, you'll see," Trey's mother repeats, but I'm not as confident as she. "I'm going to go down to the basement to grab some more ingredients. See if you can calm her down," I hear Mrs. Johnson tell Trey as she steps away.

Sympathy only makes it worse. The feel of his familiar arms replace those of his mother's, along with a strong shudder against my head as he firmly holds it down against his chest.

Pulling my head back, I ask, "Are you laughing at me?" He snorts, unable to contain his laughter. "You're so cruel. This is all your fault!" I yell, completely taking out my anguished emotions on him as I swat him with the dishtowel.

Balking at my declaration, he bellows back, "How is this my fault?"

"You left me here to fail!"

He brings his laughter down to a small chuckle before speaking. "My momma has been making those biscuits since she was a kid. I didn't think it would be that hard."

"It's clear baking is not my forte," I admit with defeat, making his laughter start up again.

His eyes fully take me in. "You have flour all over your face," he points out with another snort.

Fuming from how amused he is at my appearance, my hand reaches into the bowl still sitting in front of me. Grabbing a fist full of the contents, I chuck it straight at him, his mouth is fully open gasping for air from his laughter when it hits him.

He spits the powdery substance from his mouth before saying, "What the hell did you do that for?" Inside, I'm filled with a sense of satisfaction from his appearance. "Now you look like me," I gloat. The moment I'm done saying it, flour comes right back at me.

Gasping, Trey is already standing to retreat away from me when I grab for another handful. "You're going to pay for that," I warn, then chuck it right back at him as I stand.

I've lost all reason why I was upset, instead it's been replaced with a bout of laughter and the need to cover Trey in as much flour as possible as I chase him around the table. My eyes can barely stay open as I try to blink through the white cloud permeating the air. I've somehow managed to catch up to Trey and am now standing directly in front of him. Reaching for the bowl, I grab it then bring it up to dump the remaining contents over his head. When I step back to observe his appearance, he's standing rigid, covered completely from head to toe with the white ingredients from the bright yellow bowl sitting perfectly balanced on his head.

I'm the one snorting as I laugh at the image in front of

me. His hands slowly reach up to remove the bowl. When his eyes pop open, his dark eyes are scowling back at me.

"What in God's name happened here?" Mr. Johnson's booming voice has both our heads snapping in his direction. His mother steps up right behind him, taking in our battlefield with an opened mouth. The cluck of her tongue is heard loud and clear when she places her hands sternly on her hips. She disappointedly shakes her head at both of us.

"Now look what you've gone and done. You've made a mess of my kitchen," she says, reminding us of our actions.

"I'm sorry," I whisper.

"Sorry, Momma," Trey says with remorse.

Clucking her tongue another time, she says, "Y'all better get to cleaning. I'm not having my kitchen looking like a mess for dinner tonight."

I'm dreading having to clean up the mess, but from the stern glare she's giving both of us, I'm more fearful of her reaction when I refuse her command.

"Yes, ma'am," we both say at the same time. Mrs. Johnson turns with a huff and walks off in the other direction while I look back to Trey, biting my lip to keep from laughing. I fail when he lets out another snort.

"This is all your fault," I repeat.

He rolls his eyes. "I'm beginning to think whatever happens between the two of us will always be my fault," he retorts.

"Good, we at least agree on something," I say in return.

Sneering back at me, he isn't allowed the chance to reply as his mother hands him a bucket with a mop, and a cleaning rag to me. "Now hurry up with the both of you. You still have to get cleaned up," she commands.

There is no chance to argue as we begin cleaning. The entire time I'm determined to do this one task correctly, making sure there isn't a spot of flour left anywhere. Nearly thirty minutes later, there is no evidence of our childish behavior and we're allowed to go get cleaned up with a nod of approval from Trey's mother.

"I swear, I don't think I've ever felt so ashamed for my actions in my life," I confide to Trey as he follows me out of the kitchen.

"Have you ever gotten into trouble at all?"

"Are we going to have this conversation again? You can't make me out to be the spoiled brat with money anymore," I throw back at him while entering the hallway leading to my room.

"It isn't what I was referring to. I'm asking if you've ever gotten in trouble."

Stopping to face him, I consider all the times I've been in trouble. "Scolded, yes. Being punished for my actions, no," I truthfully admit. "Had what we'd done happened at one of my houses, it would have been the staff cleaning up the mess while we got a good tongue lashing."

"Lucky you," he says with a twist of his lips. "Had I been a kid and done this shit, I would have gotten an ass whooping and still had to clean it up."

"Would it have been worth it?" I dare to ask.

Smiling wide, he says, "Fuck yeah." Exactly what I

knew he would say as I begin to laugh along with him.

Trey's personality and responses have always been a form of amusement for me. I find myself always asking questions just to hear his response. Our laughter eventually dies down and we stand in the hallway gazing into one another's eyes. Silence overcomes us, however I don't want to chance saying anything to send us back into the darkened mood we somehow seem to find at times.

His hand reaches out, brushing through the strands of my hair. "What is it you're doing to me, Victoria?" he asks as he stares into my eyes

Completely at loss as to what he means, I say, "I don't understand."

"You're making me feel shit I hadn't expected," his husky voice expresses with a serious tone.

A shiver radiates throughout my body, starting at the spot where his hand is still gliding through my hair and traveling all the way down my spine. Excitement builds when I see him inch forward, closing the distance between us. My eyes begin to drift closed, anticipating his kiss, only it never comes. A squeal from down the hall breaks the moment.

"You're really here?" a girl shouts, startling Trey to step back.

He opens his arms to the young girl launching herself at him. "Chrissie!" he shouts, indicating his younger sister. "Damn, girl, you've grown up." Letting her slide down his body she steps back, disgusted with how her clothes are now covered in flour.

"Why are you all white?" she asks Trey before her

eyes catch me off to the side. "And her too?" Her head tilts as she considers me. "Who is she, by the way?"

Holding out my hand, I say, "I'm Victoria," gently shaking her hand as she smiles back and forth between Trey and me.

"You brought a girl home," she teases him.

"She's a friend," he informs her, but the title no longer offends me. "She'll be staying in your room, squirt. Is that okay?"

"Are you staying with her?" Chrissie asks, his brows arched high.

"No." He wraps his arm around her neck. "Let's go catch up. I need to know who you've been bringing home," he says, dragging her away without a backwards glance in my direction.

"Why, so you can beat them up?" I hear her ask with a giggle as they leave me behind.

Being left alone, I turn to enter the room I was loaned to find Mr. Whiskers still laying on the bed where I had left him. The sound of my footsteps awakens him, and he lifts his head to give me his usual meow. Sitting on the bed next to him, I ask, "Was your day as exciting as mine?" I pet the top of his head, earning me a wide yawn. "I take that as a no."

"At least you're not left with questions," I say, thinking back to Trey's comment, still at a loss.

I may never come to understand the terms Trey keeps throwing at me, or the meaning behind most of his comments, but deep down inside I know I've fallen for a man not wanting more than to be *"just friends."*

Chapter Fourteen

Feelings

Trey

I'M A LIGHT sleeper. I've been a light sleeper for as long as I can remember. It drove my mom insane when I was a child and I'd wake in the middle of the night at any little noise. The only way for me to be completely out for the night is to be drunk, which is not the case tonight, and the reason why I can hear Victoria's footsteps as she walks to the bathroom. When she's done, instead of her footsteps leading her back to my sister's room, they're leading her to my bedroom instead.

Anticipation builds inside of me, my entire body going stiff in the bed I'm lying in. Peering directly at my open door, her silhouette appears in the doorway. She stands at the entrance, her body leaning into the doorframe as if she's sleep walking. The room is blanketed in darkness, keeping me from being able to make out her facial features. However, from the sigh she lets out and casualness of her stance, I know she's staring directly at me.

"Couldn't sleep, princess?" I ask, coming out more of an assertion than a question. She lets out a startled gasp.

"How did you know I was standing here?"

"You were loud when you went to the bathroom," I tease back to her.

"Was not," she responds with a snarling whisper.

Silently laughing in the dark, I ask, "Why the creepiness?"

"I wasn't intending to creep." I remain still, watching as she steps forward until she is standing at the side of the bed. "You're right. I couldn't sleep," she conveys.

"Could be all the sweet tea you drank at dinner," I suggest, remembering how she practically drank the entire pitcher herself.

"No. It's the house."

This response has me chuckling out loud. "I can assure you, my parent's house isn't haunted."

"I didn't say it was haunted. I just don't sleep well unless it's in my own bed."

Thinking back, I recall all the nights she slept soundly in a strange bed . . . with me. "You never had a problem with it when we had sex," I remind her.

"I was drunk most of those times," she points out.

There is no arguing on my behalf as I was there every single time. There wasn't a night we had sex that didn't begin with her being intoxicated. It makes me wonder if those were the only terms for her to sleep with me.

"I meant to say thank you earlier and just forgot," she mentions, drawing me back to the present.

Turning to lean up on an elbow to better look at her, I ask, "For what?"

"I know you hate being stuck with me and I don't blame you, but . . ." she pauses and I hear her sigh. "Thank you for everything," she utters.

"I didn't have much of a choice," I respond, regretting the words the moment I hear them out loud.

"Why do you do that?"

"Do what?"

"Purposely find ways to remind me of how much of a burden I am to you," she claims with a frustrated huff.

I remain silent, fearful of saying the wrong thing this time. "Never mind," she grumbles, turning to leave.

Sitting completely up and reaching for her, my hand clasps her wrist to stop her from taking another step. Stunned, she turns to look down at me and with the faint glow from the window on the side of my bed, I can see her pained expression.

"I'm sorry. I shouldn't have said that." I sigh, ashamed of my earlier answer now that she's pointed out how resentful it may have sounded. "Come here," I tell her, tugging her towards the bed while I hold the blanket up with my other hand.

"Why?" she asks, testing my motives.

"I want to help you sleep." Letting go of her hand, I scoot over on the bed, making the springs creak with the movement. She remains rooted to her spot while I continue holding up the blanket, waiting for her reaction. She finally steps forward and climbs into bed with me.

"Only you would think of sex as the answer," she says when I drape the blanket over both of us.

"We're not having sex."

She grows rigid. "We're not?" she asks, sounding disappointed.

"And you were the one saying all I think about is sex," I quip back.

She remains silent while adjusting her position at my side. Her entire body is practically entwined with mine, and when her thigh brushes up against my groin, I begin to reconsider my *"no sex"* proposition I had declared in my mind when I offered for her to climb into bed.

Nudging my nose in her hair, I inhale her scent. "You're not a burden, Victoria. You're just an unexpected surprise," I find myself saying. She stiffens for a moment before I feel her body begin to relax.

"I take it you don't like surprises."

Her interest makes me smile. "I'm not used to them anymore."

"I think you've just grown to expect them," she says. "Especially with the way you started out with your career. You've learned to adjust to whatever is thrown at you."

Yanking my head back so I can face her, I ask, "How is it you think I started out?"

She seems hesitant to answer. "It's not what I think, but what I know," she explains. "You told me yourself you became Abigail's manager because she was in trouble at the time. I did some research and discovered she was accused of murdering her previous manager." The admission she was snooping into my past displeases me. "I'm assuming you took on a difficult situation and handled it appropriately, which is why she kept you as her current manager."

"Now you're Ms. Know it All," I banter back at her.

I tighten my hold when she squirms in my arms, and I'm afraid I've offended her and she's trying to leave. Instead, I discover she's making herself more comfortable on my chest.

"I already told you, I prefer details. I hate it when information is withheld from me," she mumbles into my chest.

"Now you're Ms. Sassy Pants," I say, unable to resist teasing her.

Gliding my fingers through Victoria's hair, a habit I've come to have while she lays next to me, my fingers get caught in a knot. "You still have flour in your hair?" I ask, feeling a cake like substance near her neck.

"I hope not. I spent almost thirty minutes washing my hair," she utters, lifting her hand and touching the spot I'm playing with. "I didn't know it would cake up the moment the water hit my head and it made it more difficult to get out."

I'm unable to contain my chuckle and envision how angry she must have gotten discovering that fact. "I should have made you wash it out."

"Had we not been in my parents' house, I would have," I answer way too quickly, causing her to stiffen. Her comment has made me realize we've never once taken a shower together. To be honest, I've never taken a shower with a girl. She would have been the first.

Squirming once more, she rubs harder against my groin, making we wince. "Why are you moving so much?"

"You're a really hard pillow, which sucks," she complains.

Rolling us both so she's under me, I settle between her thighs. "Tell me something I don't know," I whisper into her ear before nipping down on the earlobe as the images of what I could have done in the shower wander through my mind. The vibration of her moan against my lips grazing across her bare neck sends a jolt straight down to my dick.

Fuck . . . my dick feels as if it's ready to burst from my damn boxers when she lifts her hips to grind against my cock. My hand is already reaching down to pull her underwear off when the sound of the toilet flushing down the hallway has me rolling off her in a heartbeat.

Lying stiff on my back, I stare at the ceiling, holding my breath as we listen to the footsteps retreat. The sound of the door shutting to my sister's room can be heard, allowing me to let out my breath.

"That was a close one," Victoria whispers from my side.

"No shit." I agree, remembering my door is still wide open and we could have been caught. Victoria's hand begins to skim against my ribs, forcing me to stop it from going any further. "No," I have to tell her.

"What? Why?" she asks, almost in a desperate whimper. It doesn't help my semi-erect shaft that I'm forcing to calm.

Tugging her so she's draping half her body on my chest, I wrap my arms around her and hold tight to keep her from moving. "Because if that were my momma we would have both been in trouble." Her stiffness advises she understands exactly what I mean. My mother had made sure to give us a stern lecture before heading off to bed.

"You two better behave. I'll not be having you two disrespect my rules while under my roof. Understood?" Those were her exact words, delivered with a pointed finger and a glare that could kill the bull in the paddock two acres over. She received two fearful nods from both Victoria and me.

"Is it crazy that your momma scares me sometimes?" Victoria asks in a whisper into my neck.

"I'd think you were crazy if she didn't," I laugh out.

"I do like her, though," I hear her whisper with a sigh. "She's sweet." Heat radiates inside of me from her comment.

Victoria isn't expected to like my family, nor them her, but over dinner she won everyone's heart. Deep down inside, I already know I'm screwed and there is nothing I can do about it. Victoria's breathing begins to slow and her limp form in my arms informs me she's finally falling asleep. The hypnotic rhythm of her breathing has my eyes growing weary, and I'm the happiest I have been in days. My last thought before surrendering to sleep is how she isn't a burden at all, but a *very welcome surprise.*

The sound of a snicker has me opening my eyes to a slit. My blurry vision comes clear to find my mother glaring straight at me. Her hands are on her hips and a twist of her lips warns me I'm in trouble.

"Why am I not surprised?" she voices, having me snap my eyes completely open in fear she's going to throttle the both of us.

"We didn't do anything, I swear," I protest as fast as I can. "She couldn't sleep. That's all." My mother shakes her head with a sigh while Victoria groans, most likely from my voice and disrupting her sleep.

"Just friends," my mother snorts under her breath turning to leave the room.

All tension follows her out of the room, leaving me with a sense of relief. Shaking Victoria to try to wake her, she snaps her head up, eyes still closed as she shouts, "I object, your Honor!" Then her head drops back down onto my chest.

I burst out in a full-fledged bout of laughter, earning me another groan. The feel of her warm breath cascading against the crook of my neck keeps me from getting up. Is it wrong to want to just hold and savor having her in my arms? I find myself kissing her temple, and this time she lets out a sound of satisfaction.

"It's time to wake up, princess," I say into her ear.

She lets out a content sigh this time, but from the way she's shifting in my arms, I know she's awakening. "What time is it?" she rasps out.

"I have no idea."

From the brightness of the sun radiating into the room,

I know it has to be after seven. She lifts her head up to rest her chin on my chest, her eyes still shut. She looks to be falling back to sleep, causing me to shake her once more.

"I thought we were supposed to be on vacation?" she says, still not opening her eyes.

"We are, but my momma has already been in here," I notify her.

This has her eyes snapping wide open in fear as she sits up. "Oh, god!" She holds the blanket up against her chest, looking around the room in dismay. "Is she mad?" she quickly asks.

"Not as mad as I thought she'd be." This doesn't reassure Victoria, as her eyes grow wider.

"She probably hates me," she fusses.

"Probably," I joke, watching her panic. I can't help it. Seeing her worry over what my mother's opinion is delights me. "You'll win her over by helping her cook dinner tonight," I say, watching her glower. "You really don't like cooking, do you?"

"I have no clue how."

Ahh, that explains her failed attempt at the biscuits. "Something the *staff* always did for you?" I mock.

Looking completely chagrined, she replies, "Or take out."

"Can't blame you. Matt or Abigail does all the cooking in our house."

Excitedly, she relays, "You know how to cook bacon." She seems hopeful when she asks, "Are you going to make some again this morning?"

Laughing at her enthusiasm, I ask, "Hungry?"

"For bacon? Yes!"

If bacon is what she wants, then bacon is what I'll be cooking for her this morning. I'll do whatever it takes to keep the smile on her face.

Victoria

I look down to the cowboy boots I'm wearing with doubt. "Are you sure you don't mind me wearing them?" I ask Chrissie, who was kind enough to lend them to me.

She waves off my question. "They go better with your dress than the ones you brought."

"Those happen to be Gucci. They go with everything."

"Gucci or not, they're full of flour." Glancing back down to them, I can't resist grinning from the memory. "Plus, you're in the country. You need country shoes," she insists.

"True," I reply, not wanting to disagree. They do go better with the dress I'm wearing, I think to myself as I start to brush my hair.

"How come you and my brother claim to only be just friends? Yet, you both get all googly-eyed around each other."

"We do not," I argue, pausing mid-stroke to think back to what could have her claiming we do. I can't argue since his actions have me asking a similar question every now and again. "Your brother is just confusing," I proclaim, knowing I am not far from the truth. Trey has to be the most confusing male I know. He can rapidly go from treating me as the princess he claims I am, to reminding me I'm nothing but a burden he needs to protect.

"He likes you," she chimes with a teasing smile.

"He's just being nice," I say in return.

"Whatever."

I'm preparing to reply to her sarcastic remark when I begin to wonder why I'm arguing with a teenager. It could be because she is the only one keeping me company after we were both sent out of the kitchen. After my biscuit fiasco yesterday, Trey's mother felt the need to cast me out, not wanting to risk a repeat of my failure and ruin dinner. Chrissie, on the other hand, refused to dirty her new outfit and whined her way out of cooking duties.

"Where is May?" I ask, wondering why Trey's other sister isn't in the room alongside Chrissie interrogating me. Other than dinner last night, I haven't really seen the girl.

She waves her hand in the direction of May's room. "She's probably in her room with her nose stuck in a book."

The only information I could learn of her is she is a freshman currently taking courses at the local junior college.

"She's not very social. It's sort of scary sometimes," Chrissie comments, sounding addled over her own proclamation.

"Why?"

She eyes me with confusion. "I mean, come on," she says, throwing her hands up in the air and shaking her head. "She's a dork," she asserts.

Disheartened with how she would label her sister, I ask, "Because she always has her nose in a book?"

"Yes! See, you understand," she replies, satisfied with my response.

"I always had my nose in a book," I confess.

She looks taken aback. "But you're pretty," she says, sounding baffled. "And rich. Why would you choose to be a dork?"

Laughing, I point the brush in my hand straight at her. "Pretty looks and money will get you nowhere if you don't have a brain," I declare.

"It will get you the hell out of this town," she utters with a roll of her eyes.

I silently disagree with her statement, because those two reasons are what got me *here,* driving me to feel disappointed with myself.

Footsteps break my concentration, making me look to the doorway. "Are you driving her nuts, Chrissie?" Trey asks in a teasing tone.

"No," she says, standing up from the bed. "Are y'all done cooking already?"

"Almost," he informs us, glancing in my direction. "I just thought I'd come to check on Victoria." I can practically feel the heat from his eyes as they rake up and down my body.

"Didn't think you owned a dress that wasn't designer," he says, referring to the sundress I have on. It happens to be my favorite, which is why I packed it.

"How do you know it isn't designer?" I tease with an arched brow.

"Designer or not, it's hot."

"See. Googly eyes," Chrissie states from the doorway as she leaves.

Completely confused, Trey turns and stares at her like she's lost her mind. "What the hell did she mean?"

I shrug my shoulders. "I have no clue," I lie.

It's my turn to take Trey in. "You look like a cowboy," I tease, remembering how his options are limited since he didn't have a chance to pack any clothing. When I'd asked where he got the clothes he had worn yesterday, his reply was, "I had some clothes I left behind in my closet."

He's wearing another flannel button down shirt, the sleeves are rolled up to his elbows and the top few buttons casually left open, same type of jeans he wore yesterday, with the pair of cowboy boots he's been wearing. All he's missing is the typical cowboy hat everyone else has been walking around in, which makes me ask, "You don't have a hat?"

His brow arches at my question. "Why you asking?"

"Everyone else wears one."

He considers my response for a moment. "I guess I just got used to not wearing it anymore."

"Just like you lost your accent?"

His lips turn up on one side. "You're very observant, aren't you?"

"Always," I proudly say.

"Good, one of us has to be," he conveys, holding out his hand for me to take.

Clasping my hand with his, he leads me through the house and straight outdoors, adding another question to my list.

Throwing my plate away, I wipe my hands one more time before adding the napkin to the trash. Spinning to make my way back to Trey, I decide to stop at the table where his mother and aunt are sitting with Becca, politely waiting until they address me. Trey's mother notices me with a smile. "Hello, dear."

"Hello, ladies," I politely address them all. "I just wanted to thank you for a wonderful meal. Everything was delicious."

"We're glad you enjoyed it," Mary Anne remarks.

"Come sit with us for a moment. Trey has had you long enough," Becca requests, patting the seat next to her.

Not wanting to be rude, I take her offer. It seats me directly across from Mrs. Johnson and for some odd reason, although she holds a smile, I feel as if I'm still being scrutinized for this morning.

"Have you had some pie?" Mary Anne asks, pushing the pie in front of her in my direction.

Holding my hand up in protest, I say, "I'm so full, I don't think I can eat another bite," while holding my full stomach.

When Luke had warned I was required to have an appetite at their family gatherings, he wasn't joking. Every meal I've sat down to partake in has been an abundance of food. A cookout was no exception, if not more of an extreme. I made sure to serve myself in moderation to be able to enjoy a taste of everything, but there was no way to eat it all. I am soon discovering the meaning of comfort food. It's filling and satisfying at the same time.

Ignoring my reasons, Trey's mother is already serving me a piece and placing it in front of me. "Everyone has room for pie."

I'm staring down at the piece of pecan pie reluctantly, holding back the urge to gag. Not out of disgust, but from knowing I will not possibly be able to finish it. As if reading my thoughts, she encourages me. "At least take a bite. Mary Anne's pecan pie is the best in a hundred mile radius," she suggests.

Taking a deep breath, I pick up the fork offered and take a bite thinking: *only one bite.*

"Viv tells us she found you in Trey's bed this morning," Becca discloses, making me choke on the piece of pie I'm swallowing. She pats me on the back to help it go down easier. Finally able to breathe, I quickly speak. "Nothing happened, I swear," I announce.

Had it not been for one of his sisters, I could not be declaring the same.

Becca leans in to whisper in my ear. "Even if you did, I wouldn't judge." Wide-eyed, I face Mrs. Johnson, still trying to convince her with a shake of my head.

She smiles and waves her hand. "I already spoke with Trey. He's assured me as well." Relieved by her statement, I stuff another bite of pie in my mouth to keep me from having to explain further. "Although, if you two want to add anymore grandbabies to the family when y'all return to the city, I wouldn't mind," she says, making me choke once more.

I really have to stop eating this damn pie or I might just choke to death because of their comments. The pounding Becca gives me this time is sure to leave me sore in the morning. Pushing the slice of pie away to not tempt myself anymore, I have to endure hearing the comments quickly following soon after.

"Oh, yes, they'd have gorgeous babies," Mary Anne says with a nod.

"Yes, they would," Mrs. Johnson adds with her own enthusiastic nod. I'm looking to Becca with pleading eyes for her to say something, but instead of helping she gives me a bemused smile.

"I'm sorry ladies, but unfortunately I don't believe it will be happening."

"Why not?" Mrs. Johnson looks disappointed.

"Because Trey has made it clear on more than one occasion there is absolutely nothing going on between us."

Mrs. Johnson clucks her tongue. "That boy just hasn't taken his head out of his ass," she snickers, making me thank God I don't have pie in my mouth. "He'll come around eventually. You just wait and see," she assures me.

Holding back the urge to roll my eyes, I instead give her a polite smile.

"Oh, look, Regina has arrived." Mrs. Johnson points to a family making their way around the house. "Please excuse us, dear," she says, already standing to leave the table with Mary Anne.

When they leave, I turn to Becca to pierce her with a glare. "Thanks for throwing me under the bus. You're supposed to be helping me here."

She's wearing a mischievous grin. "I'm sorry, honey, but I'm on their side." She stands up from the table. "I'm going to go look for my husband and make sure he's keeping out of trouble."

"You're ditching me?"

Becca laughs. "I'm sure Trey wouldn't mind if you start working on those babies," she says with a wink, leaving me to gawk at her.

Alone, I have no choice but to make my way back to Trey. I find him where I left him. He is sitting at the table with Jimmy and I take a seat, a frown upon my face.

"What's up with you?" he asks before he takes a drink of his beer.

"Nothing," I clip out. There is doubt in his eyes when he looks to me, but doesn't question me any further. "I'm so full, I don't think I can eat another bite," I complain.

"I think it's all the sweet tea you keep drinking," Trey teases as I watch him take another bite of his fried chicken. I have to wonder where he puts it all.

"I like the sweet tea," I say, taking another sip of the refreshment we're discussing.

"It's your crack at the rate you're drinking it." He laughs. Frowning at his response only makes him laugh harder. Sticking my tongue out at his comment, he gives me a humorless gaze. "Don't make me put that tongue to use," he says in a husky whisper close enough for only me to hear.

A feverish thrill takes over my blood with his heated stare. I want nothing more than to request he follow through with his threat considering how he left me feeling frustrated last night. Before I can torment him in return, Jimmy asks, "Did you enjoy dinner, Victoria?"

"Yes, very much, thank you."

"Good, because it's almost time to start burning it off," he expresses with a smile before he takes a drink from the mason jar in his hand.

"You better slow down on that shit before you end up in the ditch on the way home," Trey suggest, pointing his chin to the drink in Jimmy's hand.

"Nah. I'm good," he protests.

Trey shakes his head at him. "He isn't drinking water?" I ask. It's what I assumed he was drinking since the liquid is clear.

"This here is genuine, home brewed moonshine," Jimmy declares proudly, holding the glass up in salute.

"Moonshine?" I exclaim. "As in the stuff that's illegal?"

Shifting in his seat with an uneasy expression, he says, "You're not going to go report us now because you're a lawyer, are you?"

"No, she isn't," Trey answers for me. "Victoria, we're in the south. Illegal or not, we drink the stuff."

"And brew it, too," Jimmy boasts in another salute.

Trey sighs from his comment. "Regardless, this is my family and the last thing I need is for you to go being a good citizen by ratting them out."

"But—" He holds his hand up to silence me. "No buts, Victoria. Just drop the subject," he commands.

Shoulders dropping in defeat, I sit and pout. Trey

holds a blank stare before his hand comes up to caress my chin. The pad of his thumb gently grazes against my lips while I stare into the depths of his eyes. The warmth of his touch has me burning inside, most likely with a crimson blush revealing my reaction.

"I don't know what I prefer, your pout or you glaring at me," he huskily delivers. His comment has my stomach spinning with butterflies. The entire world around us has ceased to exist in the last minute, until his cousin speaks, reminding me we're not alone. "You want to try it?" he asks.

Trey withdrawals his hand, leaving behind the tingle he'd placed at the first contact. I have to resist touching the same spot with my own fingers.

"She won't be able to handle it," Trey replies, taking a sip of his beer. "She's an amateur." He's broken all optimistic emotions I held for him mere seconds ago.

"Amateur or not, I was able to handle your tequila."

"It's not the same."

"Still doesn't mean I won't be able to handle it," I challenge.

"Oh, really?" His eyes light up with amusement. "Let's find out." He reaches for the glass sitting across the table near Jimmy's hand.

"Hey, that jar's mine. Get your own," he whines.

"I'm only giving her a sip. You'll get it right back," Trey snaps, eyes focused on me when he pushes the glass in front of me. "Go on," he urges with his eyes.

Wiping my now sweaty palms against my dress, I swallow, wondering what the hell I got myself into. Not only do I know the beverage is illegal, I will be partaking in drinking the contents, which is against the ethics of my profession.

"That's what I thought," Trey says, already reaching to pull the glass away. Stopping him, I grab the glass before he can take it and lift it to my mouth. I knew the liquid was known for being potent, however I never expected it to feel as if it is burning my throat the entire time I am swallowing.

Gasping for air while coughing at the same time, my nostrils feel like they're on fire. "What the heck is that stuff? Gasoline?" I breathlessly ask. Both Trey and Jimmy are laughing in unison. If I weren't already fuming from the aftereffects of the alcohol, I would be from their reaction.

Trey takes his own sip, grimacing when he, too, swallows. "Shit, I forgot how strong that shit is," he tells Jimmy, already sliding the glass back across the table. Jimmy catches it and lifts it straight to his lips to take his own sip.

"It'll grow some hair on your balls, that's for sure," he voices.

My throat is still trying to extinguish the flames when I reply, "I don't have balls, so I'm fine."

Trey throws his head back and lets out a full bout of laughter. Bringing his head back down, he leans forward and kisses the side of my mouth. "Damn, I love some of the shit that comes out of your mouth sometimes." His laughter slowly dies down to a chuckle when he shakes his head.

My mind returns to the hallway we stood in yesterday,

his admission leaving me with all sorts of questions. His current comments only send me one step back, instead of forward.

Enthusiasm

Trey

VICTORIA SWAYS TO the music, a hint of a smile on her face as she watches those dancing around in the small clearing we've designated as the dance floor. The music has been blaring for the last twenty minutes and I haven't been able to ignore the way she lightly sways to the rhythm. The moment the music began, she lit up like a candle. Apparently, she isn't used to hearing such enthusiastic music. The extent of her musical experience probably consists solely of classical ballads.

"Come on," I tell Victoria, holding out my hand for her to take.

"Why?"

"Just trust me," I say, still waiting.

Nervously looking at my hand for a moment, she exhales before taking it, guiding her towards the patch of land where her eyes have been fixated. "We're dancing?" she asks.

"Worried I'm going to step on your toes, princess?" I tease, wrapping my arm around her waist, pulling her body flush to mine when we reach the area.

She stares down at her feet. "Yes, these aren't my boots," she replies.

"Really?" I find myself asking. All the enthusiasm she carried earlier is gone. My brows arch in question, waiting for her to voice what it is she's thinking, because I know she's trying to conjure an excuse. "I just don't know how to dance to this kind of music," she admits.

That's the reason. She doesn't want to embarrass herself. "It's not that hard. You just move," I tell her, urging her to take her first step.

She seems slightly aggravated by my response, but she follows my lead and starts to move. "I know that," she clips out with a twist of her lips. "But my kind of dancing normally has a routine to it, this . . ." She pauses to look around at the other people dancing, " . . . seems far more difficult to me," she says, sounding disappointed with her admission.

"Let me take care of it," I tell her, thinking I may have lost my mind for doing this. I don't normally dance anymore. Shit, I don't even know if I remember how to country dance.

The current song comes to an end while the new one slowly blends in. Her eyes light up with the widest smile I've ever seen Victoria deliver. "This is the song!" she exclaims.

Listening to the opening tune, I try to place the song. "*Play it Again,*" I reply, tying to figure what could have her so excited. "What about it?"

"It was the song playing on the radio when we drove here. I've had the words stuck in my head ever since," she beams, singing me the chorus when it comes on while her beautiful lips cheerfully move to the lyrics. I swear I've never seen such an animated side of her before and it fuels my desire to keep the smile on her face.

Holding her tight, I spin her in an entire circle and she giggles. It encourages me to do it again, this time faster and repeatedly, my smile starting to match her own.

She's giggling when she says, "I'm so dizzy." Her jubilant laughter vibrates into my ear. Letting out a contented sigh, she reclines her head onto my shoulder and sways along with me when the song comes to an end. The next song has a much slower pace, allowing me to clutch her tighter, closer, if possible, than I've ever had her before.

"I have to go inside," she tells me with a frown while I still sway her.

Unable to resist provoking her, I say, "You should have slowed down on that sweet tea, girl."

"I don't tell you anything about your beer, so back off my sweet tea," she jests, already pulling me in the direction of the house.

"I feel sorry for you when we leave," I express, wondering just how she will handle the thought of no longer having the brew to drink.

She stiffens for a moment, worrying me. "I hadn't

thought of that." She drags her feet as we walk. Seeing the disappointment it's brought has me saying, "I'll make sure to have my momma teach you how to make it before we leave." Her smile returns.

"*That* I will make sure not to screw up," she says, reminding us both of how she won't let the biscuit incident come to an end. Every mention of cooking since has earned me a unpleasant comment and a twist of her lips.

Entering the house a minute later, we depart ways, her going straight to the bathroom and me to the fridge near the back of the house where the beer is stocked. My mother has always had a thing with having alcohol in the house, but she knows how much we love our beer here in the south so a spare fridge is where it's kept.

I reach it, halting in my steps when I find Callie closing the fridge with a beer already in her hand. She eyes me with pinched lips and narrowed eyes, a reaction I am not surprised to receive. I've purposely been avoiding her all night because of Victoria's company. I didn't want to give Callie a reason to ruffle Victoria's feathers and upset her.

"Callie," I greet with a nod, reaching for the handle of the fridge to open and retrieve my own beer. I'd expected her to leave after her casual nod in return, but instead she retreats only a step.

"Where's your new friend?" The bitterness in her tone advises me she isn't asking with genuine politeness.

"She's around," I nonchalantly answer, closing the fridge with a loud thud, taking the brunt of my hostility out on the door.

She steps forward, wrapping her arms around my

waist, catching me by surprise. Her mouth reaches up to whisper into my ear. "Does that mean I have you all to myself now?"

Grabbing her arms, I try to dislodge myself from her embrace, but she only tightens her arms and tugs me closer to her. "Callie, you need to stop," I insist, but she refuses my dismissal.

"Oh, come on. One more time for old times' sake. She won't even know," she purrs into my ear.

I can smell the alcohol on her breath, telling me if she isn't already drunk, she's close to it. There is no fucking way she would be initiating sex considering our past.

Standing firm that I want nothing at all to do with Callie, I dislodge myself completely from her hold. "You're not getting anything from me anymore," I remark, making her glower back at me when she steps back.

"Is that why you're ignoring me? Because of her?" Her anger is exposed as her nostrils begin to flare.

"She doesn't need to be around your venom, Callie."

Growing angrier, she says, "How can you say such a thing to me?"

"Callie, you're no different now than you were growing up. You were always throwing yourself at me. Shit, had I not come to my senses, I would have fell for your trap?"

She seems astonished at my remark. "You think it was a trap?" Callie squares her shoulders and takes in a deep breath. "It takes two and I didn't see you telling me *no* each time you fucked me."

Taking just as deep of a breath, I try to keep from exploding. "You knew damn well I was going to leave and you were the one who got the idea you could get me to stay."

She's completely raging at his point. "How was I *not* supposed to get ideas? You knocked me up and left me when I needed you the most."

"You were no longer pregnant when I left, Callie," I say, reminding her of that fact. "You lost the baby long before I left, so don't try to pin that shit on me," I point out, feeling a pang of sadness at the memory. "What did you expect me to do, marry you?"

"Yes! Step up and be a man," she declares, throwing her hands up in exasperation.

My blood is completely boiling from rage. "How many times do I have to tell you, Callie? I'm not stupid enough to let any girl tie me down! Just because you were pregnant doesn't mean I would have married you. Thankfully, it never came to that."

"You're a bastard," she declares, bringing her hand back, ready to slap me. I catch it mid-air, holding tight to her wrist. "I'm not the only one who was lucky," she says through clenched teeth before yanking her hand from my grip and stepping around me to leave.

Finally alone, I twist open the bottle and take one giant swig. The cool liquid travels down my throat, helping to douse the flames of rage still boiling inside of me.

Swallowing the remaining contents of the bottle in one more chug, I toss it into the trashcan next to the fridge. The loud clatter of the bottle hitting the others already in the trashcan echoes in the small room. Opening the fridge, I grab for another and head off in search for Victoria. My mind is still lost in the conversation I had with Callie, but I know it will be Victoria helping to soothe my shattered soul. Her smile is the answer I need to push the demons of my past aside, especially those I chose to leave behind.

Victoria

The conversation renders me breathless, not knowing how it's possible. What would have happened had the bathroom not been occupied as it were? I would have never gone searching for Trey. What I hadn't expected was to find him having a conversation with Callie. I knew she was at the cookout, as I'd seen her when she arrived, but what I heard has shocked me.

She was pregnant? With his baby! They continued to argue before I decided to turn and leave, but not before I'd heard Trey's declaration: *I refuse to be tied down to any woman.* It was a blow I was *not* expecting.

I don't need to hear anymore. His statement is proof he isn't worth my time. In the beginning, I'd kept my distance to allow me time to resolve my own dilemma, but it seems to have backfired on me.

My legs automatically walk me outside the house, my destination unknown. All I care about is putting distance between Trey and myself. Eventually, I reach the table where Jimmy and his friends are sitting, their laughter a welcome ambiance.

"You have any more of that moonshine you can

share?" I ask him, determination in my eyes to erase what I've just heard.

He looks stunned at my request, but shakes it off just as quickly, pushing his mason glass in my direction. "Changed your mind about the hair?" he laughs out.

Grabbing for the glass, I comment, "I've got a really great aesthetician to take care of the problem." Lifting the glass off the table, I take a giant gulp. As the first time, the smell alone has me gagging, but I push past the aroma and swallow as fast as I can. Fire is the only description I can give as the liquid travels down my throat.

Coughing for air as I receive a bout of cheers from Jimmy and his friends, I still can't believe I've done it. "I believe we may have just made a country girl out of you!" Jimmy cheerfully boasts.

City or country girl, it doesn't matter which I am, because neither one will ever be good enough in Trey's eyes, regardless of how hard I try.

Trey

Why the fuck is Victoria taking so damn long? Standing outside the bathroom door, I'm drinking my third beer in the ten minutes she's been gone, wondering what's taking her so long. The door finally opens, only instead of finding Victoria exit, it's my Uncle Finn.

"Where's Victoria?" I ask. He gives me a baffled look when he comments, "Is she the one who was knocking earlier?"

The foul smell coming from the small bathroom informs me of why she must have left. "Light a damn match, Uncle Finn," I advise with a wave of my hand in front of my nose.

Walking away, I go search the other bathroom in the house, which is in my parents' room. She isn't in there, so it leaves me confused as to where the hell she could have gone. I didn't see her leave. Exiting the house, I return to the cookout and spot her from a distance and make my way over to her. She's sitting at Jimmy's table with his friends, the only girl in attendance. The sight has me rushing my steps to get to her faster.

Reaching her, she is lifting the all too familiar mason jar containing Jimmy's moonshine to her mouth. She takes a sip and her face grimaces.

"What the hell are you doing?" I ask, yanking the glass from her hand. She scowls at me before saying, "Hey, give that back," as she reaches across the table for the glass.

Ignoring her protest, I look to Jimmy. "How much of this shit did you give her?"

He shrugs. "I don't know. She took the glass from me. I guess she was looking to grow hair after all," he laughs out, initiating a round of laughter from his friends.

Victoria stands, trying to leave the table. "Where are you going, princess?" Jimmy asks her.

"Don't call her that," I snap at him, hating the way he's slurred the pet name I've given her.

"Why not? You do," she slurs.

"I'm going to pretend you didn't say that because

you're already drunk." Furiously glaring at Jimmy, I say, "Her name is Victoria. Use it," I order.

"No!" she argues. "I never gave you permission to use it, either, yet you still do," she declares with a slight sway. "I used to like you calling me that because I thought you cared, but you're nothing but a liar."

Jimmy is grinning at me when he says, "Maybe she'll like it better when I call her *princess.*" He takes a sip from his glass while giving Victoria a wink.

Raging mad he winked at her, I say, "Shut the fuck up, Jimmy."

"What's got up your ass? You're the one throwing out she's just your friend. What if I want her to be my friend, too?"

I'm about to tell his ass he isn't allowed to look at her anymore when she exclaims, "He doesn't deserve for me to be his friend!" She issues the declaration at me before stumbling away from the table.

What the fuck did she mean by that comment? Realizing she's completely escaped my presence, I begin to follow her. It's clear from the way she's looking around at her surroundings she has no clear destination in mind. I don't protest, but follow knowing it's best to let her walk off her drunken stupor. She's completely overwrought, for whatever reason, I have no clue.

She's far enough from the cookout for me to ask, "Where the hell are you going?"

She keeps marching as she shouts over her shoulder, "I don't know, but at least it won't be here!"

Her walk is turning into a drunken sway with each

step. It's a bit entertaining, so I keep following her, staring straight at her swaying ass. She must have decided the stables are her destination since she's walking in that direction.

Entering the stables, she pauses, looks first left then right before resuming her steps. She keeps looking back and forth between the horses until she stops directly in front of Betsy's stall. The horse already has her head sticking out and greets Victoria with a nudge to her head. I silently observe her until she reaches for the padlock to open the stall door.

"What are you doing?" I ask, practically running to stop her. My hand closes around hers and I pull it away. With scorn, she faces me.

"I'm leaving."

"You are not taking the horse. You're drunk out of your damn mind and will probably break your neck."

She releases an exasperated growl. "Fine. Then I'll walk." Stepping around me, she tries to exit the stable in the opposite direction she came from.

"You plan on walking all the way back to D.C. from here, princess?" I ask toward her retreating back.

"Yes!"

"Now that's just stupid. You'd never make it on foot." I know it's the alcohol speaking for her.

Still stomping forward, she reaches the back of the stable, lost as to where to go. "I tried to take Betsy but you wouldn't let me," she cries out.

Rolling my eyes, I step up behind her. "Victoria, you need to calm down." I exhale when she turns to face me, furiously searching for what to say. Crossing my arms over my chest, I wait for her to speak.

"I hate you!" Not what I was expecting. Her eyes are full of rage, matching the feeling coursing through my veins earlier.

Rolling my eyes at her, I say, "What's new, princess?"

"I already told you not to call me that!" she screams, fuming mad.

"Why not?"

"Why do you do that?"

"What?" The question is beginning to become old. Quirking my brow, I wait for her to clarify, because I *know* she will. "You either never answer or answer with a question. *You're* frustrating," she growls. "Just answer the damn question for once!" she demands.

"What was the question again?" I'm completely at a lost as to what she wants an answer to.

Grumbling, she says, "Why do you have to be such an asshole?" Before I have a chance to reply, she adds, "I don't want you to be an asshole, but you are," then shoves at my chest. Now I know it's the moonshine making her irate.

"What is it you want me to be?" I ask, testing her.

With the full moon coming in through the opening of the stalls, I can clearly see her eyes flickering back and forth, searching her mind. Her bottom lip is trapped between her teeth as she bites down on it. My thought of wishing it were my teeth biting down on it is broken when she declares, "*My asshole!*"

Shaking my hazy mind, I say, "I don't understand you

right now. Either you don't want me to be an asshole any longer, or be *your asshole.* Which one is it, princess?"

Without answering what I've asked, she says, "Why do you keep calling me that?"

"What? Princess?"

"Yes. It makes me believe you care when I know you don't."

She has my attention now. Stepping forward, I close the distance between us. "What makes you think I don't care?" Her mouth gapes open then closes. "What's wrong, *princess?* Got nothing to throw back at me?"

"Then prove it!" she demands.

I don't need any more encouragement than the demand she's given. My lips slam down onto hers, unable to resist kissing her, something I've wanted to do all night. My palms are possessively digging through her hair to keep her in place, not wanting to let her go. Our tongues duel, matching the need I know we've both been denying each other. The taste of the moonshine mixed with the sweetness I will forever associate with Victoria's kiss has me groaning with want.

My hands leave her hair to grab her ass, picking her up to take her into the only stall I know will be empty. Her legs are wrapped around my waist as I stumble forward into the stall and dropping down, my knees take the brunt of the fall. Lowering her down onto the hay covering the ground, she thrusts her hips up against my groin, having me practically lose my mind. Her hand reaches between us to squeeze my already hardened cock through my jeans. There is no way she will escape tonight without me making love to her. I won't be able to hold back.

Her fingers find the clasp of my jeans, unbuttoning them and reaching inside. The warmth of her palm wrapping around my shaft has me nearly coming when she begins to stroke it.

"Princess, you better be careful or I may just explode in your hand," I murmur into her mouth.

Unexpectedly, she shoves me off her so I'm now the one lying on the bed of hay.

"I'd rather you explode in my mouth," she says with a smile, already lowering herself down my body.

Dear Lord, I'm going to blow.

Squeezing my eyes shut to ward off the images of her sucking my cock in order for me not to explode like a randy teenager, I have to take a deep breath to say, "Another day. Right now I need to be inside you." I pull her up my body to kiss her.

Our kiss is fervent, urgent, no resistance in hiding how desperate we are for one another. I'm about to roll her back underneath me when she rapidly pulls her head back. "*You're mine,*" she growls, her nails digging into my chest. "I don't care what you say."

"And *you're mine,*" I declare in return.

"Are you sure?" she asks for confirmation, sounding sad and unsure.

"Of course." I don't know why, but there is no denying how true the words are.

"Then prove it," she demands, her hands reaching for the waistband of my pants to pull them down. Lifting my hips to help her remove them, she releases my erection and grabs it to guide it to her entrance. I don't know what has gotten into her, but it's fucking hot and has my dick demanding to be inside her.

"These are a lost cause," I notify, before ripping her panties away from her body. Her heat meets the head of my shaft and we both moan as it glides into her center.

The faint glow from the moonlight glistens off her face to highlight her features. Her eyes are full of desire as they stare down at me. Rocking her hips back and forth, she finds her own rhythm, leaving me to keep my eyes locked onto hers. Her palms push down onto my chest with every whimpered moan she lets out. My own hands are digging into her waist, helping to encourage her movements; not that she needs any; she is doing a well enough job of keeping a perfect rhythm to push us closer to completion.

Her whimpers grow into desperate moans. The walls surrounding my cock begin to tighten, a sign she is near to coming. Her speed increases and her fingers grasp onto my shoulders, and will most likely leave marks to match the scrapes from the hay digging into my ass; a souvenir of my reckless thinking from having sex outdoors. Better my ass than hers because I can't imagine marking the perfection of her skin.

"Oh, God, Trey!" she moans louder, encouraging me to say, "Fuck, princess. You feel so fucking good." And she does, along with how beautiful she looks above me.

She throws her head back and the tips of her hair stroke against my thighs, increasing the fire traveling through my veins. She looks like a fucking goddess as she rides my dick. With a powerful cry, she reaches her completion.

One . . . Two . . . Three more strokes in and out of her and I follow her over the edge, groaning out her name in return.

Exhausted, she slumps down to lay across my chest. Both our chests are rising and falling in unison as we pant to catch our breath. Releasing my grip on her waist, my one hand wraps completely around it while the other strokes up and down her back.

"I never believed that crap about make up sex until now," she breathlessly laughs out into the crook of my neck. "Totally worth the fight," she says, making me laugh along with her.

She snaps her head up to look down at me, her finger grazing across my lip. "You should smile more often," she says, her own smile beaming down at me. "You're much more handsome when you do." She leans down to place a quick kiss on my lips.

"Are you trying to say I'm an ogre when I don't?" I ask.

"No, but I love it when you smile," she says, making me grow soft inside.

"Aren't I the one who's supposed to feed you all these mushy compliments?"

She lowers her head back down onto my shoulder. "I wish you would."

Her request leaves me speechless. I've never had to compliment a girl to catch her attention. Had they wanted them, I would have sent them walking. I wasn't going to waste my breath chasing after them, yet Victoria's comment has me regretting not doing so with her.

My dick begins to soften inside her and normally it

would be when I'm tossing the girl off me. However, I'm clutching tighter to Victoria's body to keep her from moving. Perplexed as to what got us in this position, I find myself asking, "Victoria? Why were you drinking the moonshine?" She doesn't respond immediately, advising me she may have drifted off to sleep.

Shaking her, she utters, "I wanted to forget."

Her response has me completely confused. "Forget what?"

Instead of a coherent response, she asks, "Why is the room spinning when my eyes are closed?"

Oh, shit, she's completely gone.

"Because you're drunk."

She grumbles into my neck, but doesn't speak anymore. Instead, I hear her breath growing heavy, letting me know she's already falling asleep, and from the bout of sex we just had, I'm a bit exhausted myself. This girl knows how to wear me out sometimes. My eyes begin to grow weary and I struggle to keep them open. Thinking to myself: *Maybe a little nap will help.* I surrender to the darkness with her happily still in my arms.

Chapter Sixteen

Aftereffects

Victoria

AN EXCRUCIATING PAIN radiates throughout my head. The sound of horses whinnying reverberates around me, adding to the pounding inside my skull. I'm in the process of groaning when ice-cold water cascades down on me, making me sit up, gasping for air.

"Rise and shine!" an annoying voice screams out.

I'm still trying to take in why the hell I'm drenched when another voice yells, "What the fuck, Callie?" Trey's voice booms and bounces around in my skull. This time I wince from the pain. Holding my pounding head, I muster enough energy to open my eyes and the piercing glare of the sunlight has me closing them shut again.

"Just thought y'all needed some help waking up this

morning." Callie's sarcastic tone sounds like nails on a chalkboard.

"Why are you two yelling?" I groan, wishing they would just shut up. The screech of a horse's whinny makes it worse. An unpleasant shiver from being wet travels down my spine, making me remember how I was awoken. Snapping my eyes, I ask, "Did you throw water on me?"

"I threw water on both of y'all. You need to get your dirty asses up and out of my stables."

I can both feel and hear Trey when he says, "Do I need to remind you who the stable really belongs to?"

Confused in regard to their conversation, I ask, "Why are we in the stables?"

Callie's snicker can be heard loud and clear in my condition. "Figures you'd screw her in here. Old habits don't die, do they, Trey?"

Habits?

Screw who?

At this point, I couldn't care less who she's referring to. All I know is I have to pee and there is a disturbing feeling in my stomach. Attempting to stand, I find it difficult because I feel lightheaded, as if I'm drunk. Maybe I am, considering how the room is spinning. Holding my head, I reach to try to balance myself, the contents of my stomach refusing to keep rooted come straight up. Hunching over, I puke up nothing but bile onto the ground. The feel of a hand pulling my hair back is welcome, yet embarrassing when I realize it belongs to Trey.

When I have nothing left in my stomach, I slowly raise my hand up to wipe at my mouth.

"You better now?" Trey asks, his voice booming in my head once more.

"Sorry," I apologize. It comes out close to a whisper since my throat is so dry.

He brushes strands of hair away from around my face. I feel like shit. I can't imagine what I look like. With pity in his eyes, he's says, "You sort of do." Wait, did I say my thoughts out loud?

At this point, it doesn't matter. All I want to do is pee and being drenched is not helping since I'm now shivering from the cold.

Rubbing at my arms, I take in my surroundings, confirming we *are* in the stables. My mind is strenuously wondering why, however my bladder is demanding I find out later. Right now, it takes precedence with its request.

"I've got to pee really bad," I find myself informing Trey, making him chuckle. Even his simple chuckle has me wincing from the sound. Taking my first step forward is more difficult than I expected as my mind is keeping me from staying balanced. The world around me only spins faster when my body is lifted up against his chest.

"What are you doing?" I utter, still trying to keep myself from repeating what I just finished doing.

"I don't think you're ready to walk," he voices, already marching with me in his arms towards the exit of the stable. With the way I'm feeling, I can't argue, nor will I. Being in Trey's arms is a much more pleasant idea than walking. The moment we exit and the sun hits my eyes, I wince, digging my face into the crook of his neck to block out the sun. It takes a couple of minutes to get to the house, the entire way I'm taking deep breaths to keep from hurling.

Entering the house, we both receive curious faces staring back at us, but Trey walks straight past them with a nod and a *"Good morning"* to everyone, not stopping until we've reached the bathroom.

Depositing me in front of the door, he asks, "You going to be okay on your own?"

Considering my condition before I reply, I say, "As long as nothing moves on me, yes." He laughs, and I grimace from the sound. Holding onto the wall to help guide me, I close the door behind me and make my way to the toilet, lifting up my dress and reaching for what *should* be my underwear, but they're not there.

Why the hell don't I have any underwear on?

Pushing the question aside because I have other concerns, I take care of my personal business and head to the sink next to wash up afterwards. Looking into the mirror, the sight staring back at me is frightful. My stomach is still in knots, but hopefully a shower will help.

Thirty minutes later, I am bathed, dressed, and making my way to the kitchen area where most of the family is gathered. When I enter, all conversation comes to a halt, eyes awkwardly staring at me. Trey is nowhere to be found, leaving me feeling out of place.

"You hungry, dear," Mrs. Johnson kindly asks. The thought of food has me gagging and my hand comes up to my mouth to keep it from coming out. "Oh, dear. Did you get into Jimmy's moonshine last night?"

Shamefully nodding my head, she sympathetically

looks at me. "In that case, take a seat. I'll get you some-thing for those symptoms." Not in the mood to dispute her command, I take a seat next to Luke, searching for his wife only to find her absent. "Where's Becca?"

"She went to go check on one of the mares ready to deliver. She should be here soon since she's been gone over an hour."

"Mare?" Why would Becca be checking on a horse.

With a smile, Luke answers my thoughts. "She's our local vet." With my brows raised high, I nod in under-standing, then just as quickly my eyes go wide in dismay. Does that mean she was in the stable when Trey had to shamefully carry me out? The notion has me feeling sick again, but I force myself to push it down.

Minutes later, Trey's mother places a glass of orange juice, coffee, and some aspirin in front of me, encouraging me to drink. Without protest, I swallow the pills, hoping they take effect soon as my head is still pounding.

"Did you have fun last night?" Luke asks after taking a sip of his coffee. Taking a sip of my own, I try to remem-ber myself.

"I think so. At least I did up until I began drinking Jimmy's moonshine. Everything after that ceases to exist in my mind," I find myself telling him as I remember why I went in search of him. The memory has my heart filling with sorrow.

Luke's booming laughter is a reminder of Trey's, but not a welcome one, as it has me wincing from the pound-ing still hammering in my head. "Trey was telling us y'all will be leaving soon. It's going to be sad to see you leave."

This surprises me. "When did he tell you this?"

"Right before you walked in. He went to take a shower in my parents' bedroom. I guess he got a phone call and was pretty upset over it."

Still not understanding why it would cause us to leave, I continue probing for answers. "Do you know why?" I'm nervous it may be concerning me.

"Something about Emily walking," he says. "He was pretty upset over it and sort of blew up, claiming y'all were leaving soon."

Oh, goodness. That would clearly upset him considering how much he cares for the baby, but it's not reason enough to leave his family when we've just barely arrived. Mrs. Johnson places a plate full of food in front of me, breaking my thoughts. And although my stomach is protesting, she orders, "Eat up. It will help settle your stomach."

I have no right to disrespect her orders, so I pick up a piece of toast and bite into it, knowing starch is the best remedy for a hangover. Maybe if I put a *very* small dent into it, she won't be too upset with me.

Eventually I'm pushing the plate away, having eaten as much as my unsettled stomach can handle. Trey exits his parents' bedroom wrapped only in a towel. He walks past without any acknowledgment that he's seen me. As Luke had mentioned, he holds a grimace on his face, clearly upset as he marches past everyone in a hurry.

Becca enters the house, pulling my attention over to her. She has a teasing twinkle in her eyes when she takes a seat directly in front me.

"All dried up now?" she asks, causing me to turn beet red when I realize she *was* indeed in the stable when I awoke.

"Dried up?" Luke asks.

Before I can conjure a lie, Becca is giving him the details. "Callie had the nerve to dump a bucket of dirty water on her and Trey to wake them. Apparently, someone isn't happy he's moving on."

Luke whistles in response while Mrs. Johnson is inquiring, "When did y'all leave to the stable?"

"They fell asleep there," Becca informs her, taking a piece of leftover toast off the plate before taking a bite.

I'm crimson red. There isn't any way to disguise my shameful actions as Mrs. Johnson's wide eyes peer over at me. "I see," she says, her eyebrows coyly raising high with her lips turned up to one side in understanding.

"It was the moonshine," I divulge, still trying to figure out why I would wake there. I'm sure by how we were both fully clothed that nothing occurred between Trey and I. All the times we've had sex, he's pretty adamant to disrobe me first, so sex could not be a reason. I'm beginning to wonder if we just passed out drunk there.

Trey steps into the room minutes later while I'm still lost in my thoughts. All eyes turn to him. "What?" he confusedly asks to the room.

"Leave it up to you to find a way to break my rules," Mrs. Johnson huffs before returning to the main area of the kitchen.

He looks completely lost as to what his mother meant, while I on the other hand am curious to ask him why we were in the stable. It'll just have to wait, because I don't want him disclosing the reasons in front of everyone.

He walks to stand beside his mother. "Are you sure you have to leave so soon?" she asks him, a plead for him to reconsider in her tone.

"Yeah, momma. I'm sorry. I've got a lot of shit going on and I should get back to it."

"Why do we have to leave?" I plead along with his mother, saddened he's considering leaving already.

His jaw is tight when he says, "Because I said so."

"*Because I said so* isn't a reason," I argue back.

"I said we're leaving, so we're leaving," he rages in return with a fury to not challenge him.

Ignoring his wrath, I say, "No. We just got here and you deserve to spend time with your family." I'm hoping by using his family as an excuse he'll reconsider.

His brows arch in shock that I challenged him. "I wasn't asking for your approval. We. Leave. In. The. Morning," he says, gritting his teeth with every word.

"I wasn't giving it." His jaw tightens again as I narrow my eyes. He closes what little distance he can between the two of us, leaning down so his hands rest on the table and his face is as close as it can be to mine. "Let's get one thing straight. We may have come because of you, but I'm tired of putting my life on hold because of your careless mistakes. We're going back because I said we are, so go get your shit packed and be ready by morning before I end up dragging your royal ass out of here against your will."

For a mere second, the room is thick with tension. Internally I'm screaming to fight, but the anguish his words fill me with keep me silent.

The sound of a hard slap has Trey's head coming forward, missing my forehead by a mere inch, frightening me. Trey holds the back of his head with his gaping mouth hanging open when he pulls his head back.

We both face his mother, who is standing beside him with her finger pointing closely to his face. "You apologize right this minute, Junior. I did not raise a boy to be disrespecting a girl with those kind of words."

With his hand still resting on the back of his head, he faces me, eyes filled with wrath. Without saying a word, he stomps off, ignoring her request, leaving without giving me the apology his mother has commanded. The slamming of the back door has me flinching in my seat as my eyes become glassy and my lips tremble from the threatening tears I'm holding at bay, refusing to make a further embarrassment of myself in front of his family.

Standing, I leave without excusing myself as fast as my legs can take me to Chrissie's room. Inside, I enclose myself in the confines of the empty room, except for my cat whose meow has the dam of tears running down my face. I don't know what it is I've done, but there is no mistaking the loathing Trey feels for me. Not even his mother can make him see any different.

Trey

What the fuck just happened?

I lost it. Completely fucking lost it without intending to do so, and my pride kept me from apologizing like my mother and my conscience were screaming I do.

My ears are still ringing as the pain radiates from my momma's backhanded slap. Maybe the embarrassment of my mother slapping me upside the head is what had me walking out. Shit, I'm not a little kid anymore, yet the woman treats me as if I were one.

I find my father near his truck, throwing a sack of feed into the back. He eyes me coming up to him and stops to take his gloves off.

"Heard what happened in the stable this morning from Becca. I've already had a talk with Callie."

"Yeah, well, can't really blame her."

He doesn't disagree, but instead asks, "Wanna talk about it?"

I want to answer no, but find myself speaking regardless. I tell him everything, starting from the beginning when I found Callie in the side room up until when we awoke this morning drenched in water, sparing him the full details of my sexcapade with Victoria in the stable.

When done, all I receive is silence, which I had not expected.

"You going to say anything?" I ask.

He looks at me uneasily. "What is it you want me to say?"

"Something. Tell me what it is I'm supposed to do," I practically plead, hoping he'll be able to give me an answer.

He shakes his head in disapproval. "This isn't my

problem to solve, it's yours." I groan in disappointment, raking my hand down my face. "Tell me something. Do you care about this girl?" he curiously requests.

I'm taken aback by his question. "What does this have to do with me caring about her?"

With a pinch of his lips, he shrugs his shoulders. "Because if you do, then you already have the answer."

I told him everything hoping he can help me figure out what the hell to do about Victoria, not to further confuse me. I told myself I wouldn't sleep with her anymore, drunk or sober, knowing it would only complicate matters. I had come to the decision of eventually returning to the city and going our separate ways after my last talk with my dad. There was no way things would work out between us with how different we are. Only after falling asleep with her the other night was I left wondering if it was the best decision. She made me smile, something which is rarely accomplished nowadays.

The phone call this morning had me reverting back to my old ways. I'd returned to the point of resenting her when Abigail excitingly conveyed how Emily had taken her first steps this morning. It threw me into a fit of rage, hating how I wasn't there to watch my baby girl take her first steps, all because I was stuck babysitting Victoria. It plummeted me into a vortex of chaotic emotions.

My father is still patiently waiting for my answer, however I can't give him one. "I don't know," I confess, not completely knowing if what I feel is real, or a figment of my imagination.

Needing a distraction, I keep myself occupied working with my father for the remainder of the day. I needed time to think. After sex last night, this morning's episode, and the conversation with my father, I'm left more confused than ever. At the end of the day, I still couldn't give myself a solid answer as to what I was going to do.

Upon returning for an early dinner, every member of my family was now playing Victoria's protector. They ensured I wouldn't be left alone with her. Especially Becca, who was glaring at me throughout the entire dinner. My balls were starting to shrivel from fear she'd castrate me in my sleep with the gazes she was giving me.

At the end of dinner, my father decided to pull me aside with my brother, requesting we head outside to have beers and just catch up. I couldn't resist. It grew late and before I knew it, we headed off to bed. The house was draped in darkness and everyone else asleep when I entered with my father late into the night.

On the way to my room, I find myself walking towards my sister's room where Victoria is staying, only instead of her being alone, my sister Chrissie is sleeping next to her in bed, doing exactly what I had planned on doing.

Unable to resist, my feet lead me over to the side of the bed, kneeling down to look directly at her sleeping form. My fingers brush away a strand of hair, causing her to lightly stir, but not fully awaken. I had hoped she would so it would give me the opportunity to finally apologize, but I'm not lucky enough. Knowing it's late and I'll have to be waking shortly to leave, I brush a kiss across her temple, whispering, "I'm sorry, princess." I know she can't hear me, but I still feel the need to say it.

She's correct. I *am* an asshole for my actions. It's who I am, and who I most likely will always be. But to be *her* asshole is asking too much of me, and this is where she'll unfortunately be disappointed in me as well.

I watch as my mother hands Victoria a bag full of sweet tea packets. Apparently, Victoria has accomplished learning how to make her favorite brew from my mother after all.

Victoria reaches in to give my mother one last hug, holding each other longer than expected. The unshed tears in both their eyes when they pull apart has my heart aching.

"You are always welcome here, with or without Junior. You hear me now?" Victoria nods in understanding. My mother looks to me next and I reach in to hug her, a sniffle coming from her when I wrap my arms around her waist. The sound has me regretting my decision. However, it's made and it's time to go.

Pulling away, she reaches up to place her palm on my cheek. With her still glassy eyes, she requests, "You be nice to her. She's a sweet girl." She whispers the request so only I can hear.

Blankly staring at her, I can neither nod nor deny her wish, but hug her one more time. My father has agreed to drive us to the airport an hour away. Russell refused to fly back in to our little crop dusting runway. I'm pretty sure my Uncle Finn didn't mind us flying in that morning, but I couldn't argue with Russell any longer. He was doing me a favor by flying us back and forth on such short notice.

Parting ways with my family at home, Victoria and I are soon climbing into my father's truck to drive to the airport. The entire drive is made mostly in silence with only the radio to entertain us. Since the truck is a single cab, it put Victoria between my father and I, her body nudged closely to mine. From her stiff posture as she clutches her cat's carrier to her chest, I can almost feel her hatred towards me. It makes for a very awkward and uncomfortable ride to the airport. Over an hour later, we're driving up to the plane as it sits waiting for us. Victoria quickly says her goodbyes to my father before making her way into the aircraft.

Sternly looking me in the eyes, he gives me one more piece of advice. "Whatever it is you decide, you remember you'll have to return home one day, so you keep that in mind when you make your decision," he says, adding another question to my ever-confused mind.

I give him one last hug goodbye and follow Victoria inside to find her conversing with Russell. I make it just in time to catch Victoria telling him, "Thank you. And of course you will be compensated for your time and fuel it requires for the trip."

"That will be fine," he happily tells her. She returns a satisfied smile before they part ways. Following Russell into his cockpit, I ask, "What was that all about?"

He's making notes in his journal when he answers. "She wants me to fly her to East Hampton Airport. I don't see it as a problem as we have the jet all day," he states, finally looking up to me for approval.

I'm enraged he's already agreed to her request, but don't argue, knowing exactly why it is she wants him to fly her there. "That's fine. Thanks, Russell." The acceptance is not out of compliance, but to keep her satisfied.

Making my way back to the main area of the aircraft, Russell follows so he can close the hatch. I find Victoria already seated and buckled, her cat safely secured in the seat next to her. Her eyes are focused on the view outside the window, never once acknowledging me when I take a seat across the aisle from her.

The sound of the engines comes to life and has me pushing my despair aside. Minutes later, as we taxi down the runway and climb into the air, I find myself looking out of the window, mourning the loss of my family.

"Are you going to ignore me the entire trip?" I ask Victoria. At first she ignores my question, until I push her, "Well?"

She snaps her head in my direction, fury radiating from her eyes. "I planned to, but please clarify which mood you're currently in so I can better prepare myself for what conversation you are trying to have with me."

I was not expecting *this* response. "I just wanted to know," I find myself uttering.

Her head twists to face the window, fury still in her features. I wait another thirty minutes before I brave to push again. "What made you decide to run to your parents after all?"

"I'm not running home. I'm doing as my father requested me to do before we left," she says into the window.

"But is it what you really want?"

She remains silent for a couple of seconds, until I faintly hear her reply, "I don't think I have much of a choice anymore."

I hate her response. It indicates she's doing as ordered. It's what she hates most in her life, to be told what to do. "You could have returned to Seattle," I inform her.

There is a heavy silence for another minute before I hear her sigh. "There's nothing for me there, anyway," she faintly murmurs, still staring out the window. "I just don't want to be alone right now."

I should be telling her she won't be alone if she were to return with me, but I can't. Instead, I foolishly remain silent.

Several hours later, we're landing in the Hamptons and I find myself asking, "Are you going to be okay? Do you have a ride or would you like me to accompany you in a taxi just in case?"

"I'll be fine," she crossly clips out.

Still unsatisfied with her response, I say, "I don't like knowing you're alone, Victoria. It's not safe."

"You've done enough, Trey. Your babysitting duties are over," she delivers as she grabs for her cat and luggage, quickly exiting the plane after she says it.

Ignoring her words, I follow her inside the terminal, keeping a safe distance between us, needing to ensure she safely gets into a cab for my own peace of mind. When she does, it's without a backwards glance. As she drives off, I stand there, watching her depart, feeling as if I've made the biggest mistake of my life, yet I did nothing to stop her.

Chapter Seventeen

Regrets

Trey

STARING DOWN AT Abigail's most recent contract Benjamin had sent over, it reminds me of the last contract I had in my hands. However, this one wasn't drawn up by Victoria. I know because she should still be on leave from work, which is why I'm meticulously reading it word for word; at least I'm trying to. I can't seem to focus. I've read the same paragraph four times; the words are beginning to blend together in a blur. I'm wishing it *were* her who had drawn it up, then I would trust it were all correct and I wouldn't have to be wasting my time.

In the background, I listen as Abigail scrambles to search for Emily's favorite toys while speaking on the phone. Today she has strength training and on these days she needs to keep Emily as occupied as possible since it's indoors. Normally Matt would accompany her when he's in town to help with Emily, but today he has other plans—plans, in which, I am to join him.

She says something into the phone, sounding alarmed, but I don't clearly hear, choosing to ignore since it's *her* conversation. I did catch the tail end of my name, though, and as much as I want to know why she's mentioning it, I choose not to at the moment. It's for the best. If not, we may end up bickering again. This past week all she's done is try to interrogate me about my trip back home, but she hasn't accomplished getting anything out of me.

"He did what?" she exclaims into the phone. Averting my eyes in her direction, I find her narrowed eyes glaring at me. She says nothing more, still listening into the phone, nodding every so often. She lets out a frustrated huff and moves on in the direction of her room, leaving me to roll my eyes at her crazy antics.

Returning my attention back to the document in front of me, I try reading the paragraph another time, but it's useless. I have no drive to focus. Why the fuck do we pay Benjamin's office so much damn money if in the end we have to review the damn contract before Abigail signs it? I already know the answer to my own question when I finish: *Because I don't trust the person who drew it up.* I never trust anyone when it comes to business.

I trusted Victoria at one point, though.

"You ready?" Matt asks, standing near me, ready to leave.

Abigail's footsteps can be heard making their way in

our direction. "Hold on. I need to have a talk with him before you leave," Abigail hails from the hallway leading her into the living room. She's carrying Emily in her arms, handing her to Matt when she reaches him. "Can you take her outside for a little bit? I don't want her to get frightened by my yelling."

Confusedly, he takes the baby from her hold and her hands go firmly on her hips with her all too familiar glare. "He has some explaining to do," she hisses.

By the way she delivered the statement, I know she's pissed.

"What?" I ask, having absolutely no idea why she's raging. "Did I forget to do something?"

"Go," she orders to Matt with a tilt of her head towards the backyard. He seems worried at first, but leans down to kiss the side of her mouth when he tells her, "Don't kill him, beautiful. You have to remember he's the one who keeps you out of jail."

Without hesitating, she replies, "I'm pretty sure Julio would help me hide the body." Matt laughs at her reply, but from the fury in her eyes, I don't doubt she's considering it.

"Vamonos, bonita, your mommy is about to get crazy," Matt tells Emily then leaves as requested through the back doors. When the click of the door is heard, Abigail attacks. "I just finished talking with your momma." The statement furiously comes out of her mouth.

I'm on the couch looking up to Abigail as she stands directly in front of me. I have to crane my neck to look up at her, but the comment has me jerking it back. "What the hell are you doing talking to my momma?" I reply, already having a clue where the hell this is going.

"I talk to your momma every now and then because she's the closest I'll ever get to having one." Shit, now she's managed to make me feel guilty about my first comment. "You know what she told me?" she asks, her head cocked to one side, not waiting for my response. "She told me what happened while you were there."

Shit. I grow nervous this may not end well. "Stay out of it. It's none of your business," I tell her, not really wanting to discuss the subject any further.

Guilt completely takes over every emotion I've carried from the moment I let Victoria walk away. I swear with every breath I take it feels as if my heart is shattering a bit more.

Abigail stomps her foot on the floor like an upset child. "It may not be my business, but dammit, Trey, how can you be such an asshole sometimes?"

I snort from the reminder of Victoria's words. "Tell me something I don't know," I grumble under my breath.

Leaning into the back of the couch, I throw the contract to my side, my arms defensively crossing over my chest as Abigail continues her speech.

"Is this why you've been acting like you have a thorn up your ass?" What the fuck? Now she's pointing out the obvious? "Is what your momma said true?"

What is it with women? They never make sense when they're pissed. "What did my momma say?" I ask, curious to know.

"She told me you came back because I said Emily began walking and acted a fool in front of Victoria."

Fuck . . . My mother has acquired an advocate. The woman has been on my ass about apologizing to Victoria and since I can't lie to her because she's my mother, she knows I haven't done so yet.

"Yeah, so," I foolishly quip back.

Her mouth falls open. "I told you on the phone she took her first steps, not walked."

I know where she's trying to go with this and trust me, I feel like the biggest dumbass in the world. "You made it sound like she began walking," I say, still regretting how I had jumped to conclusions. "She's walking now, isn't she? Had I stayed I would have *really* missed it," I say in my defense.

Emily hadn't actually started walking, but only took assisted steps by holding onto the couch. Abigail was so excited when she explained that I had blown it out of proportion by thinking she had actually begun walking.

Shamefully, I admit, "There's nothing I can do about it now, Abigail."

Shocked, her mouth gapes open. "Nothing you can do about it?" she exclaims. "Apologize to her!" she yells. "Maybe then she'll forgive you!"

"I can't."

"Why not?" she asks, still yelling.

"I just can't!" I throw back at her, frustrated because I don't have a reason. I hate the fact that I don't have the balls to apologize to her. Plenty of times I've tried calling her phone, but the moment I bring her number up, I can't push the button to deliver the call. Fear of rejection is my worst enemy at this point.

She throws her hands up in an exasperated growl. "You need to get your head out of your ass and do something about it! Your momma has already given me permission to slap you upside the head!" she says, reminding me of the last time I got slapped upside my head by my mother. "She's hoping I can knock some sense into you!" My mouth opens to argue, but another angry outburst interrupts me.

"You had one good thing. One!" She holds her finger up to show how many I had. "And you go and screw it up!" Her voice pitches higher with each sentence. Now I know why she asked Matt to take Emily outside. She would have been crying by now from hearing Abigail's screams.

Rising out of my seat because I'm tired of having to look up to her, I say, "I didn't have shit. She was never mine to begin with. Do I need to remind you she was engaged when I started fucking her?" Shit, wrong choice of words, but the resentment of being reminded of how this all started encouraged my words.

"She wasn't engaged the last time you saw her, Trey. Or have *you* forgotten that?" Abigail challenges. "I like her, and I'm not the only one. Your entire family likes her. So you better do something to fix this so you at least have a chance with her," she says, shoving her finger into my chest.

It's meant to frighten me, however all it does is irritate me further. Her declaration adds to the guilt my soul has been harboring.

"What if I don't want a chance with her?" I croak out.

Abigail looks taken aback by my response. Slowly she retreats, shaking her head in disappointment. "I don't believe you," she chokes out in clear denial. "I've known you since the beginning of *this* life, Trey," she says, referring to her present memory, what's she's known since the day she awoke in the hospital. "And I know you want more than one night stands. You want what Matt and I have."

She appears saddened from her speech, and to be honest, I'm feeling the same way. "Love, and you deserve it." Her lips quiver and her eyes turn glassy when she finishes.

Pulling her to my chest, I engulf her in my arms to soothe her. She wraps her arms around my waist, holding tight. "I just want you to be happy," she says into my chest.

As I hold her, I stare outdoors to watch Matt playing with Emily, my heart swelling. She's correct. At one point in my life, I had wanted what they have: Love. I never thought I would ever have the chance at it, though, so I gave up the notion of believing it was possible. Is she right? Did I fuck up the only chance I had at finding out if I could have love?

Matt takes his seat in the chair as I lean up against the wall at his side.

"I don't understand your fascination with tattoos. The shit is permanent, man. They're forever," I say with a slight protest of his decision.

"Exactly, which is why I'm getting it," he replies, seemingly satisfied with himself. "I want to die happy knowing I have their names branded on my skin."

I can't really argue with that since he's getting the names of the two most important girls in his life permanently inked on his skin. If I weren't against tattoos, I would consider doing the same with my mother's name.

"How is it Abigail agreed to this? You've both been arguing about it for months," I say, remembering the bickering whenever the conversation arose.

With his mischievous grin, he says, "I promised to not get *her* name." I'm confused since I haven't seen the design he's chosen.

The tattoo artist removes the white film he'd placed above Matt's heart. Lifting a mirror up for Matt to view, I lean in to take in the design, shaking my head in awe. The fucker found a loophole in his promise.

"Abigail is going to flip, you know that right?" I ask, reminding him how much of a protest she put up. She refused to allow him to *"permanently mar his beautiful skin with her name."* Matt, on the other hand, thought otherwise. In his heart, he knows Abigail and him are meant for each other. They are forever, hence getting a tattoo to prove it.

"Does it look okay?" The tattoo artist asks in regards to the design.

With a wide smile, Matt replies, "Perfect." I can't say I disagree with him. The design is perfect.

"She did make you promise not to get her name," I say, affirming the obvious reason for his choice.

Above his heart is a design with two names to form the shape of a heart. On one side is Emily's name, on the other is *Beautiful.* The buzz of the machine begins and Matt looks to me for a distraction.

"Care to explain what was going on with Abigail?" he asks, because he really has no clue. Julio arrived minutes after Abigail and I were done, not giving Matt a chance to find out why he was sent outdoors with Emily.

"She's berating me about Victoria," I find myself shamefully admitting as I return to our earlier conversation, which is still fresh in my mind.

"What's going on between you? You didn't look too happy when you came back last week," he says, stating the same as Abigail had claimed. They're most likely conspiring against me; only Matt wouldn't push me as hard as Abigail has been doing.

"She's claiming I should go after her."

"Why haven't you?" Obviously, he would side with his wife on the subject.

Raking my hand through my hair, I say, "I don't know." I sigh, frustrated from not knowing myself. "I know I fucked up, but . . ." I trail off, unable to finish my thought.

"What made you run?" he asks, knowing exactly what happened without me having to tell him.

"I got scared," I confess. "The night before we left, something happened. Something I wasn't expecting."

This earns me an arched brow. "She started getting possessive over me. I panicked. I've never let a girl get close enough for that to happen. Yet she did it without trying."

This causes Matt to laugh and the tattoo artist warns

him to keep still. Clearing his throat, he comments, "So you dumped her because she was calling you her boyfriend."

"Not exactly," I grumble under my breath. I recall the memory of Victoria above me, her nails possessively digging into my skin when she declared, "You're mine," and I'd furiously repeated it back to her. "I woke up the next morning realizing it was time to run."

The buzz of the needle overtakes our silence, although the tension is thick in the air. "Tell me something," he requests. "How did you feel when you found out about the tabloids? Like *really* feel?"

"I was fucking pissed. You know that," I remind him.

He has a gleam in his eyes when he asks, "Why?"

I'm taken aback by his question. "Why the fuck do you think I was pissed? They were claiming she was engaged."

His grin widens. "Exactly. You were pissed because you thought she belonged to someone else and not you," he reasons. "I would have been just as furious had they said the same about Abigail."

I cannot argue. I was pissed for that specific reason.

"It's probably too late," I voice, wondering if it really is. It's been too long since I've seen her. Her family has probably brainwashed her and she's most likely back on track to her debutant lifestyle.

"It's never too late," Matt claims. "Imagine had I given up on Abigail after Lisa showed up at our door. I would have married her instead of Abigail."

"Really?" I ask, not realizing he had thought of it at one point.

He shrugs the shoulder not being worked on. "Good thing I didn't. Love is worth fighting for."

What the fuck is up with everyone claiming I'm in love? "I'm not in love," I utter in denial.

"Love. Lust. Like. They're all the same and start somewhere, right? The point is, you should never give up."

Leave it up to the want-to-be love doctor to be the voice of reason.

Victoria

Two weeks have passed since Trey left me at the airport. The Hamptons were not the answer I needed to forget Trey. On the contrary, I had constant reminders with the lectures and glares I received from my parents. After two days of constantly being reminded of my mistakes, I left. It wasn't a tough decision to make, however it was one I will most likely live with for the rest of my life. My father gave me one ultimatum while I was there: marry Andrew as planned, or be disowned. I chose the latter. There was no way I was going to allow anyone to dictate my decisions anymore, and marrying Andrew would have been a trap. I'd be forever captive in a life without happiness.

Having returned to Seattle, I started work the next day, throwing myself into my cases to help keep me distracted. It aided to an extent, until I arrived to my condo at night and was reminded of the only man who has ever stepped foot into it.

The ping of a new message breaks my thoughts. Opening the messenger app on my laptop, dread swells up inside of me when I read the message.

Benjamin: Have you gotten the contract back from Abigail Adams?

Victoria: No, I haven't.

Benjamin: The company needs it by tomorrow afternoon, so find out what's taking them so long.

Shit . . . I don't want to have to follow up with them. I was hoping they would have just returned the document in a timely manner after I had it couriered last week. I made sure there was nothing missing from the contract, having read it over six particular times myself before I sent it off. So why is it taking them so long to return it?

I'm left with no choice but to do as requested by Benjamin and contact them. Opening up my email, I begin the formal message needed to be sent to the both of them. Minutes later, I send it off. Closing my email out and returning my attention back to the file I was working on, my office phone rings a few moments later.

"Victoria Montgomery speaking."

"Why didn't you just call me?" A deep, familiar voice asks from the other end. My stomach bottoms out as my breath lodges in my throat.

"Hello, Mr. Johnson." I remain cordial, regardless the fury traveling through my blood.

"Princess?" The endearment comes out low and husky from the other end.

"Don't call me that," I find the strength to deliver.

"Why not?" Why am I not surprised he would answer with a question? I ignore the stab of pain I receive from it, because in all reality, I do miss him huskily calling me that name.

"Because you don't deserve to call me that anymore," I grit out, holding back the anguish to scream the words. "Mr. Johnson," I repeat, trying to keep my professionalism. "It's imperative the contract be signed and returned by tomorrow morning at the latest."

"So you drew up the contract yourself?" he asks, somehow sounding delighted with the fact.

Taking a calming breath, I say, "Yes, I did. So if you'd please have Ms. Adams sign it as soon as possible, I'd be forever grateful."

"Forever, huh?"

Why is he continuing on with this conversation? I'm starting to become aggravated from the restraint I have to use to keep from going off on him. "Mr. Johnson, just have her sign the damn contract and let me know when I can send a courier to retrieve it," I inform him before slamming the phone down onto its cradle.

The conversation has my stomach in knots. Taking a deep breath to ward off the sensation arising inside of me, my eyes close and I try to focus on a happier thought. It's useless since my happier thoughts are all of him, and it's contrary to what I'm attempting to accomplish: forgetting him.

The night guard walks me to my car as he's been doing for the past two weeks when I leave work. The week I was gone achieved the desired result, and the paparazzi realized it was time to move on. There was no story to pursue if the source was no longer around.

Nevertheless, Benjamin insisted I have a security guard escort me to my car every night since I always left the office so late. Better safe than sorry, he claimed.

Arriving at my condo thirty minutes later, I enter it and immediately go to my room to change. Now in more comfortable attire, I move into the kitchen next. These past couple of days I have been keeping a strenuous schedule to distract myself and I haven't been eating properly, which is most likely the cause of my unusual symptoms. I'm fatigued and nothing seems to appeal to me.

Opening my fridge and staring at the empty shelves, I make a mental note to bribe the housekeeper to stock the fridge this week. I'm about to grab a bottled water when the doorbell rings.

That's odd. I'm not expecting anyone.

I stiffen with alarm. Swallowing, I grab for my new phone, since I never got my old one back from Julio, and call downstairs to the doorman. He answers my call on the second ring and when I ask if he had sent anyone upstairs he replies with a "No."

It can only mean they must have come through the parking garage. The doorbell rings again and I'm still hesitant to answer. This time there is a knock, and with leaded footsteps I head to my door.

"Do you wish for me to call the police, Ms. Montgomery?" The doorman requests as I look through the peephole to find Trey standing on the other side.

Letting out my breath, I tell him, "No. I'm fine. Thank you for your time," then end the call and open the door. "What do you want?"

Holding up the contract I had delivered over a week ago he claims, "I got the contract signed for you."

Narrowing my eyes at him, my blood slowly rises to unusual temperatures.

"How did you get into the building?" I ask, addressing the question still lingering in my mind. In his usual Trey form, he nonchalantly shrugs his shoulder.

"You gave me the code to get in, remember?"

Shit. I did at one point.

I'm ready to tell him to fuck off, yet the yearning from seeing him again keeps me from doing so. "I told you I would have a courier sent for it," I tell him, my teeth clenched tight as I struggle to bring my erratic heart under control as it pounds against my chest.

He stares back at me, sorrow in his eyes. "I know, but I really wanted to see you," he says, an admission I was unprepared for. "Please, Victoria, just let me say what I need to say and I'll leave afterwards," he pleads.

Considering my options, I find myself stepping back to grant him entrance. His broad body brushes past me, my knees becoming weak, threatening to buckle from the simple brush as his body passed mine.

Closing the door after he enters. I find him waiting for me near the doorway. He holds out the contract with his extended arm and I take it from him, walking over to place it inside my portfolio bag.

Turning, I find Trey patiently waiting, mere feet from me. Knowing he's in my condo has me lightheaded. The memories of the last time he was here are rapidly coursing through my mind. He gave me both arousal and despair in the course of twenty-four hours.

Feeling the need to sit before I collapse, I'm the one now brushing past him to my couch, wrapping my legs under my body, vigorously gripping my thighs to keep me from reaching out to him when he takes a seat on the other end.

He remains silent, simply staring at me until I command, "Speak," putting a little too much anxiety into the single word.

"I see you're still saucy," he professes.

Not liking his response, I reply, "It's no different than what you've delivered many times to me."

I watch him swallow. "I guess I deserve that," he utters, clearing his throat. He fidgets in his seat, having me grow perplexed over his behavior.

His eyes are full of despair when he begins speaking. "I'm sorry, Victoria, about everything. I shouldn't have been such an asshole to you and I regret my actions. If I could take them back, I would, but I can't." He swallows again, this time grief overtaking his features. "I shouldn't have said those things. It was wrong of me and it was my stupidity speaking."

His declaration is what I have been wishing for from the moment we stepped onto the plane to leave Tennessee, yet now that he's delivered it, the sense of satisfaction is lacking. Instead, I'm full of remorse. I've been carrying around the pain of his rejection for the past two weeks, and it's as if I've become immune at this point to any apology he could have given.

"I wish I wouldn't have heard your words, either, but it's not easy to forgive and forget, Trey. What I would have preferred is for you to not have a reason to have to apologize," I inform him.

I give him time to respond, however he remains silent as he looks to the floor. His silence only fuels my resentment. My mind is screaming to tell him what I heard, but it would be too easy for him. Breathing to keep the nausea rising in my stomach, I remain glaring at him, waiting for a reaction. An imaginary dark cloud looms above us.

"So that's it?" he asks when his head rises.

I'm filled with the same sorrow he's staring back at me with, however the painful words I heard him declare to Callie are forever scarred in my mind. Those words are the reason for me saying in return, "That's it." I hold my breath, waiting for the rejection to come.

It never comes as he stands looking directly into my eyes when he says, "It was nice knowing you, princess." His final words slowly roll off his tongue.

He's almost at the door when I call out to him. "Trey." This brings him to a halt. My heart is heavy when I ask, "What was I to you this entire time? I deserve to know that much."

He looks taken aback from my request. "You were my friend," he says, answering as if I should have known.

With a forced smile, I reply, "Thanks for being a

friend when I needed one," feeling just as much the hypocrite Trey can be.

Giving me a curt nod, he resumes his steps and exits my condo. The sound of the click from the door closing has me taking my first breath since I saw him standing on the other side of the closed door. My heart is demanding I go running after him, but my sorrow is reminding me of why it's for the best he leave.

"How many times am I going to have to tell you, Callie? I'm not stupid enough to let any girl tie me down!"

Those are the words guiding my shattered heart.

Teetering on the verge of my most recent heartache, I've come to discover life will always find a way to test your decisions. I stare down at my bathroom counter in shock, wondering why fate is being so cruel to me. A positive blue cross stares back at me from the center of a long white stick, the answer to what is now my future, a future without Trey because I chose to send him away. Now it's only this baby, and me, because I refuse to tie Trey down.

Chapter Eighteen

Compelled

Victoria

DARK CLOUDS. SHATTERED heart. Endless sorrow.

These are the emotions surrounding my days for the past month, along with my continuous nausea. Regardless of my constant attempts, there is no particular remedy this baby likes to stick with. Already it's being as stubborn as the other half who created it. When I find something I believe it likes, it chooses to change its mind. Although, I can be appreciative I am no longer constantly throwing up. Thankfully, that period lasted a week. It's what drove me to take a test, and the fact my period never came.

"Victoria, can you meet me in my office, please," Benjamin requests on his way past my door.

Taking one last bite of my saltine cracker and washing it down with a sip of my ginger ale to ward off the bout of nausea refusing to leave this morning, I rush my way over to his office, not wanting to keep him waiting any longer.

Entering less than a minute later, I find him already peering at the door, waiting for my arrival. "Sorry," I say, feeling guilty for taking the extra minute at my desk after he summoned me.

He waves off my apology with a smile. "I called you in because I need a favor."

His request isn't odd, as it's how he always begins what is usually a command. I've grown up around lawyers my entire life and Benjamin's persona is far from that of the ruthless lions I was used to being around. He is always polite, carries a smile, and is friendly with his employees. You would think it'd make him a pushover in the court-room, but it's the total opposite. Once he steps in front of a judge, it's then the lion is unleashed.

"What do you need me to do?"

Holding out a file, I happily retrieve it. "I need you to fly out to Los Angeles to represent Matthew Garcia during the renewal of his contract."

My already nauseated stomach flips and threatens to bring up the contents sitting in it. "Why me?" I find myself blurting out.

He doesn't catch the uneasiness in my tone. "I was supposed to go myself, but I'm in the middle of litigations on my current case and I don't want to leave it to someone else."

"I'm only a junior associate. Wouldn't you prefer to

send another partner in your place?" I ask him, trying to use it to my advantage. "It would seem more professional, don't you think?"

He gives me a hard smile. "You're my *best* junior associate, and we both know if I could I would have already made you a partner."

Taking the compliment with a gratified smile, I still feel the need to try to get myself out of having to go. "Can't you send Melissa? I'm in the middle of preparing for a case and I'd hate to leave it to someone else."

He denies my request. "I was going to, but his manager refused, declaring I send you instead. Give the case to Melissa." I inwardly groan. Of course Trey would order Benjamin to send me.

"I refuse to leave it to someone else. I started it, I should stick with it," I try to protest.

"Do we need to discuss the terms of insubordination?"

Oh shit, now he has me.

Swallowing, I answer, "No, sir."

Reading the anxiety radiating off me, he asks, "Does this have anything to do with what the tabloids reported about his manager and you?" he inquires with a tilt of his head. "You've assured me that everything is settled and there was never anything going on."

Although I had to admit to Benjamin that, yes, I had indeed kissed Trey out in public, it was my bad luck it was discovered and blown out of proportion by the paparazzi. I reassured him there was absolutely no relationship between us, which was not false at all. There wasn't. Ever. I blamed our kiss on a lapse of judgment from my heart-stricken emotions of coming off of a broken engagement. He sympathetically ate it up.

"You're correct," I reassure him.

"Good, then you shouldn't have any problems representing Mr. Garcia," he expresses, sounding satisfied. "See it as a working vacation for the next several days."

"Days?" I choke out. "Why are we handling their contracts, anyway? Shouldn't he be working with an entertainment lawyer instead? We're family law," I state, pointing out the obvious.

"I've been handling Abigail and her husband's contracts from the very beginning. I've advised them in the past to seek another lawyer if they'd like, but apparently they don't trust very easily and prefer I keep handling everything since they started with me." He laughs out as if it should amuse me as well. "To be honest, I agree with their manager. I would rather you go than Melissa. You don't let anyone step on your toes and it's exactly what they want. Someone who is going to get them the best deal possible."

I sigh once more. "I figured you could take advantage of the California air to bring you back from the mood you returned with. You haven't been yourself since returning and quite frankly, I'm beginning to get worried." Of course I haven't been myself. I feel like shit and the cause of my problem is the same person Benjamin is sending me to. He takes advantage of my silence. "It's settled, then. You'll go and return at the end of the weekend," he states, as if I've already agreed.

Benjamin's intercom starts speaking with the receptionist's voice. "Benjamin," she says, since we're all on first name basis in the office. "There's a Mr. Julio Valdez here for Victoria."

"Tell him she'll be out in just a moment," he informs her. The click of her hanging up her phone is heard loud and clear. "Your escort is here," he tells me with his cheerful smile.

"Why did they send Julio?"

"All I know is they insisted on sending their private jet for you," he says, not seeing anything bizarre about the situation. "Just be happy you don't have to travel commercial. Have a safe trip," he adds.

I want to scream in frustration. If I didn't value my job so much, I would quit. I *do not* agree with what he has me doing, nor do I want to do it. With a polite smile, I exit his office and return to my own. Entering, I find Melissa has returned from her morning in court.

Grabbing the files I am currently working on, I walk them over to her desk. "Benjamin would like for you to take over these cases for now." Placing them gently on the desk, I try not to disturb the order of the files. "This one is near complete. You just have to review the contract, send a copy to her lawyer and it should be ready to file with the court," I say, indicating the file sitting on the top.

"Where are you going?" she asks, concern in her features.

"Benjamin is sending me to California to handle Matthew Garcia's negotiations."

"Why you?" she protests, looking upset over not being offered the opportunity to go herself. "Trust me, I tried getting him to send you," I utter. This has her frowning in disappointment.

Being the busybody she is, she quickly asks, "When are you coming back?"

Returning to my desk to retrieve my laptop and personal items, I say, "Monday, but sooner if I can."

Several minutes later, I'm meeting Julio in the lobby area where he greets me with a smile. "Hello, Victoria."

I give him a nod in greeting. "Hello, Julio. I'm glad it's you and not Trey," I find myself blurting out loud. He responds with a sorrowful expression. With his hand extended, he returns my old phone. "Thank you," I say, not that I really need it any longer.

"Do you want to follow me to my condo so I can pack?"

"I was hoping you'd allow me to ride with you. I took a taxi straight from the airport, but Trey has arranged for a car service to drive us there."

I can't help but reply, "How thoughtful of him." I'm still holding a grudge against him, regardless of his consideration.

As we're walking to my car, Julio comments, "He wanted to be here himself to pick you up, but he got caught up with another one of his clients. He sends his regards." I ignore Julio's message from Trey.

Julio offers to drive us to my condo and I don't protest since I still feel slightly ill. I don't know how I will make the trip in one piece if it continues. Entering my address in my navigation system, I leave Julio responsible for getting us home.

"Not that I'm upset you're here, but shouldn't you be

with Abigail? She's your main priority."

Keeping his eyes focused on the road ahead, he answers, "She's with Mateo and they're occupied with planning Emily's birthday party. She insisted we use the jet and I accompany you for your safety."

Ah, yes, Abigail did mention Emily would be turning one soon. Curiosity getting the best of me has me asking, "So they're going all out for the baby's first birthday?"

"Actually, no. They're planning something small. Just them."

"You're not going to be there?" I'm appalled they didn't invite Julio. He must have caught my expression because he quickly explains, "No, my mother has a very important doctor's appointment tomorrow and Abigail has given me the weekend off to be with her."

"Is she okay?" I ask, responding to his saddened features.

"We discovered a little over four years ago that she has cancer. She went into remission, but the cancer has returned. She's on her second round of chemo."

My heart aches at his admission, but he holds a gratified smile as he continues. "Thankfully, Abigail is very understanding. She gives me the time off to be at every appointment and has been generous enough to pay for all her treatments."

"That's sweet of her," I say, earning Abigail more of my respect than she already had.

Julio nods his head in agreement. "I refused at first, but she already had Trey take care of all the expenses when I called to set up payment arrangements. They've always been generous when it comes to me and my mother and I'm thankful to be in her service," he states.

It reminds me of how selfish my father can be with his employees. Had Julio still been in *his* service, he would have not had the opportunity for time off to be with his mother. My father would have seen his request as a weakness. It was for the best Abigail pursued him for her protection. It's clear she is compassionate and understanding when it comes to family.

The conversation helps the time pass quickly and before I know it, I'm walking into my condo. "I shouldn't take too long. Make yourself at home," I tell Julio once we've entered the condo.

Heading straight to my closet, I grab the same Louis Vuitton suitcase I took with me to Tennessee, which is still packed from my previous trip. Opening it up, I begin pulling out clothes and tossing them aside to make room for a fresh set. One of the last items is my favorite dress, still tattered and smelling of the stable I awoke in that morning. Normally, this would have been the first dress I packed, however in the condition it's in, it can no longer be worn.

Closing my eyes, I return to the night of the cookout. My mind fills with memories of the joyful night of dancing with Trey and enjoying the company of his family, thoughts I will forever hold in my mind. Tossing the dress aside with my other discarded items, I rush to finish packing. Considering my options, I take a mix of business, casual, and sleepwear, hoping this trip won't take more than three days because it's all I'm packing for, positive I will wrap this deal up by then.

Mr. Whiskers watches me from outside the closet door, giving me the perfect opportunity to snatch him up and place him in his carrier. As expected, he gives me a protesting meow, but I ignore him, placing him inside and zipping up the bag. With my cat and luggage ready for departure, I start making my way back into the living area.

Julio meets me at the end of my hallway, taking my luggage from me. Mr. Whiskers chooses the moment to continue protesting. Julio curiously raises his brow. "You still have the cat?"

"Of course I do. What would you expect me to do with him?"

Eyeing the carrier hanging from my shoulders, he carefully replies, "I just thought he'd be dead by now."

Irritated, yet expecting the comment, I say, "Well, he isn't because I take very good care of him."

"Are you sure it's a good idea to bring him?" he asks, skepticism clear in his tone as he eyes the animal complaining at my side.

"Trey knows I don't travel without him. So he doesn't have a choice."

Not defying my decision, he replies with a curt nod. "The car is already waiting downstairs. We should go."

The ride to the airport is thankfully short and quick. Upon arrival, the all too familiar aircraft is already waiting for us when we arrive. It's déjà vu, only this time we are lacking the presence of Trey. Thirty minutes later, we're in the air and my symptoms decide to worsen.

"Do you normally get airsick?" Julio comments, looking concerned. "You don't look okay."

My illness is the cause of my rude replying. "Thanks for pointing out the obvious." Julio apologetically peers at me. "I'm sorry, but no, I don't usually get airsick."

"Is there anything I can do to help?"

My mind is conjuring the words, *"Yeah, kill Trey for making me feel this way."* But instead, I shake my head at his offer.

Still insisting, he says, "I can check to see if the fridge has any ginger ale." I take another deep breath.

"Thank you. I'd appreciate that." I surrender.

He ventures off to the front of the aircraft while I stare out the window, wondering how exactly I will react when I see Trey again. I've made my decision to not inform him of my pregnancy. We've parted ways and it's for the best.

Julio returns, looking regretful when he hands me a small container of baby cookies. I'm questionably looking at him, wondering why he would be handing me these. "There was no ginger ale, but I found some of Emily's snacks hoping they may help."

I grant him a pleasant smile. "Thank you," I reply for the consideration.

Opening the container, I take a cookie and begin eating it, hoping they may help. If this nausea doesn't ease up soon, I don't know what I'm going to do. With my stomach slightly settling thanks to the cookies, I pull out Matt's file and begin reviewing the details to be better prepared when I enter the meeting.

Soon, we're landing and I'm thankful to be breathing fresh air when we step off the aircraft. An hour later, due to Los Angeles traffic, we are arriving at our destination, only it isn't a hotel as I had expected.

"Where are we?" I ask, taking in the building facing the Santa Monica Beach.

Helping me with my luggage, Julio informs the driver of our hired car, "I'll be right back down in a minute," before turning to face me to reply, "We're at Trey's condo."

"He never said he owned a condo in Los Angeles," I find myself saying out loud, while at the same thinking: Another detail Trey kept to himself.

For some odd reason, the fact leaves me feeling embittered from not knowing. Leading me into the building, he explains, "He rarely uses it."

Regardless, he still has it. Stepping onto the elevator, he continues, "He only stays here when he has business in town. He prefers to spend most of his time in Portland."

Minutes later, we're entering the condo, but immediately I sense the loneliness in it. The thought of staying in a personal residence belonging to Trey has me wanting to bolt back to the car waiting downstairs.

"Why am I not staying at a hotel?" I dare to ask. "Isn't it the professional thing to do?"

"His instructions were to bring you here. My job is to follow orders," he answers, without hesitation.

At the very moment, I am ready to defy those orders.

"I'm sorry, Victoria, but I don't have time to escort you to a hotel. I have to leave within the next couple minutes if I'm going to make my flight back to Portland," he states. "And to be honest, I would much prefer to know you're staying here," he finishes in a flat tone.

Knowing the situation I would put him in if I defy his

orders, I reluctantly follow him without any further argument. Peering around, Trey's condo holds the appearance of the typical bachelor pad. Casual, yet still kept in an orderly fashion.

"Trey isn't expected until tomorrow, so you have the place all to yourself tonight. The guest room is through here," he says, escorting me to one of the rooms off the living room. Placing my luggage on the side of the bed, he turns to face me. "I don't know if the fridge is fully stocked, but on the counter I believe he keeps a stack of menus to restaurants that deliver." He hands me a single key. "This is the key to the front door. Please, I beg you, don't leave unless you absolutely need to," he pleads.

I give him a nod in agreement. Satisfied with my reply, he continues, "There is a car service expected to pick you up in the morning to take you to the meeting. They are a trusted service I hired myself, so you have nothing to worry about in regards to your safety."

At least this comment has me feeling slightly better, but only a tad bit.

"I'll pray for your mother's health," I tell him, seeing how anxious he is to leave.

"Thank you, I appreciate it." He walks around me. "If you need anything at all, please don't hesitate to call me. I may not be nearby, but I'll call Mateo if needed. He, too, has a key to the place."

Closing the small distance he's placed between us, I hug him. "I'll be fine, Julio. I'm not a little girl anymore."

A flat smile forms on his lips. "I know."

I don't know how to take his comment, but he's already exiting the condo, insisting I follow to lock the door behind him. Minutes later, I'm leaning against the door staring off into the distance, wondering how in the world I've allowed myself to be manipulated into this situation. First with the negotiations, now with having to stay as a guest in the home of the one person I am desperately trying to keep distance from.

Regardless of the reasons, I'm too exhausted to dwell on them at this time. For now, I'm going to take advantage of my free time to prepare for tomorrow. The last thing I want is to look like a fool by not being prepared.

Trey

I'm exhausted, frustrated, and just want to sleep for the next couple of days. The last four days I was stuck in New York trying to salvage what little of a career my most recent client has, only I gave up on the cause. It didn't take me long to realize he couldn't care less how his actions will affect his career, so I made the executive decision to let him go; a first on my part. From the beginning of Abigail's career, I've had every type of dilemma thrown at me between the many clients I represent, but my number one rule is: If you work with me and follow orders, I'll make sure to keep your ass out of jail.

Apparently, this client didn't like to follow orders very well, so it was time he moved on. I wasn't going to waste my time trying to cover his drug problems when he refused to do anything to kick the habit. Thankfully, with him now in my past, I am able to return in time to deal with Matt's negotiations, and I won't miss Emily's birthday. Regardless if I would have kept the mess of the client, I would have moved mountains to get to her in time. An added bonus is knowing Victoria is in Los Angeles, and with any luck I'll find her awake.

My plane lands and nearly an hour later I'm walking into my condo. It's completely draped in darkness. At first, I grow fearful she's refused Julio's request of staying here, but when I make my way over to the guest room, I find her already curled up under the blankets in bed asleep. With the glow of the city lights through the windows, I am able to take in her features. Even in sleep she has a beauty beyond what words can describe; she takes my breath away, as she's always done.

Staring at her, my heart grows heavy just watching her take her shallow breaths. I know I fucked up by walking away. My stubborn mind had me leaving without a backward glance. It wasn't until I was back in my own bed, mourning the memory of having her in my arms, that I'd come to my senses. The hurt staring back at me when I delivered my answer to her final question is still engraved in my mind, as if it were written in stone. It wasn't the answer she was seeking, and it wasn't until later I figured it out for myself. By then, it was too late. I'd left her.

Her cat greets me with his scowl while I remain standing at the doorway. Walking over to the bed where he is curled up at her side, I scratch the top of his head.

I ask him in a low whisper, "You pissed she brought

you?" He replies with an immediate meow, making me chuckle. "You better get used to it because if I have my way, you'll be earning your frequent flyer miles." This time I receive an unsatisfied scowl before he begins licking at his paw.

The scent of her fragrant lotion has already overwhelmed the smell of the room. Glancing around the room, I see her luggage near the entrance, bringing a smile to my face. Originally I had a room reserved for Benjamin near the location where the meeting will take place, but I immediately nixed the idea when I learned he wouldn't be able to attend the meeting himself. It was then I demanded he send Victoria in his place. This meeting was my chance to start earning her forgiveness without her discovering my intentions.

"See you in the morning, old man," I say to the cat with one last pet before exiting the room.

On the way out, I take one last glance over my shoulder, resisting the urge to scoop up Victoria and bring her to my bed, or curl up at her side. I know doing so may upset her. I'm so exhausted I know it's best to go to my own bed to sleep, or risk keeping us both up all night.

The beam of light coming from the guest room awakens me. Knowing Victoria is up has me climbing out of bed and making my way over to her. I hadn't expected her to awaken in the middle of the night.

I find her sitting crossed legged in the center of the

bed, deeply concentrating as she stares at her laptop in nothing but a skimpy negligee. Holy fuck, the sight of her has me silently groaning inside as I command my dick to ignore the sight of her. If not, I will be growing stiff within seconds.

"Couldn't sleep?" I ask from the doorway, holding back my need to finish with *princess.*

I've startled her, as she brings her hand up over her chest with a gasp. "What are you doing here? You weren't supposed to be back until tomorrow," she shrieks, bringing her knees up to her chest as if to guard herself.

I keep a safe distance to try and gain her trust. "I got back early," I say with a shrug. *And I couldn't wait to see you again* is what I want to add, but I can't risk pushing her further away.

"Shouldn't you be sleeping?" I ask, hoping to distract her.

Frowning, she exhales. "You know I have difficulty sleeping in strange environments. I figured I'd go over Matt's statistics to better help with his negotiations tomorrow."

Resuming my steps to take me over to sit next to her, I expect for her to scoot away when she becomes stiff, but she doesn't. As stated, on the screen is Matt's statistics. "What for?"

"According to most of the articles I've read, Matt's career has been on the rise since he first signed."

"It has," I agree, proud of the fact myself.

"According to this website . . ." she says, switching over to the NFL statistic's page and pulling up Matt's profile, " . . . he's the highest ranking player since last year."

"I know. Last year the star quarterback had a torn ligament in his shoulder. Matt replaced him," I say, remembering how it was a blessing in disguise. Matt was able to prove his worth and was now one of the starting players.

"So why is he settling for a little more than what they'd given him when he first signed? He should be demanding more."

"I've discussed it myself with Matt and he's afraid if we push them too hard they'll have him traded off to another team. He likes where he's at right now. It doesn't put him too far from both locations and challenging them would risk them trading him off," I explain. "I pull in enough endorsement deals to exceed his current salary, so it's not like he's in it for the money."

Her lips go flat as she considers my explanation. "But wouldn't he prefer to be the star player?"

"Of course he would, but in this career, if you piss off the wrong person, you're out, contract or not. Those can always be bought out."

She snickers at my response. "Well, that's just stupid."

"It's the way it is."

She stares back at her laptop, deeply concentrating on the screen as she switches from one website to another. Staring at her, I can see the exhaustion and stress in her eyes. I dislike it.

Reaching forward, I close the laptop, making her gasp as she glares at me. "Hey, I was working."

Grabbing her hand, I stand and bring her up with me. "You're not officially on the clock until tomorrow. Time for bed," I inform her, turning the light off on the table next to the bed. Guiding her along with me back towards the exit of the room, I feel her resist when we reach the doorway.

"I'll be fine in this room," she protests, trying to pull her hand from my grasp.

Holding firm, I continue pulling her towards my room. "Didn't you just finish saying you don't sleep well in strange environments?" I ask, repeating her words.

"I'll be fine," she utters in return, still following, though.

Now at the side of my bed, I pull back the rest of the cover and urge her to get in. "You need your rest if we plan on wrapping this up tomorrow. The last thing I need is for you to zombie out on us and get Matt screwed over."

I don't need light to know she's scowling at me. It's typical for Victoria to react this way. Using the small of her back, I push her forward with my hand and this time she doesn't resist.

"No sex," she declares, reminding me of another time she issued the order.

The command has my dick hardening from the memory. I hadn't considered sex until she mentioned it. "No sex," I find myself agreeing against all protests from my now aroused state.

Lying on my back, I tug her to drape half her body across my chest. The feel of her warm breath gliding against my shoulder while she lies snugly in my arms makes me joyfully delirious.

"Goodnight, princess," I huskily whisper against her

temple as my lips touch her skin. There is no response on her end, but the arm wrapped around my waist tightens in acknowledgment. I don't need words to satisfy me. What I need is lying luxuriously in my arms.

The feel of her ass pushing against my groin is what awakens me. My hand is firmly gripping her breast while the other pulls her harder against my dick. Finding the hollow of her neck, my lips begin trailing kisses along her bare skin, earning me a whimpered moan. There is no way I can control my yearning any longer. My erection is demanding relief and from the way Victoria purrs, she wants the same.

Gliding my fingers down her abdomen, they find the warmth of her center then dip inside. She's wet and ready and I can't wait any longer to be inside of her. Pulling my erection out through the gap in my boxers, I lift her leg and push her underwear aside, guiding myself to her entrance. In one single plunge, I'm inside her. Her body goes rigid one second, the next she's jumping away from me, clear across the bed.

"What are you doing?" she exclaims, pulling the cover up to her chest. "I thought I told you no sex!"

Fuck . . . She's cock blocking me. My dick is already mourning the loss of her warmth it was wrapped in a couple of seconds ago. "You wanted it, too," I argue back. "You're the one who was rubbing up on me."

"I was not!" She peeks downward, causing my shaft to jump.

Smirking at the direction she's peering at, I say, "I didn't get this hard all by myself," referring to my still erect dick.

Her brows furrow in fury. "Screw you, Trey," she huffs, climbing off the bed. "Go find another friend to fuck," she hisses on her way out.

I'm left sitting alone, absorbing her words.

Shit . . . Fuck . . . Dammit.

There isn't enough curse words to equal how angry I made her feel. I should have held better control over my yearning for her. I knew this would happen if I pushed her too fast, yet can you blame me? Staring down at my dick, it's pathetically still palpitating against my abdomen. "Calm down, you're not getting any after all," I find myself telling it, feeling as miserable as it looks.

One cold shower later, I go in search of Victoria to apologize, but find her already gone. Looking down at the time on my phone, I notice it's twenty minutes past the time I had Julio schedule the car to pick her up.

Shit.

I had forgotten to cancel the damn thing.

A little over an hour later, I'm driving into downtown Los Angeles. Having called ahead to inform them I was back in town, I requested they wait to begin the meeting until I arrive. Arriving on the floor where the meeting is to take place, I immediately spot Victoria sitting off to the side reviewing a file, most likely Matt's. Matt is on the other end with the NFL representatives having a private discussion, allowing me to head in Victoria's direction.

Stopping directly in front of her, I fully take in her

pencil skirt with its matching, feminine blazer. Seeing her in professional mode does nothing to stop my libido from rising. Especially since I know exactly what she looks like under those clothes. With our close encounter this morning, and the images coursing through my mind, I have to take deep breaths to calm my raging hard-on.

Clearing my throat to catch her attention, her head snaps up in bewilderment, alarmed she hadn't seen me step up to her. Rising, she clutches the file she was reviewing tightly against her chest, using it as a shield. "Hello, Mr. Johnson," she professionally greets, posture stiff and her eyes locked with mine.

I struggle to keep the smirk threatening to spread under control, knowing the effect I can still bring out of her. "Ms. Montgomery," I reply with a curt nod, keeping with her professionalism. "I see you made it here without needing a ride from me."

She lifts her chin. "I used the car service you hired. It was best."

Oh, she's just as saucy as I like her. She is making the situation in my pants worsen without intending to.

One of the representatives steps over to us, along with Matt, making Victoria stand to greet them. "Mr. Johnson, Ms.—" He looks to Victoria for an answer with a flirtatious smile.

"Ms. Montgomery," I reply for her. The look in the man's eyes has me using every ounce of restraint to keep from punching the smile from his face. No one is going to fucking look at her that way, except for me.

Leaving her with a cheerful smile, he follows his colleagues into the conference room, leaving just the three of us behind.

Matt is about to follow them when Victoria stops him. "Mr. Garcia," she greets. "Before we enter that conference room, I need to know I have your complete trust." Her request has both Matt and I apprehensively looking at her.

"Victoria?" She holds her hand up to silence me, eyes locked directly onto Matt's.

"Mr. Garcia. Do I have your word?" He has no chance but to nod his head in agreement. "Thank you," she relays, marching off ahead of us.

Within a heartbeat, Matt and I are both following her, however I've grown a knot in my stomach wondering what she's up to. Everyone takes their seats, Matt to one side of Victoria, I on the other, the representatives across the table from us.

Their lawyer quickly begins. "Your client and office has had a chance to review the terms of the agreement. Not much will change except an increase in pay, so unless you have any concerns, I do believe all we need is a signature from both parties and we can all be on our way," he happily delivers.

"I've reviewed the terms of the contract and found some discrepancies with your terms and I do believe it is in my client's best interest we go over them today."

"I'm sorry, Ms. Montgomery. We were unprepared for this," Mr. Low Blow Flirtatious replies after clearing his throat.

"I understand that, but I've had a chance to review the contract myself on behalf of Mr. Garcia and I feel he has been cheated out of what he fully deserves. As his lawyer, I believe it's in the best interest of both parties to try to come to an agreement. My client has fulfilled his contract to term, so he is now considered a free agent. He's free to find another team who he will gladly guide to the Super Bowl next season."

"You sound so sure your client can make that a possibility," their lawyer says. Victoria reaches into her leather portfolio to retrieve a document, sliding it across the table, eyes directly facing the representatives when the lawyer catches it for review. "This is a print out of his statistics from this previous season. As you already know, he's the highest-ranking athlete in the NFL. I'm sure you'll agree?" They nod. "So you all know if I were to advise my client to walk out of here right now, you'd be losing one of your most valuable players. One I *know* will get you to the Super Bowl this upcoming season," she claims. "So, you need to decide whether you're willing to fulfill Mr. Garcia's new requests, or watch him take another team to the championship. I'm sure the moment I walk out of here Mr. Johnson will have an offer to present to Mr. Garcia within ten minutes."

From the way she has delivered the words, she has *me* squirming in my seat. I don't know if it's from fear she may just screw up the chance at Matt having the opportunity to continue with his dream team, or the tone she used. She is all business. No questions asked.

My phone vibrates on the table and normally I would ignore it, but the alert banner on the locked scene informs me it's a message from Matt. Swiftly grabbing the phone,

I unlock the screen to read it.

WTF is she doing?—Matt

I have no fucking idea, but you told her you trusted her.—Trey

I can't deny I am just as worried as he is.

"Then I believe we should discuss what new terms Mr. Garcia is seeking," the leader of the NFL representatives expresses, still looking nervous. With a grin, Victoria proceeds to list her demands.

Three hours later, the NFL representatives decide to call it a day. We were all unprepared to stay this long and by the way the meeting ended, there is no doubt we are returning tomorrow.

To be honest, it couldn't have come at a more perfect opportunity. I haven't been able to keep from glancing at Victoria every so often during her negotiations, and after the first hour she began to grow pale. At this point, she looks like she isn't feeling well.

The NFL reps stand when we bring the meeting to an end and we all politely excuse ourselves for the day. I'm about to ask Victoria what is ailing her when she rushes as fast as her legs can carry her straight out the door.

"Is she okay?" Matt asks with concern.

I'm still staring at the door Victoria just ran out of. "I have no idea," I reply, trying to figure it out myself. Ten minutes later, she has returned to the lobby area, still not looking any better.

"You could have warned us you were planning on pulling that shit in there," I inform her with a pang of resentment from being left in the dark.

Directing her comment to Matt, she says, "I'm sorry, Mr. Garcia, it wasn't until I arrived this morning that I decided to challenge them. To be honest, it wasn't until I started to research you as an athlete that it occurred to me you weren't being compensated enough with their current offer."

"What happens if they decide not to sign me again? I'm out of a career."

She turns to face me. "I'm sure your manager will get you out of the deep end. He's done it plenty of times before for all his clients," she confidently airs. "Are you having the car service retrieve me, or should I call for a cab?" She's quick to change the subject.

This has both Matt and I arching our brows. "Why would I call for a car?"

Victoria looks to me as if I'm the one not making sense. "Because I need to get back to your condo."

Matt has an amused smile on his face. "Good luck, man. See you in a bit," he says, giving me a quick pat on the shoulder. He leaves Victoria and I alone and it's for the best, because from her loathsome expression, I know this battle isn't going to be easy.

"You're riding with me. We're heading over to Matt and Abigail's for Emily's birthday," I inform her, watching her eyes widen.

Spinning to walk away, I catch her arm and turn her to face me, earning me a glare. "I'm fine. You go enjoy yourself," she snarls, withholding the anger I know she wants to spit at me.

"Victoria, I am perfectly capable of driving you."

"I'd rather you didn't. I'll find my own way back to your condo."

This is exactly what I was expecting, so I'm prepared. "Victoria, Abigail is expecting you to join us. Do you want me to inform her how you rudely turned down an invitation to her daughter's birthday?"

Remorse overtakes her features. "No, I wouldn't," she rasps out, delivering it with sincerity.

Satisfied with her response, I grin from ear to ear when I say, "Good, let's go. I'm hungry."

I don't give her a chance to react as I began to guide her with my hand on the small of her back towards the parking garage. She remains silent the entire way and when we reach my car, a less than amused expression mars her face.

"So you do own a sports car?" she asks, referring to my Audi R8 convertible.

Starting the car with the remote start feature, I lock her against the car when I reply, "If Grey can have one, why can't I?" She looks completely baffled by my response. "50. You've read it, haven't you?"

She's still at a loss about what I'm referring to. "Do you ever read?" She seems annoyed by my question. "Of course I read. Legal law," she points out.

This has me throwing my head back to laugh. Stepping forward to close the distance between us, my hand comes up to prod into her hair, my other gripping her waist to lock her in place. "Damn, princess. I can't wait until the day I can show you exactly what you're missing." The words come out as a promise I unintentionally expected to make.

Her silent gasp and widened eyes inform me she's just as aroused from my declaration as I am. Swallowing hard, she replies, "I don't think that will be necessary."

From her labored breathing and dilated eyes, I know she's far from telling the truth. She tries pushing me away, but I remain firm to my spot and it causes her brows to furrow. Resistance is no longer my virtue as I kiss her.

Our mouths fuse as one as my tongue demands entrance to her mouth. She opens, the warmth and taste of her mouth the ambrosia I've been craving for weeks. Her hands fiercely grip at the stands of my hair, tugging and pulling, refusing to allow me to escape. Minutes later, we are separating. Our mouths gasp for breath, as she remains mere inches from my lips.

"I've been wanting to do that for weeks," I find myself confessing against her chin. My mouth is still trailing kisses across her throat when the sound of a honking car has us frantically pulling apart. Victoria's eyes widen as she comes to her senses. Shame mars her features before she spins to open her door and steps into the car. I want to chuckle, but the erection I'm sporting is keeping me from doing so. At the moment, all I can do is close my eyes and picture the most hideous image I can conjure; if not, I won't be able to drive. Damn, fucking celibacy. It's a bitch.

Chapter Nineteen

Decisions

Victoria

HOW IN THE hell can he make me weak in the knees with a single kiss? All my pent up anguish evaporates in the time he's kissing me. It's as if he's done no wrong and I have no reason to be angry with him, instead demanding more from his kiss.

My emotions are in an uproar because of Trey. He's a complicated case I fail to win; regardless of the many times I object to his advances, my weakness for him prevails over my fight to push him away. My heart warns me he's bound to hurt me again, which is why I've chosen to keep my secret to myself. Telling him would mean risking his refusal to accept our child, which would only add to the betrayal of my damaged heart.

I'm so lost to my thoughts during the drive I lose track

of time during the trip from Trey's condo to Matt and Abigail's house. It went by faster than I expected. Upon leaving the meeting, my one insistence was Trey drive me back to his condo to allow me to change into more comfortable attire. As Julio had mentioned, the celebration would be small and casual, so there was no need for me to attend in a business suit and feel completely out of place.

Trey had hesitated at first, but after making me *promise* him I would still accompany him, he agreed. Strangely, he was pretty adamant I promise.

Taking in the small house, it's quite similar to their Portland residence, only this one doesn't have a huge gated fence to keep intruders out. Maybe because it's already in a gated community.

With Trey at my side, he leads me up to the front door. Without knocking, he enters the house as if it's his. The moment we walk in, the squeal of Emily's laughter is immediately heard.

"Tey!" She wobbles over with her hands held high to be picked up. Trey rushes the couple of steps to close the distance and lifts the child up into his arms.

"Happy birthday, baby girl!" he cheers out loud.

His face lights up with a radiant smile as he proceeds to coat her with raspberry kisses all over her chubby cheeks. There is no doubt from his expression he loves this child. The sight has me wondering if my decision is a mistake. How do I know he won't be this way with our baby?

Matt meets us. "Hello, Victoria." He smiles, facing Trey to give him a half hug. "Thanks for her gift, man."

"They installed it already?" Trey asks, sounding

shocked by the news.

"A couple of days ago. I wanted to make sure Julio would still be here when they installed it." Trey nods in agreement before glancing down into Emily's eyes. "Did you like your swings, baby girl?"

She lets out another squeal, pointing straight out the back window to where a large wooden play-set is assembled. "Sly!" she shouts with excitement.

Abigail's laughter is heard behind me as she walks over to us. "She hasn't wanted to come inside since they put it up," she tells him. "Hello, Victoria, thank you for coming," she tells me before pulling me in for a hug and placing a gentle kiss on my cheek.

I hadn't expected the affection and I'm shocked rigid for a moment before returning her welcome. "Thank you for having me," I say in return.

Releasing me, she turns to Trey to hold out her arms. "If you'll excuse me, I have to put Emily down for a small nap or else she'll be cranky when we cut the cake."

Still holding her in his arms, Trey turns to protest her request. "I just got here," he whines. Abigail ignores his reply to reach in and take the child from him. "You'll have plenty of time to play with her later. Matt and I need a break from being outside, thanks to you."

Her words simply encourage Emily to begin shouting, "Sly! Sly!" Her hands excitedly reach out into the air in the direction of the backyard. Abigail lets out a frustrated groan before walking away with a screaming Emily.

Sighing, Matt asks, "Why do you always have to buy her shit that drives us nuts?"

"Dude, she needed a swing set," he nonchalantly responds. "By the way, they're delivering one to Portland as well." Matt blows out his cheeks and drops his chin down to his chest in defeat. "What are you bitching about? I made sure to order the biggest slide they had so we can play on it, too." Matt's head snaps up, his lids completely wide.

I don't know whether to laugh at Matt's reaction or join him. "I need a beer," he simply replies instead. "Sounds good," Trey agrees.

"Want a beer?" he asks me on the way to the kitchen.

Shaking my head in refusal, he snickers, "City girl."

He has me wanting to bash him upside the head with his beer from his comment. I want to scream at the top of my lungs it has nothing to do with me being a city girl. My reasons are not because I'm *too* good for beer, nor why I have refrained from drinking caffeine, which is proving to test my patience in more ways than one. They're because I am trying to do what is best for *our* child.

I love my coffee! It was my source of fuel to calmly get me through the day. But no, I've had to replace it with water to ensure I'm hydrated enough. On top of it, I have to watch what I eat when I *do* have an appetite, or risk blowing up to the size of an elephant. Let's add the fact that in a little over eight months from now I will be squeezing what will feel like the equivalent of a baby elephant out of an opening the size of a lemon.

So, no, me being a city girl has nothing to do with me not wanting a damn beer. It's what I want to tell him now that he's standing back in front of me drinking his beer.

GABBIE S. DURAN

Glaring back at me, he appears lost as to why I would look at him this way.

"What's up with you?" Trey asks.

"I'd prefer some water, thank you," I say through clenched teeth.

My request has him frightened, for his eyes grow wide as saucers before he scurries off to retrieve my water. Matt, who was standing at his side, is wearing a puzzled expression. Trey returns with my water in hand.

"I'm fine," I reassure them both, grabbing for the bottle, but they're still both apprehensively staring at me.

Abigail returns and is a welcome distraction. "Victoria, would you mind joining me in the kitchen while the guys start the grill?"

"Yeah, grill," Matt utters, pulling Trey along with him.

"What the hell was that all about?" I hear Trey ask as they both walk away.

"Do you need help with anything?" I feel the need to ask on the way over. "No, I just felt like you needed a distraction. Was Trey driving you nuts again?" She laughs, and I join her.

"When isn't he?"

"Don't worry, after a while it'll grow on you," she expresses going about her tasks of preparing what is needed for the grill with a coy smile on her face.

She's rendered me speechless. What makes her think I'll be around long enough for it to *grow* on me? Leaning against the counter, I watch Abigail moving around the kitchen when I spot a bowl of pickles at my side. Taking a quick glance to make sure Abigail is distracted, I grab for one and eat it. The tang of salt mixed with vinegar has been a taste I've been craving for days. One spear was not enough, as I'm now grabbing for another. This time when I place it into my mouth, I am caught as Abigail says, "I hope you don't mind eating hamburgers," while adding spices to the ground beef in a large bowl in front of her.

"Hamburgers sound perfect," I truthfully tell her, my stomach already growling at the thought of the meal to come.

She begins kneading the meat in the bowl as she continues. "Matt was telling me you didn't feel well this morning. Are you feeling better?"

Around the slice of pickle, I say, "I am, thank you. My stomach has just been in knots lately."

Abigail stiffens, looking alarmed. "You don't have the flu or anything, do you? I have to ask because of Emily. I don't want her getting sick."

"No, I'm fine. It's just . . ." I have to carefully search my mind for what to tell her. "It's not the flu. I swear," I simply answer.

My response is unconvincing, but she takes it and resumes her mixing. "Matt also told me the details of the meeting this morning. Do you really think you can get him a better deal?" I would have expected her question to be full of resentment because of my actions, instead she seems full of curiosity.

"I wouldn't have risked going up against them if I didn't. I believe in him and *I know* he deserves better."

She sighs. "I do, too. Matt and I both love what we do, which is why we don't do it for money. But, like you,

I believe he deserves more," she conveys while I continue to eat the pickles. "To be honest, we probably wouldn't be making as much as we both do had it not been for Trey. He works really hard to get us the best deals." The sincerity in her statement matches her grateful expression.

"I hope everything works out," she sighs, now forming the ingredients of the bowl into patties.

I chew what's in my mouth before replying. "It will, or else I'll make sure to keep my word and find him the team he needs to get him to the Super bowl," I promise.

Her smile in response to my comment has the small doubt I have in myself disappearing.

"Victoria, may I ask you a personal question?" she slowly draws out.

I'm confused by how uneasy she seems. "Sure."

"How serious are things between you and Trey?"

"Serious?" I ask, taken aback.

She giggles at my reaction. "I know what's been going on between you and Trey," she admits. "Trey is a really great guy and I just hope you two work things out. He deserves someone who can make him happy." She sighs.

Her declaration has my heart aching. She's claiming *he* deserves happiness, but what about me? I do, too. "Have you tried telling him that?" I unexpectedly murmur.

"Actually, I sort of bitched him out about it," she claims, and I slightly choke on what I'm eating. As I catch my breath, she continues. "Trey can be a bit reserved at times. He doesn't really open up to anyone very easily."

"Tell me about it," I say with a grimace, knowing from experience how closed up he can be. Trey keeps himself guarded, withholding secrets no one but himself is allowed to know.

"Once you get past the obnoxious humor and get to *really* know him, you'll find he has a heart worth fighting for," she continues explaining. I take in her advice with silence, unable to find the correct words to respond until a wail from down the hall breaks my thoughts.

"That will be the birthday girl. Excuse me, I'm going to go get her," she informs me, leaving me alone to my thoughts once more.

It's soon Matt who is breaking them again when he enters the kitchen. "Are these the patties?"

Staring down at the raw meat formed into what looks to be hamburger patties, I say, "I think so?" Matt simply chuckles and takes the platter away.

From the corner of my eye, I catch Trey entering the house and I immediately become worried he'll head in my direction, seeking to make conversation. Luckily I'm saved when Abigail walks over to him to pass Emily off. With a heartfelt smile and open arms, he receives her, allowing Abigail to return to my side.

"You must really like pickles," she teases when she enters the kitchen, making me glance down to the bowl, which is now only a quarter of the way full.

"For some reason, I've been wanting pickles lately. Good thing we were having hamburgers," I laugh out, trying to disguise the real reason why I've been craving them.

Catching a glimpse of Trey sweet-talking with Emily has me smiling at his charisma. "He's so confusing sometimes," I catch myself commenting out loud.

Abigail gives me a heartfelt laugh. "It's not you. He's always been that way. Right when you think you know him, bam," she relays with a clap of her hands. "He shocks you speechless."

"But in the end, Trey really does have a heart as big as his head." We both begin to laugh from her comparison.

"I don't know what would have happened had I got my memory back." She sighs when our laughter comes back under control.

"Memory?"

"Trey hasn't told you how we met?"

Recalling what I know of the story, I say, "Trey mentioned you had an embezzling fiancé and that you moved in with them, but that's the extent of it." She doesn't appear too satisfied with my response. "Am I wrong?" I quickly ask.

She lightly shakes her head. "That's not all of it," she utters. "Actually, I'm surprised you don't really know all of it."

I feel resentful because I know exactly why I don't know all the facts. "Yeah, well, Trey doesn't tell me anything at all. What little I do know I've had to practically strangle out of him," I grumble under my breath.

"The tabloids pretty much spilled my entire story after the Bill incident."

"I don't read gossip magazines," I quickly reply.

"It wasn't gossip. I woke up not knowing anything," she points out.

I'm rendered speechless. "Actually, I did know one thing. A number. It's what lead me to Portland to Trey and

Matt's doorstep."

My mouth is slightly gaping open from her admission. "Not even your name?" I push.

"Not even my name. I had to be told who I was and what put me in that coma," she informs me. "Or at least, that's what he wanted me to believe."

I stuff another pickle into my mouth before saying, "By him, I take it you mean your ex-fiancé?"

She nods her head. "Matt and Trey were strangers to me, but they never once hesitated to protect me."

I can feel the sadness radiating off her, but I'm curious to know if the smile she's conveying is truly happiness, or sadness in disguise. "It doesn't sadden you to not know your past? Who you were? If you had any family?" The questions are grave, but curiosity has gotten the best of me. I expect her to curse me to hell and walk away, but she surprises me.

"It used to, but not anymore. I don't think I really had a family, anyway," she answers with a sigh. A smile soon forms seconds later. "It doesn't matter. My true family is my friends who have been there from the day I met them. They're all I need to make me happy."

"Even Trey?" I laugh out.

Her smile widens. "Yes."

At that precise moment, Emily lets out a wail, which draws our attention. "See, you made her cry. Give me back the remote!" Trey bellows, yanking the remote from Matt's hands.

"Come on, man. The game is on," Matt complains, extending his arm toward the flat screen.

"If baby girl wants to watch Mickey Mouse Club-house, then that's what we're watching!" The iconic mouse appears back on the flat screen within seconds. A cheerful squeal and the sound of tiny clapping hands have replaced her cries. "See. She's much happier now," he triumphantly relays, taking a seat with her on the couch.

"Fine, I'll go check on the burgers," Matt whines as he stands and exits through the back doors.

Abigail rolls her eyes. "Why does it not surprise me? We rarely get to watch television when he's around." She laughs, but gives me a wink when she says, "Obnoxious," in a drawn out voice.

Squeezing my hand, she says, "That's what I meant by his big heart. More than once Trey has proven he'll do whatever it takes to make one of us happy. He stood strong by my side when I needed him and I know he'll keep doing it. You can't give up on him, Victoria. Please don't," she pleads. "Want to help me prepare the sides?" she asks, as if knowing it's best to change the subject at this point.

Her request is more than welcome, although my eyes keep glancing in the direction of the living room where Trey is sitting comfortably with Emily at his side, both sets of eyes focused on their show.

Thirty minutes later, Matt enters the house with our cooked patties and while preparing his burger Matt looks down to the bowl that once held pickles looking perplexed. "What happened to all the pickles?"

Oh shit! I didn't realize I ate them all.

Before I can apologize, he adds, "I think there's more in the fridge," spinning to retrieve the jar from the fridge.

He refills the bowl, grabs his pickles for his hamburger then moves on to the next condiment. The entire time I'm grateful he never once asked why they were gone.

An hour later, the cake is brought out and with Trey at my side we begin to sing *Happy Birthday.*

Candles are blown out and Trey impatiently exclaims, "Let's eat some cake!" He fist pumps the air. I can't help but laugh with everyone over his enthusiasm. Emily has even joined the laughter before reaching down with her little hand to grab a fistful of cake.

"Baby girl, I didn't know it was that kind of party," Trey claims, dragging his finger across the icing on top of the cake and bringing it to his mouth to sample the morsel with a satisfied groan.

"Trey!" I shout out to him. "Use a plate," I scold, appalled over what he's done.

He has the audacity to ignore my scolding as I watch his finger dip back down near the same spot he drove it in seconds ago, repeating the same action. He brings the sample he's most recently dug for and brings it an inch from my mouth. I've been eyeing the decadent confection for the past ten minutes and I can't find myself denying his offer.

Taking his fingers into my mouth, my tongue explodes while savoring the sweet taste of sugary perfection. I watch as Trey's eyes roll back and he lets out another groan. Yanking my mouth away from his fingers, I feel as if I'm burning with humiliation because of his reaction. I swat at his chest. Trey catches my hand, bringing it up to kiss my palm.

His dark eyes are peering down at mine with a hunger that is all too familiar. "I'll make sure to take some cake home. For later," he huskily says to me.

My jaw is biting down on the inside of my cheek to ward away the tears threatening to emerge. Damn hormones. They have me wanting to cry, while at the same time drag Trey down the hall to the nearest room to have my way with him.

"And you both claim there isn't anything serious going on," Abigail snickers, breaking our eye contact and adding to my crimson cheeks. Putting a small distance between us to get my emotions under control, Emily is commanding Trey pick her up.

Without protest, he heeds her command. "Come on, baby girl. Let's go see what Uncle Trey bought for you." Taking my hand with the arm not holding Emily, he leads us out to the backyard.

Releasing her when we reach the play-set, we both carefully keep an eye on her as she walks around. The entire time my eyes glance at Trey and his reactions to Emily. My mind has once more returned to wondering if and when I will tell Trey about my pregnancy. Seeing how he is with Emily is the only reason why I may tell him now. However he takes the news, whether he resents me or not, I have to believe that deep down inside of this stubborn man there truly is a heart.

Trey

We're finally leaving Matt and Abigail's, but the entire time we were there I couldn't help but notice Victoria's mood. From the moment I informed her we were going over there, she appeared uneasy about something. I brush it off as her feeling nervous about going to their place. I keep reminding myself Victoria isn't much of a social person. Nevertheless, even after Matt and Abigail made her feel welcome, she still kept up her walls of defense. It's starting to frustrate me. It's as if she's choosing to keep herself guarded against me.

Gazing over to her, she's facing the window, her focus entirely on the scenery outside. Maybe she's holding the whole "asshole" persona against me? I wouldn't blame her if she did. I haven't truly put forth my efforts to woo her.

"I'm hungry. You hungry?" I ask, attempting to catch her attention. It works, as she's facing me with a stunned expression. "We just finished eating a couple of hours ago."

Giving her a half shrug, I say, "So."

"I'm not hungry, but if you want to grab something, I don't mind."

"Good. I'm up for hot dogs."

Giving me a questionable expression, she asks, "Hot dogs? Really?"

"Ever been to Hollywood?"

Forty minutes later I'm parking my car in the center of Hollywood, praying the guy I just paid twenty-five dollars will keep an honest eye on my car and it still be there when

I return. I couldn't care less if they break into it, shit in the car is replaceable, but I *do* need a car to drive us home.

"It isn't anything like the movies make it out to be, is it?" Victoria asks, stepping around a homeless guy. Making sure I drop some cash on the way around him, I respond, "Far from it."

Tucking Victoria securely at my side, I continue walking with her until we cross the street and are in front of the Kodak Theater. Her attention turns to the performers in the midst of their act. She's completely lost in awe. When done, I resume leading her down the street to the Chinese Theatre. Her eyes light up when she takes in the ground.

"This is where all the actors sign and leave their imprints in the cement, isn't it?"

"Yup," I happily reply, loving how her eyes are lighting up. She practically yanks my arm off as she pulls me, weaving around people to take in each individual piece.

"Oh my God. Those are the Harry Potter characters!"

This girl has never read *Fifty,* yet she's going crazy over some wizards? The thought has me laughing out loud.

"What?" she scowls at me. "You're going to mock me for reading Harry Potter, aren't you?"

I try to swallow my laughter, but fail miserably. "I just can't believe you've never heard of the most talked about movie of the twenty-first century, yet you know about a bunch of kids."

With her hands on her hips, she eyes me with a glare full of fury. Oh shit. My dick just went from limp to hard in two-seconds. Pulling her flush to close the gap between us, I gently kiss her lips. "I'm sorry. It's just amusing."

She rewards me with a cute little pout, causing me to kiss her again. "Books were what I used to help me escape. This series was one of my favorites. It took me to another world."

"Book junkie, huh?"

She giggles. "Yeah, I even wear glasses," she says, adding to my amusement.

Blowing the air out of my cheeks, I try to keep my dick from hardening any more. Fortunately for me, Victoria can feel what effect she has on me when she delivers a gasp and looks down towards my shaft. She tries to pull away, but I don't allow her. "Don't move, princess, or I may end up getting arrested for indecent exposure," I tease.

She swats me on the chest. "Whatever." She pulls herself away anyway to look around our feet. "I heard Marilyn Monroe is here, too."

"I remember seeing her somewhere. Let's go find her," I say, guiding her off in search of the iconic figure. For the next hour, Victoria's smile remains on her face, her eyes alight the entire time. We walk back and forth down the block, taking in every name on the stars along the way. The sightseeing adventure ends with us at the Disney Store for dessert. Before we leave, she goes off in search of a souvenir, a classic Mickey to take with her. She clutches the plush toy tight to her chest as we wait to pay for it. "I had one growing up, but I think the staff must have eventually thrown it out while I was gone. I've been meaning to replace it," she explains after I'm done paying for the toy.

"Thank you," she continues when outside the store.

She places a quick peck on my mouth, delivering it

with a thankful smile.

"You're welcome," I say, only allowing a breath of separation to tell her before I'm holding her head in my palms, wanting more than just a peck. I completely forget we're out in public until someone says, "Get a room," causing Victoria to jump away.

Her breathing is labored and her cheeks are flushed with color. She shyly bites down on her lips, holding her Mickey up. "Thank you," she repeats.

I can only laugh. "Come on, I smell my dinner."

"You're still hungry after all that ice cream?"

"You ate most of it," I tease, although I'm telling the truth. I only got a couple of bites from the dessert. She was devouring it like there was no tomorrow. "Plus, I came here for hot dogs," I say, leading her towards my destination of choice.

On the side of the street is a vendor with a small makeshift grill cooking hot dogs.

"You're going to eat that?" she asks, sounding disgusted with my choice of food.

"Don't knock it until you've tried it. They're fucking good," I tell her, choosing to ignore the scrunch of her nose. "Want one?" She looks pale, as if she's holding herself back from gagging when she shakes her head.

"I'm good," she says.

"Don't know what you're missing."

Two hot dogs later, we walk back to the car, my belly full and satisfied. "Are you sure those were safe to eat?"

"I don't know how you didn't want one. The wiener was wrapped in bacon. I thought you like sausage and wiener," I remind her with a wag of my brows.

Pressing her hands to her stomach, she says, "I don't even think they had their food license."

"They didn't, which makes them taste better." She doesn't seem too optimistic with my reply and a roll of her eyes makes me laugh.

Her pursed lips turn up into a smile, and knowing I put it there gives me more satisfaction than the hot dog I just ate.

Chapter Twenty

Vagina Cramps

Victoria

TREY WALKS OUT of the bathroom looking like death is about to claim him. Throwing himself on the bed next to me, his groan overtakes the room.

I give him a suspicious look. "What is wrong with you?"

He groans as he curls himself into a fetal position.

"Vagina cramps."

This has my eyes going wide. "Vagina cramps?" I say, as if he's lost his mind. "How in the world can you have vagina cramps, Trey, if you don't have a vagina?"

Instead of immediately answering, he lets out another pained groan, clutching at his stomach. I have to watch him take heavy breaths.

"I'm over here dying, princess. Can't you see that?"

Now I'm rolling my eyes as I sit next to him on the bed.

"You're not dying, and I told you not to eat those hot dogs. This is all your fault," I tell him, only the sense of satisfaction from being correct does me no good.

"I swear this is worse than giving birth to a child. Have a little sympathy for your man," he pleads.

I swear I may just strangle him for being a sissy.

"First of all, you aren't my man," I clarify as an ache from having to point it out overtakes me. Before I can add any more reasons, he groans again.

"Fuck!" he exclaims.

"Second of all, *you do not* have a vagina. And third, you would not have one clue what it's like to have a child, so you cannot compare the two."

He lets out another groan while he turns his body in my direction.

"I was there when Abigail was having Emily. I was in the room," he explains. "I felt her pain, and this is worse."

With those words, I come to believe he truly has lost his mind. I'm about to continue arguing simply for my own entertainment but he lets out an earth-shattering fart.

"Oh my God, Trey!" I yell, which is the worst mistake in the world as I begin to taste the vapors his body has released.

Now sighing, he clutches at his stomach. "Sorry, princess, I couldn't help it."

Gagging, I run straight for the bathroom, emptying the contents of this afternoon's meal. Trey's footsteps can be heard behind me while I'm still clutching the porcelain bowl.

"I'm sorry, princess, but you know what they say. When you fart in front of someone, it's because you love them."

Love?

Did you just say love?

I'm still pondering the thought as I begin hurling again.

My hair is pulled away from my face and the smell of Trey is strong at my side. When I'm able to calm myself, I flush the toilet and grab for a piece of toilet paper to wipe my mouth. Sitting back against the counter, I close my eyes and force myself to take deep breaths.

Trey brushes my hair away from my temple and when I can bring myself to open my eyes, I find him earnestly gazing back at me.

"I'm sorry," he conveys, truly looking apologetic.

Taking a deep breath, I reply, "You should be, this is all your fault."

"Everything is always my fault," he laughs out. "I just didn't know you had a sensitive stomach."

"I usually don't." He grimaces after saying the words, the appearance all too familiar. "If you plan on farting again, you better leave this room," I order, pointing at the door.

"I'm sorry, but my fucking vagina cramps are a bitch."

"Trey Johnson, you *do not* have a vagina so get over yourself. Be lucky you won't have to endure the pain of having a child eight months from now."

He's completely taken aback by my statement. I hadn't meant to say the words, but his claims to have a vagina were irritating me.

"Forget I ever said that," I correct myself.

"What are you trying to say?" Crap, now he's asking questions.

"Nothing," I state, trying to stand. His hands on my shoulders keep me rooted to the floor.

"Victoria," he sternly demands. "Is that why you've been acting weird?"

I remain silent, unwilling to answer. I'm expecting him to pressure me to reply, but he shocks me by asking, "If I need to go buy you a test or something, I will. I've done it before and I'm not ashamed to do it again." He's completely serious.

"Why would you have experience with it? Do you have to do it with every damn *friend* you have?"

"No!" he defensively answers. "I had to buy them for Abigail a long time ago. They didn't want the paps to find out she was possibly pregnant so they sent me," he explains.

Oh. Well, that was considerate of him.

"You still haven't answered if I need to go buy a test for you," he reminds me.

My eyes find the floor before his finger lifts my chin to look at him. "No. I already know." Sincerity overtakes his features when I confess, "I'm pregnant."

It's as if time comes to a stop with those two words. There is no one in this world but Trey and me. No one else matters, except for the child currently nestled in my womb.

"You're pregnant?" he chokes out.

Tears begin to build and my vision becomes cloudy.

I don't want to cry, but I know if I don't remove myself from Trey's proximity, I will begin to do so. The shock of my admission allows me to shove him away and stand this time. Leaving him behind in the bathroom, I find myself escaping to the bedroom, but change paths when I notice the unpleasant scent still lingering in the air.

His heavy footsteps can be heard following me. "Are you sure?"

Without turning around, I tell him, "I'm sure."

"How do you know?" I hear him ask from behind.

I'm standing in the safety of the living room when I stop to face him. "I took a test," I tell him. "Three to be exact," I add for reassurance.

He remains silent, adding to the dread already coursing inside of me. "Why didn't you tell me?" he asks.

I'm still trying to consider how to confess that I wasn't planning to, but as if reading my mind, he says, "You weren't going to, were you?" There is no denying my guilt, as it must be overtaking my face. "Tell me, Victoria, is it even mine?"

"Of course it's yours," I throw at him, offended he would think otherwise.

His brows furrow in doubt. "Do I need to remind you of our most recent dilemma?" he mentions as if intending to wound me.

Seething, I say, "I haven't slept with Andrew in nearly a year. Say what you may about me, Trey, but unlike you I don't believe in throwing myself at every man for sexual exploitation." This wounds *him* as his eyes turn dark in anger.

"I just want to make sure you're not trying to trap me with a baby that isn't mine," he states, further plunging the dagger of hatred into my heart.

Rage overtakes me. My blood pressure has risen beyond any level it has ever reached in the past. I'm no longer fueled by pain, but hatred when I deliver, "I'm not like the women of your past, so don't you *dare* compare me to them. You've made it clear you would never commit yourself to anyone, which is why I chose not to tell you about my pregnancy. I don't need you, or *anyone,* to help me raise *my* child. The last thing I need in my life is a worthless, no good bastard claiming I tried to trap him by getting pregnant."

I don't bother waiting for his reaction as I walk as fast as my legs can carry me out of his condo. There are no words he can say to pardon how I feel for him. I meant every word spoken. I don't need him, nor will my child in the future. If there was any doubt in my mind he would have been a supportive father, my hopes were crushed when he claimed the child wasn't his. It only goes to show, he will never change his ways, which includes settling down.

I don't know what led me to give the taxi driver this address, but it was the only other address besides Trey's I knew of in Los Angeles. Knocking on Matt and Abigail's door late in the night has me fearfully wondering if they will answer. After several minutes, I find Matt gazing back at my tear streaked face. It's not how I would have liked to arrive, let alone have to beg them for cab fare, but they don't turn me away. Without hesitating, Matt pays the driver while Abigail pulls me into the house and leads me to the couch.

"What happened? Where's Trey?" Abigail is worriedly asking.

Convulsing from my tears, I say, "I left." I sob into my hands.

Rubbing my back, she tries to calm me. "Tell us exactly what happened. Maybe we can knock some sense into him," Abigail says.

Matt brings over a bottle of tequila and a shot glass, but I push away the offer.

"Are you sure? It works for Abigail," he laughs out.

"I can't," I whimper. This has them both taken aback. "I'm pregnant," I blurt out.

"Oh shit," Matt says, while Abigail sighs, "Oh, dear."

"He tried claiming the baby isn't his and I'm probably just trying to trap him." I continue to sob.

Abigail's furious eyes turn to Matt. "He wouldn't have told her that if it wasn't for you and Lisa," she hisses up to him, making him turn pale the moment she makes the statement.

I'm left in the dark as to why she would say such words, but being reminded of Trey's doubt has me weeping all over again. Abigail instantly resumes comforting me while Matt paces the room. "He's going to get pissed at us if we don't tell him you're here. He's probably worried sick over you leaving."

"I really doubt it," I utter around my tears.

UNSPOKEN *Temptation*

He stops, sympathetically looking down to me. "I believe what you said, but I know Trey, he didn't really mean it. He can sometimes say shit he doesn't mean," he proclaims. "Trey is a dumbass sometimes and he just . . ." he pauses, as if searching his mind for what to say next, " . . . just word vomits without thinking."

The word vomit reminds me of how sensitive my stomach still is. Bringing my hand up to refrain from puking again, Abigail scowls at Matt for his choice of words. "Sorry," he says quickly.

The arm wrapped around my shoulders squeezes me for encouragement. "Are you sure you don't want to call him?" she suggests. I shake my head at the thought. Crap, I hadn't thought clearly when I came here. Where the hell am I supposed to go now? "I'm so sorry. I know I'm imposing on you, but I really didn't know where else to go."

"I understand," she says then sighs. "You're always welcome to stay here. I remember what it was like to feel lost. We don't really have a spare bedroom, but this couch is pretty comfortable according to Matt," she says, making me giggle from wondering why she would say such a thing.

"Thank you," I earnestly reply.

"I'll get the extra covers," Matt says before walking off. He returns minutes later and Abigail begins to scold Matt. "He has some major ass kissing to do before he gets near her."

Matt holds his hands up in surrender, but doesn't argue.

Lying down, I feel overwhelmed from the night and I

immediately begin to sleep the moment my head lands on the pillow. I have no thoughts as I drift to sleep, simply because I refuse to dwell on the troubles I know are to come. Regardless of what my future holds, I *will* prosper, and I *will* survive.

Trey

I'm numb. Breath stealing, mind fucking, dumbstruck to the core numb. My knees give out. Strength completely vanishes as I drop to land on the couch. Her words echo throughout my mind.

Pregnant . . .

Worthless bastard . . .

I don't need you . . .

The last sentence strikes, aimed directly at my heart. Regret over my words begins to take over. I went from being delighted of hearing her news to being crushed in the end; it's no one's fault but my own. I should never have doubted the baby was mine. Anguish over past mistakes was what fueled my words—words which should have never been spoken from either of us.

Realization finally hits me she's left. Standing to race after her, my legs lead me outdoors, frantically searching the streets. Pulling out my phone, I call her, only to get directed to voicemail. I keep trying over and over again as I return upstairs to my condo for my car keys. Entering the front door, I hear the ringing of a phone coming from the guest room. Within seconds, I discover why it is she wouldn't answer. Her phone is sitting next to her laptop in the center of the bed.

Dread courses through me. She's out in public, alone, without her phone or protection. Hundreds of frightening possibilities of what can occur to her travel through my thoughts. Running back into the main living space, I grab my wallet and keys then rush right back out the door to my car. Even if I have to drive around all fucking night to find her, I will, but I am not coming back without her.

"I told you not to come over here," Matt scowls, denying me entrance to his house as he checks over his shoulder. "She doesn't need the stress right now, and Abigail will have your balls if she finds out you're here."

Matt called me soon after I left my condo. During our phone conversation, he informed me she told them of the news. I'm grateful. At least I know they will take good care of her. Raking my hand though my hair, I let out a frustrated breath. "I know, but I just want to make sure she's okay."

"She's fine," he replies.

I hate how he's championing her. Now that the tables have turned, it isn't so amusing.

"How pissed was she?"

He frowns at my question. "She wasn't pissed, but wounded by your words." His admission feels like salt on an open wound. "If Abigail finds out I called you, she'll have both our balls when she finds out that you're here." I cringe because I know she will, and I know I'll never hear the end of it from her.

"Is Abigail still awake?" I ask, fearing for my balls.

Matt shakes his head, allowing me to let out the breath I've been holding. "She fell back to sleep with Emily."

Remembering how late it is, I say, "I'm sorry she woke you."

"It's no big deal. I'm glad she came here and not somewhere else."

"Me, too," I sigh.

A moment of silence passes before Matt speaks again. "You should probably go home and rest. She'll be here in the morning."

"It seems like all I ever do when it comes to Victoria is let her walk away," I shamefully admit. "I don't want to leave."

He passively considers my words. "I thought you would have learned from my mistakes," he declares.

His words are the reason for my actions. Ignoring his protest to not enter, I push past him. "What the fuck are you doing?" Matt loudly whispers.

"Learning from your lessons. I'm taking my woman back, no questions asked."

With the dim glow of the kitchen light, I make my way over to the living room where I know she'll be. Kneeling so my head is directly in front of her, my lips find her temple to place a kiss upon it. "I'm sorry, princess," I whisper to her, knowing it's just the start of the many times I imagine myself saying it. Bending forward, my arms scoop up her entire body and bring her to my chest. I turn to find Matt currently blocking my way.

I challenge him with a glare. "You're taking the blame for this shit," he glowers back.

"Whatever."

"You have to remember you're dealing with Abigail and a pregnant woman," he reminds me.

"Nothing a little makeup sex can't fix from both of us," I suggest, remembering the last time the statement was mentioned.

It was the night my life completely changed.

He doesn't look too confident over my suggestion. "I know it may work on Abigail, but if I recall you still haven't been forgiven for the first time," he smirks.

Shit. Way to kick a man when he's down by reminding him of his faults. "I'm working on it," I inform him, already taking my steps forward to begin walking with Victoria to my car.

Thankfully, Matt has renounced his efforts to stop me from taking Victoria, but it doesn't mean I've relinquished my fear she'll awaken and protest leaving with me. She doesn't stir at all when I place her into the car, or the entire ride home. It isn't until we reach my place that she releases a protested groan from being disturbed. I lift her out of the car, tensing all over again. She remains asleep, most likely exhausted from today, while I lay her into my bed and undress her.

I cannot help but grin when I recall her commanding words, *"No sex."* Climbing into bed next to her, I promise tonight I will heed the words, simply to not frighten her.

But tomorrow is a new day and I plan on reminding her of exactly how pleasurable it is to *make up*.

Feathering kisses across her chin, my lips find the center of her mouth. "Good morning, princess." She releases a protested groan, as I'd expected. "I've made you breakfast," I inform her, continuing to trail kisses down her chin. She murmurs her sweet purr, still engulfed in sleep, persuading me to continue trailing my lips down her neck. Wearing simply her bra and underwear since I removed her clothes the night before, her body is half bare, and too enticing to not kiss or touch.

Her hands slide into my hair. Her nails dig into my scalp as she pulls my head flush to her body. Her encouraging whimpers, along with her hands pushing my head further down her torso spurs my mouth, resuming its trail further south to her breast. Hating the barrier of the fabric separating me from my prize, my fingers tug it down, taking her nipple into my mouth, she holds my head in place with her palms.

This is not how I planned to wake her, but who am I to deny giving her pleasure? Suckling hard, she thrust her chest up as if demanding more. Moving on to her other breast, I give it the same attention. I'm about to begin making my way down her abdomen when I feel her stiffen. Her body thrust up, nearly knocking me off the bed.

"What are you doing?" she screeches. Taking in her surroundings, she asks, "How did I get back here?"

"I was trying to wake you so you can eat, but you had other plans."

"What other plans?"

I point down at my erect shaft. "Is that all you think about?"

Oh, hell no. "You are not laying the blame on me this time, princess. You're the one who was encouraging me."

"Was not!"

I run my hand down my face. "We're never going to get anywhere this way," I let out with a frustrated sigh.

She shields herself with the thin sheet of the bed. "You still haven't answered how I got here. I'm sure I fell asleep at Matt and Abigail's," she states, eyes searching the room. "And why am I naked?"

"You're not completely naked. You still have your bra and underwear on," I casually say.

She chucks a pillow directly at my head with a growl, nearly hitting me had I not caught it in time. "You still haven't answered my question," she says.

"Which one?"

Mistake. Not the response she was wanting as another pillow comes flying at my head. Dropping the one in my hands, I catch this one. "Stop throwing pillows at me," I holler, throwing it back onto the bed, realizing I've made another mistake. I just refueled her ammo.

I reach out to grab it, but she predicts my move and grabs for the other end, tugging hard while I tug back. It's a tug of war between the two of us over a fucking pillow. "Let go!" she growls. Heeding her command, I do, watching her fly completely back off the bed. The last I saw of her were her legs up in the air before a thud is heard.

She lands on the floor with a yelp. Scrambling over the bed and landing on her side, her eyes are glaring up at me. "I hate you," she seethes through clenched teeth.

I can't help but laugh at her expression, which is yet another mistake as the pillow we were battling over seconds ago whacks me upside the head.

"What the hell was that for?" I bellow out while holding the side of my head. She got me good. I think I saw stars for a moment.

"For being an asshole!"

"What's new?" I grumble under my breath.

Holding her abdomen, she lets out a pained groan and I panic. "Oh, shit. Did I hurt the baby?" Lifting up the cover to dive underneath it, my hands come down on her hips.

The cover is lifted and Victoria's head peeks through. "What are you doing?"

"I'm making sure I didn't hurt the baby," I say, gently feeling, probing her skin.

"Trey, the baby is fine," she laughs out.

Glancing up to her, she's still holding the sheet up with her hands in a makeshift tent. "How do you know?"

With a roll of her eyes, she replies, "Because all my research says so." As if it that answer is sufficient enough.

Jerking my head back, I ask, "You've done research?"

"Of course. You know how I prefer facts."

Of course, I mimic in my mind. It then occurs to me I'm not so ignorant in the facts of pregnancy, either. I know a couple of my own.

"What else did your research say?" I ask with hooded

eyes.

"A lot," she breathlessly replies while I slowly begin to crawl up her body.

Her breathing is progressing to a pant the higher I go. Now directly above her, I look down into her eyes. "Are you getting most of the symptoms you read about?" I ask, recalling one very important detail Matt had no complaints about.

Her breathing becomes heavier. "Some," she squawks out before my lips find the spot below her ear.

Dropping the blanket, it lands to drape above us. With me straddling her waist, I grab for her arms, holding them up above her head. Mistake number, what? I've lost count, but this one has her exposed breast thrusts straight towards me. My mouth is back to watering, remembering what they tasted like as I suckled them.

"What are you doing?" she chokes out. Her attempt to buck me off once more brings me back to reality.

Taking a deep breath to clear my mind, I say, "I came in here to talk, so we're not leaving here until you listen." Now I'm the breathless one. "And to feed you. I came in here to feed you, too," I add recalling my true intentions.

"We have nothing to talk about, Trey." She tries bucking me again.

This isn't working. "We're never going to get anywhere if you keep moving."

"Then get off me!" she yells as she squirms underneath me.

Her fury has returned and there is no escaping it. Lowering myself so I'm completely blanketing her chest,

I thrust my hips down into her pelvis as I whisper into her ear. "I've had a raging hard-on for the past month and you're not helping with those angry eyes of yours." She goes stiff as a board. "That's right, princess. When you glare at me I get hard." I thrust again. "Really fucking hard." Did she just whimper? I'm pretty sure she did.

"Trey?" she croaks out.

Nibbling at the skin at the hollow of her neck, I say, "Yes, princess?"

This time I feel the vibration of a groan. "You have to get off," she repeats, the command full of agony. Yanking my head back, I watch as her cheeks puff up with air, her appearance completely pale. Leaping completely off her, she rolls to her side, her hand coming up to her mouth.

"You okay?" She holds up a single finger in the air while her eyes close and she takes in a deep breath, blowing her cheeks out when it releases.

"Are you barfing in the mornings?" She responds by shaking her head, still taking deep breaths.

"I stopped throwing up a couple of weeks ago. It's just a lingering nausea that won't go away," she exhales in a deep breath.

Oh, this has me recalling another fact Matt shared. "Do you want some of my cum?"

Her eyes snap open in shock. "What the hell?"

Gleefully, I state, "Yeah, I read somewhere that nausea is the body's way of trying to fight off a foreign body, which in this case is the baby." I point at her flat abdomen. "If you swallow my cum, your body becomes immune to it and the nausea then ceases to exist."

"I'm not swallowing your cum!" she exclaims.

"Why not?"

Her eyes narrow down into a slit. "First, I'm going to pretend you didn't ask. Second, I've never even given a guy a blow job, so the method to get said fluids would be pointless to try since I don't know how to retrieve them."

I scoot closer to her while grabbing my shaft. "I'm an excellent teacher," I relay with a wag of my brows.

The same pillow from earlier is thrown at my chest. "UGH! You're intolerable," she growls while standing and stomping off in the direction of the bathroom.

Holding my arm out wide in the air, I say, "What? It's for the sake of the baby."

"Asshole!" she shouts before slamming the door.

Well, that didn't go as planned.

Confessions

Victoria

OH. MY. GOD.

I may just strangle the man!

Gripping at the edge of the bathroom counter, I'm still taking deep breaths when Trey comes barging into the tiny room, pointing his finger directly at me. "Yes, I'm an asshole, but I'm your asshole now, princess, so learn to deal with it." I'm staring back at him wide-eyed, still full of rage.

"You denied the baby was even yours," I indicate, reminding him of his own words. "I shouldn't forgive you."

"I fucked up, I know I did, but it's not going to be the last time because I'm not perfect. I make mistakes. Dumb ones. But it doesn't mean I can't learn from my mistakes."

Has he lost his mind or does he always babble this

way? Before I get a chance to ask, he resumes his rambling.

Raking his hand through his hair, he releases an exasperated sigh. "I don't know what the fuck you've done to me, but I'm fucked. Screwed in the head, fucked." He points at his head.

Arching my brow at his admission, I refrain from nodding my head to agree with him.

Pointing his finger back at me with a glare, he says, "But you made me this way. I always said I wasn't going to let some girl tie me down. I saw how stupid Matt got with Abigail when he got all love-struck and I thought he was a fucking pansy for acting that way," he declares. "Now I'm the fucking pansy!" His hand rests on his chest above his heart.

Looking at him in doubt, I say, "You are?"

"Yes, I am!" Throwing his hands up, he looks at me as if I'm the one who's lost their mind.

Cutting him off before he can resume, I say, "You think I wanted to make you this way?" I glare at him. "You're the total opposite of what I was looking for."

"I know!" he agrees. Instead of his admission satisfying me, it makes me angrier.

He grabs his crotch in warning. "You know what that glares does to me," he delivers with a low husky voice.

Oh, shit.

I'm already on fire from feeling just as strung out from my sexual frustration. With his hooded eyes, his hand grabbing at the object I deeply want inside of me, and that deep voice of his, I'm done.

GABBIE S. DURAN

Swallowing to force myself to speak, I regain my courage. "I can't . . ."

Tilting his head with curiosity, he asks, "Can't what?"

"I can't risk being hurt anymore," I choke out.

Stepping forward to close the distance between us, his dark eyes are gazing into mine. "Sometimes risks are worth taking, princess."

My eyes meet his, but I know it's best to break eye contact to allow me to properly think. The feel of his finger forcing me to look back up has me peering back at him. "It seems like all I ever do is take risks with you," I rasp out around the lump lodged in my throat. "It feels like an endless cat and mouse game with you," I add.

His jaw turns hard. The veins in his throat begin to bulge. Moments pass before he replies, "I'm done chasing. No more. I've caught you and you've captured me. There will be no more running," he declares.

My lids close. The tears in my eyes now glide down my cheeks. "It's too late. There's nothing you can say or do now to make me change my mind."

Ignoring my protest, he says, "Do you want to know when I think I fell in love with you?" My eyes snap open. "The first time I saw you standing across the room with Abigail," he conveys, tucking my hair behind my ear. "It was almost three years ago at that charity event. You looked like a princess in a room full of peasants. I always thought the whole 'love at first site' saying was bullshit, but when I saw you . . ." he pauses. "I knew I was fucked."

His last sentence has me in giggles from his choice of words. He laughs along with me. "When I took you back to the hotel and we made love, I was a goner." His head tilts again. "Now that I recall, you were the one who started this cat and mouse game by leaving the next morning." The memory has me frowning.

Lifting his hand to palm my cheek, he says, "You were once a temptation, Victoria. One I knew I could never have. You've broken me for all other women. No one will ever compare to you. I will never have anyone, unless it is *you.*"

There is that word again . . ."Love?" I whisper, my heart begging for it to be true.

Slowly, his head nods up and down. "I love you, Victoria."

My rapid pulse has my head spinning. "Love is an infatuation." My father's words echo in my head. "We barely even know each other."

His shoulder goes up into a shrug. "We've got the rest of our lives to get to know each other. What's the hurry?" A sheepish grin spreads across his lips.

I release a burst of laughter at his rebuttal, knowing only he would declare such an objection to my statement. "What am I going to do with you?" I ask, laying my forehead against his chest. "I'm so scared, but I'm pretty sure I'm falling for you, too," I confess.

"So no love?"

Pulling my head back, I look up to face him. "We'll see." From his sorrowful expression, it's not what he wanted to hear.

"Trey, I'm pregnant. I just started my job. My family has disowned me. I work too many hours, there is no way

I'm going to be a perfect mother. I'm not used to being around children. How in the world will I know what to do with one? This is not exactly how I had planned out my life when I was a child daydreaming of my own fairytale."

"Is anything ever planned out with us?" he laughs out. "You'll be a perfect mother," he assures me.

"I wouldn't be so confident just yet. Have I mentioned I've never held a baby before? What if I drop it?"

Adding to our amusement, Trey says, "I'm pretty sure I was dropped a couple of times as a child and I turned out just fine." This makes me groan. It's not exactly what I needed to hear for a boost of confidence.

My stomach takes this moment to disclose its hunger by releasing a roaring grumble. We both laugh as I acknowledge it. "I'm hungry," I say, as if it isn't obvious.

"No shit," Trey replies. "If you wouldn't have been so damn stubborn, you would have been fed already, woman."

"You made food?"

He lowers his mouth mere inches from my ear. "I made bacon," he whispers into it.

My eyes close and I don't care if he's heard me whimper because I may just have a reason to fall in love with this man . . . He cooks me bacon.

Trey

Victoria lets out a contented sigh and the sound will never

get old. "Full?" I ask from the edge of the bed, feeding her cat another piece of bacon.

The tip of her toe shoves into my thigh. "Stop feeding him bacon, you're going to clog his tiny arteries."

"He's probably going to croak any day now. Let the beast die happy." I know it's not what I should have said because her eyes become glassy. Fucking hormones. "Sorry, princess," I apologize, hoping to redeem myself, while shoving the cat to the edge of the bed, but making sure to drop the piece of bacon in my hand to make up for the rejection.

"Did you like my peace offering?"

"Very much," she replies with a smile, her eyes peering over the top of the ginger ale she's drinking. Pointing my chin at the can, I ask, "Did it help settle your stomach?"

"How did you know I needed ginger ale?" she curiously asks.

I move up the bed so I'm next to her. "I called my momma to ask her what would help with your upset stomach." I pause, waiting for her response. As expected, she goes stiff. The second sip she was going to take has come to an abrupt stop, her eyes peeking over the can she's slowly brings down.

She swallows hard. "What did she say?" she rasps out.

My mouth curves up to one side. "You mean when I finally got her to speak after she started crying?" Victoria's shoulders drop down and her eyes grow soft with sadness. "They were joyful tears, I swear," I explain, allowing her to let out a breath. "She went screaming to practically the whole neighborhood how she was getting a beautiful new grandbaby soon."

There was one particular comment I'm still trying to decipher. "Would you happen to know why my momma and Aunt Mary Anne would both agree you know how to listen when asked to do something?"

Her mouth forms into a small 'O.' "They may have mentioned how they wanted us to work on making a baby when we got back to the city."

This has me intrigued. "Really? Should I have told her the baby was really made back home?" Victoria's expression instantly turns confused. "The stable," I remind with a smile.

Her eyes go wide and all color leaves her face. "We had sex in the stable?" Biting my lips, I stifle the laughter I want to release. "We had really hot sex in the stable," I repeat. Her only response is a groan and a frown. "I don't even remember," she replies in a whisper.

Now I'm the one with a frown. It reminds me of the many times we've had sex because of her intoxicated state. This is a joyful moment of creating our child and she doesn't remember. Thankfully, I've got time to make up for it. With her condition, there will be no drinking.

"If you'd like, we can go back and reenact the entire process." My head is playfully wacked with a pillow. "I swear you always have sex on your mind," she lectures. I'm not going to argue, for two reasons: One, Victoria would find a way to twist my words to prove me wrong, and two, she's correct. I do always have sex on my mind when it comes to Victoria.

"You're thinking about sex, aren't you?" she laughs

out.

"Well, yeah, now that you've mentioned it," I reply. She picks up another pillow, already aiming at my head. "I thought you were going to stop that!" Yanking the pillow from her hand, I toss it off the bed. She lets out a heartfelt laugh.

Seeing her cheerful smile returned almost makes me not want to ask a certain question. Her earlier words have been lingering in my mind and I have been carefully choosing when to approach her with the subject. Better now than never. "Victoria, what did you mean when you mentioned your family disowned you?"

She stiffens and I'm expecting her to run, or least change the subject, but she surprises me. "Exactly what I said, they *disowned* me."

Her emotions are strong in the air. I can practically feel the sadness she's trying to disguise while picking at the invisible lint on the bed. "Was it because of me?" I brave to ask. Her saddened eyes find mine. "Sort of," she whispers.

I *am* the asshole she declares me to be.

I've cost her her entire family.

As if sensing my self-loathing, she reaches forward to place a gentle kiss on my lips. "It's not what you think," she attempts to reassure me, but fails.

"What am I supposed to think? I know I'm not good enough for you and they even know it, or else they wouldn't have made you choose." I roll over to step up off the bed when she brings me to a stop. Trapping me by straddling my waist, she shoves at my chest to keep me down. "They were still trying to force me to marry Andrew when I returned. Had it not been for you, I probably would have already been married to him long ago."

Hearing her remind me of the fucker has my blood boiling. Her heartfelt chuckle helps calm me a little, though.

"Somehow you always come back into my life when I need you the most," she proclaims.

I'm not exactly jumping for joy quite yet because the realization hits me that every decision has consequences.

"What's going to happen now? Isn't everything you have because of them?" Her eyes cast downward, the sadness growing tenfold.

"Most of it," she relays. "The condo in Seattle isn't mine, but they've given me a year to vacate. The car was a graduation gift, but it's not exactly a baby carrying vehicle," she states.

Eyes wide, I'm quick to respond, "Don't even think about a mini-van. Over my dead body are we driving a fucking mini-van." She throws her head back and laughs. Her laugher is welcome in the darkness of our moods. "No mini-van, then," she grants me.

I never thought I'd get so irate over a fucking vehicle, but from the look in her eyes, I knew she would have suggested it. "Anything else?" I press. Her abiding silence worries me. "My trust fund. They revoked everything I had in the account in regards to my trust."

I'm shocked. "They can do that?"

She nods her head. "The account was in their name to begin with, so legally they can." Her shoulders drop down.

"I guess I could try to fight them for it, but I don't want to bother."

Brushing the hair away from her face, I say, "It isn't worth it, Victoria." Her skepticism has me asking, "How much was it?"

"A little over five million."

Holy. Fucking. Shit.

Had I been standing, she would have knocked my legs out from under me with her response. My shock amuses her. "Still not worth it?"

Swallowing the lump lodged in my throat, I say "No," trying to reassure her.

"Good, because I'm no longer considered a spoiled rich girl," she says, lowering herself so she's draped across my chest.

Caressing her bare spine, I let out a sigh, resenting ever throwing the words at her. I've said so much shit I now regret. Victoria is far from what I portrayed her to be in the beginning, yet regardless of the countless times I've thrown the angered words at her, she allows me to come crawling back.

That shit has got to stop.

Rolling us so she's below me, I stare down at the one girl who has captured my heart. Then my eyes roam down her body right where she holds our baby. Lowering myself so my mouth is right above her abdomen, I glance up to her to say, "You both will never need for anything as long as I'm around." I place a kiss upon her bare skin. "You don't need your worthless family. I've got more than enough to give back to you. We may not be all prim and proper, but sometimes dysfunctional is better in the end." I brush my lips back and forth against her skin. "We'll be sure to shower you with the love you never had." Her eyes grow glassy before the first tear falls. I'm already kicking myself for making her cry. Crawling my way up her body, this time her hands are not pushing me away, but instead holding tight to my head to guide me up to kiss those tears away. Finding her mouth, I eagerly kiss her.

She breathlessly says into my mouth, "You're going to make us late." She giggles, but doesn't protest by pushing me away.

"We've got a couple of hours. Right now we've got weeks of being apart to make up for," I beam above her.

She playfully shoves at my chest. "See, I was right. All you think about is sex."

"I'm pretty sure with the way you've been looking at me for the last couple of days, I'm not the only one." Her throat vibrates with a stifled groan. "See, *I was right, too,*" I chuckle in return.

The playful Victoria is gone, replaced with the shark from yesterday. They had no chance when it came to her. The same glare that has me growing hard in seconds does the opposite for the men gazing back at her from across the table; she has them cowering with their tails between their legs.

It didn't take them long to agree to her terms. I was sweating bullets along with Matt the entire time, but she sat there confident as ever. No doubt in her mind she would get her way. From her demeanor, I can already predict a future of us battling from our stubbornness, but then I'm reminded it was her stubbornness that attracted me to her. It will be worth it if our relationship is going to be full of constant make-up sex.

"Thank you, gentlemen. It was a pleasure doing business with you and I'm sure I will be seeing you again this season in our private box during the Super Bowl," she confidently claims, shaking each individual hand with a satisfied smile.

They laugh at her enthusiasm then exit the conference room, leaving the three of us to celebrate. Matt engulfs her in a hug, lifting her up to spin her around, her playful giggles echoing in the room. "Hey, be careful with her, she's carrying my precious cargo in there." I gesture towards her, but know well he'd do nothing to hurt her.

Gently placing her back on the floor, both of them laugh back at me. Pulling her to my side, my arm protectively wraps around her waist.

"Thanks, Victoria. It's more than I would have ever asked for," Matt announces.

Shyly accepting his compliment, she says, "My pleasure."

"Celebration at the house tonight," Matt gleefully says without taking no for an answer.

"Sure, we'll be there," I inform him.

"I'll see you guys later." He whoops on his way out.

Turning Victoria so she's directly facing me, I say, "Thank you." Kissing her hard, she opens up, pushing her tongue into my mouth, demanding more than a simple peck. My dick is already jumping in my pants. "Princess, unless you want me to properly thank you on this table, we need to leave," I say against her mouth.

"Then you better decide where exactly you plan on rewarding me, because I'm pretty sure I earned it."

My eyes roll to the back of my head. "Princess, you better not expect to see the light of day for the next couple of days," I say, picking her up and throwing her over my shoulder.

She lets out a protest, but not what I expected to hear. "Trey, my briefcase. Don't forget it," she states, pounding at my back to catch my attention.

Rapidly spinning her around to retrieve the item, she lets out another bout of giggles. The sound will never get old and I intend to make sure to hear it every day.

Several months later . . .

After an exhausting round of sex, Victoria props her head up on her hand.

"How about this one," I ask Victoria, handing her another flyer. She apprehensively looks down to it. She doesn't look satisfied with my suggestion. "What's wrong with it?" I ask, peering down at the details of the penthouse.

She considers it for another moment. "Nothing, I guess." She sighs. Dropping the flyer aside, I prop my own head on my hand, mimicking her stance.

"What's really wrong, Victoria?"

Her lips twist up to one side as she considers her words. She's thinking, hard.

"Do you resent that I work so much?"

The question has taken me aback since this is the hard-core, driven Victoria asking. It's who I fell in love with.

"No. Do I make you feel that way?"

"I'm just worried about when the baby comes. How are we going to do it?" The worry in her eyes is practically eating at her.

"We'll figure something out," I relay. "There's always a nanny." I grimace, not really liking the idea myself, but knowing it may be our only option due to our schedules.

She sighs again, rolling onto her back to rub at her small mound of a belly. Victoria is now six months pregnant . . . with our boy. I would have been fine with the sex being a surprise, but Ms. I Need to be Informed of Everything demanded to know. I can't complain, though, knowing a future linebacker is baking inside the woman I love. The thought has me overjoyed. Placing my hand over one of hers, I kiss her belly as she relays, "It would be the life I had." The hurt is evident in her tone. "I don't want our baby being raised solely by a nanny."

Sighing, I acknowledge the truth in her words. Victoria and I both work hard and with it comes long hours. I'm not ignorant, knowing it may get worse with the rise of her position.

"Where is this going, Victoria?"

She remains silent. I don't need to look at her to know

the wheels in her head are turning. "We've been looking at place after place and there isn't one I'm happy with." Shit, she didn't have to tell me. I've discovered the fact on my own. I'm beginning to grow frustrated over it.

"You want to know why I'm not happy with any of them?"

Arching my brow, I patiently wait for her to tell me. "Because they're all condos, or apartments, not houses."

Understanding where she's going with this, I say, "Victoria, we've discussed this. If you want a house, I'll buy you a fucking house, but you're the one who wants to be close to work in case something happens with the baby."

"I know," she murmurs under her breath. "Sometimes I wonder if my career is worth sacrificing my child's happiness for." I don't disagree. "I want the typical fairytale." Turning so she's facing me, she holds a radiant smile. "I've already got my prince, why can't I have the castle I truly want?"

"Prince? Princes are pansies, Victoria."

Giggling, she says, "If I recall, you called yourself a pansy once." Fuck, I didn't think she'd remember that detail. "It doesn't have to be a castle, but a house will do," she clarifies.

If it's a fucking castle she wants, I'll find a way to get it for her. She's worth it. But knowing Victoria, if I presented her with said castle, she'd roll her eyes and give me the many reasons why I am taking everything she says out of proportion.

"Okay, I'll call the realtor and tell her to start searching the suburbs. What area are you thinking?"

Her eyes shyly look down between us as she says above a whisper, "Portland."

Taken aback because my hearing must be failing me, I ask, "Did you just say Portland?"

Coyly smiling up to me, her lips are lost between her teeth when she nods. "It would be closer to Matt and Abigail's house. And I know how much you love it there."

"What about your job?" I ask, watching her grow a little apprehensive and her earlier comments dawn on me. "If you want to stay home with the baby, Victoria, I wouldn't hold you back. I make more than enough money to support all of us."

"I know, money isn't my concern," she conveys, and I know she's speaking the truth. Victoria may wear all designer clothing, but it's the lifestyle she was provided, not one she chose. She won't hesitate to remind me money doesn't grant you happiness, it will only fill a void. It's the happiness you make with those you love that is the true wealth. Every day she's made me a richer man with how she proves how much she cares.

"I just feel as if I'd be failing if I stop practicing law for a while to stay home with the baby," she says, still sounding saddened when she declares the words.

"How is staying home with our baby failing?"

Her hands move over her abdomen. "It's not. I just don't want to regret my decision."

Pulling her to my side, her belly between us, she drapes her arm over my chest, holding tight. Fully kissing her, I know this helps calm her when she's restless. Giving me a satisfied smile, I know I've accomplished my task.

"Do you want to know what I think?" I bravely ask. She nods, allowing me to speak. "I want you to do what makes you happy. If working and kicking ass in the court room is what turns you on, then do it," I remark. "But if you want to stay home to raise our family, then I'm all for it. But you have to do what makes you happy."

Resting her chin on my chest, she smiles. "You make me happy."

"You bet your pretty ass I do," I say, reinforcing my words with a slap of my hand on her butt cheek.

She yelps before laughing. "I'm serious!" she exclaims, slapping my chest in return. Catching her hand, I kiss the inside of her palm, earning me her contented sigh.

Returning to the subject, I say, "It's your decision, not mine, Victoria."

Those are our last words on the subject. As much as I would like to demand she stay home, regardless of her final decision, I know it's a death trap. I have to let her decide, if not, I risk losing her forever.

Victoria

The next day I walk into Benjamin's office, my heart erratically racing while my anxious mind keeps reminding me why this is the best decision I will ever make. With a trembling hand, I lay my resignation letter on his desk. Taking the document, he quickly looks it over before peering directly in my eyes with a smile—far from the reaction I was expecting.

"I knew this day would come," he vocalizes.

Astonished he would say so, I ask, "Really?"

He chuckles while giving his head a light shake. "I've known for a while, Victoria."

His comment has me wondering when I lost my touch with reading people. It was my strongest point in court. This leaves me disappointed I've failed as a lawyer.

"Was I lacking?"

Eyes-wide, he answers, "No, but I know you, and I know the man you've come to call your *partner.* I wouldn't expect anything less than for you to put your future first." His chin points towards my belly. "I have faith everything will work out."

"I appreciate everything you've done for me."

He gives me a genuine smile. "You'll always have a position here with us if you ever decide to come back."

"Thank you."

I walk away feeling happier than I have in the days it took me to ponder over this decision. I have no regrets. My unborn child already means just as much to me as my love for Trey, only I still haven't proven the extent of how I feel to him.

He continues to declare his love for me every day, regardless of my silence in return. It wasn't because I doubted my love for him that I didn't return the words, it was because of the fear he'd return to his old ways and walk away, but not anymore. I know Trey is worth keeping. Obnoxious and all, in my eyes he's perfect just the way he is.

There will never be a dull moment as long as we're together, which is why I plan on spending the rest of my life with him from this day forward.

Epilogue

Trey

"I HATE YOU!" Victoria hisses through clenched teeth.

The words no longer mean their true intention, but are Victoria's endearing words for me. Beneath those words she is declaring her love in disguise. There isn't a week that doesn't go by that she doesn't hiss those words, along with her other usual statement.

Kissing her forehead, I say, "I love you, too, princess." I point at the Mickey in front of her to give her something to focus on.

She lets out a heart-wrenching scream. Grabbing a fist full of my shirt, she glares into my eyes. I don't suppose this is a proper time for my dick to grow hard, is it?

"This is all your fault!" And there it is. Her proclamation of love would not be complete without the other. I've come to love hearing those words thrown at me. The day she stops is when I know I should grow worried.

355

Nodding my head in agreement, I say, "Yes, it is," knowing it's best to agree with her in her state or risk having my balls dismembered. "Although, I'm pretty sure it was you who was raping me in the stable that night," I bravely add.

With her contraction dying down, she turns to me with a puzzled look. "The stable?" she questions, completely at a loss of what I'm referring to.

Pushing her hair from her eyes, I kiss her lips that are swollen since she's been biting down on them for the past hour. "Yes, the stable. At my parents' house," I remind her.

Realization comes to her. "Oh, my God. The day I woke up with no underwear!" she utters while taking a deep breath. "Damn moonshine," she protests under her breath, having us both laugh from the recalling of our story.

"Right now I'm thanking the moonshine," I whisper, kissing her below her ear.

I feel her contentedly sigh before her abdomen under my hand grows hard, indicating another contraction. All the fucking books said she would have hours before she would be close to deliver. According to the nurse who checked fifteen minutes ago, she's already dilated to six centimeters.

Her screams confirm she's getting closer and I look to one of the nurses still in the room. "Go see what's taking that fucking doctor so long! This baby is going to kill her!"

"Trey, calm down, you're scaring the poor girl," my mother says in a calming voice while wiping Victoria's brow. "You're doing great, honey. Now keep breathing like they taught you and focus on the mouse over there," she says, indicating the stuffed animal at the edge of the bed.

"Those fucking classes were lame. I can get her to breathe better when we have sex."

The damp towel my momma was holding lands hard against my chest. "Trey Johnson, don't make me come around this bed and knock you upside the head." The towel I can handle, her knocking me on the head, not so much.

"It's almost over, princess, I promise. Just hang in there." I feel helpless because I can't take away her pain. If I could, I would.

Mimicking the little girl from the exorcist, she says, "Easy for you to say. You're not the one squeezing a baby elephant out of you!" she growls into my face.

"I doubt you have an elephant in you," I joke. "Unless you were cheating on me?"

Looking down at her belly, I can't disagree with her size. She is huge. *Very.* There were some days I thought she would topple over from how big her stomach had gotten. I made the mistake of informing her of my opinion and got one of the new Jimmy Choo's I bought her to the side of my head. Though, the shoes were what led to my comment. She cried when I gave them to her, but not tears of joy. They were tears of misery since her feet were so swollen.

The make-up sex was totally worth the goose egg she found minutes later. I'll take a shoe to the head any day for what I got in return.

Victoria's latest scream has me panicking. "Tell them to hurry up!" I shout at the air because I can't particularly shout at the two women in front of me. Lifting up the cover, I look down into Victoria's vagina, or at least what she'll let me see as her hand shoves me away. "Get out of there!" I hear her screech.

Coming from out of the covers, I say, "I was checking to see if the baby is coming. It's not like I don't know what it looks like. My face is down there practically every night."

She groans, landing back on the bed while throwing her arm over her eyes. "Your mother doesn't need to know that, Trey," she hisses.

"No, I don't," Momma agrees.

"Titi!" Emily shouts to Victoria, entering the room with Matt and Abigail. "I'm sorry, baby girl, Titi can't hold you right now," I inform her, watching her frown. Victoria's hands clutch her belly and she lets out a loud groan. It worries Emily. "Titi crying?"

Breathing through clenched teeth, Victoria says, "Titi's okay, baby. I'm just—" but doesn't get to finish as she tightens her grip on my hand. "Argh!"

Emily cries along with her and Abigail does her best to calm her. "I think we'll wait in the waiting room for a while," Abigail expresses, while Matt's eyes go as wide as saucers. He's speechless, following his two girls out of the room, but I still manage to hear him say, "Still want to keep trying for that second baby?"

Victoria lets out another scream, bringing my attention back to her. Gripping at my shirt, she yanks me down so our faces are mere inches from each other. "Get me the fucking anesthesiologist before I cut off your balls for doing this to me."

It isn't a threat. From the fury in her eyes, I know she's serious.

Looking to my momma, I say, "I value my balls. Go get the nurse." She chuckles at my reaction before turning to leave the room.

Brushing back the hair off her sweaty forehead, I smile down to Victoria and give her soothing words. Minutes later, her contraction must have died down as she's smiling back at me. "I love you."

Since the moment she delivered those three words a couple of months ago, I've been the happiest man alive. Lifting up the hand holding her wedding ring, I kiss the inside of her palm.

Victoria came home the day she submitted her resignation, declaring her love for me. It was the same day I asked her to marry me. She hadn't known I already had the ring. Up until then I didn't have the balls to propose to her in fear she'd turn me down. I've seen what a denial can do to a man's emotions. For the couple of minutes it took her to respond, I practically lost my dinner thinking she would deny me, but with an ecstatic smile she gave me a "Yes!"

Knowing the condition she was in, I worked fast. Gathering my small little crew, I flew us all back to Tennessee and married her in front of my entire family. At first, I was hesitant, unsure if it was good enough for Victoria, thinking she preferred a luxurious wedding. But the radiant smile she kept holding the entire time until she met me at the altar was all I needed to push any doubt away. And I made sure to keep my word to reenact our night of conceiving our son, sans moonshine.

Her stomach tightens again. "I hate you, and you're an asshole for doing this to me," she growls through clenched teeth. Is it odd that those specific words make me light up inside?

"I vowed to be your asshole until the day I died when I married you, and you can hate me all you want, because I'll still love you," I promise her.

She yells loud enough to break my eardrums. I'm about ready to leave her to start my own search for the doctor when my mother returns with a cheerful, scrub-wearing doctor. "Victoria Johnson?" he says, the most perfect name I've ever heard.

She nods, panting through the slit of her mouth. "You better be the one to give me the juice or I may strangle you."

After the words she's delivered, I find it amusing he's laughing. "I've got your juice," he replies, while I'm over here thanking God.

Looking to me, he asks, "Are you her husband?"

"Better believe it," I declare.

"It's his fault I'm in this condition," Victoria adds. "I swear I'm going to kill him."

Her comment has the entire room laughing.

The doctor looks to me. "They all say the same thing."

Giving me instructions on how to hold her, he begins the procedure to give her the epidural. Soon she's juiced up and loopy with a smile as if she was never in pain.

An hour later, Madden Everett Johnson makes his way into the world.

Madden was my choice, needing a touch of my favorite sport in him. Everett was Victoria's. She wanted our child to be named after one of his grandparents, and we both agreed it wasn't going to be her worthless father's name we were blessing him with.

I never thought my heart could expand any more than it already had, but seeing Victoria nursing our son at her chest has tears forming in my eyes. She looks up to me with an exhausted smile, looking more radiant than ever. "Isn't he beautiful?"

"I'd prefer to call him handsome."

She nudges me with her elbow. "Next to you, he's the second most precious person I've ever laid my eyes on."

I see her lips begin to tremble and I lean down to kiss the frown away. "I love you, princess." She smiles against my lips. "I thank God everyday Matt got shot and I had to wear a monkey suit to find you."

We both let out a bout of laughs, understanding why I would say such words.

Cradling our son between us, she replies, "And I thank God I drank too much champagne that same night."

The End . . .

Acknowledgments

To my husband and children. You stood by me during the frustrations that came with the process of writing this book and I love you so much for never giving up on me.

To every single one of my readers who begged me to write Trey's story. You all own a little piece of his heart. If it wasn't for your persistency, this story would have never been written.

Trey and Victoria, I never thought the day would come when I'd write your story, but without a doubt, I am glad I did. You two will always hold a place in my heart.

To my editor and heroine, Edee Fallon. You are always a text message or phone call away when I am in doubt. I love you.

Skye, Missy, Barbara, Carrie, Michelle, and Tyf, thank you for the text messages that kept me sane through this crazy ride.

Carrie Renteria, I may have just found you, but I am glad you came into my life.

To the awesome photographer and models who helped make my characters come to life: Mandy Hollis, Julio Elving, and Ashley Edmund. Third time was definitely the charm. I thank you more than words can ever express.

Rebecca Pau, thank you for delivering such an amazing cover. I knew from the beginning you would never disappoint me. Hugs and kisses, girl, I love you.

Stacey Blake, I am lifting my glass of wine in salute to your awesomeness. Thank you for making my story so beautiful.

To my street team, The Beautiful Girls, thank you for all your support and for believing in me.

To my beta group, thank you for guiding me in the right direction.

Last, but not least, to all the readers and bloggers who took the time to read *Unspoken Temptation.* Without you, I wouldn't have a reason to write. Thank you from the bottom of my heart.

Discover the series that begin it all with Matt and Abigail in *Unspoken Memories*.

Chapter One

I CAN HEAR voices, two to be exact, a man and a woman. They're speaking quietly, but loudly enough that I can clearly make out their conversation. I can't open my eyes, no matter how hard I try, and they feel heavy, so I keep them closed.

"I can't leave her, she's our money ticket!" he says in a very stressed tone.

"How much good is she to you now? She's in a coma! We don't know if she's ever going to wake up." This comes from the woman, and from the way she says it, I know she isn't happy.

"Well, it doesn't matter, I need a little more time to try to figure out how to access the rest of the funds. The longer she's in this coma, the more time is on my side, and the more money we get."

Okay, this is where the conversation is getting really interesting to me. At this point I'm trying hard to open my eyes, but I keep getting pulled somewhere else, back into the darkness. My gut feeling is telling me keep my eyes closed and keep listening, so that's what I'm trying to do, I'm fighting the pull that wants to take me away.

"Well, I'm tired of being your fuck buddy, I want more!" she demands of him in a very loud whisper.

Fuck buddy? Why is she being a fuck buddy, and whose? But by the way she tells him this, I have a feeling that she's been his fuck buddy for a while.

"Look, when we started this you knew to never expect more, but if she's going to be a vegetable for a while, I'm thinking things are going to change very soon."

This doesn't sound good. I start to freak out, especially since I feel like a vegetable right now. No matter how hard I'm trying, I can't move a muscle. I wonder, are they speaking about me?

The room suddenly grows quiet, and I start to hear footsteps fading in the distance. I believe they're leaving, because I hear the opening and closing of a door.

I give it a couple of seconds, but the room is still silent. I can finally relax. Then all of a sudden, the darkness begins to take over again.

I FEEL MYSELF slowly waking up again and I let out a light moan. I can feel the grumble of it traveling down my chest, and it aches. I feel so groggy and weak. I don't want to wake up, but my body is not allowing me to fall back asleep and I try to slowly open my eyes. It's hard at first, but after a couple of blinks, I'm successful at bringing them to a slit. My body is aching as I try to lift my arm. It feels like weights are holding it down, but I'm able to move my hand, I think.

What is that sound? It's a constant beeping, coming from the side of my head, and it's speeding up as I move in that direction. I try to lift my arm to get to it, with little success because there's something tugging at it. When I look down, I see an I.V. attached to my arm, why would I have an I.V.? I attempt to completely open my eyes. I see an older lady who is wearing nurse's scrubs walking towards me. She must have done something, because the loud beeping is finally gone. It was making my head hurt, so I'm grateful she finally made the thing shut up.

"Good, you're awake," I hear her say next to me.

I feel her warm hand grab onto my wrist while she looks down at a watch she is wearing. I'm still confused. I have no idea where I am.

I manage to move my head a little and take in my surroundings. It looks like I'm in a hospital room. It's white, and almost empty, with only a couple of chairs in each corner. There's a flat screen on the wall directly in front of me, with a clock to its side, stating it's almost six. Underneath the clock there's a white board with writing on it. I guess my nurse's name is Karen, since that's the name on the board.

"How are you feeling Ms. Adams?" Karen says, still focusing on her watch.

I lie there wondering why I'm even here, and how did I get here? Wait, what did she call me? Is it my name? It doesn't sound familiar.

I have no clue where in the world I am and I don't like it.

"Where am I?" I ask Karen, wondering why I would

be in a hospital room.

She looks up from her watch, with a blank face. "You're at Washington Memorial Hospital, Ms. Adams." Then she goes back to looking at her watch.

I'm still confused, why is she calling *me* that name? "Who's Ms. Adams?" I ask her, confused.

She lightly snaps her head up again to look down at me, and draws in her eyebrows. Her smile has disappeared and goes directly to a frown. "Why, you are, of course," she informs me.

She places my wrist down back on the bed, patting it lightly. "I'll just page your neurologist and we'll go from there, okay?" she says as she turns and walks out of the room, leaving me there still baffled by the whole situation.

A couple of minutes later, another lady walks into the room. I'm assuming she is my doctor because she's wearing a white coat. She looks Indian and young. But as she's walking in she has a smile on her face and it gives me a bit of hope.

A bit.

"Ms. Adams, I'm Dr. Kumar, your neurologist. How are you feeling, dear?" she enthusiastically asks me, while swiftly grabbing my chart, opening it, and beginning to review it.

Knowing the truth will never hurt, I say bluntly, "I feel like shit and I really have to pee."

This makes her laugh, as she pulls out what looks like a pen from her coat pocket, walks to the side of my bed and leans above me. I realize it's a flashlight as she starts flashing it back and forth between my eyes, making me flinch. It burns my eyes and if my arms didn't feel so weak, I would have swatted that darn thing out of her hand.

Trust me, I try, but I quickly give up the notion. Once she's done shining the death light at me she replaces it in her coat pocket and walks to the end of my bed to pick the chart back up and starts scribbling notes into it. I lay here staring at her.

As she's still scribbling, the nurse walks in again with a new I.V. bag and busies herself with changing it while the doctor asks me, "Ms. Adams, would you be more comfortable if I have Karen here remove your catheter so you can go to the bathroom yourself?" She is still staring down at the chart making notes.

I nod my head in agreement, but can't help asking again, "Who is Ms. Adams? You both keep calling me that name?"

The doctor quickly snaps her head up, while the nurse stops fiddling with the bag and they both stare at me in shock.

The doctor immediately looks at the nurse. "Call her fiancé, and order a CAT scan STAT." Then she looks down at me and says, "We'll just order some more tests to make sure there isn't any swelling remaining and go from there, okay?" She finishes with a smile.

Still very confused about what is going on, I nod my head in acceptance and hope that I'll remember something in a couple of minutes. Right now the only thing I keep thinking about is the conversation I heard earlier. Or I think it was earlier. I really have no idea when it took place. It almost feels like it only happened a couple of minutes ago and I'm really anxious to find out who was in my room. But more than anything I still have to pee.

My thoughts must have taken me away for a couple of minutes because the nurse has managed to remove my catheter and with a lot of assistance, I'm able to sit up on the bed. At first my body is wobbly and unbalanced, but after a few minutes I find the strength I am searching for and make my merry way along, holding onto the nurse for dear life. The metal stand holding the I.V. bag follows me the whole way.

It's hard to walk when you have something attached to your arm following you around. After the first tug at my arm, I want to yank the thing out myself. However, the nurse keeps saying I have to leave it in, since it is providing me with the fluids to increase my health.

That is the only reason it stays in.

After some major maneuvering, again with the nurse's help, I'm finally able to relieve myself in the attached bathroom. I can't go at first, knowing she is standing there staring at me. But even after asking her for some privacy, she only moves to the doorframe of the bathroom.

Finishing up what I needed to do, and washing my hands, I take a moment to stand in front of the mirror and stare at my reflection. Other than needing to take a brush to my hair, I look perfectly fine.

Or at least I think I do for someone who is in the hospital.

Actually, I don't recognize myself at all. You would think that I would at least recognize my reflection, but it doesn't come to me. So I stand there staring at myself and take in my features.

My hair is blonde, very long, and my eyes are a very bright green. I'm also tall. I remember being at least half a foot taller than the nurse, towering over her a bit. Another noticeable thing is that I'm very skinny. Don't I ever eat?

When I hear the nurse knock on the bathroom door making sure that I'm still okay, it distracts me from my thoughts, also reminding me that we have to go get my CAT scan done right away. I exit the bathroom and allow her to lead me to the bed, laying me back down.

An hour later, after being put through a cocoon-like machine, as I'm being wheeled toward my room, I see a man rushing in my direction. He's practically running when he walks and he looks exhausted. I don't know who this man is, but by the way he's looking straight at me and still walking in my direction, he knows me.

He looks to be in his mid-thirties and he's wearing an expensive looking suit. He's lean, and tall, but not too tall. He has disheveled black hair, as if he's been running his hands through it. He has stress lines around his face, but at this moment his face is lit up and he's happy to see me.

"Oh honey, you're finally awake, I've been so worried about you," he says as he reaches me, giving me a kiss on my forehead. I'm really confused about who he is because I don't recognize him. But when my mind takes in his voice, realizing that it sounds very familiar, I panic.

If I were still hooked up to the monitor at this moment I'm pretty sure it would be making the crazy noises from earlier, because my heart rate is going crazy. First it feels like it had stopped, and now it's accelerating because I'm freaking out.

This is the voice, the male voice I heard the last time I heard anything, but he's alone this time. I immediately start looking around, thinking about the other mystery voice, the one that belongs to the woman, expecting to hear it any minute. But I don't.

He follows, as the nurse continues to push me back into my room and once we're all in the room, he starts attacking the doctor and nurse with different questions. There are so many, it's even confusing to me. Although the most important one is how much longer I'm going to be here now that I've woken up. That particular question is the one I care about the most, because I'm pretty sure when I leave here I don't want it to be with this guy. The uncomfortable feeling I'm getting from him is not making me feel good.

I keep staring at the guy, hoping that I would recognize him somehow, but I can't. He seems worried about me, so obviously he must be someone important. However, I think about the ominous conversation that took place that included his voice.

Wanting to know who he is, I demand, "Who are you?" I say out loud, looking directly at him.

He snaps his head to look at me and he's disoriented, like I just asked the stupidest question in the world. At this point it sounds pretty stupid to me too, but I really need to know who this stranger is.

He frowns, bringing his lips into a flat line, and finally he says, "I'm Bill, your fiancé."

Now I'm screwed, I think. I'm pretty sure that this was

the voice I heard with the woman the last time I tried waking up. But, why would my fiancé be someone else's fuck buddy? I don't understand. Right now my life is starting to feel like some kind of soap opera and I'm obviously the starring actress.

They're all still looking at me, as if they're waiting for me to say something.

"Abigail, are you sure you're feeling okay?"

If my throat weren't hurting so much, I would be saying right now: *No you dumb ass, I just woke up, my body feels like shit, and you guys keep calling me a name I don't recognize.*

Another thing to add to the list is that I don't trust them! But I keep my mouth shut knowing this is the best thing to do. However, I ask again, knowing that I still need an answer. "Who's Abigail?"

Ignoring my question, Bill turns to the doctor. "What's wrong with her, why doesn't she know who she is?" he demands, pointing his hand in my direction.

Looking perplexed over the whole situation herself, she answers him, "She seems to have had a bit of a memory loss." The doctor gives him a calming look like this is normal. "She may just need time to recover properly; it can happen with patients in her situation."

Shaking his head, Bill grabs the bridge of his nose with his thumb and forefinger, sighing to himself. He's still quiet, like he's concentrating on what he's going to say next. I think he's still shocked.

I hate that they won't give me any detailed answers.

"What happened to me?" I ask, looking between Bill

and the doctor.

Everybody is looking at me, still very uncertain whether to tell me or not.

Bill walks up to my bedside, taking one of my hands into his, and drops his head, looking gently at my face.

He takes a breath and begins, "A friend of ours was having a party at a hotel downtown, and as usual we had a room there so you could get ready. As we were waiting for the elevator to go down to the party, you became impatient, and decided to take the stairs instead. You were wearing some really high heels and lost your footing on one of the steps and hit your head pretty badly on the way down." He pauses like he's concentrating on what to say next, then carries on, "When you arrived at the hospital you had some really bad swelling in your brain, so the doctor here suggested that we put you in an induced coma."

I'm trying to absorb all the information he's just given me, then I look over to the doctor, still really confused about the whole situation.

"How long have I been in a coma?" I whisper, staring at the wall ahead of me, holding back the tears that are fighting to come out.

She looks to Bill first, then directly back at me answering, "It's been a little over four months since the swelling in your brain reduced and we reversed the medication. You didn't wake up right away," she calmly states, as if reassuring me everything is fine.

I look over in Bill's direction and ask again, "Who are you?" I want confirmation.

He's now starting to look irritated by my question, but

he responds again. "I'm Bill, your fiancé, baby."

His answer still throws me for loop and I panic a little.

Why would my fiancé want me to stay in a coma? He had looked relieved to see me awake, but I keep replaying the conversation in my head, wanting to doubt it. I know what I heard. It was loud and clear, even if my eyes weren't open.

Another thing that comes to mind, is why does he have someone else as a fuck buddy?

My panic is obvious to Bill, so he says, "We've been together for over a year now. We met at one of your shows over two years ago when I became your agent and we started dating a little while later. It was love at first sight for me." He tries to reassure me with a smile. But I'm not buying it.

I look over at the doctor with a look like, "Please tell me he's kidding." From the way she's looking at me, I know she believes his story. Bill looks up to the doctor and begins asking how soon I'll be able to go home.

While she goes over the lecture about needing my rest before leaving, I block out their bickering at each other.

This is when I start reciting a number in my head, 951-555-2945. It comes to me naturally, like I've called it regularly.

That's weird, why would I be thinking of a phone number at this moment? I'm happy that at least something is coming back to me.

"Bill, what's your number?" I ask, loud enough so they both can hear me.

They both snap their heads in my direction in confusion for asking such a question, but Bill automatically answers. "555-6213, why?"

Mmm, not the answer I was expecting, so I try again, "Is there any other number I would call you at?"

I must have excited the doctor because her face is beaming. "Are you remembering something Abigail? Whatever it is, it might help. What is it you remember?"

Bill looks excited as well, but knowing that it isn't his number, I just fib. "I thought I remembered, but it was only a glimpse of an area code, then it disappeared." I lie to both of them, keeping the number to myself.

"By the way, what is the area code here?"

The doctor is the first to speak up, "206."

That is definitely not the area code I'm remembering. They're both still patiently waiting for me to say something, so I answer with the only excuse that I can think of at the moment. "That's why I asked Bill to recite his number hoping it would spark something, but I was wrong… I'm sorry." I look at them, disappointed.

Seeming just as irritated about the whole situation, Bill turns to the doctor, barks at her to order more tests, wanting to know why I've lost my memory.

The neurologist decides to steer the conversation by saying, "Although she has a bit of a memory loss, she might get it back in time, especially once she goes home and begins to see things more familiar to her. Give her time; she's just woken up," she says before her lips go into a frown of disappointment as well.

"Then how soon can she go home so she can start remembering?" he barks at her, making me flinch from the anger in his tone.

He turns to me and with a nicer voice says, "Baby, your name is Abigail Adams. You're a famous model. Is it ringing a bell?" he questions with desperation.

I shake my head and pick at the imaginary lint on my blankets. The name doesn't ring a bell at all. I want it to, but it doesn't.

Bill notices my lack of response and begins fumbling with his phone like he's looking for something and once he's found it he brings the phone close to my face for me to look into the screen. On it is a photo of myself with a whole bunch of make-up, and I'm half-naked.

"See, that's you at your last photo shoot, it's for *Vogue*!" he says with enthusiasm. "Of course you know who you are, you're legendary since this cover came out." The phone is still in front of my face as if he expects the light bulb to turn on in my head.

When I shake my head at him he only sighs again, clearly disappointed. I think I'm really beginning to irritate him.

He moves to the corner of the room dragging the doctor with him, by the arm, and in hushed tones he begins speaking with her. The nurse walks in at this moment saving me from having to look at both of them, knowing that they are discussing me and leaving me out of the conversation. The nurse entertains herself by fluffing my pillows, in an effort to make me more comfortable, but I know she's really just trying to be nice about the whole situation.

They both stop talking and look over in my direction and he smiles. The only trouble is that his smile is worrying me and I want it to go away. It's the type of smile meant to reassure me that everything is okay, when in reality it's not.

Knowing the situation is not going to get any better until my memory comes back, I bring up the excuse that I'm tired so they will leave me alone. Right now I want to be alone and sleep. My body feels drained, even though I just woke up a couple of hours ago. What I really want is for Bill to leave, so whatever excuse I can give them to make him leave works for me.

They all leave me to get my rest and as I'm left alone with my thoughts. I wonder again if I'm wrong about Bill. I keep trying to convince myself that maybe it was someone else, or maybe I had dreamt the whole conversation. I begin to get drowsy and my eyelids start to feel heavy, dragging me into sleep once again.

In my dream, I feel happy, and I see this guy who's laughing with me.

He's young, early twenties, good looking, and really fit. He's taller than me, enough so that I have to look up at him. He has a narrow looking face, his hair is a dark color, with dark chocolate brown eyes, and thick lashes that are long, curl, and make you jealous that he has them. But what really catches my attention is his smile. He has a smile that just makes you melt inside and it makes you smile with him. He's all sweaty and I note that he looks like he just finished working out. Or has done something that has made him breathe really fast and heavy. His shirt is soaked and he's chugging water from a water bottle like he's dying of thirst. I look at my surroundings and notice that we are in a park, at the end of what I think is a trail, and in the background there are a lot of tall trees. He then throws his arm around my shoulders and says, "Keep up that pace and we're definitely going to PR this race."

What race and what PR event is he talking about? My dream begins to fade away, and I'm trying really hard to ask him what's going on, or who he is?

Unfortunately, I can't get the words out of my mouth. I want to know his name, but he quickly fades away.

As I open my eyes, I notice it's morning again, with the light coming in through my hospital room window and a new nurse is taking my blood pressure, which is what must have woken me up.

Now that I'm awake, I take the time to focus on trying to bring back some type of memory. When the nurse sees that I'm awake, she informs me that Bill came by early this morning while I was still sleeping and dropped off my stuff.

I turn my head and notice an iPad on the side table and I reach over and grab it. Wanting answers fast, I start to Google my name, "Abigail Adams." Right away all kinds of articles and images come up.

According to the Internet, I'm not a world famous model, but I am in high demand in the states. Thanks to my current fiancé, slash agent and manager, I was on the way to becoming the most highly sought after model in recent history. Before my accident, I had wrapped up an interview and photo shoot with *Vogue* that was going to get me those international shoots I was working towards.

I was born in Seattle, but raised in the foster system.

My mother died when I was twelve, leaving me to be raised by the state in different foster homes until I was discovered at the age of eighteen. I had begun with small photo shoots for a local agency that kept me financially above water for a couple of years, until I met Bill, making him my current agent and manager.

On the Internet there were a ton of pictures of me, some from different interviews, photo shoots, or pictures that must have been taken by paparazzi when I was out and about. There were so many, it's almost like I wanted to be constantly photographed or spoken to, which feels a bit disturbing.

After reading a couple of articles and flipping through what seems like thousands of photos, I feel even more confused than when I started. The only thing it's proven to me is that I was a shallow and conceited person who only cared about herself. For some reason this makes me feel like crap.

After sitting in my room for most of the day, I notice that I start to feel jittery and stressed. Eventually, I start twitching my leg, swinging my foot back and forth and feeling trapped like I want to get out and do something. It is driving me crazy.

I blame it on being immobile for so long.

On this second day since I've woken up, the doctor is in my room giving me my routine daily check-up. Bill showed up this morning, but most of the time he's on the phone barking commands at someone about a deal that he's trying to close. He's been coming to visit me as often as he can, but I have a feeling that he'd rather be at his office than with me.

He claims that he is really busy at work, but that he misses me badly and wished that he could spend every waking hour with me, but I doubt it. It takes all of my willpower not to roll my eyes at his response. Even when he kissed me that first day, it didn't feel right. There was no emotion in it on my part. As if to confirm that my body didn't really know him. It had worried me, but I had made it a point to Bill that I just needed time and space, giving him an excuse to stay at a distance.

Before I could even allow him to think things were back to normal, I had to figure out what normal was.

About the Author

Gabbie is a Southern California native, who lives with her wonderful husband, two amazing kids and a senior citizen kitty. When she's not writing you can find her reading or sneaking off for a run. Some might say it's a crazy life, but she wouldn't change anything about it.

Email: author.gabbiesduran@gmail.com

Website: http://gabbiesduran.com/

tsu: https://www.tsu.co/gabbiesduran

Facebook:
https://www.facebook.com/authorgabbiesduran

Twitter: @gabbiesduran

Goodreads:
https://www.goodreads.com/author/show/7093957.
Gabbie_S_Duran

Instagram: http://instagram.com/gabbiesduran/

Pinterest: http://www.pinterest.com/gabbieduran/

Spotify: Gabbie S. Duran

www.ingramcontent.com/pod-product-compliance
Lightning Source LLC
Chambersburg PA
CBHW051938240626
47153CB00005B/1540